Irish author **Abby Gre**
career in film and TV—
of a lot of standing in
trailers—to pursue he
she'd bombarded Mil
they kindly accepted
She lives in Dublin, Ireland, and
for distraction. Visit abby-green.com or email
abbygreenauthor@gmail.com.

Carol Marinelli recently filled in a form asking
for her job title. Thrilled to be able to put down
her answer, she put 'writer'. Then it asked what
Carol did for relaxation, and she put down the
truth—'writing'. The third question asked for her
hobbies. Well, not wanting to look obsessed, she
crossed her fingers and answered 'swimming'—
but, given that the chlorine in the pool does
terrible things to her highlights, I'm sure you can
guess the real answer!

MISTAKEN AS HIS ROYAL BRIDE

ABBY GREEN

VIRGIN'S STOLEN NIGHTS WITH THE BOSS

CAROL MARINELLI

MILLS & BOON

First published in Great Britain 2023
by Mills & Boon, an imprint of HarperCollins*Publishers* Ltd,
1 London Bridge Street, London, SE1 9GF

www.harpercollins.co.uk

HarperCollins*Publishers*, Macken House, 39/40 Mayor Street Upper, Dublin 1, D01 C9W8, Ireland

ISBN: 978-0-263-30702-3

11/23

MISTAKEN AS
HIS ROYAL BRIDE

ABBY GREEN

MILLS & BOON

This is my 60th story for Harlequin Mills and Boon.

I never dreamed, when I first picked up a
Mills & Boon novel in my grandmother's house in
the 1980s, that I would one day be writing for the
iconic publishers. It is literally a dream come true.

I couldn't have done this without the patience,
love and cheerleading of my friends and family.

I couldn't have done it without the expertise of
my editors.

And, most especially, I couldn't have done it
without the readers. You are the ones who make this
job worthwhile.

Thank you!

This is for my mother

CHAPTER ONE

IT WAS LIKE a scene from a futuristic movie. They were in the middle of the desert under a scorching sun and around them were all manner of eye-popping spectacles.

On a huge stage in the far distance a world-renowned band was blasting out their hits to an ecstatic crowd. There were food and drinks stalls selling everything from healthy smoothies to tequila shots to burgers and Asian street food.

Otherworldly giant figures appeared through the heat haze—people on stilts. At that moment a couple walked past Maddi Smith, hand in hand, and she only realised belatedly that they were entirely naked except for body paint.

There was a circus ground nearby, and Maddi watched a trapeze artist in a sequined leotard with a mane of long bright red hair fly through the air against the bright blue sky like an exotic bird. She held her breath and let it out again when the trapeze artist was safely caught by the hands of her partner.

Huge temporary art installations made of wood—intricate houses, windmills, even ships—were silhouetted against the sky. A man drove across the desert in the distance on a fish-shaped motorbike.

The crowd around them were an eclectic mix of young and old, but with a common theme of eccentricity, a zest for life and wearing costumes that bared acres of flesh and wouldn't look out of place on the cover of a steam punk novel.

'This place is wild, Mads. How on earth did you hear about it?'

Maddi's half-sister Laia put her arm through hers. Maddi's heart swelled. She loved her so much, even though they'd only met for the first time a year ago.

And right now the two half-sisters fitted right into the crowd around them milling through the teepee tent village where they'd slept the night before. Laia was wearing a black diamante bra-top and tiny shorts, fishnet tights and sturdy black boots. Her hair was backcombed and threaded through with tiny plaits. They'd had their eyes painted with sparkles and glitter and bright green eyeshadow.

Maddi was wearing something very similar, but instead of shorts she was wearing a tiny gold mini skirt. They both had huge goggles on their heads, part of their costumes but also protection against the sun and sand.

Maddi squeezed Laia's arm. 'I heard about this place when I was working at the club in Dublin. It's been on my bucket list ever since.'

Laia smiled. 'Is that the place where you had to dress like a French maid?'

Maddi shuddered. 'Don't remind me. I could have worn that uniform here and not looked remotely out of place.'

Laia laughed.

At that moment a man walked past wearing nothing but a thong and a large rug around his shoulders. His sunglasses had a third lens to cover his third eye.

He looked at them and tipped an imaginary hat. 'Ladies.'

The sisters giggled and then Maddi took Laia's hand. 'Come on, let's find some food. I'm starving.'

Laia responded dryly, 'When *aren't* you hungry?'

Maddi made a face at her and led her through the crowd, conscious of the ever-present security detail that accompanied them at a distance. Because Maddi's sister was someone important. Very important. She was Crown Princess of a small kingdom in the Mediterranean called Isla'Rosa. She was due to turn twenty-five in mere weeks and then she would be crowned Queen.

Maddi was the product of an illicit affair Laia's father the King had had about a year after his beloved wife had died while giving birth to Laia.

When Maddi's mother had fallen pregnant the King had panicked and sent her into exile, with an allowance to bring up his illegitimate daughter and an edict to stay away from Isla'Rosa for fear of causing a scandal.

Her mother was a proud woman and had left, taking her broken heart and her pregnancy with her. One of Maddi's abiding memories from growing up was her mother's bone-deep sadness. Her mother had never hidden the origins of her birth, and Maddi had always felt in some part responsible for her pain. If Maddi hadn't been born then they wouldn't be living in exile. Her mother would still be in the country she loved.

Laia had explained to Maddi that she'd only found out about her when her father had been on his deathbed, racked with guilt and remorse, nearly four years ago.

He'd confessed to Laia that he'd had the affair because he'd been grief-stricken and overwhelmed by becoming a widower with a young baby daughter. It was no excuse, he'd said, but it had been a moment of weakness that he'd always regretted. He'd begged Laia to look for Maddi to try and explain and ask for forgiveness for his behaviour.

But Laia hadn't gone looking for Maddi straight away. She'd been fearful of what she might find. Afraid that Maddi would hate her for being ostracised, and possibly not want anything to do with her. Maybe even be bitter and want to lay her own claim to the throne or harm Isla'Rosa.

But eventually Laia *had* gone looking for Maddi and had

found her in Ireland, and from the moment the half-sisters had met, all of Laia's concerns had dropped away. There had been a powerful connection between them. An instant bond. As if they'd already known each other on some level.

When Laia had found Maddi she'd explained that she fully intended to reveal Maddi as her half-sister, and a true Princess of Isla'Rosa—but they agreed it wouldn't happen until the coronation, when Laia would announce Maddi as Princess, once she was Queen.

Their father the King had been much revered by the people of Isla'Rosa and the world over, especially for his lifelong devotion to his deceased wife, so news of an illegitimate daughter and a lover would come as a huge shock—not just to the people of Isla'Rosa.

Maddi didn't want to be the cause of any adverse headlines before the coronation and she'd made it very clear that she had no designs on Isla'Rosa. The most important thing for her was to get to know her sister. She'd never expected Laia to come looking for her. And she'd had no intention of seeking her sister out, even though she'd known where she was. That whole existence…a royal life of duty and privilege… was so far removed from Maddi's very ordinary upbringing as to be on another planet.

She harboured no bitterness or resentment at having lived a parallel life. She was inherently shy and not academic. In the infrequent moments when curiosity had driven her to look her sister up online, and she'd seen Laia's poise and confidence in social situations, she'd always felt totally intimidated and relieved not to be in that position.

Her sister spoke five languages fluently!

Maddi spoke one.

So in fact she still felt very ambiguous about taking up her rightful place as a Princess of Isla'Rosa. The prospect was terrifying, and she wasn't remotely ready, even though she'd spent the last year working as Laia's lady-in-waiting. It had been Maddi's suggestion when Laia had said she wanted her to return to Isla'Rosa with her.

Working for Princess Laia as one of her staff had afforded Maddi the chance to get to know her sister undercover, and also to get to know her ancestral home.

The last year had been a revelation.

She hadn't expected to fall in love with the small island and its rocky landscape dotted with flowers, its pristine beaches and charming medieval main town, Sant'Rosa. Or the smiling, friendly people she'd immediately felt connected to.

She hadn't expected to feel as if she belonged somewhere for the first time in her life.

She hadn't expected to fall in love with her half-sister, older by nearly two years. She wasn't just a sister—she'd become a best friend.

For most of Maddi's life she'd kept people at arm's length, aware of the huge secret she carried within her. Aware of the fact that her father had chosen to reject her before he'd even met her. She'd carried it like a bruise all her life, on top of the guilt and responsibility she felt for her mother's exile.

Meeting Laia and going to Isla'Rosa had gone some way to soothing some of those very complex emotions. Maddi even hoped that her mother and Irish stepfather might return to Isla'Rosa for an extended period. But as yet her mother hadn't decided what to do...

As they stood in the queue for food, Maddi smiled at Laia's obvious enjoyment of the spectacle around them. She'd noticed in Laia a growing preoccupation recently as the coronation drew closer, and had suggested this trip as a diversion.

She'd said, 'It'll take your mind off things, and it'll also help maintain your image of feckless socialite with nothing on her mind but fun, even in the face of huge responsibility.'

Laia had looked at her and then stood up from behind her

desk in her office at the castle on Isla'Rosa and said, 'Brilliant. Two birds with one stone. When do we leave?'

Maddi felt a prick of guilt that the burden of becoming Queen was all on Laia's shoulders and always had been, even though it was totally irrational for her to feel guilty— she'd never been recognised publicly as a member of the royal family.

And, as much as becoming a princess terrified her, she knew deep down that it was her destiny now, and she owed it to Laia and her own mother to at least do her best to fulfil it. At least then her mother's exile and heartbreak might not have been completely in vain...

At that moment Maddi noticed the sun glinting off something in the distance. It was a small sleek plane—a private jet—touching down on the runway. For some inexplicable reason a tiny shiver went down her spine. A sense of foreboding.

She kept looking back, and now she saw the tiny dot of what had to be a motor vehicle coming towards the festival, a plume of dust and sand in its wake.

'What is it?' Laia asked. 'What are you looking at?'

'A plane has just landed—a small one. Someone is coming.'

'People are arriving all the time.'

Maddi couldn't explain why *this* arrival felt different. But now Laia was watching too, and as the vehicle got closer they could see that it was a black SUV with tinted windows. It looked official in some way. Officious. The opposite of the crowd and vibe around them.

Laia tensed beside her and said, almost to herself, 'He wouldn't have followed me here... I mean, I wanted him to see the pictures we leaked to the press, but to actually come all this way...'

Maddi knew who she was talking about. The man who had been growing more and more frustrated by Laia's reluctance to meet with him, to discuss the fact that they were due to be married. She'd been promised to him in marriage since her birth. An archaic arrangement that had shocked Maddi when she'd first heard of it.

'He' was King Aristedes de Valle y Montero of Santanger, the neighbouring kingdom to Isla'Rosa. Their marriage was to be a union to unite the two kingdoms, which were enjoying a rare period of harmony after hundreds of years of bitter enmity and war.

The only problem was that Laia did not *want* to marry King Aristedes, because doing so would endanger Isla'Rosa's independence. As the smaller country, it would naturally be dominated by the bigger, richer entity of Santanger.

Laia had a vision for Isla'Rosa. She wanted to solidify peace between the countries *not* through an archaic marriage pact but through modern diplomacy, agreements and trade deals. And she was afraid that King Aristedes—known for being a stickler for tradition and rules—wouldn't listen to reason. That he would insist on the marriage and force her into it by appealing to her sense of duty and responsibility.

Laia was passionate about her country retaining its independence, and since she'd come to know and love it so was Maddi.

The car drew to a halt on the edge of the crowd and as Maddi watched, the driver got out and opened a back door. She held her breath. A man uncoiled his tall body from the back of the car, and she knew from Laia's indrawn breath that it was indeed King Aristedes.

Maddi had never seen him in the flesh. Even though he was still at some distance she could see that he stood head and shoulders over most of the crowd. He was wearing a dark three-piece suit which made him stand out even more among the outlandish costumes. He started to walk through the crowd with a couple of men who had to be his security detail, also dressed in suits and wearing sunglasses.

If Maddi hadn't been as tense as her sister, she might have giggled at how out of place they looked.

Laia's fingers were digging into Maddi's arm painfully. 'I can't believe he came all the way here,' she said.

'You've been dodging meetings with him for months now,' Maddi pointed out. 'We left Manhattan the morning he arrived to try and take you for lunch.'

That had been one among many other similar occasions. Maddi could understand that he must be frustrated. He'd made no secret of the fact that he was ready to wed his convenient bride and have his Queen by his side.

Beside her, Laia said, 'I only have to hold out another couple of weeks, until my twenty-fifth birthday, then I'll be crowned Queen and I'll have much more power to renegotiate the marriage agreement and encourage him to think of other solutions.'

King Aristedes was tracking closer. Moving swiftly through the crowd. Maddi couldn't help but notice how he moved with loose-limbed grace. He was even taller than she'd thought. Shoulders broad, chest wide. He oozed such power and masculinity that the people in the crowd around him noticed and stopped to watch. Which, considering the other eye-popping spectacles around them, was no small thing.

Not just imposing and charismatic, he was also gorgeous, with short dark hair and a strong-boned face. A trim dark beard hugged his jaw. Maddi couldn't see his mouth from here, but she'd seen it in photos. Well-defined. Sensual. Firm. *Sexy*. His eyes were covered now, but they'd appeared dark in the photos.

Maddi realised at that very inopportune moment that she was way more transfixed by King Aristedes than she should be.

She tore her eyes off the man coming towards them and

turned to her sister, who was pale. Maddi gripped her arm, 'Laia, look at me…are you okay?'

Laia's gaze went to her sister. She shook her head. 'I feel sick. I can't believe he's still determined to marry me, even after everything I've done to put him off.'

Laia was referring to her well-documented campaign of appearing in public at every glittering party and social event with the sole reason of deterring the famously conservative and staid King Aristedes from pursuing their marriage by making herself look like a party girl.

Maddi said, 'Look, is it really that hopeless? What if you use this opportunity to talk to him and make him see your side?'

But Laia shook her head. 'I tried to talk to him after my father's funeral, but he wouldn't listen. He said very clearly that our marriage would happen the way it had been agreed and he would not discuss the matter further. He showed no interest in who I was. He sees me only as a means to an end.'

'Won't you be risking the peace if you're crowned before the marriage takes place?'

Laia shook her head. 'No, he wouldn't want to look petty. *We* know the marriage is due to take place before the coronation but it's not common knowledge among the greater public, yet. The itinerary was going to be revealed much closer to the day to minimise the risk, albeit small, of old rebel elements from both kingdoms stirring things up. I can use that to my advantage now. Santanger prides itself on being a modern, forward-looking country, which makes it so ironic that he's intent on this marriage. He'll see it as an inconvenience that things haven't gone exactly to plan, but if he thinks the marriage is still in play he won't care too much. That'll give me the time I need to go to him as an equal head of state.'

Passion mixed with panic made Laia's eyes wide and very green.

'Mads, I don't want to let Isla'Rosa be swallowed up by Santanger. We've fought for our independence in so many battles! Our father set up the marriage agreement under pressure from King Aristedes's father, who engineered it so that the marriage would take place before I turned twenty-five—before I could be crowned Queen—ensuring Santanger maximum leverage over Isla'Rosa.'

She shook her head.

'I think Father thought it would be for my benefit, having my husband by my side before I was crowned Queen but over the years he saw how capable I was and I think he regretted bowing to the pressure. He told me on his deathbed that he didn't want me to marry for anything less than love, no matter how high the stakes, so maybe he was preparing me to rebel against it, if I wanted to.'

She continued, 'He wanted me—*us*—to be happy. I know I can persuade King Aristedes that a marriage is not necessary to create lasting peace between us, but I need to be Queen before I'll have the power to do that. Until I'm crowned I'm still vulnerable, and King Aristedes knows that—which is why he's so hell-bent on pursuing this marriage as soon as possible. It shows he hasn't changed his view on how this should happen. He still wants his marriage of convenience and to have power over Isla'Rosa.'

Love and loyalty swelled in Maddi's chest for her sister. She knew this was her chance to do something really useful.

She took Laia's hands in hers and said quickly, 'When was the last time you met King Aristedes face to face?'

Laia frowned. 'A few weeks after my—' She corrected herself. '*Our* father's funeral, when I tried to talk to him about the marriage agreement and he refused to listen. I haven't seen him in years.'

Maddi hid her pang of pain at the reminder that she'd

never met her father behind a wry smile. 'Wow, you've really turned avoiding him into a sport.'

Laia shrugged and smiled back weakly. 'I did what I had to, to avoid the inevitable.' She looked over Maddi's shoulder and gulped. 'But it didn't work. He's getting closer.'

The back of Maddi's neck prickled, as if she could feel his presence. Strange... She'd never met the man. But she was about to.

She squeezed Laia's hands. 'You need to go—*now*. Into the crowd. Get lost.'

Laia frowned more. 'But...what do you mean? You're coming with me.'

Maddi shook her head. 'No, I'm going to take care of this. You just need to disappear till your birthday, right?'

Laia nodded.

'Then I will make sure King Aristedes is distracted until it's too late.'

'How?'

Maddi smiled even as her insides knotted with apprehension. 'What was apparent the first time we met? How much we look alike. We could pass for twins.'

Maddi had heard the castle staff whispering about the likeness between her and Laia, but no one had had the nerve to speak of it directly.

Understanding dawned in Laia's eyes, but she shook her head. 'No, Mads. I can't let you do something like this. It's too crazy...'

But Maddi was firm. 'You've borne the weight of massive responsibility all your life. Let me do something for you and our country.' Before she lost her nerve she gestured to their bodyguard, who came over. She said, quickly and quietly, 'You need to take Princess Laia away from here. There's a serious security threat.'

He needed no more instruction. He bundled Laia in front of him and they were soon lost in the crowd.

Maddi couldn't believe what she'd just done, but she didn't regret it. She and Laia *could* almost pass for twins. Apart from their eyes. Laia's were green and Maddi's were hazel.

They both had long, wavy dark brown hair. Olive-toned skin. Wide, almond-shaped eyes. Straight noses. The same mouths. Except Maddi's had a more rosebud shape. And she had a small gap in her front teeth.

They were of similar height, and the only other real difference was one that Maddi lamented, she was curvier than Laia, whose figure ran to being more athletic.

Maddi took a deep breath and turned around. King Aristedes was even closer now, his head swivelling back and forth, tracking everyone in the crowd. She drew her shoulders up straight and looked at him.

As if sensing her gaze, King Aristedes stopped and his head turned towards her. He went very still. Like an animal scenting its prey. The tumult of the crowd around them died away.

He lifted his sunglasses from his face. Maddi's heart thumped. His eyes were deep-set and unfathomably dark. Impossible to read. His jaw was clenched. He moved towards her.

King Aristedes stopped in front of her and she had to tip her head back to look up. He looked at her for a long moment and said nothing, his dark gaze roving over her face and body.

Maddi's skin prickled all over and her insides turned to liquid. Maybe she'd overestimated just how similar she was to her sister. But then King Aristedes spoke. His voice was deep and it resonated all the way inside her.

'The elusive Princess Laia. I think it's time for you to come home and fulfil your obligations, don't you?'

CHAPTER TWO

MADDI WATCHED AS the festival below them in the desert became a smaller and smaller dot. Laia was down there somewhere, watching this plane leave. Maddi sent her a wish that she would escape somewhere until it was safe for her to emerge and become Queen.

She was aware of King Aristedes on the other side of the aisle. She could feel his gaze on her but she was avoiding looking at him. It was like looking at the sun. Too dangerous.

She felt very self-conscious in her costume, which, out of context looked cheap and tacky and bared far too much flesh.

'What on earth was that spectacle?'

Maddi bristled at his scathing tone. Reluctantly she looked at him. 'It's a famous festival. It brings art and music and people together in an extravaganza of creativity and innovation. There's nothing else like it in the world.'

'It looked ridiculous.'

Maddi turned her body to face him and opened her mouth, but then she saw his gaze drop to her chest for a split second. A zing of electricity skated over her skin and it shocked her so much that she forgot what she was going to say.

He raised a brow. 'I think you can remove your...glasses now.'

Maddi frowned, and then realised he was referring to the goggles on her head. She pulled them off, wincing a little as they caught on her hair.

The air inside the private jet suddenly felt cold, and it wasn't just the chilly atmosphere caused by King Aristedes. Air-conditioning. She shivered and he noticed.

He frowned. 'You're wearing next to nothing. Do you have other clothes with you?'

He and his security team had allowed her to go to their tent and collect her bag and other things. So she did have a change of clothes with her. She wasn't sure it was going to be much of an improvement, though. But she jumped at the chance to get out of his disturbing presence even for a few minutes and collect her thoughts.

'Yes, I do. I'll go and change.'

'There's a bedroom and bathroom at the back.'

Maddi stood up with as much grace as she could muster, considering she looked like an extra from a Mad Max movie, and went to the back of the plane.

She closed the door to the bedroom suite behind her and took a deep, shaky breath. She'd done it. She'd fooled King Aristedes into thinking she was Laia. Even if it only allowed Laia enough time to get away it would be worth it.

Maddi looked around the suite. It was sumptuous, but understated, in a palette of cream and gold and beige like the rest of the plane. There was luxurious carpet underfoot.

She'd grown used to luxury since living in the castle on Isla'Rosa, but this was another level.

She put her bag down on the bed and opened it, choosing some clothes to change into.

She went into the bathroom, and the sight of the massive walk-in shower made her very conscious of the thick layer of grime and dust she'd acquired over the last twenty-four hours.

Stripping off, Maddi turned on the water and stepped under the hot steaming spray with a little groan of satisfaction. It took her an age to do her hair and scrub at her face until she was sure all the make-up was off.

When she stepped out, she wrapped her hair in a towel and pulled on a robe. She looked at herself in the mirror and balked—because suddenly the difference between her and her sister looked much starker. She would never get away with convincing the King that she was Laia now.

She was much paler than Laia, having grown up in Ireland, so she hadn't cultivated the natural tan her sister had. Her hair was also a bit darker because she hadn't grown up in the sun. Her eyes looked much darker now, too.

This had been a nuts idea. But it was too late to turn back. And if it allowed Laia to get away to somewhere she could hide out then it had to be worth it.

Maddi got dressed, dried her hair, and then, fully prepared for the King to realise instantly that she wasn't Laia, went out to meet her fate.

Ari heard the door open behind him and didn't like the way a sizzle of anticipation skated along his nerve-endings. It was most unwelcome. But from the moment he'd locked eyes with Princess Laia in that godforsaken circus amusement park something in his awareness of her had shifted. As if a gear had clicked into place.

She'd never had that effect on him before. Granted, he hadn't seen her in almost four years, and perhaps now that she was a fully grown woman...

'Sorry, I took a shower. I hope that's okay.'

He could smell her before he saw her. Musk and rose. She came alongside him and he turned his head. His eyeline was at her slim waist. She was now wearing short cut-off shorts covered in sequins. Bare, shapely legs led down to a pair of pretty feet in gladiator sandals. Nails painted a coral colour.

His gaze tracked back up and he saw that she was wearing what looked like a lurid pink Spandex leotard under the shorts. No bra. Nothing to disguise the most beautifully shaped breasts he'd ever seen. Full and teardrop-shaped. Nipples hard and pushing against the material.

In an instant Ari was engulfed in more than heat. It was white-hot lust—for a woman he'd been promised to in marriage since she was a baby. And who he'd never had this reaction to before.

Her face was clean now. Paler than he remembered. But still beautiful. She'd grown into her beauty since he'd seen her last.

Those distinctive almond-shaped eyes… He'd always had the impression they were green in colour, but here on the plane they looked darker, almost more golden than green.

And her mouth… Had it always been that provocative, with a naturally pouting bow shape?

His conscience pricked. Did he not even recognise his own fiancée? He doused the heat in his body with ice and said sharply, 'Don't you have something to cover up with?'

Laia sat down in the chair and the movement made her breasts sway under the thin material. Ari could not understand this horny schoolboy reaction to a woman when he'd never indulged in such behaviour even when he had been a schoolboy. Control had always been key and he'd never lost it.

But her body was like a siren call.

He shook off his jacket and handed it over. 'Here, put this on.'

He watched as the Princess slid her arms into his jacket and pulled it over her chest. He immediately lamented her hiding her body from view even as he welcomed it.

Was his reaction due to sexual frustration? Possibly. He'd let his last mistress go a few months ago, to focus exclusively on tracking down his wayward fiancée and making her his Queen. His last few lovers had been disappointing—not just sexually, but on every level—and he'd actually relished not having to play that game for the last few months.

It had galvanised him to follow through on this royal pact. He was ready to settle down. He was resigned to the fact that he would soon be committing to one woman, no matter their compatibility, because he'd vowed that he would never be unfaithful to her.

His father had been serially unfaithful to Ari's mother and it had broken her. Turned her into someone unstable and bitter. Love was for fools. And so was chemistry. It didn't last.

He knew he would like Laia enough to bed her, even if she wasn't his usual type. So this unexpected *heat* he felt was…surprising. A distraction. Princess Laia Sant'Roman of Isla'Rosa had never so much as caused a blip of awareness in him. Another reason why she was so perfect.

What the hell was going on now?

'I can't believe you came all the way to the festival to find me.'

Maddi was still trembling from the excoriating look King Aristedes had just given her. It was clear that he couldn't be more disgusted by her. She cursed herself again for not taking more care to pack her clothes in the tent. For not at least grabbing a sweatshirt or jacket.

King Aristedes's jacket was warm around her shoulders. His scent was tantalising, deep and complex. Tones of leather and wood and something more exotic. She imagined a dark flower, blooming in the rocks against the odds, sending out a musky scent…

King Aristedes said, 'I was growing tired of having my invitations ignored or rescinded. Enough is enough. We have a pact to honour, and it's time to get on with our lives as King and Queen of Santanger.'

Maddi felt a spurt of loyalty to Laia. 'And of Isla'Rosa. You'd be King of our—' She corrected herself quickly. '*My* country too.'

He inclined his head. 'That is part of the agreement, yes.'

Maddi's hands curled into fists. 'I don't want Isla'Rosa to get lost in this agreement. The pact doesn't say that we have to lose our independence—and yet that is what will happen, isn't it?'

He said with casual arrogance, 'Your marriage to me can only benefit Isla'Rosa, it needs investment to reach its full potential.' And then, 'There's no reason why the privy council who are ruling until you come of age or marry can't go on doing their very fine work. Let's face it: they've proved their ability to rule during your...frequent absences.'

Maddi went cold. Laia had been right. He had no interest in her or her desire to be ruler of her own kingdom. Maddi knew that the members of the privy council appeared to be the ones with all the power, and in many ways they were. But Laia had been assuming more and more control since their father had died, and the council now deferred to her on almost every decision. She was no mere figurehead.

But of course King Aristedes didn't know that, because her sister had been promoting an image of pleasure-seeking sybaritic socialite at every opportunity, in the hope of putting him off.

It was common knowledge that King Aristedes was famously serious and strait-laced. Unlike his playboy younger brother, Crown Prince Dax, who seemed to be his opposite in every regard.

Thinking of the King's intransigence, Maddi said, 'Are you sure this is a good idea? We're not very alike.'

One of Laia's complaints was that she wasn't even his type. He seemed to favour tall, leggy blondes. Ice-cold and perfect. Laia and Maddi bore the features and colouring of their mixed ancestry—Roman, Greek and Moorish.

King Aristedes's deep voice pulled Maddi back to the conversation.

'It's not about whether we're compatible—it's bigger than that. Our marriage will honour a peace pact made by our fathers to ensure long-standing harmony in the region.'

The father Maddi had never met.

It was as if King Aristedes was pushing against that wound, bringing it back to life.

Hadn't her father ever wondered about her? Cared what had happened to her?

Loved her at all?

In a bid to stop her mind going to dark places, Maddi focused on the conversation at hand, while trying not to let herself notice how King Aristedes's muscles moved and bunched under his shirt and waistcoat. She'd somehow imagined the King to be…softer. But this man was the opposite of soft. He resembled a prize fighter in civilised clothing.

'So you have no objection to a marriage that is not built on common interests or love?' she asked.

'None. And nor should you. This marriage is an important strategic alliance. Maybe if our countries had done this a long time ago we wouldn't have suffered so much war and hardship.'

Maddi had studied the history of Isla'Rosa, and by extension some of the history of Santanger, and from those early battles in the Middle Ages right up to the last battle in the last century, it had been brutal.

Maddi still found it hard to get her head around the thought of such carnage on the pretty streets of Isla'Rosa's main town and in the clear blue-green seas around the island. Maybe King Aristedes was right.

Maddi immediately felt disloyal to her sister.

It wasn't that Laia didn't want to do her duty—she did, passionately—but she'd revealed that she wanted to do it with someone by her side who could offer a real relationship. Love and respect and loyalty to the crown of Isla'Rosa, as well as her, of course.

Maddi admired Laia for her idealism about love, but she couldn't understand it personally because she had grown up watching her mother do her best to hide her broken heart. She'd married eventually, and she was now relatively happy, but Maddi had always been aware of the deep sadness inside her.

So Maddi couldn't envisage what it was to strive for love. As far as she could see it just brought pain and destruction. It was somewhat disturbing to realise that King Aristedes was making some sense to her...

'Where are we going?' she suddenly thought to ask, belatedly.

'Straight to Santanger. The wedding will take place in a couple of weeks and there will be a lot of preparation.'

Maddi gulped. Further confirmation that King Aristedes was clearly set on having their marriage take place exactly as planned. No deviation.

A small rogue inside her was tempting her to test him. She said, 'What if we delay the wedding until after I'm crowned Queen of Isla'Rosa?'

King Aristedes looked at her. Stern. No emotion. No softness. 'That is impossible.'

'Nothing is impossible,' Maddi said, hoping to sound defiant but fearing she sounded hesitant.

He shook his head. 'This will happen as per the agreement. You'll become Queen of Isla'Rosa when we marry.'

Yes, but not before you become King of Isla'Rosa through that marriage and its precious independence is gone for ever.

King Aristedes looked impatient. 'You've always known this was the agreement. You've had your whole life to prepare for this moment.'

That was true. She had to be careful. She was responding as Maddi, not Laia. Laia would be cool, calm and collected.

'You're right. I have.'

'And I can trust that you won't do a disappearing act once we land?'

Maddi envisaged Laia on another flight, hopefully to the other side of the world. No way would she jeopardise that.

She forced a smile. 'Of course not. I'm committed to this.'

Right up until he realises I'm not Princess Laia and kicks me off Santanger.

Or, worse, locks her in a dungeon. She wouldn't put it past this brooding taciturn king who had obviously reached the end of his patience to do something so drastic. Laia had shown her the terrifying dungeons in the castle on Isla'Rosa. They'd given Maddi nightmares for weeks.

Clearly satisfied that he had his errant fiancée under some kind of control at last, the King turned back to his laptop.

Maddi could understand Laia's misgivings now. She could see how her sister had clashed with King Aristedes and his arrogance, and had taken the drastic actions she had to try and deter him. But he was like a rock. Immovable.

As for Maddi...she could only imagine what his reaction might be when he discovered the truth about who she was.

'Are you sure you've nothing more substantial to change into?'

Maddi had an absurd urge to giggle at the look of distaste on the King's face. Well, it was an urge either to giggle or melt in a puddle. Because when he looked at her like that he caused all sorts of illicit flutterings deep in her belly.

She glanced down at her attire. The hot pink Spandex leo-tard and cut-off shorts sparkling with plastic diamonds. Bare legs. Flat sandals. That little rogue inside her was almost glad on Laia's behalf that she was causing such a spectacle.

'I really don't have anything else. It's this...or what I was wearing before.'

They were due to land in the next few minutes.

King Aristedes made a sound and said ominously, 'That will be rectified as soon as we get to the palace.'

Maddi looked out of the window and her heart quickened at the sight of Santanger in the distance. It was officially winter time now, but the sun glinted off the sea and the rocky island as if it was summer. Maddi knew the temperature would still be comfortable. Like Isla'Rosa, it had the perfect all-year-round climate.

A big change from growing up in damp Ireland, where you were lucky to get a summer and rain was a far too frequent reality.

Isla'Rosa was somewhere in the distance, to the west of Santanger. Too far away to be visible. It took an hour to fly from Isla'Rosa to Santanger. As Maddi had heard Laia say under her breath more than once, *'Too close for comfort.'*

As the plane grew closer and closer, Maddi could see a very impressive palace high on a hill overlooking the city down below. The palace made the castle on Isla'Rosa look like a shed. It was seriously impressive, both as an obviously defensive fortress but also as a royal palace, with whimsical towers and turrets.

Waves crashed against jagged rocks and Maddi shivered involuntarily again. She spotted some pristine beaches in the distance. White sands.

They were approaching the airport now, and the runway spread before them, a long black ribbon. The airport building was surprisingly modern. Perhaps an example of progress on Santanger, the vastly richer country.

The airport on Isla'Rosa was not modern, and that was being kind. That was another reason there was so much pressure on Laia to marry King Aristedes: for a much-needed financial injection into the economy. But Laia was determined to haul Isla'Rosa into the modern age in her own way. Maddi admired that.

The plane touched down and Maddi could see an entourage of people and cars waiting. Cars with flags. Suddenly the magnitude of what she was doing hit her and she went clammy with nerves.

'Are you all right? You're very pale,' said the King.

Maddi nodded her head and smiled weakly. 'Might have been something I ate.'

King Aristedes all but snorted derisively. 'That wouldn't surprise me.'

He was standing up now, and he filled the space effortlessly. Maddi stood up too, and felt momentarily light-headed. Actually, contrary to what she'd just told King Aristedes, she hadn't had a solid meal in about forty-eight hours.

She must have swayed, or something, because suddenly her arm was in the King's hand. Not even his jacket could act as a barrier to the shock of his touch. Firm and strong.

His voice was gruff when he asked, 'Are you okay?'

Maddi nodded quickly. 'Fine…just stood up too fast.'

The King took his hand away and Maddi started to take off his jacket. 'You'll probably need this.'

'*No.*' His voice was sharp. 'Leave it on. There are clothes for you at the palace.'

Maddi frowned. 'But…you don't know my size.'

He looked at her. 'Of course I do. I have all your information, as you have mine.' His gaze swept her up and down. 'Although I'll admit you've changed a little in the four years since I've seen you. It's not a big deal—we can find clothes to fit you.'

Maddi felt his look like the lick of a flame over her skin. Yet she was pretty sure his words weren't complimentary. How humiliating that she found him attractive…

The discreet staff on the plane appeared and helped King Aristedes gather his things. The security men emerged again, from the front of the plane.

Maddi could see more people outside now. The clammy panic was back. She clutched the King's jacket around her like armour, as ineffectual as it was. She put her bag over her body. She felt very self-conscious.

Staff whispered into the King's ear and he looked stern again. Steps were brought to the plane. The door was opened. At the last moment Maddi remembered she had sunglasses and put them on.

King Aristedes stood at the door and gestured to her. 'Time to go.'

Maddi stepped into the doorway, glad of her sunglasses against the glare of the sun. She started to walk down the steps, very aware of her bare legs. The air was a lot cooler than it had been in the desert, but still pleasantly mild.

Out of the corner of her eye she spotted flashes of light and looked over. A crowd of photographers were just beyond a chain-link fence. She heard a curse behind her, and then there was a hand on her waist.

She almost lost her footing on the last step when King Aristedes said, 'Don't look at them. Come this way.'

She was bundled into the back of a sleek SUV with tinted windows and one of those little flags denoting a state car before she could think straight, and then they were moving out of the airport in a cavalcade, along wide roads lined with trees.

The roads soon brought them into the city, also called Santanger. It was a very substantial city, and an intriguing mix of old and new. The old part was full of small winding streets and honey-coloured stone buildings with terracotta tiles. Window boxes overflowing with flowers added bright pops of colour.

There was a massive cathedral overlooking the sea, Baroque in design and also of honey-coloured stone.

Glossy-looking boutiques on the winding road down to a

marina told the story of wealth in this large island kingdom. And Maddi wasn't prepared for the vista opening up into a thoroughly modern part of the city, with soaring steel and glass buildings. It was the financial district. Which reminded Maddi that King Aristedes was renowned for his financial acumen and hosted one of the world's most prestigious global economic events on the island every year.

Apart from his inherited royal wealth, he was also one of the most independently wealthy men in the world. Not that Maddi cared a fig about that. The kind of wealth she valued was in getting to know her sister and finding a place she could really call home on Isla'Rosa.

The car turned away from the marina and went up a hill, out of the city. Soon they were driving under a massive stone arch guarded by men in uniform. Now they were clearly on private property.

Still, Maddi wasn't prepared when the cars drove into a massive courtyard with views straight out to the Mediterranean as far as the eye could see under a bright blue sky, not a cloud in sight. Water sparkled from an elaborate central fountain.

Her mouth dropped open. Beside her, King Aristedes said, 'Anyone would think you'd never been here before.'

She hadn't.

But of course Laia had, over the years, albeit infrequently.

Maddi clamped her mouth shut. Then, weakly, she said, 'It just…never fails to take my breath away.'

The car had come to a stop now, and King Aristedes stepped out. A man in what looked like a butler's uniform stepped forward and opened Maddi's door. She saw his eyes widen when she got out in her garish outfit.

Thankfully there didn't seem to be many other staff waiting for them, apart from the entourage from the airport and the security men. God only knew what they were thinking.

The palace up close was even more intimidating. A vast soaring entrance led into an open courtyard with another fountain. Off the inner courtyard there were numerous passageways.

A woman about her own age approached Maddi, smiling.

King Aristedes said, 'This is Hannah. She will take you to your rooms and show you where to find other clothes.'

Suddenly, at the prospect of the King leaving her to her own devices, Maddi felt very alone. 'Where are you going?'

King Aristedes looked at her as if she had two heads. Clearly he wasn't used to being questioned.

'As you can imagine, I have some work to take care of,' he said. 'We will have dinner together this evening. I will send for you.'

And then he walked away, flanked by about a dozen very officious-looking people.

Hannah said, 'Please come this way, Princess Laia.'

Maddi followed the girl through a warren of corridors, each more sumptuous than the last, with murals painted on the walls depicting scenes from around the island. They passed more inner courtyards with a distinctly Moorish influence. Evidently they shared the same marauding ancestors…

Then they took an elevator up a few floors. This level was hushed and even more opulent. It had to be where the bedrooms were. Hannah stopped outside some massive double doors and opened them with a flourish. Maddi stepped inside and it was like stepping into a dream.

A vast bedroom with a carpet so soft underfoot it felt like walking on air. A huge four-poster bed dressed in crisp white and blue linen.

The sleek bathroom featured two sinks, a walk-in shower, and a bath that oozed decadence, with shelves stocked with exclusive products.

There was also a lounge area, with a couch and a TV,

books on shelves and all the latest glossy magazines spread out on a coffee table.

But the jewel in the crown of this room was the terrace, just beyond the open French doors. It was wide and generous, overflowing with colourful flowers from pots and planters trailing over the edge of the stone balcony. From there, Maddi had an unobstructed view out to sea, and far down below to where the city shone in the sunlight.

The palace spread out on either side of her...majestic. She could see formal gardens. An inviting pool. There was a larger terrace, presumably used for social gatherings but for now it was empty except for a peacock, which chose that exact moment to puff up its gloriously hued feathers, as if showing off just for Maddi.

She couldn't help smiling at the sight. And then she promptly stopped smiling when she thought of Laia.

Hannah cleared her throat behind her. 'Princess Laia, would you like some lunch?'

Maddi turned around just as her stomach rumbled. She made a face. 'Yes, please. I'm starving.'

Hannah's eyes widened. Maddi cursed silently. She had to remember she was pretending to be a princess. Well, she *was* actually a princess, but...

Her head started to throb lightly.

Hannah asked, 'Anything in particular?'

Maddi was about to say she'd eat everything and anything, but she stopped herself and said, 'A chicken salad would be lovely. With some bread. And fruit...and cheese. If that's okay?'

Hannah smiled. 'Not a problem. I'll return shortly. Please help yourself to whatever clothes you like in the dressing room. They're part of your trousseau from the King.'

Maddi had almost forgotten she was still in the King's jacket, which reached only to the top of her thighs.

Hannah left and she went into the dressing room. It was huge and stuffed with clothes as far as the eye could see. And shoes and jewellery.

Maddi touched the iridescent colours of an evening gown. It shimmered as it moved slightly. She let go, afraid she might dirty it. With a growing sense of futility she searched in vain for some more casual clothes—jeans and a T-shirt, or ath-leisure wear.

Eventually she found a loose pair of trousers and a silk shirt. She opened the drawers and gasped when she saw the wispiest items of underwear. She pulled out a bra and it al-most floated away it was so delicate. She grew hot at the thought of the King approving such purchases.

But of course he'd be too busy to bother himself with such things. He'd probably given someone a brief and they'd re-searched Princess Laia. Because all of these items were defi-nitely suited to her sister more than to Maddi.

Maddi's style ran in a more eclectic direction. And she definitely needed more support from her underwear. Espe-cially if that censorious look from the King on the plane was anything to go by. Just thinking of it again made her skin prickle and warmth bloom between her thighs.

These bras wouldn't go near fitting her, so she'd have to do without. She grabbed underwear and the shirt and trousers, and slipped out of her own clothes and into the new ones. They felt as light as air against her skin. She tied the ends of the shirt around her waist.

Hannah returned with a delicious lunch and left it on the table on the terrace. Maddi ate it with relish and savoured the view.

And then she thought of Laia and felt guilty. She got her phone out of her bag—it had been turned off since she got on the plane. She switched it on and there were numerous messages from Laia.

Are you okay? Where are you?

You're completely crazy, you know that?

Thank you, Mads, you've saved my life...

Where are you? Please let me know you're okay...

Maddi smiled and texted back.

I'm fine. We came straight to Santanger. The King has no idea I'm not you...yet. I hope this gives you enough time to get away...let me know where you are. By the way, I'm wearing clothes from your 'trousseau'. I hope you don't mind! I miss you! xx

Maddi sent the message and waited. Nothing. She presumed Laia must be travelling and put the phone down.

She sat looking at the view for a few more minutes, sipping her water, and then she started to feel restless.

She wanted to explore, but she wasn't sure if she was allowed to roam around. But then...she wasn't a prisoner, was she? Why shouldn't she explore the palace a little bit?

CHAPTER THREE

ARI WAS STANDING in his formal office at the palace. He'd showered and changed and allowed himself to feel a sense of satisfaction at having finally tracked his errant fiancée down.

But something about that niggled at him. It had been a little bit too…easy. His mouth thinned. If you discounted the fact that he'd had to fly to a remote desert to find her.

He went over to his French doors and opened them, the view of Santanger laid out below him never failing to make his blood surge with pride. He put his hands on the stone wall of the terrace and breathed in the familiar scents of his home—wild herbs, native flowers and the very distinctive salty tang of the sea.

He didn't take his inheritance for granted for a moment. Unlike his father, who had seen it as some sort of God-given right.

Maybe if his father hadn't displayed such feet of clay Ari might have been the same. But from an early age he'd known that his father was much closer to the earth than to God.

He'd witnessed the tawdry reality of his father's very earthly desires—namely for other women. So he'd always had a sense that he didn't want to insult the people of Santanger by being a hypocrite—presenting the facade of a happy royal family when in reality it had been anything but.

Ari wasn't perfect by any means, but when it came to him marrying for the sake of his country he would do so with the utmost integrity. He would not be unfaithful. He would not do that to his Queen. He'd witnessed his own mother crumble and become a shell of a person. Belittled and made insecure.

She'd married for love and she'd never got over the betrayal of that dream. Ari could only be grateful that he'd learnt early in life that such a fantasy didn't exist.

Maybe for normal people. But not for people like him. Or Princess Laia.

Something caught the corner of his eye and he looked down to his left. As if conjured out of his thoughts, Princess Laia was walking around a courtyard, stopping to sniff flowers.

She'd changed into a shirt and loose trousers, and she was… Ari squinted…*barefoot?* A flash of heat went through him before he could stop it. She'd pulled her hair up into a loose knot and tendrils fell down around her face.

She'd always seemed neat to him before. Somehow fastidious. Here, with her shirt tied around her slim waist, she looked like a student who'd wandered in from outside the palace. As he watched, one of the palace dogs came into the courtyard, big and shaggy, of indeterminate breed.

He tensed. He knew Princess Laia had an aversion to dogs because her father had been attacked by one as a small child. Ari had never noticed dogs in or around the castle on Isla'Rosa on his few visits over the years—understandable, if a little regrettable, because he himself loved dogs.

The dog ambled along behind an unsuspecting Princess Laia. Ari's hands gripped the wall. He didn't fear for her safety, only that she might get a fright. But, as if sensing the dog, she turned around and immediately dropped to her knees to greet him with smiles and soft words. Like any other dog-lover. Except Princess Laia was not a dog-lover—unless she'd had some kind of immersion therapy since he'd last seen her.

Ari frowned. He could distinctly remember her visiting

Santanger when she was younger, with her father, and how they'd both tensed when the palace dogs had appeared. He'd had to have them put in the palace kennels until the visit was over. But Laia was crooning over this dog now, and scratching behind his ears.

A cold finger traced down Ari's spine as a suspicion started to form in his head. A suspicion that he couldn't even fully name yet. Just a feeling. He turned away from the view and went back to his desk, which was covered with newspapers and grainy paparazzi photos. He'd been about to throw them all in the bin—part of his efforts to track down Princess Laia that he no longer required. Except…maybe he did.

He pushed the papers and photos aside, growing more frustrated when he couldn't find what he was looking for—he wasn't even sure what he was looking for—but suddenly there it was.

A picture of Princess Laia in Central Park in Manhattan with another girl. Named under the photo as merely 'a friend'. They were arm in arm, heads together. Clearly close. And also…far more intriguingly…very physically similar. In fact they could almost be twins.

Similar height and build. Except the 'friend' was a little curvier. Both had long, wavy dark hair. They were wearing sunglasses, but Ari sat down now and searched online for a better image of Princess Laia. A formal photo popped up, showing very clearly that her eyes were a striking shade of green. To his shame, he couldn't have said for certain what colour her eyes were before. But now he could.

The woman he'd just brought to Santanger did not have green eyes. They weren't far off—a kind of hazel—but they weren't this very distinctive green.

The cold finger tracing down his spine became a burning sensation. Anger. When she'd been in Manhattan that time, he'd interrupted a trip to South America and had flown in at short notice to try and meet her. But when he'd arrived she'd already departed, leaving a paltry message of apology, saying that something had come up. Once again slipping through his fingers like mercury.

Another picture caught his eye. It was the grainy paparazzi photo of Princess Laia in the desert that had pinpointed her location for the first time in months. When Ari had read the caption under the photo his patience had snapped: *Is Party Princess Laia ever going to settle down?*

What he hadn't noticed until now was the same 'friend' with her in the picture. Arm in arm again.

Ari knew it now with cold certainty. The woman currently in his palace, wearing clothes from the trousseau he'd bought for his fiancée, was *not* Princess Laia. No wonder she'd seemed so different. So if she wasn't the Princess, then who the hell was she? And where on earth—literally—was Princess Laia?

He picked up his mobile phone and made a call to his younger brother. He was grim. 'Dax? I need you to do something for me…'

'Princess Laia? The King is ready for you to meet him for dinner. If you'd follow me, please?'

Maddi felt unaccountably nervous. When she'd come back to the suite after exploring earlier she'd thought she might be tired enough to nap a little, but she'd been restless.

She wasn't used to just doing…nothing. Waiting around.

She and her mother had received a modest level of financial support from her father the King. Her mother probably could have got more, but she'd been too proud to ask for it.

It had been enough to give Maddi a good education, but not so much that they hadn't had to work for their keep. Her mother had worked as a receptionist for the local doctor in the small town outside Dublin where they'd lived. And Maddi had taken part-time jobs to help out from a young age. So she was used to working. To being active.

That was why she'd asked Laia if she could be her lady-in-waiting. It gave her something to do.

She followed Hannah down endless labyrinthine corridors, wondering if she should be slightly insulted that King Aristedes had put so much space between himself and his 'fiancée'? But then they stopped abruptly at a set of double doors at the end of a corridor. There were guards outside. Stony-faced. They made Maddi want to try and make them smile, like she did with the guards on Isla'Rosa, but she controlled herself.

She suddenly felt self-conscious about what she was wearing, but it was too late. Hannah had knocked on the doors and the guards were opening them. Hannah stood back to let her into what was clearly the private apartment of King Aristedes, and the formal splendour of the foyer area alone told Maddi that she was dressed completely inappropriately.

What the hell was she wearing now?

Any thoughts Ari had had about confronting this stranger pretending to be Princess Laia dissolved in a rush of white-hot lust.

She was standing in his reception area and his mind couldn't even compute what she was wearing.

Black liquid trousers clung lovingly to long shapely legs.

Leather, Ari, it's called leather, supplied an atom of his brain that was still functioning.

The trousers showcased a very lush but firm bottom.

Blood rushed to every erogenous zone before he could stop it.

Above the waist she wore a black silky top overlaid with lace that highlighted her curvy but toned physique. And those amazing breasts.

His mouth went dry. She looked as if she wasn't wearing a bra—*again*.

Her hair was down, wavy and untamed. He could see that she wasn't wearing much make-up, but she didn't need it. Like Princess Laia, she had a natural beauty and stunning bone structure.

At least she was wearing shoes this time, even if they were spindly high-heeled sandals that added inches to her height. Which would put her even closer to his mouth.

Basta. Enough.

This woman, whoever she was, was intent on making a total fool out of him and she would be punished for that. And, *worse*, for making him want her.

He willed the lust in his body down to a dull throb and stepped forward out of the shadows.

'Princess Laia, thank you for joining me.'

Maddi started and turned towards where the King's voice had come from. A door leading out of the reception area. He looked mouthwateringly handsome, wearing dark trousers and a white shirt open at the neck.

He came towards her and she had to stop herself from moving back. Not because he intimidated her—but because of her own reaction. Her pulse was suddenly thundering, her skin prickling all over with awareness.

'King Aristedes.'

She suddenly wondered if she should curtsey, but maybe it was a bit late for protocol.

He stopped and held out a hand, indicating to the room beyond. 'Please, come in.'

She walked ahead of him, a little wobbly in the high heels, very aware of him behind her. The room she entered was vast, and had stunning views straight out to sea. French doors were open and a light breeze brought in scents of the island—wild flowers and the sea. Intoxicating.

The room was as opulent as the rest of the palace but also surprisingly not as decadently decorated as she had imagined it might be for a monarch. It was almost minimalist in style, with a few pieces of furniture and some abstract art on the walls. Maddi liked the unfussiness of it.

'And, please, I think there is no need for formalities. Call me Aristedes.'

Maddi turned around. Her breath hitched at just how gorgeous he was against this backdrop. Tall and vital and *sexy*.

Somehow she found her voice. 'Okay... Aristedes.' It felt unbelievably decadent, just saying his name.

He asked, 'Would you like a drink?'

He walked over to a drinks cabinet with that loose-limbed grace. For the life of her Maddi couldn't understand why Laia thought this man was staid...boring. He oozed a dynamic energy that made her skin prickle and her blood thunder.

He looked at her. Her mind was blank. Wiped clean because he was so distracting.

Drink, supplied a helpful voice. He'd asked her if she wanted a drink.

She was losing it. She wasn't sure what she should ask for, but the thought of something to take the edge off her self-consciousness sounded good. 'What are you having?'

He looked a little surprised by her question. 'A small whisky.'

Impetuously she said, 'I'll have the same.'

He brought over a tumbler with rich dark golden alcohol covering the bottom. She took it from him and sniffed it appreciatively.

She looked up. 'Scotch?'

He took a sip and nodded. 'How did you know?'

'My—' Maddi stopped. She'd been about to say, *My step-*

father is an aficionado. 'I took an interest on a trip to Scotland once.' She mentally crossed her fingers, hoping that Laia had been on a trip to Scotland.

Aristedes said, 'Ah, yes, I think you went there with your father?'

Maddi made a non-committal sound and took a sip, hoping he'd move on. The drink was fiery and immediately warming.

The sun was starting to set outside and the sky was turning a golden pink. Entranced, Maddi walked over and stood at the open French doors, beyond which there was a balcony and then nothing but a precipitous drop to the crashing sea below.

She sensed him coming close behind her.

She said, with genuine emotion, 'I would never get tired of this view.'

The similar sunsets on Isla'Rosa were also spectacular.

'I always had the impression that you were eager to travel and see the world beyond your own country. You've certainly spent little enough time on Isla'Rosa since your father died.'

Maddi tensed. Out of her and Laia, she was definitely more of a home bird. Laia—apart from trying to promote an image of a globe-trotting socialite—did have more of a wanderlust.

Maddi avoided his eye and looked out to the view again. She shrugged minutely. 'I'm young. I knew I would only have a finite amount of time before my ability to travel freely would be curtailed.'

A sound from behind them made Maddi turn around. There was a butler in uniform.

He bowed his head. 'Dinner is served, Your Majesty.'

'Thank you, Felipe.'

Aristedes stood back and said, 'This way, please.'

Maddi followed the butler and sent up silent thanks that Aristedes hadn't had a chance to pursue that last line of conversation, presumably relishing the chance to vent his ire about having to chase down his elusive fiancée.

Felipe led them into a relatively small private dining room. It was more elaborately decorated than the first room, in a rococo style. A table was set with a white linen tablecloth and silver service. Crystal glasses. More French doors were open, allowing that soft fragrant breeze to enter the room. There was another small balcony outside.

They sat down at the table and Maddi put the clutch bag she'd brought with her on the corner of the table. At the last minute she hadn't known what to bring, so she'd just stuffed her phone into the bag.

The butler left and the King took his napkin and flicked it open before laying it on his lap. Maddi locked eyes with him and for a moment saw something that made a little shiver go down her spine. *He knows.* But then whatever she'd thought she'd seen was gone and she robustly told herself she imagined it.

She put her own napkin across her lap. 'The style of these two rooms is very different…is there a reason for that?' she asked.

A shadow passed across Aristedes's face, but it was so fleeting Maddi thought she might have imagined it.

He said, 'I had the palace redecorated throughout on the death of my father.'

Maddi was about to ask, *When was that?* but as Laia she should know.

She took a quick gulp of water. 'I like what you've done. It's very…elegant. But this room is different.'

That was an understatement. She looked up now to see a mural on the ceiling—cherubs and clouds and voluptuous women.

'This room was my mother's favourite. When it came to it, I couldn't change it.'

Maddi looked at him. 'You were close?'

His face became expressionless. 'Close enough.'

On that succinct and distinctly chilly response the butler and some maids appeared with their starters. A light salad of sweet pear with walnuts and parmesan. White wine was poured and it tasted light and slightly fizzy.

'That was delicious,' Maddi said after she'd cleaned her plate.

'All locally grown.'

'As is most of the food on Isla'Rosa,' Maddi felt compelled to point out.

Every weekend one of her favourite things to do was to go down to the farmers' market and buy ingredients to cook. She'd been teaching Laia how to cook recently.

Her heart squeezed. Where was she? Had she got away somewhere safe? There hadn't been another text message yet.

Aristedes lifted his glass in salute. 'We are very lucky to have such wonderful resources.'

He sounded faintly mocking. But then Maddi wondered if she was hearing things. Being paranoid. The staff came back and removed their plates, then returned with the main course—a light and flavoursome beef stew.

'You have a good appetite.'

Maddi put down her fork and felt a dull flush climb into her face. Her endless capacity for food was an affectionate joke between her and her sister.

'I like food.'

Maddi knew she sounded defensive. And she knew she wasn't exactly behaving like a delicate princess. What she wanted to know was how they had got the beef so tender and tasty. Had they marinated it?

'When you were here with your father as a teenager you were a vegetarian. Obviously that was a phase?'

Maddi went panicky and cold inside as she thought furiously of when she'd last seen Laia eating meat. And then she relaxed. It had been a week ago—she'd eaten a burger. Well, she'd eaten half and Maddi had eaten the other half.

'Yes, it was a phase,' Maddi said with some relief, and picked up her glass of wine to take another sip.

'And have you always had that gap between your front teeth? I've never noticed it before.'

Maddi almost spat out her wine, but somehow managed to keep it in her mouth and swallow it without looking as if she was choking. She did have a gap in her front teeth. Not hugely prominent, but enough of a feature to be noticeable.

She decided to try and brazen it out. 'Are you sure you've never noticed it before? We haven't exactly been…close.' A frisson of awareness skittered over her skin.

Aristedes shook his head, eyes on her. On her mouth. 'I think I would have remembered a feature like that. It's… noticeable.'

'Maybe my teeth are just…growing apart?'

'In that case perhaps you should see the palace dentist?'

Maddi wanted to squirm. 'I'm sure it's nothing to worry about. Teeth shift all the time. I remember when I had braces—'

'I don't remember you with braces.'

He knew, and he was toying with her.

The suspicion lodged in her head, making Maddi even more trenchant. 'I didn't visit here all that often, I had them as a young teenager.'

Laia had told her she'd always tried to duck out of visiting with her father over the years.

'Clearly I should have paid more attention.'

His tone was perfectly bland, but Maddi looked at him suspiciously. He watched her lazily. She had an impression of a big jungle cat, toying with a morsel of food. The air around them felt closer. Heavier.

The staff came back, breaking the weird moment, and cleared the plates.

The butler asked, 'Would Princess Laia like some dessert? Tea or coffee?'

'Or perhaps a digestif?' the King interjected.

Maddi looked at her wine glass. It was empty. The wine together with the whisky was already having an effect. The thought of dessert was tempting, but she didn't want to draw attention to her appetite again and she knew Laia didn't have a sweet tooth like her.

She shook her head and smiled at Felipe. 'Just a coffee would be lovely, thank you.'

'I'll have the same. Thank you, Felipe.'

Alone with him again, Maddi felt pinned under Aristedes's gaze. She stood up and went to the balcony, looking out over the sea. It was dramatic and awesome. She looked down. And not a little terrifying. A suspicion slid into her mind. Had he brought her here on purpose, because he was going to expose her and then tip her into the sea as punishment?

Felipe returned with coffee and biscuits and Maddi went back to the table. She tried to ignore the tension once they were alone again and busied herself with milk and sugar.

'Sweet tooth?' Aristedes enquired.

Maddi cursed herself and put back the second spoonful of sugar. 'Sometimes. But not in general, no.'

Then he said, almost idly, 'I'm glad you're finally here. We've been waiting a lifetime for this moment.'

Laia had. Maddi, up until relatively recently, had been living a very normal life.

Well, normal except for the fact that she hadn't had a boyfriend yet. Or a casual lover. Or a one-night stand. All the boys she'd met had seemed like…boys. Not men. She hadn't been remotely interested. She hadn't felt anything.

Until she'd seen Aristedes climb out of his car in the desert in his ridiculously out of place three-piece suit.

Maddi cursed her hormones for being triggered by the worst person in the world for her to develop a crush on. Literally the worst. The most inappropriate.

She tried to focus on what he'd said. 'I… Yes, I guess we have been waiting a lifetime.'

'And only another two weeks until you will become Queen of Santanger and of your own kingdom.'

'Of which you will also become King.'

He dipped his head. 'As has been the agreement since you were born and since I was eight years old.'

Curiosity got the better of Maddi for a moment. 'And it really doesn't bother you that this is a marriage purely for business purposes?'

'And succession purposes. We will have children, Laia.'

Heat bloomed between Maddi's thighs at the thought of making those children. She pressed her legs together under the table. She was not here to make children with this man!

He went on, 'Not to mention for all the very good reasons of promoting peace and fostering economic growth on Isla'Rosa. You have nothing to lose.'

'Only my autonomy—my country's autonomy.' Maddi knew Laia would have wanted her to say that.

'*We* don't get to have autonomy. We have responsibilities to our people.'

Maddi leaned forward. 'But don't you want to be happy? I mean, I'm no idealistic romantic, but surely a marriage will thrive better if there is a sense of companionship and…' She stopped.

He arched a brow. 'And?'

Maddi's face was hot now. 'Mutual…attraction?'

'Oh, I think we have something we can work with.'

Maddi balked. 'You do?' It came out as a squeak.

Aristedes stood up on the other side of the table and held out a hand. This was heading into territory that Maddi had no idea how to navigate. Reluctantly, but also with an electric buzz in her blood, she put her hand in his and let him help her up. He moved closer, so they were standing only inches apart by the table.

Maddi couldn't look away from his eyes. They were dark, but she could see golden lights, very deep. Like fires burning. She was burning too, inside. She couldn't breathe.

Aristedes lifted her hand and held it close enough to his mouth for her to feel his breath. Her breasts felt heavy, and something completely new and alien coiled and writhed, alive in her lower body. She felt hungry, but it wasn't for food.

His mouth was…sinful. Firm. Sculpted. She desperately wanted him to touch his lips to her skin.

But he didn't bring her hand to his mouth. He said softly, 'Exactly how long are you planning on keeping up this charade?'

The heat haze in Maddi's body went cold. 'I'm sorry… what did you say?' Maybe she'd misheard him?

He said, slowly and distinctly, 'We definitely have something we can work with—which would be very convenient if you were, in fact, my fiancée, Princess Laia. But we both know you're not, are you?'

He knew. Had he known all along? Since when? The plane?

Maddi's brain went into freefall. She tried to pull her hand back but the King held on. Not too tightly. But tightly enough.

He said, 'Who are you?'

Desperately scrabbling for time to think, Maddi asked, 'When did you know?'

He looked at her for a long moment and then let her hand go, pacing away to the French doors. Ridiculously, Maddi felt almost rejected. She held her hand to her chest.

He turned around and looked at her, and at her hand. Sharply, he said, 'Did I hurt you?'

'No, not at all… I just…'

She dropped her hand. How could she explain that when he touched her it had burned, but not in a bad way?

He folded his arms across his chest, but that only made her notice the way his muscles pushed against his shirt. 'So, who are you?'

Maddi swallowed. 'I'm Princess Laia's lady-in-waiting.'

'What's your name?'

Rapid-fire questions.

'Maddi Smith.'

'You look very alike.'

Maddi scrabbled to find an explanation. No way could she tell him she was Laia's half-sister. He would use the information to draw Laia out of hiding, or God knows what else.

'Have you never heard of doppelgangers? We're just very alike. My mother was from Isla'Rosa…' She stopped there.

'Did you grow up there?'

She shook her head. 'No, I grew up in Ireland.' To stop him asking questions for a minute she repeated her own. 'When did you know?'

'I don't think you're really in any position to ask questions, are you?'

Maddi bit her lip and she saw his gaze move there. The air between them snapped and crackled.

He looked back up. Almost as if he couldn't help himself, he finally said, 'The dog. I saw you with the dog. I remembered Laia has a fear of them because of her father.'

Of course. Maddi had stopped to pet a dog one day, when she and Laia been walking somewhere, and she'd only noticed that Laia had turned to stone behind her after a few seconds. Laia had explained about her irrational fear. She wanted to like dogs, but her father's fear after being attacked as a young boy had seeped into her consciousness too, and she couldn't seem to let it go.

'So what happens now?' she asked.

Aristedes sat back on the wall of the balcony and Maddi felt her insides swoop as she thought of the perilous drop on the other side.

Before she could stop herself, she put out a hand, 'Could you not do that, please?'

He frowned. 'Do what?'

'Perch on the only thing between you and crashing to your death on the rocks below.'

He didn't move. 'These walls have been here since the Middle Ages and they'll outlast us.'

Something about her face must have transmitted how terrified she was and he stood up. 'What happens now? What happens now is that you tell me where Laia is.'

Maddi's hand dropped back to her side. 'I don't know.'

The King's mouth compressed. 'I don't suppose you went through all this just to turn around and give me her location.'

Maddi almost felt sorry for him. 'No. But the truth is that I have no idea where she is. Honestly. All I was doing was giving her a chance to escape.'

'Escape the life she knew she was destined for? A life of privilege?'

'She wants more. And she wants to be Queen of her own country.'

Aristedes, clearly frustrated, ran a hand through his hair, messing it up. 'She *will* be Queen of her own country.'

'Yes, but it'll become just a smaller state—part of Santanger. With the best will in the world, you can't guarantee that it won't. She doesn't want to be Queen of here.'

'I'm afraid she doesn't really have a choice. Where is she?'

Maddi was beginning to feel annoyed. 'I told you—I don't know.'

At that moment there was a *ping* from behind her. She went cold. *Her phone.*

She turned around and grabbed her bag. She opened it and looked at the screen. All she could see without unlocking it was the start of a message from Laia:

Mads! It's all cool. I'm safe and very far away in...

She couldn't see the rest of the message without unlocking the phone.

She looked up. Aristedes was in front of her, holding out his hand.

'That's a message from Laia, isn't it? Give it to me.'

No way.

Maddi clutched the phone tightly in her hand and dropped the bag to the floor. She slowly moved sideways around the King and backed towards the open French doors.

He kept his hand out and turned to face her. He said warningly, 'Maddi...the phone.'

But Maddi could feel the air behind her now, and before she lost her nerve she turned around and hurled the phone out into the sky that was now dusky.

She wondered vaguely how long it would take for the phone to reach the rocks and smash to bits. Or had she thrown it hard enough to land all the way in the sea?

CHAPTER FOUR

AN HOUR LATER, Ari was still pacing back and forth in the private dining room, filled with so many volatile emotions and, worse, *desire*, that he didn't know what to unpick first.

He couldn't get the image of Laia—*blast it!*—Maddi out of his mind's eye, when she'd been standing in front of him with huge eyes and biting her lip. In that moment, in spite of her deception, all he'd wanted to do was cup her face in his hands and kiss that treacherous mouth until she was soft and pliable in his arms and—

Mierda.

He'd never been so distracted by his hormones. And for it to be happening now was particularly galling. He needed all his wits about him. Maddi had been returned to her suite of rooms with a guard outside. He couldn't afford to have her disappear now. Not when she was his only link to Princess Laia.

He couldn't believe she'd thrown her mobile phone into the sea. But there would be other ways for them to communicate. He just had to make sure he knew when they did.

He left the dining room and went back to his offices and paced some more there. He was about to call for his senior advisor, but at the last moment he stopped when something occurred to him.

He was the only person who knew about this. Who knew that Maddi Smith was *not* Princess Laia.

The last thing he needed now was a tabloid frenzy if the story slipped out. He had his brother Dax on the case, tracking down Laia. There was no one he trusted more in the world. Dax would find her and return her to Santanger.

In the meantime...everyone believed Princess Laia was here. And that their engagement was progressing. So why shouldn't he take advantage of that situation? He would have to delay the wedding preparations that had been put into motion as soon as he'd found Laia—*Maddi*. But he would just explain it as wanting to extend their engagement for a short time. After all, they'd spent hardly any time together.

As it was, the specific details of the wedding date etc hadn't been made public yet, out of a very small but real risk of rebel elements using the wedding to stoke up unrest in the kingdoms. So, if anything, he could use this to his advantage now.

Clearly when the real Princess Laia did arrive they *would* have some things to discuss. As much as he would have liked simply to switch the fake Princess for the real one, he could recognise that that wasn't practical. Laia had certainly made it clear that she wasn't coming into this marriage willingly.

So, no matter what happened the wedding was on hold. But not derailed. Not as long as he had 'Princess Laia' here, sticking to the engagement schedule.

Until the real Princess got here, no one would be any the wiser, and they could get on with planning the wedding.

The thought of Laia shirking her duty sent fresh anger through him. They didn't have the luxury of shirking their duty. He didn't. And neither did she. Their marriage was the next step in the process of making Santanger even stronger. Creating a new royal dynasty. Creating the next generation of rulers.

The fact that it would also ensure lasting peace between their two countries was an added bonus. In an unstable world, people wanted assurances of longevity and stability and their marriage would permanently defuse any of the small, but lingering rebel elements in both kingdoms. It was time to let the past go for good and move into a new harmonious future.

Ari had never entertained any notions of marrying for love—he'd witnessed what love had done to his mother. Made her weak and bitter. And all the while his father had shown his callous disregard, taking lovers into his private rooms while his wife, his Queen, had self-destructed.

Something Maddi had said came back to him...

'But don't you want to be happy? I mean, I'm no idealistic romantic, but surely a marriage will thrive better if there is a sense of companionship...'

He didn't disagree with that sentiment entirely. He knew exactly what he expected from his marriage to Princess Laia. Mutual respect. Integrity. And, yes...ideally, companionship. From which they would create a stable union and a secure foundation for their heirs. With none of the drama and emotion and histrionics he'd witnessed in his parents.

But as for happiness...? Happiness wasn't something Ari had ever expected or craved. It wasn't something he needed. He would find happiness in knowing that things were proceeding as they should. As they'd been planned. Meticulously.

And right now he was *not* happy.

An image of Maddi popped into his head...standing there so defiantly after she'd thrown her phone away. Tall and strong and curvaceous. Like some sort of amazon warrior. She'd looked regal in that moment. *And sexy as hell.*

Ari shook his head to dispel the image and the thought. He would control this entire situation—including his rogue hormones. She would not get away with this audacity.

But there was one thing he needed to attend to, with possibly the only other person in the world he trusted as much as his brother. An old friend who now ran a security company that provided his protection and that of every other high-ranking individual on the planet.

After a small amount of chitchat, Ari said, 'If I give you a name, can you investigate and ask no questions?'

'Of course. Consider it done.'

'Thank you.' Ari gave his friend the name and terminated the call. If there was anything he needed to know about Maddi Smith, his friend Antonio Chatsfield would unearth it.

The following morning

'You are welcome here as my guest, until such time as Laia arrives. And I can assure you she will. I have someone looking for her right now.'

'Who?' asked Maddi.

She hadn't slept well last night—unsurprisingly. But not just because Aristedes had found out about the deception. No, her fractured sleep and dreams had been populated by very disturbing images of him punishing her for her transgression by hauling her into his hard body and kissing her until she was dizzy and molten. Senseless.

She'd been woken early by Hannah, who had told her the King would join her for breakfast in her suite. A small dining table had been set up in the sitting area.

She hadn't known what to expect of the King this morning but he seemed perfectly sanguine. She didn't trust it.

'Who, what?' he asked as he plucked a grape from the fruit bowl and popped it into his mouth.

Maddi couldn't help but feel slightly jealous of the grape as those firm lips closed around it. He was wearing a light blue shirt today, and dark trousers. Beard neat and trim. Hair thick and pushed back from his face, revealing all its hard-boned beauty. He really was spectacular.

'Maddi?'

She blinked. She was losing it. 'Who have you sent to look for Laia?'

'The best person for the job. My younger brother, Crown Prince Dax.'

Maddi's eyes widened. If there was anyone in the world Laia disliked more than Aristedes—and, to be fair, she didn't *not* like him…she just didn't want to marry him and thought he was too serious—it was his brother. The renowned playboy, the 'spare' heir, Crown Prince Dax de Valle y Montero.

Maddi had been surprised at the level of Laia's dislike for the man. Whenever she saw pictures of him with yet another beautiful model, stepping out of a club, or lounging on a yacht, she would make dismissive comments about his lack of a work ethic and/or his lack of responsibility to his duties.

It was ironic, really. Laia was perceived as being not unlike Crown Prince Dax, but in reality she couldn't be more different. Maddi felt sorry for the guy if he did manage to find Laia.

'Anything you'd like to share?' asked Aristedes.

He'd obviously noticed her reaction.

Maddi shook her head and wiped her face clean of expression. 'No, nothing at all.'

She put half a croissant in her mouth to stop herself from blurting anything out. She had a habit of speaking whatever was in her head. It was a miracle Aristedes hadn't figured her out as an imposter sooner.

When she'd swallowed the croissant, she said, 'What if I don't want to stay here as your guest?'

'But I insist.'

'You mean, you're going to keep me here as a prisoner?'

He made a face. 'So dramatic… Nothing like that. Considering the fact that you've offered yourself up in place of Laia, I'm merely accepting your offer.'

'Offer…? I haven't offered anything.'

'The moment you stood in front of me and let me believe you were Princess Laia, the offer was made. Everyone here believes you are Princess Laia, and that's how it shall remain until she assumes her rightful place by my side.'

Maddi went cold inside. She hadn't really thought ahead to what would happen if she was found out. 'You can't keep me here against my will.'

'Oh, you'll stay, and it'll be your choice—as it was your choice to come here. You'll be doing what's best for Princess Laia and Isla'Rosa and her future marriage.'

'How's that, exactly?'

'I could expose you in a second. That would cause lurid headlines for Princess Laia and potentially draw her out of her hiding place... But it would also be a scandal for me, and I don't particularly relish adverse headlines—I never have.'

No, he hadn't. Contrary to his younger brother's behaviour, since Aristedes had ascended to the throne on his father's death he'd always stayed within the margins of propriety and respectability. If he took lovers they were from a pool of socially acceptable peers. The moment it looked as if things might be getting serious, he cut things off. He'd never jeopardised the wedding pact with Princess Laia. As much as she'd wished he would.

But he hadn't lived as a monk, and along with his brother he'd garnered a reputation as a skilful lover. His reputation, of course, was less lurid than Dax's—whose lovers invariably kissed and told. In vivid detail.

He went on, 'There's no need for anyone to ever know about this. You'll keep up the fiction that you are Princess Laia, and you will accompany me to all the events she was scheduled to attend during her time here.'

'But...' Maddi's brain felt foggy. 'What if someone notices I'm not her?'

'They won't get close enough to see the small differences. You fooled me, and I've met her. You really are very similar.'

'Doppelgangers,' muttered Maddi.

'When Laia gets here no one will be any the wiser and we can all get on with our lives.'

His calm self-assurance made Maddi feel prickly—or was it his insistence that as soon as Laia arrived she'd be jettisoned in favour of her half-sister, even when there was this palpable...*thing* between them, like a current of electricity?

'You're very certain it will all work out in your favour.'

'Things generally do.'

That made her even pricklier. 'And what's to stop me from leaking the truth and flushing Laia out so I can let her know what your plan is?'

His gaze narrowed on her. 'Do you really want to see your future Queen embroiled in more salacious headlines than the ones referring to her insatiable appetite for partying? No matter what happens, she turns twenty-five soon and she will be Queen. Do you think this stunt will really inspire her people to believe she's ready to rule?'

Maddi was silent. Maybe he had a point. Laia's privy council knew that she was hard-working and hadn't let her responsibilities slide, in spite of her social life. And the people of Isla'Rosa were fiercely loyal to their Crown Princess. But negative press so close to her birthday and the coronation could be damaging.

Then Aristedes said, 'Not to mention the peace agreement. Do I need to remind you of what's at stake if the marriage doesn't go ahead?'

Maddi felt sick. 'But there are other options...'

'Options that I'm not willing to entertain when this dynastic marriage will comprehensively ensure peace for generations to come. To be perfectly frank, whether or not Laia becomes Queen of Isla'Rosa before or after our marriage isn't really all that important, but the marriage must take place.'

Maddi felt defeated by his determination. He'd obviously come to terms with the fact that Laia might be crowned Queen of Isla'Rosa before they married, but he still expected her to marry him. He didn't know Laia had other plans, but Maddi had met him now and could appreciate how persuasive he was.

Laia could still find herself getting backed into a corner where she might feel she had no option but to go ahead with the marriage. What if he refused to discuss peace plans unless they were married? If anything, the stakes would be even higher if she'd already been crowned Queen! Then all of this would have been for nothing.

Maddi longed to warn Laia. But she had no way of contacting her now, after throwing her phone away. She couldn't reveal to Aristedes Laia's plans for another route to peace— he would do something to thwart them. It was more urgent than ever that she do all she could to protect Laia and make sure she got to her birthday and the coronation. She had to trust that Laia had considered all this and knew what she was doing.

'Okay, I will agree to pose as Laia...until she is found.' Maddi crossed her fingers on her lap under the table.

The King's eyes flicked down. A muscle pulsed in his jaw. 'The table is made of glass, Maddi.'

She hadn't noticed. She went puce and uncrossed her fingers. 'I'm just saying that my priority is protecting her wishes, and if that means pretending to be her then so be it.'

'Don't worry. I have faith in my brother. He hasn't failed me yet.'

Maddi privately wondered how accurate that was, when the guy was never not partying, but she kept it to herself.

'So what happens now?'

He flicked another glance over her attire. She'd dressed in a hurry, pulling on a silk shirt and a pair of designer jeans. She'd had to go braless again, and the shirt was straining a little across her chest. Treacherously, she could feel the tips of her breasts pucker and tighten. She wanted to cross her arms, but didn't want to draw even more attention to the area.

Aristedes said briskly, 'I've postponed the wedding plans for now. My staff believe it's so that we can spend more time getting to know one another, so you'll be spared a wedding dress fitting. But I'll arrange for a stylist to order some more...suitable clothes. Then you'll be slotted into the schedule we had already arranged to introduce the people of Santanger to their future Queen.'

Maddi's heart palpitated. She tried desperately to stop images of herself trying on wedding dresses from forming in her head. 'Schedule...? That sounds busy.'

'It is,' agreed the King. 'There's an event most days, and you will need lessons in Santanger's history and etiquette. Laia would have known what to do, but you'll need all the help you can get.'

Suddenly Maddi realised that, whether she liked it or not, she was about to be thrown in at the deep end of being a princess. Her insides swooped sickeningly. She hadn't considered things would go this far...but there was no turning back now.

Two days later, Maddi's head throbbed from an overload of information and her body ached from being poked and prodded and waxed and buffed and pummelled. All in the name of transforming her into a sleeker version of her. Into Princess Laia.

She now had an entirely new wardrobe of clothes. Specifically to fit *her*. The wispy, floaty bras were gone and had been replaced by items a little more...supportive, but no less provocative or wispy. It was good to feel a little less exposed again.

She had just had a lesson in Santanger royal etiquette from one of the King's aides, and was now waiting for Hannah to take her to meet the King for lunch.

Maddi hadn't seen him in two days and she was embarrassingly nervous. Like a teenager, with butterflies swooping around her belly. She was wearing a sleeveless plain shift dress in dark caramel tones. It came to her knees, but had a discreet little slit up one side. She wore matching court shoes. She fidgeted in the dress. She felt as if she was going to an interview for a job in a bank.

She'd pulled her hair back earlier into a low ponytail—she'd had it trimmed yesterday, to take some of the unruly heaviness out—but now, in a fit of something rebellious, Maddi pulled her hair free and left it loose, falling around her shoulders.

There was a knock on the door. Hannah appeared. 'Princess Laia? If you'll come with me, please, the King is ready for you.'

Maddi dutifully followed Hannah who was quickly becoming her only real touchstone in this vast and dizzying place full of labyrinthine corridors, dead ends, and spiral staircases disappearing to who knew where—towers for impersonators?

Maddi almost slammed into Hannah's back before she realised they'd stopped outside a door. This was a different door from the one leading into Aristedes's private suite of rooms. Once again, guards were present. One of them opened the door, stepped in, announced Maddi and then stood back to let her enter.

She realised immediately that it must be his offices. Bright and airy. Surprisingly modern. She saw an anteroom to one side with desks and staff. A couple looked up curiously. She seemed to be in a reception area.

And then a door opened to her right and there he was, effortlessly filling the frame with his tall, powerful build. He looked slightly hassled. A little bit grim.

'Princess Laia, please come in.'

He stood back to let her pass and his scent washed over her and through her. Evocative and potent. His office was huge, with a separate seating area where there was a TV with a rolling news channel on mute. Floor-to-ceiling bookshelves filled one side, and vast windows looked out to the vista of the sea and the island on the other side.

There was a table set up for lunch. Aristedes gestured to it. 'Please, take a seat.'

Maddi did so, aware of his eyes on her as he sat down too. Would he approve of her slightly more put-together appearance? She sneaked a look at him and flushed. His dark eyes were boring into her.

'What is it? Do I not look the part? They spent hours working on me—'

'My brother has gone AWOL.'

Maddi felt a jolt of relief. She put her hands in her lap. 'Oh. Well, maybe he's gone to a party somewhere.'

Aristedes's expression darkened. 'What are you suggesting?'

Maddi refused to let him intimidate her. 'That he has a reputation for…such things.'

'He would not be distracted in this instance. Not if it's a request from me.'

Maddi shrugged minutely. 'Well, you know him better than me. I've never met him.'

Aristedes stood up and paced back and forth, muttering to himself—something about it not being like Dax to just disappear. Secretly, Maddi wondered if Laia had anything to do with it. Maybe he'd tracked her down and she'd managed to disable him in some way?

Aristedes turned around and glared at her. Maddi felt a very illicit throb of awareness.

'Are you sure you don't know anything about this?'

She lifted her hands. 'No phone. No means of communication.'

Aristedes made a sound of frustration and sat down again, flicking out his napkin before laying it across his lap.

Maddi felt guilty then, and leaned forward. 'Don't worry. I'm sure he's okay.'

Aristedes made another sound—a snorting one. 'Oh, I don't doubt that. He can handle himself better than my most experienced security guards.'

A staff member came in with plates of salad, light and zesty, served with fresh crusty bread. Maddi's mouth watered, but she stopped herself from falling upon the food. She hadn't eaten much over the last two days, with all the lessons and fittings and beauty treatments.

When they were alone again she asked, 'You're close to your brother?'

He looked at her suspiciously for a moment before saying, 'Yes, very. It was just the two of us.'

'This must have been a fun place to grow up. Hide and seek could take days.'

As if she'd caught him by surprise, he said, 'We did have fun...but when we played hide and seek it was usually us hiding from our nanny or the security guards.'

Maddi smiled. She could imagine two dark-haired imps turning the hair of everyone around them grey. 'I bet you were handfuls.'

'We were—until I had to be prepared for inheriting the crown one day.'

'How old were you?'

'Eight.'

Maddi sucked in a breath. 'So young.'

His gaze narrowed on her. 'I was happy to bear that responsibility.'

'I can't imagine what that must have been like.'

She'd had a carefree childhood. Unlike Laia. And Aristedes. They had that in common. She felt a prick of jealousy and quickly quashed it.

'Do you have brothers and sisters?' Aristedes asked.

Maddi avoided his eye. 'I grew up an only child.' That was factual, at least.

Before he could quiz her on her meaning, their plates were cleared and main courses brought in. Sea bass in a delicious herb sauce with new potatoes and vegetables. Maddi concentrated on eating to avoid making conversation.

'You like your food. I don't remember Laia having such a healthy appetite.'

Maddi swallowed a mouthful and fought back a wave of self-consciousness. She wiped her mouth with the napkin. 'I appreciate food, yes. I enjoy cooking it too.'

He arched a brow. 'A cook and an impersonator? That's impressive.'

That stung. But it was a fair comment.

He went on, 'What else do you do? I have a feeling you could turn your hand to pretty much anything.'

Maddi was fairly sure he didn't mean that as a compliment. Self-consciousness struck again. 'I didn't go to university. I was never academically inclined. When I left school I went to work in Dublin in a…a casino.' She almost winced as she said this.

'As a croupier?'

She shook her head. 'No, a waitress.'

She shuddered slightly as she recalled the wandering hands of some of the male clients. Especially after a few drinks or winnings.

Quickly, she said, 'But I also worked in restaurants, and

as a nanny for a while. I'm an expert in cooking for kids of a certain age and convincing them that broccoli is fun to eat.'

Aristedes looked mildly horrified. Princess Laia *had* gone to university, to do a degree in international relations and economics. She was able to navigate a state dinner for up to a hundred people without breaking a sweat. *She* was obviously ideal to become the wife of King Aristedes. No wonder he was so intent on pursuing her.

For the first time in her life Maddi felt inadequate, when before she'd always held a certain amount of pride in her ability to jump into any situation and do well in spite of her lack of academic qualifications.

Feeling defensive, she asked, 'What did you do at university?'

He looked at her. 'I didn't go.'

'Oh? Why not?' Maybe he'd already had all the information. She wouldn't be surprised.

'My father died when I was eighteen and I became King. There was no time to go to university.'

'Did you want to go?'

'I had a place at Harvard. Yes, I would have loved it.'

Maddi's heart squeezed. He actually sounded wistful.

'What were you going to study?'

His mouth quirked slightly. 'Engineering.'

Maddi sat back. 'That's impressive.'

'I still did the degree. I just had to do it remotely. Here.'

'Not quite the same experience as living at a university and being relatively carefree for four years.'

'No. But then I was never destined for a carefree life.'

'Do you mind that your brother got to have that life and you didn't?'

He blinked. 'No, of course not. He has his own set of challenges that I have never faced.'

Like what? Maddi wanted to ask.

But their plates were being cleared now, and coffee was served with little delicious biscuits.

Ari cursed the woman opposite him. Her innocent questions were precipitating a slew of memories. One of which was particularly vivid. He'd been playing chase with Dax, the two of them scuffed and dusty. He remembered that his stomach had hurt from laughing. Suddenly he'd been hauled up by the back of his shirt to see his father's humourless chief advisor glaring at him.

'It's time for your lessons. You've been told you can't play in the palace like this any more. It's not seemly for the heir to the throne.'

Ari remembered the stone-like feeling sinking into his belly. All the happiness gone. The look of disappointment on Dax's face as Ari had been led away to the dusty and musty schoolroom.

Not a hugely traumatic memory, to be fair, but it had signalled the end of the only time in his life when he remembered being free. When he'd had his brother by his side all the time. Before they'd effectively been split up.

He remembered that had also been around the time that his parents' marriage had fractured in plain sight. He'd been told not long afterwards that a princess had been born in another country and that one day she would be his wife. The thought had terrified Ari as a child. Especially when he'd seen his own mother so upset and unhappy.

He'd vowed all the way back then, with a child's logic, that he would never cause his wife to be that unhappy. It was only as he'd grown up that he'd realised what that would mean. No emotion. No love. Because love only caused things like jealousy and insecurity and ultimately tragedy.

'What is it? I ask too many questions…is that it?'

Maddi's voice broke Ari out of the past. He looked at her

and was surprised at the concern on her face. It made something shift inside him. What was he doing, sitting here having a surprisingly easy conversation with this woman who, together with Princess Laia, had thrown the marriage pact between Santanger and Isla'Rosa into complete disarray?

Today she looked…less wild. But no less beautiful. Because she *was* beautiful. More beautiful than he had initially given her credit for. Her bone structure was that of a classic beauty. High cheekbones. Firm jaw. Straight nose. Big eyes, beautifully framed by dark, arching brows and long, luxurious lashes.

She was also now wearing clothes that *fitted*, and in a colour that made her skin look golden and silky. The dress enhanced her curves without being provocative. Yet she was still provocative to him. Even though she wasn't wearing a shirt that strained over her very obviously braless breasts. Even though she wasn't barefoot.

He shook his head. 'It's fine. You didn't say anything that hasn't already been said a million times.'

She shrugged minutely. 'Okay.'

She dunked a biscuit into her coffee and popped it into her mouth, between those lush lips. He caught a glimpse of that maddening gap between her teeth. Everything about her seemed designed to get under his skin like a thorn and *itch*.

She pushed her hair behind her ear at that moment, and Ari caught a glimpse of something twinkling high on her ear.

He leaned forward. 'What is that?'

She looked at him, eyes amber and gold. 'What is what?'

He pointed. 'In your ear.'

Maddi touched it. 'It's a diamond stud.'

'It'll have to go.'

She looked crestfallen. 'It was a gift from someone… special.'

Ari immediately felt hot all over—and not with desire. With something far more volatile. 'A lover?'

She shook her head, making her glossy hair slip over her shoulders. It looked like burnished brown silk.

'No, just a friend.'

The volatility in Ari calmed a little. 'Like I said, you'll have to remove it. It's too…unconventional.'

She lifted her chin. 'Maybe a little unconventionality wouldn't be such a bad thing?'

The volatility was back. No one spoke like that to Ari. Yet, as much as it angered him, he hated to admit that he also found it…refreshing.

He said, '*If* you were Princess Laia I would be happy to pursue a conversation about the merits of unconventionality within the parameters of a royal marriage, but you're not. We have a function to attend this evening. Remove the stud.'

Now Maddi went pale. 'This evening? What event?'

He almost felt sorry for her. *Almost.* 'A garden party here at the palace. Relatively informal. To introduce you to some staff and members of parliament. Important people in Santanger society.'

A few hours after lunch Maddi was standing in front of a mirror in her bedroom, nerves coiling in her belly like restless snakes. She'd got used to dressing formally when working as Laia's lady-in-waiting, but she'd always been dressed to fade into the background, in muted colours.

Now she was dressed to stand out. It was a royal blue silk dress, loosely fitted and mid-length. Sleeveless. Deceptively simple, yet so elegant it took Maddi's breath away. It flowed and moved like air around her body.

She wore matching high heels, and her hair was pulled back into a low bun. Some wild tendrils fought to get loose—

the hairstylist had given up trying to tame them. Her make-up was minimal, yet effective.

She was wearing a string of pearls around her neck and simple pearl drop earrings. A matching bracelet. The diamond stud high in her ear twinkled at her. She had a rebellious urge to leave it there and see how Aristedes would react. But the fact that Maddi wanted to provoke him made her take it out quickly, placing it onto a little tray.

When Laia had noticed her numerous ear piercings, she'd given the stud to Maddi, saying, 'I always wanted to have loads of piercings, but I wasn't allowed. Wear this for me and I'll get to enjoy it through you.'

So that was why it was special to her. It was one half of a pair owned by Laia.

She hadn't expected Aristedes to be so incensed by a fairly conservative piercing, but when he'd asked her earlier if a lover had given it to her he'd looked as if he might explode.

It really shouldn't be attractive to her that he was so incensed by a tiny piece of jewellery, but Maddi found that it only made her want to push him more. To see him react. He was so cool. So sure. It was intoxicating to know she had the ability to affect him—even if it was just by irritating him.

Because irritating him was preferable to thinking about the fact that she was about to go out in front of people and be seen as a princess. Something she wasn't ready for—not even when she was pretending to be Laia. A persona she could hide behind.

'Princess Laia? The King is ready for you.'

Maddi's insides plummeted with fear, but she turned around and forced a smile for Hannah. It wasn't as if she had any reason to *really* care about this event, but she found that she was caring about making a good impression.

On Aristedes, whispered a sly voice.

As Maddi followed Hannah to meet the King, on wobbly

legs she had to admit that, yes, she had a massively inconvenient crush on the guy—but she had to remember where her loyalties lay. With her sister. She wasn't here for herself.

As the King had pointed out so brutally earlier. *'If you were Princess Laia...but you're not.'* That had stung far more than it should. But it was a necessary reminder. She was here under sufferance only, for as long as it took to ensure Laia got her freedom.

CHAPTER FIVE

'THIS IS FOR YOU.'

Maddi looked down at the small velvet box in the King's palm. She looked back up at him, nonplussed. He emitted a sound like a frustrated sigh and opened the box, revealing a ring.

Maddi couldn't help a small gasp. It was beautiful. A large round diamond, surrounded by smaller round emeralds in a gold setting, with more diamonds forming a V shape on either side of the centrepiece before tapering into a gold band.

It was intricate and it looked like an antique. She asked, 'How old is it?'

'It's been passed down from bride to bride in my family for generations.'

Maddi dragged her gaze up. 'But I can't wear this. What if I lose it?'

'You have to wear it. It's the ring people will be expecting Princess Laia to wear. If it's not on your finger, people will talk.'

The King put down the box and took Maddi's hand. She wanted to pull away. Not just because of her reaction to his touch, but because suddenly this was becoming very...real.

The ring was heavy and, amazingly, it fitted. Almost like a mockery of what she and Laia were doing. As if they were doomed no matter what they did.

She shivered a little.

'Cold?'

Maddi shook her head.

Aristedes said, 'Good, then let's go.'

Ari was ultra-conscious of the woman at his side. And for all the wrong reasons. She was dressed perfectly appropriately—exactly like a crown princess, elegant and sophisticated. But he felt the energy emanating from her—unpredictable and electric.

He realised, as they stood and greeted people, that she might very well do something to subvert the marriage pact, even though he thought he'd convinced her that it would be bad for Princess Laia and Isla'Rosa to do anything rash.

It was for that reason, he told himself, that he kept a hand on her elbow—so that he could move quickly if she dared to say anything out of turn. But after a moment he realised that she was trembling lightly. He slanted a look down at her and realised she looked like a deer in the headlights. Terrified.

He said something to his chief aide and suddenly the line of people waiting to greet them was diverted discreetly, leaving them alone for a moment. He turned Maddi to face him. She looked up, still wide-eyed.

'What's wrong?' he asked.

'What's wrong?' she squeaked. 'What's wrong is that I've never done this before and I shouldn't be here.'

Anger and irritation made him stern. 'And yet here you are—precisely because that's how you have engineered it.'

His conscience pricked. He took situations like this completely for granted. He'd been facing them since before he'd hit double digits. He could sleepwalk his way through a meet-and-greet and no one would even know. He might get some satisfaction out of Maddi squirming, but it wasn't going to do him any favours if she didn't at least look comfortable.

'Just let me do all the talking. No one expects you to say

anything. Just smile. But keep your mouth closed so the gap in your teeth isn't so obvious.'

A spark came into her eyes. 'I'm surprised you haven't insisted on dental surgery to correct it.'

Ari was surprised to feel a rush of negativity at that suggestion. 'Don't be ridiculous.'

He was aware of the crowd around them, eyes all over them. He acted on impulse. He took Maddi's hand, the one on which she wore the engagement ring. He lifted it to his mouth and pressed his lips against the back of her hand, keeping his eyes on hers.

Flashes went off around them as the press pack seized their photo opportunity.

It was an old-fashioned, chaste gesture, but even as he made the move entirely cynically, Ari's nostrils were filled with Maddi's scent…light, floral tones with something more complicated underneath.

He saw how her hazel eyes flared, amber and golden. The way colour stained her cheeks. Then she bit her lip. By the time Ari had lifted his mouth from her hand he was on fire all over, and had an urge to wrap his free arm around her, haul her into him and press his mouth against hers in a very public display of desire. Not his usual style at all.

But something about her made him feral, a reversion into some sort of man guided by base instincts and lusts.

This is why she's dangerous.

She wouldn't have to say a word. She'd cause carnage just by fusing his brain cells into a heat haze.

With an effort he really didn't appreciate, he took her hand and tucked it into the crook of his elbow, and then turned back to face the room.

At a discreet nod of his head, his aides let the guests approach again.

* * *

After what felt like hours, Maddi's cheeks and feet were aching. And her hand felt as if all the small bones in it had been crushed by the countless firm handshakes.

The King must have seen her cradle her hand, because he said wryly, 'You'll learn not to let them take your whole hand.'

Maddi huffed. 'You could have given me a heads-up.'

They were standing by the wall of the terrace, with the sea far below. Dusk was starting to stain the sky with lavender hues. Maddi hated to admit it, but she did feel a little mesmerised by the beauty of the place. And its scents...the smell of wild flowers and the salty tang of the sea.

Guards stood nearby—a merciful buffer between them and the now dwindling crowd.

She felt Aristedes's gaze on her and looked at him. He arched a brow. Fair enough, she supposed, considering everything she'd put him through.

Then he said, 'It was a success.'

Maddi tried not to notice how tall and broad he was. He really was stupendously gorgeous. He'd been impressively indefatigable all afternoon. She felt as wrung out as a dishcloth.

'It was? I barely said a word.'

'Everyone saw you and believed what they thought they saw. Princess Laia. That's all we needed.'

'What if we meet someone who really knows her, though?'

The King must have made a gesture, because a waiter materialised with a tray holding two flutes of sparkling wine. Aristedes passed Maddi a glass. She took a big sip, relishing the sensation of relaxing her face muscles. She wished she could slip off her shoes.

'One thing in our favour is that there isn't much traffic between Santanger and Isla'Rosa because of the centuries of conflict. Hence the marriage pact—to encourage peace and unity between the two nations.'

Maddi took another gulp of wine to avoid meeting his eye. She had to admit that, in spite of Laia's feelings, she could understand the benefit in promoting peace. But she was with her sister in not wanting Isla'Rosa to be consumed by the much bigger and richer Santanger.

The wine was making her feel a little reckless, so Maddi said, 'Have you thought about who you'll marry after you've acknowledged that this marriage pact is all but null and void?'

King Aristedes went still. He'd been looking out to the sea. His gaze swivelled to her. 'This marriage pact is not "null and void". Princess Laia was born to a life of duty—just like me. In the end she will do what is right. She is merely behaving like a petulant teenager who knows that ultimately she has no choice. The sooner she realises this, the sooner this tedious game will be over.'

Maddi shook her head. 'But it's an archaic agreement. Surely there are more modern ways to foster peace? She couldn't be making it more obvious that she doesn't want to marry you.'

The King's jaw clenched. Maddi realised then that he probably wasn't used to people speaking so plainly to him. But she had nothing to lose here. And it felt a little exhilarating.

He said tersely, 'I was told at the age of eight that I would marry Princess Laia.'

Maddi held in a gasp. 'But she would have only been a baby.'

'Just born.'

She couldn't help but see an image of a small, serious child, trying to understand such a monumental thing. It made her heart clench.

'That's a lot to put on an eight-year-old's shoulders. Never mind a baby's.'

'Nevertheless, this is how marriages between royal families have happened for generations. It's what we expect.'

'And how many happy royal families do you know?' Maddi asked.

Aristedes's face tightened. 'That's not the point. The point is—'

Maddi put up her hand. 'Duty, responsibility, stability... I get it.'

A discreet cough sounded from nearby.

Maddi flushed at the King's warning look.

He looked over her head. 'Yes, Santo?'

'Sorry to interrupt, Your Majesty, but the call you were waiting for is on hold.'

'Thank you. I'll take it on my phone.' He put a hand into his jacket's inside pocket and took out a sleek mobile phone. He looked at Maddi expressionlessly. 'That is all. Santo will escort you back to your suite.'

His cursory dismissal filled Maddi with conflicting emotions. Chief of which, though she hated to admit it, was *hurt*. He obviously hadn't appreciated their exchange. Hadn't appreciated her opinion. It reminded her that she wasn't of this world. That she'd been rejected by it long ago.

Not for the first time the difference between her and her sister couldn't be starker. On her birth, Laia had already been promised in marriage to a future king. On Maddi's birth, she'd been born to a single unwed mother, heartbroken and abandoned, promised to no one.

If anything, this event had just demonstrated how out of her depth she was. And how far removed she was from being a princess.

She hated the feeling of insecurity that washed over her. Worse, the feeling of rejection.

Before Aristedes turned away she said, in a low voice, 'Is this how you'd be treating Princess Laia? Wheeling her out for viewings and then shutting her away again? Making no attempt to get to know her?'

'If Princess Laia was here, you can rest assured I would, of course, be making an effort to get to know her—after all, she will be my wife. But you are not her, and after Laia and I are married, you and I will never meet again.'

So why would I bother with you?

He didn't have to say it. The words hung in the air.

Aristedes turned and walked away to a quiet corner of the garden and took his call.

Maddi felt stunned. Well, she'd asked for that. She suddenly saw the ruthlessness that had been hiding in plain sight underneath his very suave exterior and it sent a shiver down her spine. *This* man would indeed track Princess Laia down and bring her back here to do her duty, of that she had no doubt.

And in the meantime, she was just an irritating inconvenience.

Somehow, in the last couple of days, Maddi had been fostering some kind of notion that he might not *like* her, or this situation, but that he was…intrigued by her. And that he too felt the electric charge between them. That…

What? asked a snarky voice in her head. *That he's become more interested in getting to know you than the woman who is destined to be the mother of his children? The next Queen of Santanger?*

Full of swirling emotions that she'd stirred up all by herself, by provoking the King into telling her exactly how inconsequential she was, Maddi started when someone coughed discreetly behind her. She turned around to see Santo, the aide, still waiting.

He put out his hand, 'If you'll follow me, please?'

Maddi blindly followed him on wooden legs, feeling ridiculously vulnerable for the first time since she'd taken the audacious move to do something drastic to save her sister.

She'd become adept at not allowing the rejection by her father to get to her, but sometimes it crept through the defences she'd built up over the years and reminded her that she had a hole inside her, and no matter how much she might try to tell herself it didn't matter, *it did*. And the fact that she'd just allowed King Aristedes to remind her of how painful this wound could be was not welcome.

How was it that a man she'd met only days ago could have such a terrifying effect on her emotions?

There was a knock on the door, and then, 'Sorry to disturb—'

'What is it?' Ari snapped moodily. And then felt immediate contrition when he turned from the window and saw the wide eyes of one of his longest-serving aides at the door.

This wasn't like him. He strove at all times to be the opposite of his father, who had been mercurial and unpredictable.

Thanks to his father's disregard for his wife, and his love of other women, Ari had learnt at an early age to depend on himself. He'd received no benevolent guiding hand from either parent. Neither had his brother. He'd had to learn from aides and watching his parents to know how *not* to be.

He'd always treated his lovers with respect. He'd never cheated. And Dax was the same, even if the tabloids made it look otherwise. And yet here he was, distracted and thinking of…a woman. Who wasn't even the woman he was due to marry.

Irritation prickled again. He forced it down.

His aide was still in the doorway, looking nervous. Ari said, 'I'm sorry. My mind was…elsewhere.'

On Maddi, and the way she'd looked after he'd dismissed her the evening before.

He cursed silently.

'I just wanted to remind you that you are taking Princess Laia out for lunch today and it's almost time to leave.'

He'd forgotten his own schedule. Again, that was not like

him. He was fastidious about his schedule and his plans. And he never let anyone down. Not even his imposter fiancée.

'Is she waiting for me?'

'Yes, sir. Down by the main courtyard.'

His aide left. In spite of his best efforts, Ari felt his blood heat with anticipation. But the last words he'd said to her yesterday still reverberated in his head, sickeningly...

'But you are not her, and after Laia and I are married, you and I will never meet again.'

He'd been rude. And she'd looked hurt. Not what he would have expected of the woman who'd had the gall to impersonate the Crown Princess of Isla'Rosa. But if he was being brutally honest he knew that his rudeness had stemmed from how she made him feel, how she pushed his buttons with such ease.

She had a way of saying things, asking questions, that seemed to undermine every belief he'd taken for granted his whole life. And he didn't welcome that. His route had been mapped out for a long time, and he'd been perfectly content to follow it. Especially when it promised smooth waters and no drama. But from the moment this woman had impersonated his fiancée those waters had become choppy and much murkier.

Ari felt defensive. Some might forgive him for being rude, considering where they were and what was happening. Princess Laia and his brother were AWOL. God only knew where. And he was being forced to act out a charade with this...this doppelganger, who just had to breathe beside him to make his blood boil over with irritation and lust.

He didn't have to woo this woman. She was a complete stranger.

Is she, though? asked a little voice. *Why does she feel so familiar, then, and yet mysterious? Why is she so easy to talk to?*

Ari scowled at himself as he pulled on his jacket. Maddi Smith was an interloper. She'd tricked him. But he had to concede that if she *had* actually been Princess Laia, then he would be wooing her. Even though their marriage was a sure thing, he would obviously want her to feel as desired and accepted as possible.

And, following that logic, he would have to treat Maddi the same and not let her get to him. If anyone sensed the tension between them it would cause whispers, and that was the last thing they needed.

He needed her to promote a picture of happy unity—because he had total faith in his brother reappearing with Princess Laia and no doubt he would be marrying the right woman in a couple of weeks.

The fact that Maddi was the first woman he'd ever met who had managed to get under his skin so comprehensively was a mere irritation en route to the start of this next phase of his life with his Queen at his side.

Maddi was down on her hands and knees, desperately searching for a small pearl drop earring. One minute it had been in her ear and the next it had fallen to the stone floor, here in the main central courtyard.

Hannah was on her hands and knees too, saying anxiously, 'I'm sure we'll find it, Princess Laia, please don't ruin your clothes!'

The bodyguards were hunting as well, using their phone torches to try and see into the cracks between the flagstones.

There was a distinct cough from somewhere far above their heads and Maddi's stomach sank. Not that it could sink much more from her inelegant position so close to the ground.

She lifted her head and came eye to eye with a pair of very sleek shoes. They led up to a pair of navy trousers, encasing very long legs, a slim waist…white shirt and matching navy jacket.

King Aristedes. She stood up, brushing dust from her black jumpsuit. She'd felt so sophisticated just moments before, but now she could feel her hair coming loose from its low bun and her face was hot.

He arched a brow in question and Maddi burned inwardly with humiliation, remembering his dismissive and cutting words from yesterday. She'd told herself that nothing he said should matter, and she'd thought she'd convinced herself she could stay immune, but within one second of seeing him again she felt as vulnerable as she had yesterday.

At that moment she really didn't like him.

'I've lost an earring.' She touched her ear.

He frowned. 'It's just an earring.'

'It's a pearl earring, and presumably very expensive.'

Hannah had moved away discreetly, to keep looking, but was no longer on her hands and knees.

The King was impatient, and he put out his hand. 'It's replaceable. Don't worry about it.'

But Maddi hadn't been brought up not to care about valuable items. She knew their worth because her mother had had to work for everything, in spite of the maintenance she'd received from the King of Isla'Rosa.

Stubbornly, she didn't move, and looked down at the ground again. And there, as if to help her out, she saw something white winking at her between two stones.

She let out a triumphant sound and bent down to pick it up, holding it aloft. 'See? Found it.'

She grinned and put it back in her ear. The King's gaze went to her mouth and stopped there. Maddi shut it abruptly, aware of what he'd told her about hiding the gap in her teeth.

His face darkened and he said curtly, 'Can we go, now that the mystery of the lost earring has been solved?'

He led the way out of the courtyard to where a sleek SUV was waiting. Maddi was sorely tempted to stick her tongue out at his back, but she resisted the childish urge.

Once in the back of the SUV, driving out of the palace

grounds and down the mountain towards the city of Santanger, Maddi couldn't help saying, 'Apart from this situation, which you're obviously not happy with, are you usually so grumpy?'

Aristedes's jaw clenched. He pressed a button and the privacy divider went up between them and the driver.

Maddi was genuinely contrite. 'Sorry, I forgot.'

He looked at her, stern. 'What on earth were you doing, on your hands and knees, scrabbling around in the dirt?'

'I told you—looking for the earring. I know it must be valuable.'

He looked nonplussed. 'It's just jewellery.'

She lifted the hand where the engagement ring sat snugly—too snugly—on her finger. 'Like this is *just jewellery?*'

He made a face. 'That's different, of course.'

'So, are you? Always this grumpy?'

And rude, she might have added, if she'd had the nerve.

Something in his demeanour changed for a second, and there was the ghost of a twitch in his lips. So fleeting that Maddi might have imagined it, but it set her heart racing.

'No,' he replied dryly. 'It's uniquely your effect on me.'

For a moment something shimmered between them. Light and delicate. Then Aristedes's phone rang from his pocket and he plucked it out, saying, 'Excuse me. I need to take this.'

He spoke rapidly, in the local dialect, a mix of Spanish and Italian. Much like the language on Isla'Rosa. Maddi had been doing her best to learn it, but she couldn't keep up with the King's rapid-fire delivery.

The SUV was now driving slowly through the charming streets of the city and winding its way up another hill, where it came to a stop. The bodyguard in the front passenger seat got out and opened Maddi's door. She stepped out and realised they were on the top of a hill that overlooked the city and the sea beyond. The views were spectacular.

They walked around a corner and Maddi stopped in her

tracks. A restaurant was perched precipitously on the hill-side. It was made of glass and wood, on several levels, with massive windows and an outdoor terrace. It was an astounding work of architecture and design. Even she could see that, with no real knowledge of such things.

Aristedes put a hand lightly at her elbow to guide her into the building where the manager waited. He was holding the door open and bowed profusely as they approached. 'Your Majesty... Princess Laia, welcome to Paradiso.'

Even Maddi could translate that. Paradise. And it was. They were led to a table tucked discreetly to one side of the upper level, with floor-to-ceiling windows showcasing the amazing view.

When they were sitting down, Maddi couldn't help saying, 'I don't think I've ever been to a more impressive restaurant.'

'And you haven't even tasted the food yet. The best the Mediterranean has to offer.'

Maddi risked a glance at Aristedes, who was the picture of casual elegance even as he exuded a masculine edge that was a reminder of the latent power sheathed in respectable clothes.

'I presume this is an exercise in our being seen and promoting the myth that we're getting to know one another?'

Even though he would obviously prefer to be elsewhere. With his real princess.

'That's exactly what this is.'

He popped an olive into his mouth.

Maddi had been aware of discreet looks from the other patrons as they'd been escorted through the restaurant. It was obviously far too elegant a place for people to rubberneck.

'Do you resent having to do this with me?' she asked, and then cursed herself for looking for punishment. Had she not learnt that lesson yesterday?

The King looked at her, and she felt pinned by that dark

gaze. It reminded her of how it had felt when his mouth had touched her hand the day before.

A waiter appeared with dips and different breads.

Aristedes said, 'I took the liberty of ordering for you, presuming that you'll enjoy most of what's on the menu.'

Maddi was about to protest that she might have liked to choose for herself, but who was she kidding? 'Thank you. I'll be interested to see what you think I'll like.'

The dips and bread were all delicious, and full of flavour. Her favourite was the tomato bread with pesto sauce.

'Try the wine.'

Maddi took a sip of red wine and closed her eyes. It tasted of sun-warmed grapes and blackcurrant. She opened her eyes again to find Aristedes staring at her.

She blushed. 'Sorry, I get a little carried away.'

'Maybe you should have been a chef?'

Maddi wiped her mouth. 'I worked as a commis chef in a restaurant in Dublin once, and after seeing the pressure chefs are under, it didn't appeal. I prefer a much less pressured environment. Like cooking for friends.'

Or her sister, who had been ridiculously impressed with Maddi's pretty basic skills.

'Why did you and your mother leave Isla'Rosa?'

Aristedes had slipped the question in before Maddi could really give herself time to consider it. Wonder what telling him might reveal.

Carefully, she said, 'We left because her relationship with my father broke down. He didn't want to be with us.'

Maddi said the words with a clipped voice, hoping Aristedes wouldn't hear the emotion behind them.

'That must have been hard...to leave her home and move across Europe.'

'To a much wetter country.' She shrugged, belying the

lingering hurt for her mother's pain. 'I was a baby. I didn't know any better.'

'I've been to Ireland…it's beautiful.'

Maddi looked at him. 'You have?' She couldn't recall any state visits from the King—she was sure she would have remembered.

He nodded. 'They were under the radar, not official. Usually to attend financial conferences. The President has extended to me an open invitation for a state visit. Maybe I'll go some day…with my Queen.'

For some reason, the thought of King Aristedes visiting Ireland with Laia at his side pricked Maddi painfully.

She forced a smile. 'You should go at the earliest opportunity. The hospitality is second to none.'

Their main courses were delivered—delicate parcels of pasta filled with ricotta cheese in a light sauce. They ate in a surprisingly companionable silence, but once the plates were cleared Aristedes said, 'I need to apologise.'

She was surprised. 'You need to apologise to me? Shouldn't I be apologising to you every day, because I'm here and you're trying to track down Princess Laia?'

His face darkened and she regretted opening her mouth. She always said too much.

'Sorry, please, go on.'

'Yesterday…what I said to you was not necessary and it was rude. You are obviously close to Princess Laia—close enough to carry out this stunt on her behalf—'

'It was my idea,' Maddi blurted out, even as she registered a soothing of the hurt he'd caused yesterday.

Aristedes stopped. 'What?'

She nodded, hating it that he was now going to retract his apology. But she couldn't let him believe this had been Laia's doing.

'I told her to run. I told her I would try and pass myself off as her.'

There was a taut moment of silence, and then he said, 'She had her chance to do the right thing, but she did as you suggested. She made her choice. This doesn't change anything, really. Except maybe to demonstrate that you're not entirely without integrity.'

A waiter brought coffee and small pastries.

Aristedes went on. 'As I was saying, you're obviously close to Princess Laia, and she trusts you. She will undoubtedly choose to retain you as her lady-in-waiting once she is Queen here, and that will be her choice, of course.'

Maddi was filled with so many conflicting thoughts that she felt a little dizzy. His apology was a surprise, and mollified her somewhat. His arrogant assumption that in spite of all evidence to the contrary Laia would still agree to be his wife was enraging. But worse than all that, and most exposing, was the way she felt to hear him declare so magnanimously that she could remain as Laia's lady-in-waiting. That he would be happy to see her every day and tolerate her presence, even though this…this current of awareness throbbed between them.

And that was when Maddi had to realise that she was being a prize idiot. Because all this awareness was obviously only on her side. This man looked at her and saw nothing but a nuisance. An obstacle between him and his Queen.

She had developed a crush on him on sight, but the only thing she aroused in him was serious irritation. He'd been pretending there was something between them to mock her.

And one thing she knew already. It would be intolerable to be in close proximity to this man every day and not be *his*.

The strength of that conviction shook Maddi.

How much he affected her!

She put down her napkin. 'I'm feeling a little light-headed, actually. Would you mind if we went back to the palace?'

CHAPTER SIX

ARI LOOKED AT Maddi across the back of the vehicle as they drove up the mountain towards the palace. She looked pale. He knew he shouldn't be feeling concerned. This woman had severely disrupted his life. And yet he couldn't help wondering if he'd said something…

Maybe it was throwing her into the deep end of Princess Laia's schedule that was overwhelming her…and it would be just punishment if it was. Except right now Ari didn't have any appetite for revenge or punishment.

What he felt was much more ambiguous. And beneath that was the ever-present thrum of desire.

Her arms were bare in the jumpsuit, and they looked slim, but strong. Her waist was encircled with a gold belt. The jewellery—those pearl earrings—were the essence of understated glamour. Perfect for a queen-to-be. Except he found himself looking for that diamond stud she'd worn high in her ear, like some sort of…free spirit.

But he'd told her to take it out…like a censorious parent. Was that who he was now? Staid and conservative? Stern?

'Are you okay?' he asked.

Maddi nodded and glanced at him. 'I'm fine… I just… needed a little air, maybe.'

She did have some more colour in her cheeks now, and Ari felt something in him relaxing. On an impulse he said, 'I was going to go to my stables and check the horses, maybe go for a ride. Would you be interested?'

She turned to him, eyes wide. More hair had fallen loose from the bun, as if it was impossible to contain her hair fully. 'I'd love to.' She made a face. 'But I only started learning to ride this year on Isla'Rosa, so I'm not very good.'

'That's not a problem. We'll give you one of the more sedate horses.'

'That would be amazing.'

She smiled, and it took Ari's breath away for a second. This woman was full of something he'd never really encountered. Her emotions rose up and she appeared to have no filter for hiding them. They burst out of her irrepressibly. She hadn't been calcified, like him and everyone he knew. It disarmed him.

He instructed the driver to take them straight to the stables and put in a call to have Hannah bring some clothes for Maddi.

Maddi was glad to be engaging in something active to take her mind off how Aristedes made her feel and the things he said that cut her when they shouldn't.

They'd arrived at the stables and Hannah had been waiting there with more suitable clothes. Maddi had changed in a room used by the grooms, and now wore khaki jodhpurs and a white short-sleeved polo top and black boots. And a hard hat on her head.

She'd given Hannah all the jewellery and was glad to feel a little less encumbered. She'd pulled her hair out of the bun and into a low ponytail. For the first time in days she felt more like herself again.

It was her sister who had taken her horse riding for the first time. Laia was a proficient horsewoman, having learnt from an early age. And Maddi loved it, even if the horses still terrified her a little, with their size and sheer power.

There was a knock at the door. 'Princess Laia? The King is ready.'

And she shouldn't keep the King waiting. Maddi almost rolled her eyes. But secretly she was excited to see him in a far less structured habitat. She could already imagine him on a horse…the effortless grace and athleticism.

When she did emerge into the yard she couldn't see him. All she saw was the back of a very tall man tending to a massive chestnut horse. He was wearing faded jeans that clung to his muscular backside and strong thighs with such explicitness that Maddi couldn't look away.

For a moment she felt a giddy sense of relief—the King hadn't had a unique effect on her after all—but then he turned around and Maddi's skin goosebumped all over.

It was the King.

Of course it was.

He was wearing a polo shirt, like her, short-sleeved, showing off impressive biceps. His olive skin was gleaming.

She walked over and he stood aside, his gaze sweeping over her. She felt warm, and tried to ignore this one-sided mortifying awareness.

The horse was saddled and ready. He patted its neck. 'Here she is—La Reina.'

Maddi squinted at him. 'Is that meant to be a joke? She's called The Queen?'

He shook his head. 'Not at all. She *is* the Queen here. She's eighteen years old and she's the dam of some of the best racehorses in Europe today. Some even in Ireland.'

Maddi came closer, nervously. 'She was a racehorse?'

'Very successful, yes. My father bought her as a yearling at a sale in Dublin, when Dax and I were younger.'

Maddi reached out and tentatively touched this great dam's back. 'So you've had her for ever?'

'Yes, I guess so.'

'Is this a stud?'

'No. We do have training grounds and a separate stud nearby, but this is just the palace stables, where we keep La Reina and other horses we use purely for riding. Her mating days are long over now—aren't they, my beauty?'

Maddi watched the King's big, graceful hand and long fingers running over the horse's neck. She whinnied softly and Maddi could empathise.

The nearest stirrup was low and Aristedes said, 'You know how to mount a horse?'

Maddi balked. 'You want me to ride her? What if I hurt her or something?'

He smiled, and for a moment Maddi couldn't think. He looked completely different when he smiled. Younger. Care-free. Less stern.

'You can't hurt her. She's survived more than a novice rider, believe me.'

Maddi stood as Laia had taught her, by the neck of the horse, and took the reins in her hand. Then she lifted her left foot into the stirrup. Absurdly conscious of Aristedes behind her, she put her other hand on the saddle and some-how managed to mount the horse without making a com-plete fool of herself.

He stood at her foot and adjusted the stirrup, bringing it up higher. He looked at her. 'Not bad. You have a good pos-ture in the saddle. You know the basics?'

Maddi was not a little terrified. La Reina was a big horse and she felt very high up. She nodded, but said, 'The very basic basics.'

'Just relax and get a feel for the horse underneath you. She'll guide you.'

A groom led another horse into the yard and Maddi gulped. This horse was a massive gleaming black stallion. He made La Reina look almost petite. Aristedes went over and adjusted the reins before mounting the horse in one effortless muscular movement.

Maddi fidgeted on the horse, to ease the sudden sensation between her legs. The horse moved under her. She stopped, suddenly terrified. Laia had only let her practise on the smallest and most sedate horses at the castle on Isla'Rosa.

Aristedes was securing his hat on his head. He looked back. 'Okay?'

Maddi was nervous. 'We're going to go slowly, yes?'

He nudged his horse with his knee and they started walking out of the yard. 'Very slowly…don't worry. La Reina will follow me and Sooty automatically.'

Maddi nearly fell off her horse. 'Sooty?'

Surely that name was an affront to the majestic beast in front of her?

Aristedes waited for her to come alongside him and then both horses went side by side out onto a wide track.

'Dax and I got this horse when we were teenagers. Typically Dax didn't want to share, so we had to fight for him.'

'What did you do?'

'We had a fist fight. First one down loses.'

Maddi winced. 'I bet your mother was delighted.'

He made a face. 'Yeah, not so much… I broke Dax's nose.' Aristedes looked at her. 'Suffice it to say it was the last fist fight we had.'

'But… Sooty? I'm sorry, but that's almost an insult. Surely he should be called Caesar or Nero or…anything else?'

'As revenge for me winning, Dax logged his name in the official system before I could. And so here is Sooty.'

Maddi couldn't keep the laughter down. It came bubbling

out and she had to throw her head back. She could just imagine a young Aristedes's appalled expression.

'I'm glad you find it amusing.'

'Sorry,' she spluttered, getting control of herself, 'That's just too…evil of Dax.'

After a couple of minutes of companionable silence Maddi found she was getting used to La Reina. She bent down and patted her neck, silently thanking her for not throwing her off as soon as she'd landed on her back.

She sneaked a look at Aristedes in the saddle and almost wept at how beautiful he was. He held the reins easily in one hand, his other resting on his thigh. His body's motion with the horse was perfectly in sync. Maddi felt as if she was bouncing all over the place, but she tried to mimic his posture and discovered an easier rhythm.

The trail was getting narrower, and Maddi was glad she didn't have to try and steer La Reina. The horse seemed happy to just follow Aristedes and Sooty.

Then Maddi spied a beach down below, wide and golden. Unusual… Most of the beaches on Isla'Rosa were stony, so she'd assumed Santanger would be the same.

They made their way down the trail, with scents of herbs and flowers and earth permeating the air around them. It was just the right temperature. Warm. The sun not too fierce.

At last they were on a level with the beach and it opened out before them, wide and pristine.

Maddi lifted a hand to shade her eyes. 'Wow, it's so quiet here. I would have expected it to be thronged.'

'We're still on palace property.'

Of course. Maddi should have realised.

Sooty was dancing under Aristedes and he said, 'I need to give him his head—will you be okay if I give him a gallop?'

Maddi waved a hand. 'We'll be fine. You go ahead.'

So she could watch him like a proper voyeur.

And they were magnificent, man and beast. They trotted down to the water's edge and then they were off, galloping through the sea foam. A vision in masculine beauty, muscles rippling, Aristedes was in total control, barely moving in the saddle.

La Reina seemed content to meander up and down near the treeline, but suddenly out of nowhere a bird was startled and rose out of a bush, squawking loudly. Before Maddi could do anything the horse had reared up.

Somehow, miraculously, she managed to cling on. But then the horse bolted. Maddi realised she had absolutely no control over this powerful beast, which suddenly didn't feel like such a sedate grand dam any more. She felt like a bullet.

Every bone in Maddi's body was rattling as she clung on to the reins for dear life. Surely she'd come to a stop at some point? But they were heading straight for a clump of jagged rocks at the other end of the beach and the horse showed no signs of slowing.

Maddi was about to close her eyes and pray for mercy when a streak of black appeared beside her. Aristedes leant out of his saddle to grab Maddi's reins and he managed to bring both horses to a canter, and then a trot, and eventually to a walk, mere feet away from the rocks—one of which was particularly spiky.

Maddi barely had a chance to get her breath back before hands were reaching for her, around her waist, and she was off the horse and standing on legs that shook like jelly.

Aristedes took off her hat, threw it aside. His was gone too. 'Are you hurt? Are you okay?'

She couldn't answer because he was running his hands all over her—arms, waist, hips—and crouching down to check her legs. He stood up and she realised she was clutching at his arms and her teeth were chattering.

He cursed and pulled her into him, rubbing his hands up

and down her back. 'I'm sorry, that was my fault. I should never have left you alone. La Reina is still powerful. Something must have startled her.'

Maddi pulled back. She was feeling marginally less wobbly, and now other sensations were piercing the shock and adrenaline rush. Like how close she was to Aristedes, their bodies pressed together. How his touch was tender and comforting, but also like an electric charge, transmitting something much more potent than comfort or tenderness.

There were still tremors running through her body but her teeth had stopped chattering. She tried to speak. 'It was a bird… I think. Flew out of a…bush.'

Aristedes looked down at her. 'She could have thrown you.'

Maddi tried to smile but her mouth wouldn't work. 'She tried.'

'Maddi, I'm sorry. The last thing you need when you're learning how to ride is a scare like that. It can put people off for life.'

Maddi didn't want to seem weak or scared. Stoutly, she said, 'I'm okay. I can get back on.' She mentally crossed her fingers, hoping she wouldn't suddenly be terrified.

Aristedes's mouth twitched. 'We'll leave it a minute, hmm?'

Something shifted in the air between them. An awareness of their bodies so close together. Of Maddi's breasts crushed against Aristedes's broad and very hard chest.

They were hip to hip. Thigh to thigh. Suddenly certain that she wouldn't be able to hide her reaction behind shock any more, Maddi tried to pull back—but his arms didn't budge.

'Where are you going?'

She looked up and swallowed. His dark gaze was intense. Surely not… She wanted to shake her head.

She said, 'To stand on my own two feet?'

'Overrated.'

Maddi's brain went into a spin. Aristedes caught some of her hair around his hand. Of course it had fallen loose. It was untameable. Maddi wanted to groan. She must look as if she'd been pulled through a bush backwards.

Then he said, almost musingly, 'I should have known you weren't Laia the moment I laid eyes on you...'

'Why?'

'Because she never made me want to look twice. She never made me *want*.'

Maddi's legs nearly buckled again. She locked her knees. She was wondering if she was dreaming. But Aristedes was looking at her mouth now...hungrily. It was a hunger that caught fire inside her, deep down. She didn't know why, but she'd always had an instinct that this fire could exist. Stubbornly, she'd hoped that it did, and now she was being consumed by it.

She whispered, 'I thought it was just me.'

He shook his head. 'You make me crazy.'

Maddi ducked her head. 'I know. Because of—'

But her chin was tipped back before she could complete her sentence and Aristedes was shaking his head again.

'Because of *this*.'

And then, before Maddi could take another breath, he was kissing her. She was suspended in time and place for a second, as his strong, firm mouth moved over hers, and then, as if coming out of a trance, she was suddenly kissing him back with a ferocity that might have scared her if she'd had a functioning brain cell left in her head.

Waves of relief washed through her.

He wanted her too.

And then there were much more potent things.

Desire fast turning to lust.

He angled her head and she opened her mouth on a breath. Everything changed. His tongue touched hers and Maddi's heart pounded at the electric shock it brought, sending a jolt through her entire body, down to between her legs, where she *ached*.

He was demanding a response from her that she willingly gave. Matching him stroke for stroke. She was intoxicated.

He clamped his hands on her waist and pulled her even closer. She gasped into his mouth when she felt the hard evidence of his arousal against her lower body.

But even in the midst of this moment of total and utter conflagration, Maddi had the very unsettling sense of something else. She felt as if she was...*coming home*.

But she couldn't unpick that now. It was too confusing. Disturbing...

Aristedes broke the kiss.

Maddi was gasping, dizzy. She opened her eyes with an effort and for a second he was a blur. Then he came back into focus. His face was stark with the hunger she felt. Eyes burning.

Her mouth was swollen.

He looked at her and shook his head. 'Who *are* you?'

Maddi couldn't speak. She knew he wasn't just asking her to repeat her name. She could have asked the same of him. Right now, he didn't remotely resemble the man that Laia had always described as uptight, strict, humourless.

This man was the most exciting person Maddi had ever met, and just moments ago he'd touched her with a tenderness that she'd never encountered before. Not even from her own mother.

One of the hands on her waist moved up, disturbingly close to the underside of her breast. Maddi's breath grew choppy again.

He said, 'I've been dreaming of you... Of touching you.'

Between her legs she felt hot and damp. 'You have?'

He nodded. His hand crept under her top. She could feel

the roughness of his palms and almost groaned. He was a king…he should have soft hands from being waited on. But he didn't. He had the hands of a worker.

And then one hand was cupping the weight of her breast.

Maddi bit her lip and Aristedes tugged it free with his thumb. He bent his head and kissed her again. This time slowly, carefully, thoroughly. He squeezed the generous flesh of her breast and she moaned into his mouth, pressing closer, relishing the hard evidence of his desire.

His hand on her breast squeezed harder. Maddi's nipples were stiff, tingling. Aching. And then his thumb found the hard tip and teased it, over and over, through the flimsy covering of lace. Maddi was turning into a boneless pool of lust. She didn't feel human any more. She'd become a creature of base needs.

Aristedes broke the kiss again, breathing harshly. 'I could take you right here and now…'

Maddi opened her eyes. She should be shocked by what he was suggesting. But the fact was that every cell in her body vibrated with agreement.

Yes, please. Take me right now.

But Aristedes pulled back, and Maddi had to stop a sound leaving her mouth. A sound of distress.

He took his hand from her breast. Pulled her top down again. 'This isn't the time or place.'

Maddi tried desperately to remember why it wasn't a good idea to throw caution to the wind.

A series of unwelcome answers flooded her brain:

Because he's the King…because he hates you…because you're a virgin…

She went still. Pulled back too. She felt wobbly without his hands on her.

He reached for her again. 'Are you okay?'

But she put a hand up. She'd just revealed *everything*. 'I'm fine.'

She looked around, as if seeing the beach for the first time. Had the earth shifted on its axis? It felt like it.

'We should get back to the palace. My security team will be wondering where we are.'

He emitted a sharp whistle that had the two horses trotting over obediently. Maddi didn't have time to be scared of getting back on the horse. She was sitting astride her again before she knew which way was up.

Aristedes made sure to stay close this time, watching La Reina carefully. He was within touching distance of taking the reins again if he had to.

Maddi was occupied just trying to get her scrambled brain back into some kind of order.

Aristedes wanted her.

As much as she wanted him.

But what would happen now? Would he regret this moment of passion with the woman who had upended his world? Would he judge her for being so...wanton? Maybe he was already cursing himself for his own weakness.

What did she want to happen?

Maddi's insides clenched.

She wanted him.

With a desperation that felt almost feverish.

This was the man she'd been waiting for. The passion she'd dreamt of.

The man who is promised in marriage to your half-sister.

Maddi sobered at that.

Surely Laia wouldn't care? After all, she'd spent the last four years doing her best to put this man off marrying her. And she was now completely AWOL in a bid to get to her coronation before they could be married.

Maddi knew Laia wouldn't care. She might care that

Maddi had taken leave of her senses, but she wouldn't feel remotely betrayed. If anything, she would see it as Maddi going to extreme lengths to distract the King of Santanger.

Maddi put a hand to her mouth as a little giggle erupted at the thought of Laia encouraging her to seduce the King.

Aristedes looked at her. They were approaching the arch that led back into the stables. People were milling around in the distance.

'What's funny?'

The full import of what had just happened hit Maddi and she took her hand down and shook her head, suddenly deadly sober again. 'Nothing.'

Grooms came to meet them, but before one of them could help Maddi off the horse Aristedes was there, his hands around her waist. She put her hands on his shoulders and let him take her weight. She slid down and stood. Her legs still weren't entirely steady.

The grooms led the horses away. Maddi could see the security men at a discreet distance. Also one of Aristedes's aides, who looked as if he needed to tell him something. But he was looking at her.

Maddi felt exposed. Conscious of her hair loose and wild.

She wasn't sure how to try and articulate what was in her head. 'Aristedes... I—'

'We have a formal event to attend this evening. Hannah will help you get ready. We leave at six.'

With that, he turned and strode away, his aide hurrying to catch up and walk alongside him. Security men followed.

Hannah appeared in a golf buggy. 'Princess Laia? I'll take you back to your rooms. Would you like a snack before preparing for tonight's event?'

Maddi blinked at the girl. The fact that she'd taken Maddi's healthy appetite into account made Maddi feel absurdly emotional. It was as if a layer of skin had just been removed from her body, leaving her open to the elements.

To emotion.

She realised she was ravenous after the overload of adrenalin and shock and everything that had happened. She smiled at Hannah. 'That would be amazing, thank you.'

The girl smiled. 'I will arrange it, Princess Laia.'

Ari adjusted his bow tie for the umpteenth time. It was perfect. But it felt too tight. He cursed softly and left it alone.

His valet asked, 'Anything else, Your Majesty?'

Ari said, 'No, thank you, Tomas. You can go.'

The man left and Ari looked at his watch. He was ready early. As if he was some eager teenager, going on a date. He scowled at himself and went out to his living area, helping himself to a generous shot of whisky.

The burn down his throat couldn't burn away the memory of the stark, cold panic he'd felt in his guts when he'd seen Maddi clinging on to La Reina for dear life, hurtling towards certain maiming or even death on those rocks.

How he'd managed to get to her on time and bring the horse to a stop was still something he couldn't fathom.

And then he'd pulled her off the horse, fearing the worst... But she'd been okay. She'd been fine. So fine that he hadn't been able to resist the temptation to kiss her.

He took another slug of whisky to try and drown how that had felt, but the alcohol only made the memory burn hotter.

She'd been everything he'd fantasised about. Soft and lush and firm and strong. Hesitant at first, and then matching him stroke for stroke. The weight and feel of her breast in his hand had been more erotic than anything he could remember experiencing in years.

He still couldn't understand where the control to stop had come from. The control not to take her from the beach and give in to the almost overwhelming need to take her there and then on the sand.

The intervening hours had done little to douse his desire. Tasting her had opened the floodgates. He wanted her more than he'd ever wanted another woman. She couldn't be more inappropriate. She couldn't be more off-limits. She was lady-in-waiting to his future wife.

A future wife who is currently hiding in some corner of the world to avoid marrying you, pointed out a small voice.

Right now that fact didn't seem pertinent to Ari. Not as pertinent as how he was going to be able to stand beside Maddi for an entire evening and not give in to the temptation to touch her again.

Kiss her again.

Echoes of memories of his father, doing little to hide his desire for his latest mistress, whispered over Ari like a chill breeze. He'd vowed to be different. He had more control than that. He'd built his life around it.

But on the beach earlier…had shown that perhaps he was as susceptible to a woman as his father had been.

It had been the adrenalin rush, he assured himself now. Maddi could have died.

A shudder went through him again.

There was a knock on the door and then a voice from behind him. 'Your Majesty, Princess Laia is here.'

The back of Ari's neck prickled with awareness. He swore he could smell her scent. His blood heated.

He gritted his jaw. She was just a woman. Like any other. Her aim since she had got here was to drive him insane and he would not allow it. He was in control.

Slowly he turned around and his gaze fell on the woman before him. His hand tightened on the glass in his hand. Faintly he heard a cracking sound.

Dios mio.

Any sense of control Ari had convinced himself he had drained out of his head and body, to be replaced with pure, unadulterated lust and the certain knowledge that no amount of control in the universe would be enough to make him resist this woman.

Maddi hovered self-consciously in the doorway. Aristedes was looking at her with such a fierce expression on his face that she asked, 'Is it not okay? Hannah and the stylist said it was the perfect dress for the event...'

It was a classic black evening gown. Strapless and ruched at the bodice, then falling to the floor in whimsical layers of chiffon. A wide length of chiffon went over one shoulder.

With it she wore a short, simple diamond necklace, matching drop earrings and bracelet. Her hair was smooth and pulled back into a sophisticated chignon, held in place by a diamond pin. When she'd seen herself in the mirror she'd wished she had her phone, so she could send a picture of herself to Laia. Because she'd never looked so...*sleek*.

She'd missed her sister acutely in that moment, because she'd never really had a close girlfriend before and Laia had become her confidante. This was the most time they'd spent apart since Maddi had met her.

From the look on Aristedes's face, he was seriously regretting what had happened earlier. He put down the glass he was holding on the table and said, 'It's fine. We should go.'

He walked towards her, and that was when Maddi took in the full impact of the King in his classic black tuxedo. He was breathtaking. Suave, debonair and dangerous all at once. And yet the image of him in those jeans earlier...the way they'd clung so snugly to his thighs and buttocks...the way he'd sat on the horse...that was even more intoxicating.

He put out a hand, to indicate that she should precede him

out of the room, and she walked ahead of him on shaky legs, clutching the little bag that matched the dress.

He didn't attempt to make conversation as they made their way to the chauffeur-driven SUV waiting in the courtyard. Once seated in the back, with Aristedes on the other side of the car, long legs stretched out, Maddi knew she couldn't bear it if there was going to be this much tension between them.

Before she could lose her nerve, she said, 'Look, about earlier...' And there she faltered. Because to put it into words how seismic it had been—what did she even want to say?

Aristedes pressed a button and the privacy screen went up. Maddi flushed. She kept forgetting.

He looked at her. 'What about earlier?'

'I...' She stopped helplessly. Because what she wanted to say was, *I want to do that again.* But clearly Aristedes had no intention of doing it again. He'd come to his senses.

'Nothing,' she said, making a huge effort to push down her emotions. 'It doesn't matter. What's this event we're attending?'

Aristedes looked relaxed, but Maddi didn't trust it. There was a sudden sense of crackling volatility in the air. As if some silent communication had taken place between them that she was unaware of.

Ignoring her question, he said, 'You were brave, earlier.'

Maddi blinked. She hadn't expected that. 'I was?'

He nodded. 'You got back on the horse again.'

Maddi's face grew hot. 'I was a little...distracted.'

The ghost of a smile made Aristedes's mouth twitch, but Maddi couldn't decipher it before he said, 'Next time I'll give you a proper lesson. I won't leave you alone.'

Maddi's heart thumped. 'Next time?'

'You said you were learning—no reason why you can't keep doing it here.'

'I... Okay.'

Then he smoothly segued into answering her question. 'The event we're attending tonight is an annual charity ball to raise funds for local hospitals.'

Maddi had been to similar events with Laia. Lots of handshaking and thanking donors for their generosity.

She said, 'I'll do my best to fade into the background.'

Aristedes made a faint snorting sound. 'Then you shouldn't have worn that dress.'

A sense of exposure gripped Maddi. Was he sending her out to make a complete fool of herself?

'You said it was fine!'

His dark gaze swept her up and down. 'It is fine. It's more than fine. You look…spectacular.'

Maddi's skin prickled all over. Now he didn't look as if he was regretting what had happened at all.

She couldn't help saying, a little plaintively, 'You're very hard to read—do you know that?'

His gaze met hers. 'Shall I make it a little clearer?'

Before she could answer he had reached for her and tugged her gently towards him across the back seat. The dress rustled around her. He snaked an arm around her waist and then cupped her jaw with his other hand, angling her face towards him.

Maddi couldn't breathe. She could see the intensity in his eyes now… Dark gold flecks like little fires burning.

She put her hand over his where he held her, entwined their fingers. On a breath, she reached up and touched her mouth to his, unable to help herself.

For an infinitesimal moment nothing happened. Almost as if Aristedes was testing himself. Testing to see if he could resist her.

But just as she was drawing back, sure he was mocking her, he stopped her movement and stopped her breath with his mouth on hers. It was an open and explicit kiss. He wasn't mocking her. He wanted her.

And she wanted him.

Time and space fell away. There was only this moment and the way it felt to have Aristedes's hard, sensual mouth on hers, tongues duelling, mimicking a far more intimate action. It was a dance that Maddi knew instinctively, even though her experience of kissing up to now had been laughably juvenile.

She'd been kissed. But not like this. Not by a man who kissed *women*. Sensual, experienced women, who could match him. But she wasn't a sensual, experienced woman. She was a virgin playing at being a sensual, experienced woman. Which was easy to do under this man's hands.

Virgin.

Maddi imagined the look of distaste on his face if he ever discovered such a fact. She tensed and pulled back, breathing raggedly. The fact that he looked momentarily disorientated was some comfort. To know she could have an effect on such a man...

He looked over her shoulder and said, 'We're here.'

Maddi's insides swooped as Aristedes put her away from him gently. Thankfully the windows were tinted, because Maddi could already see a throng of press photographers outside a beautiful building with wide steps leading up to an elaborate foyer.

Aristedes got out and there was a roar from the crowd. He was an undeniably popular monarch. Maddi only had seconds to check her make-up before he was opening her door and helping her out.

She'd been to such events with Laia, but had never been the focus of attention until now. She'd have to remember not to look startled.

Aristedes put a hand at her lower back, lightly guiding her up the steps and into the stunning gilded and golden lobby.

CHAPTER SEVEN

ARI COULDN'T CONCENTRATE. That didn't bother him unduly—he could sleepwalk his way through this event. The reason for his lack of concentration was a few feet away, talking to the French ambassador's wife, a little frown between her eyes as she focused on what the woman was saying.

He'd told Maddi on their way in to let him do the talking, lest anyone spend too much time with her and start to get suspicious. Although he was fairly certain most people here wouldn't ever have met the Princess in person. And Maddi certainly looked enough like her to fool all onlookers.

He wondered at that again. They were so alike…could it really just be a coincidence? Simply the fact that they came from the same place? He hadn't heard from his friend Antonio Chatsfield yet—which was unlike him. He made a mental note to chase him up.

He made his excuses to the people around him and went over to Maddi, taking her arm. He felt the way she reacted to his presence, as if a little jolt had gone through her body. A body he had every intention of exploring so thoroughly that she would cease to have this hold over him…

'She's never been to Santanger or Isla'Rosa before, and she's never met Princess Laia.'

Maddi felt unaccountably defensive after Aristedes had

come over to interrupt her conversation with the French ambassador's wife.

'That's not why I pulled you away.'

Maddi looked up at Aristedes. 'It's not?'

He shook his head. 'I pulled you away because we need to be the first on the dance floor.'

Dread pooled in Maddi's belly as Aristedes led her into another room, where the sounds of a waltz enveloped them. Laia had told Maddi about the endless hours of dance practice she'd had to endure when growing up.

She hissed at Aristedes, 'I've never danced like this before. I don't know what to do.'

If people didn't already suspect she might not be Princess Laia, then surely when they saw her wooden dance movements they'd guess in an instant.

Aristedes, unconcerned, swung her into his arms and said, 'It's fine. Just follow my lead and try to relax.'

Try to relax!

Maddi might have laughed if she hadn't been so terrified. Doing something for the first time, surrounded by hundreds of people scrutinising her every move!

Aristedes's arm was high across her back and he held her hand in his, close to his shoulder. He said again, 'Just relax. Don't look at them—look at me.'

That would be even worse than the hundreds of curious eyes. But she did it, and it worked to an extent. The world narrowed down to Aristedes and those amazing, unfathomable eyes.

A question came to her, unbidden, and it came out of her mouth before she could stop it. 'Does anyone call you Ari?'

'My brother does, and my mother used to call me Ari. Sometimes women would call me Ari, but it was an attempt to foster an intimacy that I didn't appreciate.'

Maddi made a *tsk*-ing sound. 'How cheeky of them.'

To her surprise she realised they were revolving easily around the dance floor, her feet following his. Other couples had joined them now, and the pressure eased a little.

Maddi was curious. 'So, these women…there were a few…?'

'Are you asking me how many lovers I've had?'

Maddi flushed. 'No.'

Yes. And did he have a current lover?

'You're very impertinent.'

Maddi winced. 'I'm sorry. I tend to speak and then think.'

Aristedes's mouth twitched again. She was beginning to love that twitch. That sign that she could make him smile, even a tiny bit.

He said, 'I've had my fair share. I'm not a monk. But I'm not going to violate my wedding vows. Once I'm married I will be faithful to my wife.'

She was surprised at the vehemence in his voice. 'Even if you don't…fancy her?'

He'd told her himself he'd never felt anything like that for Laia.

'Dynastic marriages are built on far more solid foundations than chemistry and emotion. They have to be.'

'Was that what your parents' marriage was like?'

For the first time she felt tension in his body. His jaw clenched.

Maddi said hurriedly, 'Ignore me. I'm asking too many questions.'

But he didn't seem to hear her. He said, 'It should have been. But my mother fell in love with my father. It was an arranged marriage. He didn't love her. He had affairs. Lots of them. No secret. He flaunted them in her face, as if to punish her for the folly of loving him. It destroyed her.'

He looked at her then.

'That's why I have vowed to be faithful to my wife. I won't

put her through what my father did to my mother, just because he couldn't control himself.'

He didn't say it, but she heard the words. *He was weak.* Maddi was genuinely moved.

'That must have been so hard to witness.'

'My brother Dax bore the brunt of it. He was closer to my mother. I was occupied with the duties of becoming King one day. She depended on him. Too much.'

Maddi stayed silent. It put his brother into a new perspective. She knew what it was like to grow up with a parent who had suffered great heartbreak. But at least her mother had managed to pull herself out of it and get on with her life.

'What happened to her?' she asked.

'She died in a car crash when I was seventeen. Dax was fifteen.'

So he and his brother had lost both parents within a year of each other.

'I'm sorry, that must have been rough.'

He looked at her. 'Any more questions?'

Maddi shook her head. But then she said, 'I can understand why you'd settle for a passionless marriage now, but you can't control someone's emotions. What if your wife falls in love with you?'

Aristedes smiled mirthlessly. 'I think all signs are pointing to that not being a problem.'

Was he admitting defeat? Giving up on his dogged refusal to acknowledge Laia's reluctance to marry him?

But then he said, 'Even if there was passion…which would certainly make the marriage more palatable…passion doesn't last.'

Maddi struggled to think of examples of passionate, long-lasting relationships, but drew a blank. 'You're very cynical.'

'So would you be if you'd grown up in my world. At least

I know not to believe in myths and fairy tales. What a waste of a life.'

No doubt he was referring to his mother. And while Maddi agreed to a certain extent, because she'd always taken a very pragmatic view of love and relationships—largely after seeing her own mother choose to move on and settle down with someone who might not set the world alight, but who loved her and was kind—she felt a surprising need to counter Aristedes's arrogant complacency.

'That's easy to say if you've never actually been in love.'

'How do you know I haven't? I might have been made cynical by a broken heart.'

Maddi ignored the pang near *her* heart at the thought of any woman capturing his.

She snorted. 'I would like to be there on the day when you're felled by love. I think that would be a very satisfying sight.'

Aristedes didn't even dignify that with a comment. He asked, 'What about you? Have you been in love?'

Maddi shook her head. 'No. And while I hate to admit it, I agree with a lot of what you say. But I'm not arrogant enough to assume I'm immune.'

'I prefer to think of it as realism.'

It was only then that Maddi realised the music was fading out and a new song was starting. They'd stopped moving and were just looking at each other. She became uber-conscious of her body, pressed against his. They fitted. Even though she was almost a foot shorter.

He said, 'By the way, you can call me Ari.'

Her insides swooped. 'Aren't you afraid I might be trying to foster intimacy?'

He shook his head. 'No, because you're not like any other woman I've ever met. And we both know the truth of what's going on here.'

Maddi felt breathless. She chose to interpret his statement

that she wasn't like any other woman as a good thing. 'And what *is* going on here, exactly?'

The band was playing something a little jazzier now. Aristedes started moving again.

'A very rare and unusual mutual chemistry. Something that I don't think either of us expected.'

Maddi shook her head. She certainly hadn't expected to still be here, impersonating her sister. She'd only started this with a view to helping Laia escape.

She couldn't take her eyes off his mouth.

'If you keep looking at me like that, I'll be tempted to break protocol.'

She dragged her gaze up. 'What protocol?'

'We can't be seen to be physically intimate before we marry.'

She frowned. 'But…we're not getting married.'

'I know that…you know that. They don't know that.'

As if waking from a trance, Maddi became aware of the avid crowd around them again. People were dancing past them, staring at them as if they were animals in a zoo.

She wanted to duck her head into Aristedes's shoulder. She wanted to ask if they could leave yet. But she clamped her mouth shut. Because if they did leave…what then?

As if hearing her thoughts, he said, 'Much as I would like to, we can't leave yet. There's more meeting and greeting to do.'

Maddi was used to this—albeit to the other side of it. She knew that it was like an endurance sport, and she'd been in awe of Laia's stamina and patience. Now it looked as if she was to be tested to see just how well-suited she was to the role of princess.

A couple of hours later, Maddi was reaching her breaking point. Her feet were killing her. Her face was numb. She was dizzy from all the names and the people she'd met.

An aide approached the King and said something into his ear.

Aristedes put his hand on Maddi's elbow. He looked at her. 'Ready?'

'For what?' She might cry if there was another room to go to, where more people waited to meet them.

'To leave?'

Relief made her weak. 'Yes, please.'

'Try to look a little less delighted,' Aristedes commented dryly.

Maddi schooled her features as they were led out of the elaborate hall and their security followed them as they made their way down to the entrance where the car waited.

Maddi had never been so glad to sit down. She considered herself to be fit—she'd run a half-marathon with Laia in the last year—but this required next-level endurance skills.

In the back of the car, she asked, 'Do you ever get used to this?'

'It's a job, Maddi. And a privilege.'

'That's what Laia—I mean, Princess Laia says.'

'You're close to her.' He said it as a statement.

Maddi nodded. 'She's my best friend, even though I've only known her a year.'

'Clearly you'll do anything for her. You're loyal.'

Maddi shifted uncomfortably. Was she, though? When she was lusting after her sister's intended? Even though Laia had no intention of marrying the man?

The car was winding through the streets of Santanger. Maddi saw people strolling along the pavements. Shops were open late. Restaurants had tables spilling out into picturesque little squares. Down by the marina sleek yachts bobbed on the water, some lit up with fairy lights. An almost full moon hung in the sky, sending out a pearlescent glow.

For some reason Maddi felt incredibly melancholic. She

wished… She wasn't even sure what she wished. And then it hit her. She wished she was here for real. That she could be herself with this man. Not hiding behind a much larger persona.

The fact that no one else seemed to have realised she wasn't Princess Laia made her feel a little invisible…

'Maddi?'

She swallowed the unwelcome lump in her throat. What was wrong with her?

Aristedes took her hand. 'Maddi? What is it? Was tonight too much?'

She looked at him when she felt she could hide her emotion. 'No, it was fine. I was just thinking it's so lovely here. You have a beautiful country.'

'I do. I'm very lucky.'

Impulsively she said, 'You see me, don't you?'

She stopped and bit her lip in case she said anything else.

He frowned. 'Of course I see you. You're sitting just inches away.'

'I mean…you see *me*, Maddi Smith, not Princess Laia.'

Strangely, Ari knew exactly what Maddi meant. Because he had that sensation too. That people only saw King Aristedes. A figurehead. Not the man underneath.

He said, 'The minute I knew you weren't Princess Laia, I saw you.'

Maddi was direct. More relaxed. A little dreamy. Barefoot more often than not. Princess Laia—from what he remembered—was much more reserved. A product of her upbringing, no doubt.

Princess Laia wouldn't bombard him with personal questions, like Maddi did, with the lack of guile of a child. Questions that he'd answered when he usually cut people off.

A sense of exposure made his skin prickle. He'd told her far too much.

His parents' sordid history was an open secret within the palace, but not among the public—and yet he'd blithely spilled it all to Maddi as if she wasn't here as some sort of Trojan Horse.

For the first time since this woman had impersonated her boss, the Crown Princess, since Ari had realised just how reluctant Laia was to marry him, he had a very fledgling sense of things shifting. Becoming less concrete. Less certain. Not least because he was about to throw caution to the wind and behave as uncharacteristically as he ever had. By ignoring the need to control everything.

Right now, none of that bothered him as much as it should. Because he was distracted by Maddi's eyes. Huge and dark green, with tantalising hints of gold and brown. Glowing with some emotion that, inexplicably, he felt too, even though he couldn't name it.

Didn't want to name it.

What he wanted was far more base and carnal.

He lifted Maddi's hand and tugged her closer. Her scent tickled his nostrils. Light and yet deep at the same time. With some mysterious base note.

'I want you, Maddi.' The words fell from his mouth as easily as breathing.

Her eyes widened. A flush of colour stained her cheeks. She really was beautiful.

'But…is it…? Are we allowed?'

He almost smiled at her question. As if there was a higher power to answer to than him. Any other woman would be sliding into his lap at the merest hint that he wanted her.

'In public we have to be relatively chaste, but within the palace, if we're discreet, we can do what we want. After what the staff there witnessed with my father, an affair between me and my future Queen will be like a Disney movie.'

'An affair…?'

'We're two consenting adults, Maddi. I'm not married yet.'

'But you still intend to get married to Princess Laia…'

Did he? Those doubts he had took root. But Ari wasn't about to reveal his inner vacillations to a woman bent on creating chaos wherever she went. Not least in his body.

He said, 'We have an agreement. If she comes to her senses then, yes, of course I'll marry her. However, if she won't agree to the marriage then I'll have to choose another bride of royal blood. I will be getting married, no matter what. I have to.'

'You have to marry a bride of royal blood?'

Ari nodded. He really didn't want to talk about this. That was all in the future. He was more interested in the present. Vastly more interested.

But his conscience compelled him to say, 'You know nothing can come of this, Maddi. I will marry according to my duty and my responsibility and I will not betray my vows. This can only be temporary.'

The car was pulling to a stop in the main palace courtyard. Ari could see the staff waiting to jump into action.

Maddi pulled her hand back. He felt her distance herself. Physically and emotionally.

Ari signalled discreetly to the staff not to disturb them. Well-worn cynicism told him she was sensing an opportunity to bargain for something in return for agreeing to this affair. Now that he'd laid out in no uncertain terms that she would never become a favoured mistress.

He'd been through this with lovers before. Usually when he ended things.

She said, 'I don't know if it's a good idea… There's a lot of…stuff between us.'

Ari felt a sense of disappointment snake through him. He really had thought she was different. More fool him. The woman had been playing him since she'd arrived.

He leaned back. 'What is it you want, Maddi?'

She looked at him. Blinked. Long lashes cast shadows on her cheeks. 'What are you talking about?'

'This game you're playing now that you know the parameters of our relationship.'

She shook her head. Her face looked pale.

Ari ignored it.

She said, 'What *game*? I wouldn't know how to play a game even if I was given a rule book.'

'Says the woman who worked in a casino?'

Maddi's eyes widened. Her mouth opened. 'You know what? I've changed my mind. You're the last man I would ever have an affair with. You're a cynical, arrogant—'

Maddi's door was opened unceremoniously and she almost fell out. An unwitting staff member obviously hadn't seen the signal not to disturb them.

Ari cursed, the feeling of having made a mistake already curdling in his gut as he saw Maddi scramble inelegantly out of the car to get away from him.

Because he realised what he'd seen in her expression along with shock just now. *Hurt.*

By the time he had stepped out and caught up with her it was obvious she was steaming mad. Ari took her elbow. She was stiff as a board.

He said tersely, 'Just keep walking and don't cause a scene.'

Miraculously, she did as he asked. They reached his private rooms and he dismissed his valet for the night.

Once they were alone, Maddi pulled away from his hand and stalked into the reception room. She whirled around. 'How *dare* you insinuate that I'm on the make for something?' She hitched up her chin. 'I grew up with just enough to get by once my education was paid for, and I've worked for every cent I ever earned. I still do. I don't expect a handout from anyone.'

Ari's gut clenched. Either she was an undiscovered award-winning actress or he'd read this very wrong. He ran a hand through his hair. He didn't usually find himself apologising to anyone.

'Look, I think I've misread the situation...'

'You *think*?'

Maddi had her hands on her hips now. She reminded him of how she'd been that first evening she'd been here, when she'd thrown the phone out of the window. Magnificent and strong. Defiant.

He put his hands out. 'Okay, I'm sorry. I definitely misread the situation. I just... I'm used to people wanting things from me.'

Maddi looked slightly less angry. She folded her arms across her chest, which only had the effect of pushing her breasts upwards. Ari valiantly kept his gaze up.

'I guess I can understand that. You're a wealthy man. A king. I know not everyone is...'

'As pure as you?' Ari supplied.

She looked at him and all the colour in her cheeks leached away, leaving her looking stricken.

He walked forward. 'What is it? What did I say?'

She shook her head. 'Nothing. I'm...fine. Look, I don't want anything from you, Ari. All I want is for Princess Laia to get what she wants—which is not to become your wife.'

Ari ignored the bit about Princess Laia. He moved closer. 'You're lying, Maddi.'

She glared at him. She looked as if she wanted to stamp her foot.

'What will it take to prove to you that I want nothing?'

Ari reached out and plucked the pin from her hair, making it tumble down around her shoulders, thick and wild. Understanding dawned in her eyes.

'Okay, fine…there is something I want,' she admitted grudgingly.

Every nerve in Ari's body tingled at being so close to her but not touching her yet. 'What's that?'

She looked up at him and his control wavered dangerously. Did she have any idea how she was looking at him? With a provocative expression of hunger mixed with awe mixed with something else he couldn't figure out.

She bit her lip for a second, and then she said in a rush, 'I want to be touched by you. Kissed. Made love to.'

'I want you, Maddi…more than I've ever wanted anyone else.'

She shook her head. 'You don't have to say that. I know what this is…you've made that very clear.'

But even if Ari had tried, he couldn't have stopped the words spilling out. This woman made him utter things he'd never have dreamt of saying to anyone else before.

He reached out and trailed his fingers along her jaw. A delicate line. But strong. She quivered under his touch. He burned.

CHAPTER EIGHT

A MOMENT AGO Maddi had been so angry with this man and now… Now she was ready to dissolve in a pool of lust at his feet. If he hadn't looked genuinely contrite for accusing her of being some sort of gold-digger she might not still be here. But she'd had the very real sense that whatever she'd said had triggered him into a response he'd given many times before.

With his other lovers.

Maddi pushed that toxic thought down. She was no different from them—she knew that. But right now she didn't care, because she wanted him. Desperately. She wanted him to be her first lover.

When he'd joked that not everyone was as pure as her just now she'd nearly given herself away. Spectacularly. Would he know she was a virgin? Surely by now it wouldn't be that obvious?

His hand dropped from her jaw and, without taking his eyes off her face, he undid his bow tie and drew it off, throwing it aside. He undid the top button of his shirt. She saw dark skin, a hint of hair.

She almost whimpered. But a sliver of doubt sneaked in like a cold breeze, dousing her feverish desire. More than a sliver. She wasn't ready for a man like Aristedes. He had the wrong idea about her. He obviously thought she was experienced. A woman of the world. The kind of woman who would nonchalantly go to his room with him and be able to do things that would please him...

Because she would want to please him.

But how could she possibly please him?

The fear of disappointing him was acute.

She forced herself to meet his eye. Regret was already burning her insides like bile. 'I'm so sorry, Aristedes... I'm truly not playing any games... I just think this isn't a good idea.'

His face was suddenly expressionless. His eyes shuttered. He said nothing for a long moment and then he took a step back. 'As you wish. If you change your mind, you know where I am.'

He turned and walked towards his bedroom suite and Maddi fled back to her rooms before she changed her mind. She went inside and leaned against the door.

What she'd just walked away from was seismic.

Ari saw her.

She knew he did. Even if his cynicism had got in the way briefly. And he wanted *her*, which was intoxicating.

For her whole life Maddi had felt somewhat invisible. She'd been acutely conscious of her mother's sadness, and conscious that it had to do with her. So she'd tried to make herself smaller, so as not to cause any more sadness.

She'd learnt not to ask too many questions about her father, but had pored over his image online and that of her half-sister, fascinated by their resemblance while knowing that they were a world apart.

It had always hurt to know that her sister had had a relationship with their father. There was a picture that Maddi had come across online, of her sister and father on a boat, fishing. Laia was about ten years old, laughing up into the King's face. He was smiling down at her indulgently. Maddi had printed it out and kept it for years—a bittersweet reminder that he hadn't wanted to know her.

When she'd told Laia about it, Laia had cried.

Maddi kicked off her shoes and padded barefoot over to the dressing room, removing her jewellery and putting it back carefully in the boxes. The diamonds twinkled at her benignly.

She felt keyed up. Restless. About as far from being able to sleep as it was possible to feel. She looked at herself in the mirror. Flushed cheeks. Wide eyes. Yearning. Aching. Pulse throbbing. Still.

She couldn't believe she'd stood up to the King like that. Called him out on his cynicism. And he'd admitted he was wrong. It had been exhilarating.

She wanted him.

Would it really be so selfish to savour this moment of someone really seeing her. Appreciating her? To take this one thing for herself, ready or not? To give her innocence to the man who had already fulfilled her fantasy of what a passionate awakening might feel like?

Sooner or later she would have to leave here. She would never see Aristedes again. Because she knew his marriage with Laia would never happen. Laia would persuade him to agree to a more modern peace agreement—Maddi knew she would. And he would weather this change in his plans and get on with his life, choose a new bride of royal blood…sire his heirs. He might *want* his Queen. He might even fall in love with his Queen, in spite of his cynical arrogance.

You have royal blood, whispered a voice.

Maddi went still. She was a princess. Albeit very much in secret. But suddenly she couldn't stop thinking of the tantalising possibility of telling Ari that she was also a princess of Isla'Rosa. That perhaps he might agree to switch marrying Laia for Maddi.

She caught her expression in the mirror, smiling moonily at herself, and immediately stopped and scowled. What on earth was wrong with her? She'd met the man scarcely a week ago and, yes, she had a crush on him, but was she really fantasising about offering herself up to him as a substitute royal wife? Before the people of Isla'Rosa even knew she was a princess? Offering herself up to a man who was cynical and jaded? Who had admitted that he was more than happy to have a marriage in name only. To breed the next generation with no hint of scandal or drama.

She wasn't ready to be a queen! She could barely get her head around being a princess. And who was to say he would choose her even if he knew she was of royal blood?

Her blood curdled at the thought. *Rejection.* All over again. She wouldn't risk that for anyone.

Maddi might have sown doubts in his head about his marriage to Laia, but there was no way she could risk revealing her full identity in case he used it against her. To lure Laia out of hiding. Or, worse, to create a scandal in Isla'Rosa by revealing her identity to the people before Laia had had a chance to do so.

It was Laia's narrative to control, revealing Maddi's true heritage as her half-sister, and Maddi would not betray her wishes. After all, she was loyal to Isla'Rosa too.

But in the meantime Maddi couldn't deny that she did want something from King Aristedes. Now more than ever. Because she fully realised how finite this was. And how much he would potentially hate her when he found out who she really was. That she'd been hiding her identity as a princess.

He wouldn't understand that she was still getting used to the concept. It wasn't as if she took it for granted. She knew that until Laia actually acknowledged her birth in front of the people of Isla'Rosa she wouldn't feel as if she truly was of royal blood.

And that betraying little fantasy she'd had of him choosing her to be his Queen instead of Laia? It would be buried deep down, where she'd buried all her very secret fantasies that perhaps things might be different for her, that she might experience a great love some day, even though she'd ruined her mother's chances for love.

So for now she was still a regular person, and suddenly things were very clear. Maddi knew she would always regret not taking the chance to be with Aristedes. To know his touch. To surrender her innocence to him. To let him be the one to initiate her in the ways of being a woman.

Maddi stopped thinking. She turned from the mirror and walked back to the door, opened it and walked out. Guided by sheer desire, Maddi retraced her steps back down the corridor and to Aristedes's rooms.

The guards were outside. Wordlessly, one of them opened the door. Vaguely Maddi computed this, and what it must mean.

He'd told them to let her in if she came back.

Maddi went into the suite. There were a few lamps throwing out golden light. It was silent. She saw a light coming from the bedroom area and walked over, barefoot.

She stood in the doorway and saw Aristedes's clothes draped haphazardly over a chair. It was only then that she registered the steam coming from under another door. The bathroom. And then he emerged, looking down as he tied a knot in the towel slung low on his hips.

He was bare-chested, and Maddi's gaze was glued to that area. The well-defined pectorals. A light smattering of dark hair. The six-pack that looked as if it had been painted in shade and light by Michelangelo. Not an ounce of spare flesh. His skin was still damp. Gleaming.

Then he spoke. 'Are you really here?'

Maddi looked up. He'd seen her. He was frowning. Hair slicked back. The bones of his face stark and beautiful.

She nodded. 'I… I think so.'

'Come here.'

Maddi walked over, the dress pooling around her bare feet, softly swishing against her legs. She stopped about a foot away from Aristedes. He reached out and traced a finger down her cheek. Took a length of hair and let it run through his fingers.

'You're real…' he breathed.

It soothed something inside her that he wasn't behaving as if he'd just been waiting for her inevitable return. He looked as stunned as she felt to be doing this.

Unable to resist the temptation, she reached out and placed her palm flat against Aristedes's chest. It was warm and hard. His heart thumped under her hand. Strong. Her little finger grazed a nipple and he sucked in a breath, putting his hand over hers, trapping it.

He reached for her with his other arm, pulling her closer. He looked down. 'Barefoot?'

She nodded. He smiled. She melted inside. Then he cupped her face in his hands and tilted it up, his gaze roving over her features hungrily for a few seconds before his mouth touched hers. A light kiss at first. A testing…a tasting. But Maddi was hungry. She moved closer and wrapped her arms around his neck, bringing their bodies flush together.

She could feel the heat from his body seeping through the thin material of the dress. Her breasts felt heavy.

The kiss changed and became harder. One of Aristedes's hands caught the back of her head and an arm wrapped around her back, holding her. Which was good, because she wasn't sure her legs were still working.

The kiss became deeper and more explicit, stoking the

fire in Maddi's blood. Tongues tangled. She bit his lower lip gently, experimentally. It was firm. She soothed it with her tongue and Aristedes growled low in his throat.

He pulled back. Maddi opened her eyes. Everything was blurry. He slowly came back into focus and the look on his face made her gulp. He looked…ravenous. She felt a moment of insecurity—should she tell him she wasn't exactly experienced? But then she imagined him looking shocked, and then maybe disgusted… Selfishly, she didn't want to risk it.

Surely he wouldn't notice?

He moved back slightly and said, 'Turn around.'

Maddi did, and felt him move her hair so that it fell over one shoulder, baring her back. Instead of going straight for the zip, she felt him trace her shoulder blades and then down the centre of her spine to the top of her dress.

She bit her lip to stop a shiver of pure desire. She was dealing with a maestro here, which was immediately intimidating but also reminded her that he'd had lots of practice. And that reminded her that in comparison she was hardly likely to make an impression, no matter how much he might want her.

Her mind spiralled right up until his fingers found the zip and started to pull it down. Then she stopped breathing.

His hands brought the zip all the way down to just above her buttocks. The dress fell away from her breasts. He tugged it gently over her hips and it dropped in a soft swish of silk and chiffon layers at her feet.

Now she wore only a strapless bra and matching lace panties. Aristedes walked around her and stopped in front of her. She couldn't look at him. He tipped up her chin with a finger.

'Breathe, Maddi.'

She sucked in a breath and it went straight to her head. Meanwhile, Aristedes's gaze was moving down, over her chest to her belly and waist, her hips, thighs, legs… She felt his touch like the lick of a flame, leaving sparks wherever it landed.

He looked back up. 'You are more than I could have imagined...'

Maddi swallowed. 'So are you.'

She wanted to touch him again, but she was shy. She curled her hands into fists at her sides.

He took one of her hands and uncurled it. Then he stepped close and reached around her to unsnap her bra in a movement so slick and deft that she only realised what he'd done when a tiny breeze skated over her bare flesh.

Her bra lay on the ground.

Aristedes's gaze got even hotter.

Maddi could feel her nipples puckering into tight buds. He came close again and cupped her breasts in his hands, taking their weight. She had to put her hands on his arms to stay standing. A tremble was starting up somewhere near her knees and travelling up her body, uncontrollable.

Aristedes's thumbs found her nipples and grazed them, back and forth. Maddi gripped his arms tight.

'Aristedes...'

She wasn't even sure what she was asking for. An end to the torture? For it never to stop?

'I told you...call me Ari.'

She looked at him. Her eyes were heavy-lidded. She felt like a cat, wanting to push herself into his hands, begging for heavier petting.

'Ari...'

He lifted his gaze from her breasts. 'Hmm...?'

'I...' She literally couldn't articulate what she needed.

He seemed to take pity on her. He led her over to the massive bed and instructed her, 'Lie back.'

Maddi did. Glad not to have to try and stay standing when she was about to collapse into a puddle at his feet. She looked at the towel around his waist and the prominent bulge. Heat throbbed between her legs. Slick.

He came down over her on his arms. Muscles tensing and bunching. She couldn't help it. She had to touch him. She ran a hand over his chest again, her fingers tracing muscles, her nail snagging on a nipple.

Ari's head lowered and his breath feathered against the skin near her jaw. He pressed a kiss there, and then trailed kisses down her neck to her shoulder. Down further. She tensed when he came to rest beside her. He cupped one breast again, and flicked out his tongue against the sensitive peak. Maddi's back arched at the exquisite sensation. Then he surrounded it with his mouth and the sucking, dragging heat almost sent her into orbit. His other hand moved over her ribcage and down, over her belly, to the top of her lacy briefs.

Maddi couldn't think. She wanted so many things. All at once.

There was a faint ripping noise and Ari had dispensed with her underwear. Now she was completely naked. At his mercy. Begging him with incoherent words… His hand moved between her thighs, pushing them apart gently and then exploring through the heat right into the centre of her body, where she ached the most.

Ari said something that Maddi couldn't understand, but it sounded guttural. Then he took his hand away saying, 'I have to taste you…'

She let out a little whimper and lifted her head to see Ari taking her thighs and spreading them wide. Looking at her with such hunger that it sent a fresh wave of lust through her.

Then he moved down and pressed kisses along each thigh, higher and higher, until he reached the apex of her legs, where she was weeping with heat. He put his mouth to her, exploring that heat. His tongue laved her secret folds and Maddi was done…

She was so far beyond any realm of what she had thought might happen that when Ari flicked his tongue against her she came in a wild rush of climaxes that seemed to go on for ever, rolling like waves through her whole body.

When the storm had ebbed away, she could feel little aftertremors still rippling deep inside her. She lifted her head and saw Ari standing looking at her. Eyes burning like obsidian.

He flicked the towel off his waist and Maddi looked down. A sound came out of her mouth that she had no control over. He was…magnificent. A virile male in his prime. She could feel her body weeping for him all over again.

He opened a drawer in a console by the bed and she watched as he sheathed himself with protection.

Good, she thought dimly, *because any hope I had of being responsible or sane has long since left the building.*

He came down over her on his hands again. Moved between her legs. Maddi's heart rate was triple its normal speed, and even though she'd just climaxed, she could feel tension coiling tight again.

Ari put his hand on her, just above her chest, and trailed it down over one breast, then the other, reigniting the fire with little more than a touch. His hand moved down over her belly, which quivered at his touch, and between her legs.

His eyes flared. 'You're so responsive, *amada*.'

Maddi wanted to beg. But just as she was about to open her mouth Ari took his hand away and moved himself between her legs. She could feel him *there*, about to breach her body, and she moved slightly, hips circling.

In the next second he had thrust into her, in one devastating movement, stealing her breath and her soul. She gasped and put her hands on his hips, momentarily resisting his body. He was big. She felt so stretched. It bordered on being painful.

Ari stopped and said, 'Maddi…?'

She knew instinctively that the pain would only be alleviated if she moved—and she did. Ari sank in deeper. He moved slowly at first, out and then in, letting their bodies get used to one another, sliding and slick. He gathered pace and Maddi no longer felt any discomfort. Only a need for *more*.

And then he was there, hitting the spot that finally gave her some relief, and the building tension was spiralling out of control, too fast for Maddi to hold on. She couldn't stop the fall, nor the onslaught of another wave of pleasure so intense that she cried out, over and over again, hands clasping Ari's shoulders, legs wrapping around his hips as if that might contain it somehow.

Ari's own movements became more frenzied, and eventually he stilled as the storm went through him too. She could feel it in her body and could only absorb it, too spent to do anything else.

Ari extricated himself from Maddi's embrace—exquisite torture—and lay back on the bed beside her. Her eyes were closed, lashes long on her cheeks. Dark hair was spread around her head. Her body was still flushed. It was the most erotic sight he'd ever seen.

What had just happened had been the most profound experience. He tried to deny it—but he struggled to remember a time when a woman had turned him on so much that the entire world might have fallen away and he wouldn't have noticed or cared.

In a bid to try and make his brain start functioning again, he got out of the bed and went over to his French doors, opening them silently and stepping out onto the terrace. It was completely private here. The night air—cool and fresh—made his skin prickle. He sucked in the salty tang of the sea air.

He heard a noise behind him and turned around to see Maddi stir. She came up on one elbow, looking sexily dishevelled and very well loved.

He moved back to the doorway and she saw him. He watched how her gaze travelled down and widened on the part of his anatomy already responding again. As if he hadn't just died a small death.

But he wasn't going to indulge again now, much as he might like to. The woman who had turned his world upside down from the moment he'd laid eyes on her and assumed she was someone else, was still hiding secrets.

Maddi felt ridiculously shy, considering what had just happened. She couldn't quite wrap her head around it. It was too huge, too seismic.

Ari was standing by the door that led outside to the terrace. The cool night breeze traced over Maddi's skin, making it pucker. He was naked. And it was hard not to be distracted by that amazingly powerful body. She couldn't imagine standing naked in front of him like that, but he was completely unashamed.

Then he came towards the bed and held out a hand. 'Come on.'

Maddi let him pull her up from the bed, a little bemused. Her head was still feeling fuzzy after an overload of pleasure.

He led her into the bathroom and leant into the shower, turning it on. Steam soon filled the space. Ari stepped in and pulled her with him. The powerful spray covered them both and Ari put her in front of him. He poured some soap into his hands before running them all over her body. She was glad she was facing away from him, because she hadn't expected this.

She didn't know what she'd expected, because she hadn't thought that far ahead, but it wasn't this…this tender, post-coital ablution.

He massaged shampoo into her hair and worked his hands over her scalp, long fingers moving slowly and rhythmically.

She wanted to lean back against him and slide to the floor at his feet. But then he rinsed the soap from her body and her hair and turned off the shower. The heat and steam dissipated. Ari wrapped a large towel around Maddi's shoulders. Then he got another towel and handed it to her for her hair.

They hadn't spoken a word.

He rubbed himself dry briskly and Maddi wrapped up her long hair in a towel, turban-like, and secured the other towel under her arms, tying it in a knot.

Ari went into the bedroom, and when Maddi followed him he was pulling on a pair of loose sweats. They hung low on his hips.

He looked at her across the room, and then he said, 'Why didn't you tell me you were a virgin?'

CHAPTER NINE

ARI FOLDED HIS arms across his chest. Partly because he was afraid that he'd reach out and twitch that towel from around Maddi's body and take her back to bed. Her legs were long and shapely, and he had a sudden vivid flashback to how she'd wrapped them around his waist and he'd sunk so deep into her—

He gritted his jaw tight.

His question hung in the air between them. He could see the colour leach from her face. How her eyes widened.

Very faintly, she said, 'I thought you wouldn't notice.'

When Ari thought of how he'd felt every single ripple of her body against his, and how explosive it had been, it made him irrationally irritable.

'How old are you?'

'Twenty-three.'

'How the hell are you still a virgin?'

She hitched up her chin. 'That's not really any of your business.'

Ari wanted to laugh. '*Cariño*, we've just been as intimately acquainted as two people can get. I think I deserve an answer.' Then he ran a hand through his hair. 'I could have hurt you, Maddi. *Dios*.'

Her chin came down. 'You didn't hurt me…it was the opposite.'

Unable to stop himself, Ari closed the distance between them. 'What was it, then?'

She looked up at him. Eyes flecked with dark gold. 'It was…amazing. I didn't… I mean, I haven't before now because I've never met anyone I wanted to be with…like that. I went to an all-girls school,' she went on. 'So I never really had a boyfriend. And then I was working, and the men there were either creepy or just…immature. I didn't go to college, so I never got to have any experience of mixing with guys… otherwise it probably would have happened. As time went on, I just felt like I wanted to hold out for the right person…'

The thought of Maddi sleeping with another man—of another man experiencing her incredible responsiveness and sensual surrender—made Ari feel almost violent.

He said, 'And was I the right person?'

Arrogantly, Ari knew the answer to that—he felt it in his blood. A deep satisfaction he'd never experienced before.

Maddi nodded. 'The moment I saw you… I felt it. The attraction.'

He had too. Which was when he should have realised something was up—because he'd never been attracted to Princess Laia.

So why are you so intent on marrying her?

The doubts whispered to Ari, growing stronger. He pushed them down. Not the time. Not when he had more interesting things to do.

'Why didn't you tell me?'

'I was afraid you wouldn't want to sleep with me.'

Ari shook his head and admitted, 'I don't think wild horses could have held me back…but I would have had reservations.'

'Why?'

'Because first experiences can be intense, and it's easy to believe that emotions are involved when it's just a physical act.'

'Is that what happened to you?'

Ari wondered how they'd got here, but he said, 'Briefly. My first lover was an older woman. She was beautiful and experienced and quite mesmerising. I thought I was in love, but she soon disabused me of that idea. And when I found out my father had asked her to initiate me, I'd never felt so humiliated in my life.'

Maddi's eyes were huge and full of emotion. 'How could he do such a thing? That's a horrific crossing of boundaries and a betrayal of trust. And as for her? There are names for people like her.'

Ari could see that she was genuinely angry, and it made him feel for a moment as if he'd lost his footing. As if he was on shaky ground.

'It was a long time ago. In the past.'

'You loved this woman?'

Ari shook his head, an old feeling of anger surfacing briefly. 'No. I was momentarily infatuated.'

Maddi bit her lip, and Ari had to restrain himself from reaching out to release that plump flesh. She said, 'So you're telling me this—?'

'Because you asked.'

She made a face. And then, 'You're telling me not to fall in love with you?'

'If you can help it.'

Now she rolled her eyes, but he saw she was suppressing a smile. To Ari's surprise, he felt a lightness bubble up inside him. A lightness he didn't feel very often. The only person who made him feel light was his brother Dax. It was an uncomfortable revelation.

He pushed it aside for now. Along with all the other things he didn't want to think about. Like how he'd already spelled out what this relationship was, but now he was teasing her about it.

She said, 'I'll do my best not to fall for you, Your Majesty.'

'Good,' he said, as he moved closer, not able to resist temptation any more.

He reached for Maddi's towel and loosened it, so that it fell to her feet. Then he took the towel from her head and her hair fell in damp dark skeins around her shoulders, long enough to touch her breasts.

'Because we both know that this situation is just a very unique temporary hiatus in our lives.'

She was breathing fast now, her breasts rising and falling, making Ari's hands itch. But before he could touch her she'd put her hands on his sweatpants and tugged them over his hips and down. He stepped out of them. They were both naked.

He led her back to the bed and told himself that this ravenous hunger was purely due to the novelty of having a new lover. Quite possibly his last lover before marriage. It wasn't specifically unique to Maddi Smith.

Because thinking about the consequences of her being different from any other lover was not something he was prepared to contemplate.

A few days later, Maddi was looking at the tabloid pictures of her and Ari that had been taken at the charity event the other evening. The evening they'd made love. His hand was on the small of her back and her face was turned to look up at him. She was smiling, and his mouth was on the verge of a smile as he looked at her. The headline said: *The look of love between King Aristedes and his future Queen!*

Amazing how misleading pictures could be…

But she knew the reality behind them. The reality being that she wasn't Princess Laia and she shouldn't be here. She was only here to try and stop Ari tracking down Laia with one hundred percent of his focus, but that was fast becoming far too easy to forget.

Especially after the other night.

Maddi put down the papers and went to the terrace and breathed in the fresh, fragrant air deeply. She hadn't slept in her own bed since the other night. Hannah had subtly moved her things to Ari's suite, and since then it had been a blur of making love, having food delivered to Ari's rooms and periodic breaks before indulging in their ravenous hunger for each other over and over again.

He only went to his office when she was sleeping.

Was it always this...intense? It almost scared Maddi how much she wanted Ari. He'd awoken something in her that she'd never even thought she possessed. A carnal hunger. She revelled in this new incarnation of herself, revelled in his touch. She craved him. And even though she knew this phase would fade, it didn't feel as if it was fading any time soon. Only getting stronger.

She had come back here to her own suite under the pretext of needing to find something, but the truth was that she needed some space and time to get her head around what was happening.

She was having an affair with her sister's fiancé. Except she knew that she wasn't really betraying Laia. If anything, she was giving her sister an even more solid reason to turn around and declare their agreement null and void.

She wondered if the newspaper pictures would reach Laia, wherever she was. Would she feel confident enough to return to Isla'Rosa? Had Dax found her? Was that why there was no contact? Maddi knew Laia was resourceful—she'd been successfully avoiding Ari for four years—so if Dax had found her, Maddi wouldn't be surprised if she'd managed to take him by surprise...

There was a sound from the room behind her and Maddi

turned around. Ari was walking towards her, in a dark suit with a light shirt, open at the neck. She drank him in helplessly, her body already reacting, softening, moistening, aching for him.

'Here you are.'

He stopped and looked at her. There hadn't been anything planned today, so she'd thrown on a pair of loose trousers and a cropped silk top.

He said, 'Do you want a riding lesson?'

A momentary frisson of fear as she recalled the terror of being on that out-of-control horse made her tense, but she refused to let it stop her. 'I'd like that.'

'Good. The horses will be ready in an hour—they're being groomed at the moment. Which leaves us just enough time…'

'Time for what?'

He came and slid his hands around her waist, finding her bare skin. Maddi's heart picked up pace.

He bent his head and said, close to her mouth, before he kissed her, 'Time for *this*.'

Maddi was fast being pulled under, weakly pushing aside all the things she'd been thinking about. This shouldn't be her reality. But with Ari's mouth on hers and his hands finding her tender flesh and making her moan, she really wanted to believe that it was.

'We're going to a what?' Maddi asked, feeling a sense of panic at what Ari had just said.

She knew he'd told her earlier, but she'd been distracted because he'd been kissing her at the time.

'A walkabout. People line the streets and we literally walk about and meet them. It's in a port town on the other side of the island. It'll be a chance for the more remote islanders to meet you.'

'Are you sure that's a good idea? I mean…it's not like they'll be meeting *me* again. Or Princess Laia.'

But Ari said, 'Until I hear from Princess Laia that she is breaking the agreement, everything is on track for her becoming Queen of Santanger.'

Maddi mentally shook her head at his refusal to believe his plans could be derailed. She had to admire his self-belief. But then, could he even be a king without an inflated sense of self-belief?

Hannah had dressed Maddi in a colourful, flowy silk dress, with buttons down the front and a wide belt. It was chic and elegant. Her hair had been pulled back into a low ponytail and she was relieved to see she'd be wearing comfortable wedges and not impractical high heels. She didn't know how Laia did these things for hours in four-inch heels.

In the car, on their way to the town, they drove over the central mountains and Maddi got a sense of how much bigger Santanger was than Isla'Rosa.

The other side of the mountain led to more fertile lands. Maddi saw fields filled with trees laden down with lemons and oranges. And olive trees. There were vineyards as far as the eye could see. It was abundantly clear that Santanger was a thriving kingdom on all levels.

They passed through picturesque villages with central squares. People going about their business. It felt quaint and old-fashioned but modern all at once. And then the sea came into view again and they drove along winding cliff roads with precipitous drops on one side.

Ari noticed her expression and said, 'I take it you're not a fan of heights?'

'I don't mind them usually, but this is a little…close to the edge.' She looked at him suspiciously. 'You're doing this on purpose, to freak me out.'

He barked out a laugh. 'Not at all. Actually, I'd usually

travel by helicopter, but sometimes I like the drive...to keep an eye on things. And I thought you might like to see more of the island.'

Maddi was inordinately touched by his easy thoughtfulness. He was proud of his country. That much was glaringly obvious. And she had to agree it was beautiful.

She quashed the little voice telling her she was being disloyal to Laia.

When they entered the surprisingly large and thriving port town Maddi was surprised—she had imagined a sleepy little fishing village. There was even a stunning Baroque cathedral, very like the one in Santanger, which dominated the main square in the city.

'For a short time in the Middle Ages, when we were being attacked on the southern shore, this town became the capital. It's known for its ancient Roman ruins. The Romans obviously had a similar idea at one point.'

Maddi heard the crowds before she saw them. Another little lurch of panic went into her gut.

She said, 'What do I do?'

'Shake hands and take their gifts. They just want to see you.'

They car came to a stop and Ari got out. The crowds cheered.

Maddi had never seen so many people in one place behind barriers.

He helped her out and she forced down the panic. He led her over to where the people were waiting and the roar was almost deafening. And then it started—a refrain that made Maddi's ears ring.

'Princess Laia, over here! Please! Princess Laia!'

So Maddi did all she could, and dived in. At first it felt forced, pasting a smile on her face to greet these people who were complete strangers, but then she relaxed. They were all so happy and had such kind faces.

Babies were lifted up to her, and as she took one young girl about one year old into her arms, she was surprised at the sudden yearning that pierced her. She'd never considered herself maternal, even though she liked children a lot. But this baby was cherubic. And then she smiled and patted Maddi's cheek with a sticky hand. Everyone laughed and Maddi handed the baby back with genuine regret. She realised she would never be here again, to see her become a little girl and grow older.

Faces blurred into other faces and Maddi's hand felt numb. She'd had so many selfies taken, and accepted and passed back so many flowers and gifts that she was dizzy. But by the time Ari came over to join her from his side of the street and put an arm around her waist, she was euphoric.

A person called out, 'When is the wedding?'

Maddi tensed. But Ari answered easily.

'As you can see, I'm enjoying getting to know my fiancée. An announcement will be made soon.'

The crowd cheered. But it tempered Maddi's happiness as they walked back to the car.

When they were in the car and pulling away, Ari saw her expression and said, 'What's wrong? That went well. They loved you.'

'Yes, but I'm not who they think I am. They liked me because I'm a regular person.'

You're a princess.

Maddi pushed the reminder down. Ari would not appreciate that titbit of information. Not now and not ever, she suspected.

It caused a maelstrom of emotions inside her. Pride to know that perhaps she *could* do this princess thing—she'd really enjoyed today. But also a sense of yearning to be Princess Maddi, at Ari's side legitimately.

Which would never happen. Because she wouldn't ever have the bravery to risk that rejection. It would destroy her. She knew that it would destroy her. Because she was very much afraid that this crush was developing into something far deeper and more permanent.

No, she told herself desperately, going cold. It couldn't be. She didn't believe in it. It was chemistry…sex. *Not love*.

'Maddi? You look as if you've just seen a ghost.'

She shook her head, struggled to regain her composure. 'It's…just been a long day.'

He took her hand. 'You were a natural. Not many people could deal with a situation like that and connect with the people, but you did.'

Maddi swallowed the lump in her throat. He had no idea how profoundly moving that was to hear.

'Thank you,' she finally managed to get out, without sounding too wobbly.

She saw that they weren't following the cliff road again and Ari said, 'We'll be back at the palace soon. We're taking the helicopter. We wouldn't see much from the car as the light is failing.'

Maddi was relieved. This whole day had been an emotional rollercoaster. 'That sounds practical.'

The helicopter trip over the island was another vision. Little pockets of villages lit up here and there. Wider roads through the middle of the island and around the edge.

The city of Santanger glittered like a bauble. Again, Maddi saw that it was bigger than she'd thought, meandering high into the hills. In the city there were wide main streets and then smaller warrens of medieval streets. The cathedral was spot-lit.

They landed on the helicopter pad at the back of the palace and Maddi—once all the adrenalin had gone—realised she was exhausted.

Ari led her back to his rooms. He said apologetically, 'I need to take a call for a few minutes—do you mind?'

Maddi shook her head and stifled a yawn. She was also starving hungry, but fatigue won out. She took off the light jacket over her dress and pulled her hair tie out. She lay down on the bed, telling herself it would just be for a moment...

When Ari came back to his bedroom a short time later, he stopped in his tracks. Maddi was lying on the bed, on her side, curled up almost foetally. Hair fanned out around her head. Face resting on her hands. Breathing deeply.

It was the first time he'd been with a woman long enough to have this kind of a relationship. Most of his affairs had been brief, and had not ever encouraged any kind of domesticity. No lover would have dared to fall asleep in his company unless sex had been involved! And even then he hadn't encouraged sleeping together. It gave the wrong impression—that he wanted them around apart from for sex.

It must have exhausted Maddi...the walkabout. They were exhausting at the best of times, and today's had gone on an hour longer than scheduled purely because everyone had wanted to see Maddi so much.

No, not Maddi. Princess Laia.

Ari's mouth tightened. He could imagine that if it *had* been Princess Laia there today they would have followed the usual strict sequence of events. The people would have liked her, but that distance would have been there. The distance that anyone growing up as a royal cultivated over time.

She wouldn't have been as open and warm with the people. Holding babies with sticky hands. Hunkering down to talk to children through the barrier. Or to an old lady sitting on a chair. Maddi had spoken to her for long minutes. The woman had been beaming when she'd walked away.

His mother had never even done that. She'd seen a walkabout as something that would dispel the necessary distance they needed to maintain, to perpetuate a vision of the royal family as sacrosanct. Perfect.

It had been anything but. Which was why Ari had always wanted to change things.

He'd changed things already in myriad ways—mainly in the sense of opening things up and presenting a more stable leadership to his people. They'd come to trust that he was different from his mercurial father. He was more dependable. He had the interests of his people at the forefront of everything he did. He was proud of his achievements.

Taking a wife and having a queen by his side was the next step. And, as much as he'd always known it would be Princess Laia, and that she'd do the job well, he had to admit that he hadn't really had a sense of how that might look until today.

Until he'd seen Maddi in action. A woman who was natural and unaffected and warm. Compassionate.

A woman who is not destined to be your Queen.

Had it been a mistake to bring her today? To let the public see her like that? The people had loved her. But, as Maddi had pointed out, they would never see her again.

Ari hadn't really paused to consider the consequences—which was not like him. He'd brought her with him, he realised now, because he'd wanted to see her in action.

As if his gut had already told him what a natural she'd be.

As if his gut was already telling him things he didn't want to consider intellectually.

Things like the fact that he had to acknowledge his marriage with Princess Laia was becoming less and less likely. Not just because of her obvious reluctance and absence, but also because something inside him had shifted.

He'd taken it for granted for so long—when you were told at eight years old that something was destined to happen, it wove its way into the fabric of your life. You didn't question it. But Ari realised now that he'd been arrogantly blinkered about the marriage. He'd merely had it slotted into his schedule like any other meeting or event. He hadn't actually considered the human factor. The possibility that Laia was an autonomous woman who might not want or expect the same thing.

It had taken meeting Maddi to make him see that. And he found, as he considered this now, that it wasn't making him angry or frustrated. If anything, he felt a sense of liberation. As if he'd been carrying a weight for a long time and someone had lifted it from him.

He felt a frisson of excitement. Tantalising possibilities he'd never considered before were opening up. The fact that he could have a queen by his side who he actually liked. Who he liked spending time with. Who he *wanted* with a hunger that grew daily.

But she's not of royal blood.

She was a commoner. Which was why she'd connected so effortlessly with his people. A revelation that Ari didn't like to acknowledge now.

Was he really contemplating a scenario in which a woman like Maddi could be his Queen? It was an impossibility.

No King of Santanger had ever married a commoner. Their family line was one of the most ancient in the world. Academics came to study their family tree because there had never been any dilution of the royal lines on either side. Ari might be intent on bringing Santanger into the modern world, and as much as the people had welcomed the changes, he knew that underneath it all was a love and reverence for their royal family, who epitomised an ancient tradition that had been lost almost everywhere else.

Ari's frisson of excitement was fading. He might not be marrying Princess Laia any more, but Maddi certainly couldn't be a contender. So, no matter what happened, this was still just an affair and he would have to choose a royal bride. Irritating, but not insurmountable.

So why did he suddenly feel burdened again?

Maddi moved minutely on the bed, her eyelashes flickering. Ari welcomed the distraction from those revelations. He took off his jacket and shoes and got onto the bed beside her.

Her eyes opened and focused on him. *Dios*, but she was beautiful.

He traced her jaw with his finger. 'Nice nap?'

She nodded. And then she made a face. 'The truth is I'm starving…for food.'

Being with this woman was not necessarily good for Ari's ego. He laughed.

A little voice whispered at him. *You haven't laughed so much in years.*

He pushed it down. 'I'll order something, shall I?'

Maddi looked almost comically grateful, 'Yes, please.'

When Ari had ordered the food, he felt her arms slide around his waist from behind and his body responded predictably. With a hunger that was as sharp as it had been the first time he'd slept with this woman. A sense of desperation made him feel slightly panicky.

He turned around. Maddi looked up at him.

'Thank you…' she said. 'Maybe before the food comes there's time for a little…appetiser?'

For a second Ari's head told him he had to stop this now. Push her away. Send her back to Isla'Rosa. Princess Laia had made her point. He needed to move on. But Maddi's body against his was a provocation that he couldn't ignore. Or resist.

Feeling reckless and desperate at the inevitable prospect of this ending soon—because it would have to—Ari cupped Maddi's face in his hands. 'I think there might even be time for a little more than an appetiser…'

A few days later

The palace garden party for frontline workers—nurses, police officers, paramedics, fireman, among many others—was a roaring success. There was a bouncy castle for their children in one corner. Face-painting. Clowns. Local vets showing off exotic animals and puppies. Buffet tables were laden with food and refreshments. There would be a fireworks display soon, as the sun set.

It was an annual fixture—something Ari had introduced to open up the palace and say thank you to the people of Santanger. His father had preferred to keep the palace closed off—a place that only the select few got to visit. A place where he could conduct his affairs in private. Hence Ari's decision to do the opposite.

One of his chief aides approached. He said, 'It's going well, Your Majesty. Princess Laia is a breath of fresh air.'

Ari's conscience pricked. More than pricked. He felt guilty. He'd been unexpectedly caught up with business meetings for the past two days, dealing with a minor financial crisis in one of Santanger's banks.

Weakly, he'd used the distraction as an excuse to avoid thinking about what to do about Maddi, when he knew exactly what he had to do. Deal with the fact that Princess Laia was not interested in their strategic marriage and let Maddi go. And yet he was still perpetuating this pretence of an engagement that could never become anything more.

He was playing a very dangerous game.

He tracked her easily in the crowd. She was wearing a teal blue-green dress. Long sleeves, flowing skirt. Hair coiled up into an elegant chignon. She was talking to a group of nurses and she threw her head back to laugh at something one of them had said. They were all grinning. He couldn't blame them. She was stunning.

After the walkabout she was all anyone could talk about. *Princess Laia this... Princess Laia that...* Exactly as he'd planned it. Except it sat in his gut now with an acrid taste. Because she wasn't Laia. She was Maddi. And he didn't like the fact that his people didn't know who she was.

Which was so messed up—because if they found out who she really was it would invite exactly the kind of scandal Ari wanted to avoid at all costs. It was impossible.

But even now, when he knew all that, all he wanted was to go over, take her by the arm and find somewhere quiet where he could taste her, fill his hands with her firm flesh, make her press against him and moan into his mouth.

But then she disappeared. He couldn't see her any more. He tensed.

His aide said, 'The special effects team are just waiting for your nod to launch the fireworks, Your Majesty.'

Distracted, Ari said, 'Let me find Ma—' He stopped and cursed silently. He was losing it. 'Let me find Princess Laia.'

He moved through the crowd, stopping and starting when people wanted a word, feeling a growing sense of frustration.

Where was she?

He couldn't help but acknowledge the uneasy feeling that if it wasn't for her sense of loyalty to Princess Laia, Maddi might very well just disappear at any moment.

Before he was ready to let her go.

And then he saw her. She was sitting cross-legged on the grass, uncaring of her dress, with a boy of about nine or ten opposite her, also cross-legged. They were locked in an intense discussion.

Ari went closer and saw that a woman was standing nearby. She turned and greeted him, curtseying. 'Your Majesty, I'm so sorry. My son has latched on to Princess Laia and won't hear of letting her go.'

Ari's first rueful thought was, *I know how you feel.*

The woman went on, *sotto voce*, 'He has Asperger's, and doesn't connect easily with people, but she came over to him and just…knew how to talk to him. He's dragged her over here to show her something…'

Ari had always known that having children would be part of his duty as King. But he'd never really thought about what it might feel like. Watching Maddi with this young boy made something tug inside him. He had a sense for the first time that his view of fatherhood had always been too narrow. Not surprising, after the hands-off treatment from his own parents. But he'd never contemplated having something different for himself. For his own family.

The idea rooted in his head, and he realised with a lurch that it wasn't totally ridiculous to want a different, *better* experience. To want more.

And who was the catalyst for yet another unsettling revelation? *Maddi*.

At that moment, as if hearing his thoughts, Maddi looked up and caught his eye.

CHAPTER TEN

WHAT HAD SHE done now? Maddi wondered, the smile slipping off her face. Ari was scowling at her.

Ari had been busy for the past couple of days, and she'd welcomed a little space to try and get her head around this whole situation, which felt as if it was veering way out of control. As if she'd ever had any control over it.

She stood up, feeling defensive and also a little hurt. It seemed that, no matter what, Ari still didn't trust her. She'd found him looking at her warily since the night they'd returned from the walkabout. As if he was trying to figure something out.

She moved to stand in front of him. He was looking at her again with a strange expression.

She said, 'He's a sweet boy.'

Ari's expression cleared. 'You're good with kids.'

'I guess I find it easy to communicate with them.' Maddi shrugged, not liking the little glow she felt at his compliment.

Ari's aide appeared again, and Ari said, 'Give the signal for the fireworks.'

He went back towards the crowd and clapped his hands, getting everyone's attention. 'Thank you all for coming— please, enjoy the end of the party.'

Maddi followed behind him. Everyone cheered and clapped and then there were *oohs* and *aahs* as the fireworks started, launching high into the sky over the sea before exploding into a million different colours and shapes.

Maddi felt absurdly emotional as she took in the joy of the crowd. Everyone was so lovely here, and they all adored their king. They'd told her that his father had never opened up the palace like this. Or treated them as human beings.

Ari turned and looked at her. He held out his hand and she stepped forward, taking it. Standing by his side when they both knew that this was not real.

'This is a really nice thing to do,' Maddi said, smiling at the joy of the crowd, hoping he wouldn't see her emotion.

She was in deep with this man and there was no way it could end well. She had an awful sense that the end was coming before she was ready for it.

On an impulse, telling herself it wasn't out of a sense of desperation and fear that everything was about to change, Maddi turned to him and said, 'Could we do something this evening? Like…go on a date? Go out for dinner?'

It was ridiculous. Her heart was thumping as if she was a teenager, asking out a boy she fancied. She'd been sleeping with this man for days now, and she knew him more intimately than she knew herself.

Ari put a hand on his chest. 'Are you asking me out on a date?'

Maddi scowled at him and tried to hide her insecurity. He was laughing at her. Reminding her that this was beyond the parameters of…whatever it was between them.

'Forget it—a silly idea.'

She tried to pull her hand out of his but he caught it. She looked up and her insides swooped at the expression on his face. He wasn't mocking any more. There was an intensity there that she hadn't seen before.

'I would love to take you for dinner.'

'I…' She felt tongue-tied. Again, ridiculous, considering how intimate they were. 'Okay…great.'

Ari signalled to his hovering aide, gave him some instructions and then said, 'Let's go.'

But Maddi stopped in her tracks and looked down. She felt self-conscious heat rise in her face. Ari followed her gaze, down to her bare feet.

She looked up, embarrassed. 'Sorry… The last time I saw my sandals a little girl was playing dress-up with them.'

She obviously wasn't ready to be a princess, no matter how much she liked talking to people. But before she knew what was happening Ari bent down and picked Maddi up in his arms and carried her back through the garden and to the palace.

Dammit, but she couldn't help relishing the feeling of being in his arms, cradled against his chest.

She also couldn't stop the soppy grin on her face.

When they got inside the palace there was a sense of infectious energy in the air. Ari put her back on her feet and Hannah appeared and took Maddi by the hand.

She was smiling, and said, 'The things you need are in your room, Princess Laia, come with me.'

Feeling nonplussed, Maddi followed in Hannah's wake as the girl led her up through the endless corridors back to her suite. Once in her rooms, Hannah went to the dressing room and in a few minutes emerged with an armful of clothes.

She laid them out on the bed. Worn jeans, sneakers, a black silk shirt and a beautifully soft cropped black leather jacket. And new underwear.

Maddi went over and touched the leather. 'Ooh, I like this.'

Maddi glanced at Hannah, as if to ask, *Are you sure this is what I have to wear?* and noticed the girl's eyes were shiny.

She immediately went over to her. 'Hannah? Is everything okay?'

She started crying in earnest, and Maddi put her arm around her, leading her into the bathroom. In fits and starts, in between apologies, the girl looked at Maddi with huge blue eyes and said, 'I'm so sorry, Princess Laia, but I'm just so happy to see you and the King like this. My mother worked here too, for the Queen, and she was so unhappy. The atmosphere was always so tense and sad… I'm just so thrilled for you both…and for us. You really love each other, and things will be so different now.'

A solid weight settled in Maddi's belly.

She wiped Hannah's tears and said, 'You're a romantic.'

The girl looked at Maddi and said, so defiantly that Maddi laughed, 'Yes, I am—and I'm not ashamed of it.'

She took Hannah by the shoulders and said, 'Good for you. Don't ever lose it.'

But her conscience mocked her. Who was she to advise someone to keep on believing in romance when she was so busy suppressing her own emotions and deepest fantasies that she had a constant ache in her gut.

What she was doing was making a mockery of Hannah's beautiful, innocent romanticism, but also making a mockery of herself—because she was getting caught up on a flight of fancy too, and the higher it went, the harder the fall would be.

But Hannah was helping her out of her dress now, and into the new clothes. The silk shirt settled around Maddi's shoulders like air. And as she was fastening the buttons, Hannah was undoing her hair and letting it fall down.

She pulled on the jeans and the sneakers. And then Hannah led her back out of the suite and in the opposite direction from the one they usually went. They came out near the palace kitchen garden. In another courtyard.

And there… Maddi's eyes nearly bugged out of her head… Ari was waiting, beside a massive motorbike. Wearing jeans and a T-shirt under a well-loved leather jacket.

She nearly melted on the spot into a pool of lust and longing. He looked so unlike the man who had stepped out of his car that day in the desert in his suit. This man looked wild and young...and so sexy he took her breath away.

He held out a helmet and Maddi walked forward. She didn't know what to say. She hadn't envisaged this at all when she'd told him she wanted to go on a date. She was speechless.

She took the helmet and put it on her head. Then he put on his own helmet and swung his leg over the bike, sitting in the middle.

He held out a hand. 'Use me to balance, stand on the little step and jump on.'

Maddi had never been on a motorbike in her life. She sat on the bike and slid almost naturally into the dip behind Ari.

He said over his shoulder, 'Put your arms around me.'

She needed no encouragement.

Maddi slid her arms around his lean torso and then he straightened the bike. With a downward push of his foot the machine roared to life and throbbed powerfully under Maddi's body.

They left the palace, and Maddi was aware of the ever-present security following them at a distance in a car. They wound their way down the mountain, passing through small villages where people were sitting outside small cafés, children running around.

They approached the outskirts of the city. The tall, gleaming financial district. And then moved into the older part, where the streets buzzed and hummed with activity on this weekend night. It was cool, but still warm enough for people to be outside, strolling around with just a light coat.

Ari pulled up in the middle of a parking area and turned off the bike. Maddi reluctantly disengaged and sat up straight. Ari took off his helmet and she took off hers too, and handed it to him.

'You get off first,' he told her.

She did, and her legs felt wobbly. Then Ari stepped off and stowed their helmets. He handed her a baseball cap and put one on himself. She put it on.

Then he surprised her by taking her hand to lead her out of the quiet square. She stopped and he looked back.

She said, 'I thought we weren't meant to do this.'

He said, 'We're incognito.'

Maddi snorted. 'I might be able to be that, but no one is not going to recognise you.'

'Wait and see—we won't be bothered.'

They emerged onto one of the main streets, busy with evening strollers and people window-shopping the luxurious boutiques. They got a few glances, and Maddi saw some stop and stare, but Ari was right—no one approached.

They wandered up and down the busy streets and Maddi tugged Ari in the direction of the more touristy area. Here there were shops selling stuff for the beach and postcards. She felt a pang. She'd like to send a postcard to her mother, but she couldn't, of course—she had no idea what was going on. She assumed Maddi was in Isla'Rosa.

Then Ari led her down a quiet street from where they emerged into a hidden square. Maddi gasped. The houses were obviously old, some a little higgledy-piggledy. Restaurants lined one side of the square, with tables and chairs spilling outside, and the entirety of the square was strung overhead with fairy lights. There was a low hum of people talking and music. It was magical.

Ari led her over to one restaurant and the owner came out when he saw them. He surprised Maddi by clasping Ari by the shoulders, looking him up and down as if checking he had all his limbs intact, and then kissing him on both cheeks. Maddi had never seen anyone greet Ari so affectionately.

And then Ari was standing back and saying, 'Alfredo, I'd like you to meet Princess Laia.'

It was stinging harder and harder now, every time someone called her Princess Laia. And yet there was nothing Maddi could do about it. She'd put herself in this position and she couldn't afford to reveal her identity until Laia did. But in a way she had to be thankful, because this trip had shown her that she really was ready to embrace her destiny of being a princess. As scared as she still was, the people of Santanger had shown her that she might just be able to do it.

Ari hadn't mentioned the wedding in days now, and she was too cowardly to ask him if he'd finally realised it was not going to happen. Because then he would have no need of her. She couldn't let herself indulge in a fantasy where she told Ari who she really was because it was too seductive. Too dangerous. And her fantasy always played out the same way in the end—it turned into a nightmare. Rejection. Her worst fear.

'Princess Laia, you are so welcome to Santanger and to my humble establishment.'

Alfredo's greeting stopped the spiral in Maddi's head and she welcomed it. He took her hand and charmed her by kissing it. She smiled. He led them into the restaurant, which looked small and cosy from the outside but opened up inside into a beautiful airy space.

The diners were all well-heeled and elegant. Maddi felt distinctly underdressed, and was glad when Alfredo led them to a booth near the back that was secluded but gave them a view of the room.

Ari said, 'The food here is astounding. Alfredo comes from generations of chefs and bakers. His family have continued the tradition and this restaurant is renowned all over the world as offering one of the best Mediterranean menus.

His wife is from Turkey and she's brought with her a Middle Eastern fusion.'

Maddi's belly gave a low rumble at that exact moment and she smiled ruefully. 'I could pretend that I'm not that hungry or interested, but what's the point? You know my healthy appetite.'

Ari smiled. 'That's why I know you'll love it here.'

Maddi's heart clenched.

Please don't smile like that.

A waitress approached with two delicate flutes of sparkling wine. She said, 'Compliments of the house.'

Maddi smiled at her, and the waitress blushed and scurried away.

Ari lifted his glass and said, 'This is from a grape native to Santanger—we're busy cultivating our wine industry.'

Maddi took a sip. It was light and dry, with just the right amount of sweetness. 'It's perfect.'

And it was. All so perfect. All so seductive. And the more she enmeshed herself in this reality that was not reality at all, Maddi feared she'd never find her way out.

He might not reject you...just tell him, whispered a rogue little voice.

But Maddi ignored it. It wasn't her truth to tell yet.

Then the food started to arrive, and Maddi let herself be distracted by a selection of starters—including calamari, crisp on the outside and beautifully tender on the inside. There was a selection of mains to share—in particular a tender chicken tagine with couscous and olives and hummus and flat bread...

Maddi was in food heaven.

She glanced at Ari at one point and saw he was just looking at her indulgently, taking a sip of his wine.

She wiped her mouth. 'I'm sorry. I know you're not used to seeing a woman really eat.'

Maddi opened her eyes wide, and brought a hand to her chest. 'You can type too?'

He reached for her and tugged her closer, saying, 'I can type sixty words a minute. But my spelling is atrocious because I'm mildly dyslexic.'

Maddi refused to let the melancholy drag her down. 'Wow, sixty words, and the skill set of a commis chef,' she teased. 'You'll never be unemployable.' And then, more serious, 'You're dyslexic? That must be tough...'

'Both myself and Dax have dyslexia. He's slightly more severe than me.'

'You never mentioned it before.'

Ari shrugged lightly. 'I've learnt to navigate around it. I don't really think of it all that much.'

Maddi lifted a hand to Ari's jaw. 'In a way it's good that you're not completely perfect. You're pretty insufferable as it is.'

He took her hand and pressed a kiss to the palm. 'Oh, I am, am I? I didn't hear you complaining this morning in bed.'

This morning...when he'd woken her by exploring every inch of her flesh and teasing her body into throbbing, aching life. She'd thought she was dreaming, but it hadn't been a dream. But this...*this*, right now, was a dream. A dangerous fantasy she was clinging on to.

They were interrupted by a discreet cough. Maddi blushed and pulled her hand back. Alfredo was looking at them indulgently. Clearly delighted for his King and new Queen-to-be.

The weight in her gut was back.

The waitress deftly cleared their plates and Alfredo deposited new plates in front of them. 'My special baklava, a secret recipe handed down by my wife's relatives.'

Maddi's tastebuds rejoiced. The weight in her gut didn't. It sat there ominously.

Alfredo left and Maddi did her best to hide the fact that

she had just realised she loved this man, and everything about Santanger, and yet none of it was hers or had ever been meant to be hers.

She knew the sweetness of the dessert would push her over the edge.

Ari was shocked. 'You're not eating the baklava? I would have bet money that you'd love it.'

Stop it, she begged inwardly. *Stop making me fall even harder for you.*

'I do… But I think I've hit the limit, even for me.' She looked at Ari. 'You have to eat my portion too, because I can't bear for Alfredo to think I didn't like it.'

He looked at her for a long moment with a funny expression, and then eventually said, 'Okay, but on one condition…'

'What's that?'

'You make it up to me…later.'

In bed. Where they shared the only real thing about this whole situation. Sex.

Maddi hid her growing turmoil behind a smile. 'If you insist.'

When they got back to the palace Ari led Maddi through the dimly lit corridors by the hand, but her mood of melancholy lingered, ominously.

In his rooms, he didn't speak to her. A sense of wordless intensity and urgency filled the air, Maddi tried not to decipher why. Ari pushed her jacket off and to the ground. She kicked off the sneakers. Desperation overtook them as their mouths met and their hands pulled and ripped at clothes until they were both naked and panting.

He led her into the bathroom and reached inside the shower, turning it on. He stepped in, pulling Maddi with him. They were drenched in seconds and surrounded in steam.

Feeling bold, Maddi pressed close and reached up. Twining her arms around Ari's neck and kissing him. Finding his tongue and biting it. His hands rested on her hips, and then he let one drift down between her legs, sliding his fingers between her thighs and making a sound deep in his throat when he could feel for himself how ready she was.

Maddi was trembling now. She dislodged Ari's hand, because he was going to push her over the edge before she was ready and he did that so easily. She desperately needed to feel some sense of control, and she knew it wasn't just about this moment.

She pressed kisses along his neck and then down further, to his chest...his nipples, biting gently and then soothing him with her tongue, making him clasp her head and pull it back.

'What are you doing?'

She shook her head and continued to kiss her way down his body until she knelt at his feet. A supplicant. But powerful. She took his erection in her hand and heard his indrawn breath.

'Maddi...you don't have to—'

She put her mouth around him, cutting off his words. He tensed. She explored him, tasting every inch of his quivering flesh. She hadn't even realised that he'd turned off the shower. That his hands were curled into fists at his sides to stop himself from stopping her.

It was completely instinctive. This need to pleasure him in a way that would make him crazy. She looked up and almost stopped when she saw the feral look on his face.

When he spoke he was hoarse. 'Maddi, if you don't stop—'

She didn't stop. She kept going until his whole body went still and, with a curse, he lost all control and his hips jerked with his orgasm.

Maddi stood up and Ari opened his eyes. He looked dazed. He was almost slumped back against the glass wall.

'Who are you...?' he said, almost to himself.

He reached out and pushed some of her hair back over her shoulder. For a crazy moment Maddi felt like Delilah with Samson, but Ari's strength soon returned. He stood up and turned the water back on. He turned Maddi so she was facing the glass. Their reflections looked back at her.

'Put up your hands.'

She did so, her whole body tingling with anticipation. First, Ari soaped her whole body, with particular attention to between her legs. Maddi was squirming, but Ari held her hips fast. He stepped up behind her. She could feel his total recovery and wanted to curse his virility. Of course he wasn't going to let her have her moment of control.

He cupped her breasts and trapped her nipples between his fingers. She spread her fingers wide on the glass, back arching, pressing into him. She could feel him taking himself in his hand and pressing the head of his erection against her slick body, sliding between her legs.

'Bend down a little,' he instructed.

Maddi did, and Ari thrust into her in one smooth, cataclysmic movement. He bent over her and squeezed her breasts as he moved in and out. Water and steam enveloped them. Maddi was half crazed, pushing back against Ari, silently begging for *more...harder*.

It was fast and furious. Maddi's body clenched tight and then exploded into an ocean of pleasure. Ari extricated himself from Maddi's embrace and she let out a little sound as her sensitised muscles released him. She was barely aware of him taking his own release safely, under the powerful spray of water. Once again showing that he had more presence of mind than she did.

Ari bundled her into a towel and dried her. Then he carried her to the bed and she passed out in a haze of lingering pleasure and satisfaction.

She woke at some point later to find herself cocooned in

Ari's embrace, her bottom snugly against his growing erection and his hand on her breast.

She moved against him and silently, only stopping for him to put on protection, they made love again as furiously as before…as if they were being driven by all the silent voices around them whispering that this couldn't possibly last…

CHAPTER ELEVEN

MADDI WOKE FEELING DISORIENTATED. The bed was empty, but only the faintest trails of dawn lightened the sky outside. She lay there for a moment, orientating herself. There had been an edge to their lovemaking last night. An edge that hadn't been there before… As if they'd both been aware that time was running out and…

Maddi didn't even want to think about it.

But you have to. This is getting ridiculous. Unsupportable.

She sat up, pulling the sheet around her. A chill breeze skated over her skin even though there was no window or door open. She got out of the bed and pulled on a robe, went looking for Ari.

Had she heard a phone ringing a while ago? Had she heard Ari's voice, low and deep? Was that what had woken her? Maybe she'd been dreaming.

He was in his informal living room, standing watching a news channel.

She was momentarily distracted by the fact that he was only wearing sweatpants, his broad back bare.

For some reason he looked remote. Untouchable. Maddi came closer and saw what he was looking at on the screen. Her insides fell to the floor. She might have fallen to the floor too, if she hadn't locked her knees.

On the screen was footage of Princess Laia, arriving back into Isla'Rosa on the royal jet. She looked both glowing and drawn at the same time. Tense. It was the first time Maddi had laid eyes on her in… How long had it been? It felt like aeons. But it had just been weeks.

Reporters were calling out to her as she emerged from the plane. 'Princess Laia, what about your engagement to King Aristedes? Why did you leave Santanger?'

Maddi realised with a jolt that they obviously believed Laia had flown in from Santanger. And why wouldn't they? She'd been here for the last few weeks with her fiancé, as far as the world was aware.

Except she hadn't been. Maddi had. Living in a make-believe land that was now collapsing around her.

Her brain hurt as she tried to untangle what this all meant.

At that moment Princess Laia looked at the camera and said, very clearly, 'I have no comment to make at this time except to say that I'm looking forward to my coronation in a few days' time.'

Laia's birthday.

Maddi realised that they had done it. Laia had managed to get back to Isla'Rosa just in time for her birthday and her coronation.

At that moment Ari flicked a switch and the TV went black. There was a heavy silence in the room. He knew she was there.

Without turning around, he said, 'As you can see, your job here is done.'

Maddi went cold inside at the detached tone of his voice. She walked to stand in front of him. He looked impossibly remote. Like a stranger. Not like the man who had made love to her just short hours before with such hunger.

'Ari…'

He looked at her and she almost took a step back. His face and eyes were devoid of all expression.

'I'll arrange for Hannah to come and help you pack your

'It's very sexy.'

Maddi's insides liquefied. She took a hurried sip of her own wine to cool down. It was the perfect accompaniment. Crisp and light and fragrant.

'I may never leave this place,' she warned Ari.

'I used to work here.'

Maddi nearly choked on her wine. She put down the glass. 'You what?'

He nodded. 'For a couple of summers when I was a teen-ager.'

'Was it your father's idea? To try and teach you the ways of humble normal people?'

He scowled at her. 'No, actually. It was my idea. My par-ents…my mother was becoming unbearable. The tension in the palace was toxic. I came down here one day and asked Alfredo if he'd let me work in the kitchen. I was friends with his son. At first he told me no way, he couldn't be seen to be making the future King work, but I managed to persuade him. I would have been happy washing dishes—anything to get away from the atmosphere in the palace—but he insisted on me working in the kitchen, actually learning something.'

Maddi felt something inside her give way. This was the exact moment when she knew she was deeply and irrevocably in love with this man…as if up to now she'd been fooling her-self into thinking it might not be real. And it filled her with such an acute melancholy that emotion gripped her throat.

It was ironic. Maybe she was destined to be exiled by a king, just as her mother had been.

Somehow she managed to find her voice and not sound as if a storm was tearing her apart inside. 'You never men-tioned your culinary skills.'

He made a face. 'It was so long ago now…but it's like learning to type. I can chop anything you want with perfect precision.'

things. You'll leave the country discreetly, to minimise the chances of anyone seeing you.'

It took a second for what he meant to sink in. *Of course.* If anyone saw her here, then it would expose both him and Princess Laia. Obviously she had to go.

'And then what?'

'And then what, Maddi? Then you get on with your life as Princess Laia's—sorry, as *Queen* Laia's lady-in-waiting. What did you think?'

What had she thought?

She'd known this was coming. She'd felt it last night. And for the last few days. Like a sword hanging over her head. In a way it was almost a relief. She wouldn't have to pretend to be someone else any more.

It was a relief tempered with such pain, though.

As if she had to hear him say it to be sure, she said, 'This is it then…? Even once Laia has become Queen you don't… we can't see each other again?'

Maddi had wanted to make it sound like a statement, but it came out like a question.

He smiled, but it was mirthless. 'No, Maddi. I told you not to confuse sex with emotion. You said you knew what you were getting into. But maybe the great sex confused you. Because it was amazing sex. I'll grant you that. For a novice you were…spectacular.'

For a second Maddi was so outraged she couldn't speak. She'd never hit another person in her life, but right now she wanted to strike at Ari and his hateful words.

She'd been such a fool to allow intimacy to grow between them. Her anger started to burn, and she welcomed it because it was cauterising her raw wound.

'Don't patronise me, Ari. I might have been physically innocent, but I'm not emotionally naive. And thank you for the compliment. You've certainly opened my eyes as to what to expect from a satisfying lover. I won't settle for less in future.'

His jaw clenched at that, but it was small comfort.

He said, 'Be honest, Maddi, what were you really hoping for? A declaration of love?'

Pain lanced Maddi's heart. *Yes.*

'No, not that. I know what you think of love. That it's an indulgence that leads only to weakness and self-destruction. But not everyone is your mother, Ari. Some people learn to get over their heartache and find another kind of love. My mother didn't let it destroy her.'

Like his had done.

'None of that interests me. It's time for you to go back where you belong.'

I belong here, with you.

The words rose up on a tide of emotion that Maddi did her best to hold back. He was right—she did need to go back to Laia and reorientate herself. It was clear she was no longer welcome here. She never really had been. Ari had spied an opportunity to have some fun while she was here, and he'd taken it.

So did you.

Suddenly Maddi didn't have the stomach for hiding behind bravado.

'You didn't have to be tender, Ari. You could have spared me that. But then I guess this was always going to be an exercise in punishment for you, wasn't it? After all, you didn't get your convenient queen.'

'I'm not so petty. The first night we slept together was the start of my letting go of the marriage agreement with Princess Laia. Did you really think I could have a situation in which I was married to a woman while my ex-lover worked as her lady-in-waiting?'

Maddi didn't know what to say.

Ari went on. Grim. 'I realised then that this whole agreement with Laia was something I'd taken for granted. Hadn't really thought about. Certainly I hadn't considered her feelings. She tried to speak to me years ago, after her father's funeral. I know that I barely entertained her concerns. I told her it was happening and that was that. I'm not proud to admit that.'

Maddi swallowed the emotion in her throat. 'What about the peace agreement?'

He looked at her. Still cold as ice. 'That'll be between me and Queen Laia, but I have no doubt we can work something out.'

'So, all's well that ends well?'

Maddi knew she should be happy for her sister that Ari had come to this realisation of his own arrogance and stubbornness, and was showing a willingness not to let their actions affect the peace agreement. But she felt hollow.

And she must be a sucker for punishment, because she said, 'I'm sorry for the inconvenience. You'll have to find a new royal bride, but I'm sure you will.'

Ari said nothing—just looked at her. Silently telling her to leave.

Maddi turned and walked to the door. She'd been right to fear the pain of this rejection. It was like a knife lodged in her gut. Sharp and devastating.

She had felt as if she had a place here—but not any more. She was unwelcome. Unwanted. The magic that she'd thought existed between her and Ari had all been an illusion. He was right. She'd confused sex with emotion, just as he'd said.

She was almost at the door when Ari said from behind her, 'You're obviously not applying for the position yourself?'

Maddi stopped dead. Had she misheard him?

She turned around. 'What did you say?'

'You heard me,' he all but spat out.

He knows.

His remote demeanour now made sense.

Maddi felt unbelievably cold. Exposed. 'How did you know?'

When did he know? Has he known all along?

Questions buzzed in her head, causing a cacophony.

'I asked a friend to have you investigated when I realised you weren't Princess Laia.'

Maddi might have objected to that if she'd had any right to. But she'd given up that right when she'd lied about who she was.

'When did you know?'

'Only a few hours ago. Your secret was a well-kept one, *Princess Maddi.*'

Maddi winced. 'It's not like that. I always knew, but my father…the King…made my mother agree that she wouldn't make any claim to the royal family on my behalf as long as he was alive and paying her maintenance. When he died…she was ill. I wasn't interested in finding out more. Thankfully she recovered but she never mentioned it and neither did I.'

Ari was facing her now, arms folded across his chest, muscles bulging. Even now distracting. His expression was almost sneering.

'If I didn't know you I'd assume you were lying. Who on earth would pass up the chance of entering a life of unparalleled privilege and luxury? No one but you.'

Maddi was sure he didn't mean that as a compliment.

Then he said, 'Maybe it's time you faced up to the responsibility you bear, Maddi Smith. Time to step out of the shadows and stop playing at being someone else.'

Maddi whispered, 'That's not fair.'

She'd only just finally begun to believe that she could.

'Isn't it?'

His words resonated deep inside. Why hadn't she wanted

to pursue her birthright after her father had died? She could have gone to Laia long before Laia had come looking for her. She'd told herself she hadn't been interested, as if she had some higher loftier ideal than wanting a life of luxury, but perhaps the reason was more prosaic than that.

A fear of rejection. Rejection by her sister. And by the people of Isla'Rosa. She'd never fully acknowledged this before now.

Fear had stopped her. Selfish fear of being hurt. She wasn't brave and selfless, like Laia and Ari. She didn't deserve to be a princess—even though these past couple of weeks had given her a real sense that she *could* be. And that she wanted to be.

Somehow she managed to make her voice sound strong. As if she wasn't falling apart inside. 'Goodbye, Ari. I'm sorry... for everything.'

She left before she could hear if he'd even said goodbye. Probably not.

Everything happened so quickly after that. Her head was spinning by the time she was being ushered onto a small sleek jet as the sky lightened in the east...heralding another beautiful day in Santanger.

First of all, she'd deceived King Aristedes. Then she'd deceived the people of Santanger. But worst of all, she'd deceived herself.

Ari watched the small plane take off into the brightening sky. Just like that she was gone. The woman who had come into his life and turned it upside down and inside out. With her bare feet and her gap-toothed grin and her insatiable appetite—*appetites*.

His blood heated and he cursed out loud and turned away from the sight of the plane.

Damn her.

Damn her.

The marriage agreement with Princess Laia and Isla'Rosa was obviously dead in the water. But Ari had come to terms with that. There would be some other way around uniting their two countries in a peace agreement, although the marriage would have been a much neater way of doing it.

As much as he didn't want to credit her with anything, he had to admit that Maddi had been the catalyst in helping him to see how entrenched he'd been about the idea of marriage. He had to concede that if Princess Laia had come to him again, to try and talk to him, he might very well not have heard her—*again*. He would have done everything in his power to persuade her.

And perhaps that was what she'd been afraid of—that he would try to appeal to the side of her that feared for Isla'Rosa's future, the side of her that had grown up with a strongly ingrained sense of duty and responsibility. As had he.

Ari went over to his drinks cabinet. It wasn't even nine a.m. but he didn't care as he threw a shot of whisky down his throat.

Maddi had deceived him. She'd come here with one agenda—to protect her Queen. *No*, her sister. Her half-sister.

He still couldn't quite believe what Antonio Chatsfield had told him. His friend had said, 'You might want to sit down for this, my friend.'

Her father was the late King of Isla'Rosa. He was the man who had abandoned her mother.

Ari considered that for a moment—how she must have felt growing up, knowing that she was a princess but being forced into exile. And not becoming bitter about that. It would take an extraordinary human not to be swayed by such temptation.

And then to work as the Queen's lady-in-waiting for a year. Why had she done that? Why hadn't she wanted the world to know she was part of the royal family?

He couldn't ask her now, because she was gone.

Maddening, infuriating woman.

Her words came back to him. *'You didn't have to be tender.'*

No, there had been no need for tenderness. But with her he hadn't been in control of his impulses.

Passion didn't last, he told himself now—desperately. It never had in the past. It had burned bright, or not even that bright, and then faded like a dying firework. *This*, however— this thing that was between them—wasn't fading. Not even now that he knew the full extent of her betrayal.

But she hadn't told him the full truth of who she was, and that stung more than anything.

He'd trusted her. In spite of her initial deception. And he'd only realised the profundity of how easily that had happened when his friend had told him who she really was. Yet she hadn't trusted him.

He'd been harsh. He'd never been harsh with a woman before. Because no other woman had ever got under his skin before. And not just under his skin. Into his gut. Into his head.

Into his emotions.

He'd learnt from his parents that uncontrollable desire and love were self-destructive. He'd lived his life believing that he was immune to those things. His life was all about control. And that included his emotions. Until now.

It burned him to admit this, but he'd actually imagined her by his side. He'd imagined somehow being able to bring her in front of his people and have them accept her, even though he'd believed she wasn't of royal blood.

Because he hadn't been able to countenance the thought of not having her by his side...in his bed. And yet she hadn't trusted him with vital information. Proof that he was the fool. The idiot who had forgotten the lessons of a lifetime...

He slugged back another shot of whisky and cursed Maddi

Smith again. He would ban her from Santanger. He would find a suitable royal princess and get on with the task at hand. Being King and siring heirs.

And all these rogue thoughts of perhaps being an actual father and wanting something different for the first time in his life, wanting *more*, would be pushed back down where they belonged.

There was a sound at the door and Ari turned around, his heart leaping, making a total mockery of his recent thoughts. But it wasn't her. It was someone else.

His brother.

He looked at Dax across the room and was filled with such a sense of incoherent rage for everything that had happened that he said, 'Where the hell have you been?'

Dax looked as grim as Ari felt. He also looked a little wild. Jaw heavily stubbled and hair too long. His brother was wearing faded jeans and a wrinkled shirt. He looked as disreputable as he always did. But there was something different about him that Ari couldn't put his finger on, but it resonated in him as if he recognised what it was instinctively.

A woman.

His brother came in and arched a brow. 'Drinking before noon, Ari? Have you decided to join my gang?'

Dax smiled, but it was mirthless as he helped himself to a shot of whisky, quickly downed it and then filled his glass with another.

Ari looked at him. 'Dax…?'

Dax looked at him. 'I'm sorry, Ari.'

'For what?'

'For not bringing Laia back in time. We were… She has this island in Malaysia. That's where we've been. I couldn't leave.'

Then a look that Ari couldn't decipher came over Dax's face. There was something fierce about it.

'You know you can't marry her, right?'

Ari said, 'Yes, I know.'

The ferocity left Dax's face. He said, 'You'll find another princess.'

Ari might have smiled at the notion that princesses could just be found—if he'd felt remotely inclined to smile. But right now he was done with princesses.

'What happened between you and Princess Laia?' he asked.

Dax avoided his eye. Guilty.

Ari said wearily, 'It's not as if I can't put two and two together, Dax. I had no hold over her. It was an ancient agreement. I barely knew her.'

Dax looked at him. 'I tried not to…but…' he trailed off.

Ari could almost sympathise. They'd both been tied in knots by the Isla'Rosa Princesses.

He asked, 'Did you know Laia was Maddi's half-sister?'

Dax nodded and sat down on a chair, long legs sprawled out. 'But I couldn't get in touch with you. She threw my phone into the sea…'

Ari thought back to Maddi, throwing her phone out the window, and barked out a sudden laugh.

Dax leant forward. 'What's so funny? This is a disaster.'

Ari sobered. Dax was right. It wasn't funny at all. And suddenly there was a weight such as he'd never felt before, settling in his gut and spreading up into his chest, tightening like a vice.

'Maddi!'

Laia flew across her office and all but jumped into Maddi's arms.

Maddi hugged her tight. Anything to avoid the awful emotion that threatened to spill over at any moment.

Laia pulled back and ran her hands all over Maddi, as if

checking for broken bones. 'Are you okay? Did he let you leave today or did you have to escape? I can't believe he kept you there and made you pretend to be me—'

Maddi couldn't let her go on. 'Laia, it wasn't like that. He found out almost straight away that I wasn't you. But no one else knew. I agreed to slot into your engagement schedule because I thought that was the best way of letting you stay hidden. But the truth is...'

She moved out of Laia's embrace and went to the window to try and collect herself.

'Mads?'

She turned around. 'The truth is that I fell for him. We... we were together.'

Laia paled. 'Oh... Oh, wow. I didn't expect that...but I guess it was pretty apparent.'

Maddi frowned. 'What do you mean?'

Laia took her hand and led her over to the desk, where a laptop was open. Laia had clearly been looking at pictures of Maddi and Ari on their public engagements. There was the walkabout, and Ari leading her away with an indulgent smile as Maddi waved at the crowd, a huge grin on her face. And someone had taken a snap of him carrying her away from the garden party for frontline workers into the palace.

She blushed.

Laia said, 'I thought he was going to keep you on Santanger as some sort of a threat. That he wouldn't release you unless I agreed to the marriage. But he let you go...'

A knife sank into Maddi's heart. 'Yes, he let me go.' She had to give him his due. 'Laia, he knows your marriage is off the table. He realised a while ago that he'd done you a disservice in just assuming you'd marry him. He told me that you'd tried to talk to him years ago and that he all but ignored you.'

'Oh, well...that's good. Did he say anything about the peace agreement?'

Maddi nodded. 'That he's sure you can discuss it at some point.'

Laia's eyes widened. 'Wow! Maybe I didn't give him enough credit.'

'He never really forced me to stay there, Laia. I... I wanted to be there, as strange as it sounds.' She looked at Laia sheepishly. 'I enjoyed it...pretending to be you...as scary as it was. But it was starting to take a toll...not being me.'

Laia smiled wryly. 'I can imagine.'

Maddi took her hands. 'But Ari doesn't want me, and none of that matters. What matters is that you're back in time for your coronation and there's nothing and no one to stop you becoming Queen.'

A shadow passed across Laia's face and Maddi was immediately concerned. 'What is it? What are you not telling me? Did Ari's brother Dax find you? Did something happen?'

Laia went pale and shook her head. 'It's okay. I'll tell you about it later.'

As if wanting to divert Maddi from any more questions, Laia said, 'I'll draft a statement, saying that by mutual agreement King Aristedes and I have decided not to proceed with our marriage. I'll send it over to him to see if he'll accept that.'

Maddi smiled, but it felt wobbly. 'I'm sure he will. He's a good man, Laia. I think you'll like him when you do have talks.'

Laia saw her emotion and touched Maddi's cheek. 'Oh, Mads, I'm sorry...is there any hope?'

Maddi shook her head fiercely and hoped she wouldn't start crying. 'No, he made that clear from the start. And at the end. It wasn't as if I didn't know.'

But that hadn't stopped her hoping.

Laia said, 'Well, you're back where you belong. And I want everyone to know who you are...if you're ready?'

Maddi thought of Ari saying, *'Maybe it's time to step out of the shadows...'*

She smiled and took a deep breath. 'Yes, I'm ready.'

Laia gave a whoop, and hugged Maddi again, and Maddi tried her best to focus on the present and the new future that would unfold for her. A new future in which she would try and forget the man who had awoken her to a dazzling new version of herself only to crush it to pieces.

She hated Aristedes.

She hated him as much as she loved him.

CHAPTER TWELVE

Two weeks later

ARI SWITCHED OFF THE TV. He'd watched Maddi being crowned Princess of Isla'Rosa on a loop since Laia's coronation over a week ago.

He'd agreed to the statement put out by Princess Laia about the demise of their engagement, and she'd had the grace to phone him and apologise for all the theatrics. They'd arranged a future date to talk about how to proceed with building peace between their countries.

He'd had to bite his lip to stop himself asking about Maddi.

He wanted nothing to do with her. He never wanted to see her again.

Except every night in his dreams, when he couldn't stop her from intruding. They veered from being X-rated, when he would wake with a raging, burning desire that only a cold shower could cure, to dreams where she was running away from him, laughing, disappearing down corridors or into rooms that were empty when he burst inside.

He was losing it. He was so grumpy that Dax had left to go back to New York, where he was mainly based. Come to think of it, Dax hadn't exactly been in good form either.

Ari had found him watching a rerun of the coronation of Queen Laia with an intensity that had made Ari ask, 'Is there anything else you'd like to share about what happened on that island with Laia, Dax?'

For the first time since they were kids Ari had thought Dax might actually hit him. His brother had snarled at him to mind his own business and stormed out of the room.

It was late. Ari had meetings in the morning. He should sleep. But he knew he'd only have those dreams again.

Damn her.

He sat down at his desk. There was a light knock at the door. Probably Santo, wondering if he needed anything.

Ari called out without looking up. 'Come in.'

The door opened and then shut again quickly. Santo didn't speak. Ari looked up, and at first he wasn't sure who he was looking at. Someone all in black, wearing a baseball cap.

Then whoever it was tipped up their face. A rush of blood to Ari's head was his first reaction. And then a wave of heat to every cell in his body.

'How dare you come back here?'

He stood up and put his hands on the table. Was he, in fact, dreaming?

She moved forward and took off the hat. Her hair spilled down around her shoulders. She was wearing a black sweat-shirt and black sweatpants. Black shoes.

Her voice was husky. 'I'm sorry… I needed to see you.'

'How did you get in here?'

'I… I contacted someone. It doesn't matter who. They helped me.'

Ari still wasn't entirely sure he wasn't dreaming.

'Come closer. I need to be sure it's you and not Queen Laia. Perhaps you're not done playing your games.'

Maddi stepped forward. She looked pale. 'It's me.'

It was her. He wasn't dreaming.

There was such a mix of volatile emotions raging in his

gut that he had to take a second to try and contain them. He'd never had to deal with emotions before.

Damn her again.

He said, 'To what do I owe the pleasure of a midnight visit from the newly crowned Princess Maddi of Isla'Rosa?'

Maddi tried not to quiver under the scathing tone and icy glare of Ari. She'd known this would be difficult, but she wouldn't be able to move on completely until she'd faced her last fears and told him how she felt. She refused to let fear rule her life again.

She swallowed. 'I came here because I want to tell you something.'

Ari put out a hand. 'Please, be my guest. Would you like a drink? Perhaps some of that whisky?'

Maddi felt a flicker of anger at Ari's bullish mood.

She lifted her chin. 'Actually, yes, that would be lovely— if it's not too much trouble.'

'Oh, it's no trouble at all.'

He went into the living area and Maddi followed him, drinking him in. He was wearing jeans and a shirt, sleeves rolled up, top button open. There was stubble on his jaw and his hair was mussed, as if he'd been running a hand through it. When he turned around to hand her the glass she noticed that he looked a little drawn.

Her heart hitched.

Because of her?

Was he having crazy dreams too?

She downed the shot and handed back the glass. 'Another, please.' She needed all the courage she could muster.

He looked at her for a long moment, but then took the glass and refilled it, handing it back. She downed this one too, and put the glass on the table. Her head was spinning momentarily, and heat flooded her upper chest.

He folded his arms. 'So, you wanted to tell me something?'

Maddi wondered if she had gone totally mad. She was literally inviting him to inflict even more pain on her than he had done already. But if she didn't do this…she'd regret it for ever.

She said clearly, 'Yes. I came here to tell you that I love you, Aristedes. When you asked me if I was looking for a declaration of love and I said no, I was too scared to admit it, but actually I was.'

She held up a hand, even though he hadn't opened his mouth to speak.

'And do *not* patronise me by telling me I fell for you because you were my first lover and all that nonsense. This is a once-in-a-lifetime love that transcends sex. I think you have feelings for me and that's why you're so angry,' she went on. 'Because you didn't want any of this either. And because I didn't tell you who I really was. I need to explain why…'

'Go on.'

Ari was grim. Not exactly encouraging, but Maddi couldn't go back now.

She shrugged minutely. 'In a nutshell, because you're right. I was hiding in the shadows. I could have come to find Laia after our father died, to claim my birthright, but I didn't. I told myself I wasn't interested in becoming a princess or living in that world. But the truth is that I was terrified of risking rejection. So I waited until she came to me. When my father sent my mother into exile it was before I was even born. He rejected me before he even knew me. That…that put a mark on me for my whole life. And I never realised how deep it went until you made me see it.'

She ploughed on.

'And then, when I came here…met you… I told myself that I couldn't betray Laia's confidence. She wanted to reveal my identity when the time was right for her. I couldn't risk

you using the information to wreak some kind of revenge…
or that's what I told myself. But really I was still tied to the
fear of rejection. I fantasised about telling you who I was…
but I was terrified you'd still reject me. So it was fear—again.'

Ari said nothing. Maddi couldn't read his expression. She
was too scared to.

'I came here tonight to tell you how I feel because if there's
any chance that you might feel the same way then I would
like to have a life with you, Ari. Loving you and getting to
know every part of you. For ever. But if you don't then at
least you'll know how I feel. I know having a life with you
would also mean my becoming Queen, and I'm barely used
to being a princess…but I would try my best to do you proud.
Because I love you. So much.'

Maddi stood there for a long moment. Emotionally naked
and exposed.

Ari was looking at her with wide eyes. She didn't know
if it was a look of shock, or disgust, or—

She realised as the silence wore on that she didn't want
to know. Clearly he didn't know how to respond because he
didn't feel an atom of what she felt.

Devastation quietly settled in her gut, cold and frigid. She
took a step back. Still he didn't do anything or say anything.

'Okay, look… Please don't use this as an opportunity to
mock me, Ari. Just let me leave with a little dignity. You
won't ever see me again. I promise.'

Somehow Maddi was able to make her legs move and she
took one step in front of another and went towards the door.

Just as she put her hand on the knob she felt movement
behind her, and the door was kept shut by Ari's hands on it,
over her head. He was caging her in.

He said, 'You are going nowhere. You are never leaving
this palace again.'

Maddi placed her forehead against the door. 'Ari, I'm sorry

for what happened, okay? And the fact that the marriage didn't happen—'

Ari put his hands on Maddi's shoulders and spun her around so fast her head was spinning again.

'Ari...?' She looked up at him, and the expression on his face dissolved any words she might have said.

It was crazed. His eyes were burning.

'I am so over that marriage not happening,' he said. 'I'm not letting you leave here because if you do I won't be able to live. I've only been half living since you left.'

'Since you let me leave,' she said shakily.

He shook his head. 'I was so angry. You came into my life like a whirlwind and upended everything I knew. My nice, neat, complacent life. You stirred up every emotion I've ever had and hidden, and some new ones that I don't think have even been invented yet.'

Maddi hardly dared to breathe. 'Is that a good thing?'

Ari barked out a laugh. 'I think it's only a good thing if you're here to help me regulate them.'

'You want me to stay?'

'Yes, please.'

'Like...as your...guest...? Before you marry someone suitable?'

Ari glared at her. 'Don't you get it yet? It's you, Maddi. Only you. There will be no one else. I'm so fathoms deep in love with you that I'm drowning, and you're the only one who can save me.'

Maddi's heart cracked open. 'Why did you let me go? Why didn't you come for me?'

'Because I'm an idiot and a coward and I was hurt that you hadn't trusted me.'

Maddi bit her lip. 'I'm so sorry... I did trust you. I just didn't trust myself.' They looked at each other for a long moment, and then Maddi said, 'What if I hadn't come today?'

'Then I probably would have stayed miserable and angry for another week, or maybe even a month, but eventually I would have realised I was losing the best thing that ever happened to me. *You*.'

Maddi jumped into Ari's arms, wrapping hers around his neck, taking him by surprise and propelling him backwards. They lost balance and fell back onto the floor. They landed with an *oof*.

Maddi was plastered to Ari's front. She lifted her head. 'I'm sorry, are you okay?'

Ari winced. 'My back might be broken, but I don't care.'

He demonstrated that he was fine by shifting them so that she was on her back under him and he was over her. She twined her arms around his neck again.

'Do you really mean it? Are you sure you're not confusing emotion with sex?'

He smirked. 'Don't patronise me, Maddi. This is a once-in-a-lifetime love. I might not have asked for it, but I'm here for it.'

'Me too.' She smiled tremulously and reached up, pressing her mouth to Ari's. He kissed her back, hard and passionate, snaking his arm under her back to arch her into his chest. She spread her legs so that he fell into the cradle of her hips, and she could feel his body responding to hers.

He stopped the kiss and Maddi opened blurry eyes. Ari was taking something out of his pocket. The engagement ring. She'd left it behind.

He said, 'I've been carrying this around since you left it behind. Taking it out…looking at it…cursing you for making me into someone I didn't recognise.' He shook his head. 'And I've been having dreams—'

'Me too!' said Maddi. 'Crazy dreams, where I can't find you.'

Ari looked down at her, and his face was filled with something that made Maddi's heart sing. Emotion and *love*.

He took her hand and put the ring back on her finger. 'Well, now we've found each other again,' he said. 'I don't want to ever lose you, Maddi. I would die.'

'Me too. I love you, Ari.'

He kissed her palm and then pulled her up to sit, and then stand. He got down on one knee in front of her, still holding her hand. Maddi's hair was dishevelled, and she wore no make-up, and she was dressed in athleisure wear. But she couldn't care less.

'Maddi Smith... *Princess Maddi*...would you please do me the honour of becoming my wife and Queen of Santanger?'

A tiny sliver of fear made her shiver. She hated herself for it, but she had to ask... 'What if I can't do it, Ari? I hardly know how to be a princess... I don't want to let you down.'

Ari stood up and cupped her face in his hands. 'You will be the perfect queen for me and for Santanger. You proved that within just two weeks. The people love you. I love you. You can do anything you want. This is your destiny, and I want everyone to see *you* and know how amazing you are.'

Maddi melted all over. 'Thank you,' she whispered. 'That's the nicest thing anyone has ever said to me.'

He got down on one knee again. 'Now, can you please answer the question? Will you marry me?'

Maddi nodded, her eyes swimming with tears. 'Yes, please. I'd like that a lot.'

Ari stood up and cupped her face in his hands and kissed her, long and slow and thorough. Then he picked her up and carried her through the palace to his rooms—*their rooms*—and showed her exactly how much he loved her with his body and his whispered words.

As dawn broke outside, many hours later, they were both awake, still revelling in the amazingness of being together and in love. Pledging their lives to each other for ever.

Maddi tilted her head back and looked at Ari. 'What if I

hadn't been related to Princess Laia…? What if I'd just been a regular person?'

Ari came up on one elbow and looked at her. He smiled. 'I'd already instructed my staff to look up the constitution and see how it might be possible for me to marry you.'

Maddi sat up. 'You had? When?'

Ari pulled her back down to his chest. 'The day of the garden party.'

'Oh, my…'

Maddi's heart swelled in her chest. Any lingering doubts or fears were well and truly gone.

'Oh, my, indeed,' Ari echoed.

After a moment, Maddi asked, 'Do you think we could have a press conference?'

'For what?'

'I want to apologise to the people of Santanger for misleading them about who I was…'

'That's my apology to make. It was my choice.'

Maddi shook her head. 'It was me too. I didn't have to agree. I could have left. But I love them, and I don't want them to think I disrespected them.'

Ari looked at her. 'You're amazing—you know that?'

Maddi shrugged, shy.

Ari said, 'We'll do a press conference to announce our engagement and wedding. And you can say what you have to say.'

A week later, they did the press conference. Maddi was nervous, but she spoke from the heart.

And then Ari took her hand and said to the people of Santanger, 'This is the woman you fell in love with…who I fell in love with. She will be my wife and your Queen.'

There was a moment of silence as the press pack and the crowd absorbed what they'd said, and then there was a spontaneous outbreak of applause and cheering. Maddi saw suspiciously bright eyes in the most hardened of hacks.

A month later, Maddi and Ari emerged into bright, early spring sunshine outside the cathedral of Santanger. She was a vision in a long white dress—simple and classic, overlaid with Santanger lace—with a long veil and a glittering tiara.

She turned to Ari and, grinning, forgot every bit of protocol she'd been taught about how to behave in public. She threw her arms around his neck and pressed her mouth to his.

He mentally threw out the protocol book too, and wrapped his arms around his wife...his *Queen*...and kissed her back with all the passion that raged between them, while the crowd cheered and clapped and cried and threw flowers in the air.

Their marriage signalled a new era for the royal family of Santanger and a lasting peace with Isla'Rosa.

A couple of days later Maddi and Ari were in their honeymoon villa, high in the mountains, with epic views over the island. Maddi had insisted on having a honeymoon on the island, wanting to share her happiness with the people as much as possible.

The sun was setting outside, and everything was bathed in a golden glow.

They'd made love and were basking in a post-coital haze of satisfaction. And not a little emotion. When Ari had reached for protection just a short while before, Maddi had stopped him. Silently they'd communicated the step they were taking, and she was mortified to admit now that she'd cried a little at the thought of creating a family and doing it with love.

She hoped that, for them, it would be different. It would. She knew it, deep in her bones.

She turned her face to Ari and kissed his chest. 'I love you...'

He squeezed her bare buttock.

She smiled.

He said, 'I love you, Queen Maddi of Santanger.'

Through the haze of happiness and satisfaction something occurred to her and she lifted her head.

'Have you heard from Dax?'

Ari shook his head. 'No—should I have?'

Maddi frowned. 'No... I guess not. It's just that I haven't heard from Laia either. She left after the wedding reception. She said something about an emergency she had to get home for, but that it wasn't too serious. I'm pretty sure I saw Dax leaving not long afterwards.'

Ari pulled Maddi down onto his chest, crushing her breasts against him. Maddi's brain immediately became fuzzy.

He said, 'Something happened between them on that island, but he's never said what.'

'Neither has Laia.'

Maddi might have thought about how she'd felt a little hurt by that, but she was becoming distracted by her husband's roving hands.

Ari said, 'They're both grown-ups. I'm sure they're fine and they'll figure it out.'

Maddi slid over Ari's body and spread her legs either side of his hips. Every inch of them was touching. Ari's eyes flashed dark and golden.

She said, 'You mean like we did?'

Ari smiled wickedly as he smoothed a hand over Maddi's buttock again, before squeezing hard. She sucked in a breath.

He said, 'Exactly. Just like we did.'

Maddi grinned. 'Then they'll need all the help they can get.'

Ari slapped her lightly, mock-outraged. 'What are you insinuating?'

Maddi kissed him. 'Nothing—except for the fact that I'm so glad we did figure it out.'

Ari flipped them easily, so he was on top, between Maddi's legs. She luxuriated in his solid weight and wrapped her legs around his waist, inviting him into a more intimate embrace. He didn't need any encouragement.

That day was a good day.

And so was every day after that.

The people of Santanger loved their Queen Maddi as much as the King did. Well, maybe not *as* much. That would have been impossible. Because theirs was a once-in-a-lifetime love and they proved it, by living a long and happy life, in love and in passion, every day.

* * * * *

VIRGIN'S STOLEN NIGHTS WITH THE BOSS

CAROL MARINELLI

MILLS & BOON

For Rosie.

Thank you for being such a brilliant friend!

Carol xxx

PROLOGUE

'*CARMEN, ESTO NO ha terminado...*'

Carmen, this isn't over.

The suppressed anger in Sebastián Romero's voice would send a chill down many a spine. But for Carmen her older brother's words provoked only a deep sense of weariness.

The three Romero siblings stood in the newly deserted stables.

Her brothers, on hearing that their sister was moving the horses, had dropped everything, driving in urgent convoy from the luxurious sherry bodega that stood in the heart of Jerez out to the sprawling property that was about to become the centre of a bitter legal dispute.

The brothers wore smart suits and shades, and both were a foot taller than Carmen, who stood in jodhpurs and, even in the mid-spring Spanish sun, a jumper.

'Papá always said that he wanted the hacienda to be left to you,' Sebastián insisted. He wanted her to stay and fight. 'Maria only came back when she knew Papá was dying.'

None of the Romero siblings referred to Maria as Mother or Mamá. The title had been dropped individually rather than collectively—one by one, each had chosen to distance themselves in an effort to protect their minds and hearts.

Alejandro chimed in then. 'If you leave now you are handing it to her on a plate!'

'Please, stop.'

Carmen put up her hand to halt them. Her father's death six months ago was still a raw wound that smarted when touched.

It was an agonising cocktail of confusion and regret, and he'd left her with so many unanswered questions…

'It's just for three months! Even before Papá died I said I needed a break.'

'She did say that.' Alejandro nodded, addressing their elder brother.

But as he went to put a protective arm around Carmen she pulled away. She felt his sudden tension as he perhaps registered the fragility of her frame beneath the heavy jumper.

'Carmen…' He closed his eyes as he chose his words carefully. 'By rehoming the horses you've made things easier on her.'

'So I should have left them for her to neglect?' Carmen challenged. 'We all know how little she cared for *us*.'

By most standards the Romero siblings were blessed— all were joint heirs to the famed sherry bodega, and properties and investments far beyond Jerez. And while they shared many features, from their raven-black hair to their passionate natures, they were all very different people—be it by nature or nurture, the fires of their childhood had forged three unique personalities.

Sebastián, ten years older than Carmen, was ruthless. His recent marriage to Anna, and pending adoption of Anna's young daughter Willow, might have softened his soul, but not his stance on business. And, to him, their mother Maria de Luca was nasty business. With José Romero dead, he wanted Maria de Luca annihilated—right down to the image of her being removed from the label of the famed sherry they produced.

Alejandro, five years apart from both Sebastián and Carmen, was more reasonable. He wanted most of their father's last wishes met, and for Maria to remain the face of the brand, but when it came to the family home he was more than prepared to stand up for what he felt was right. The place belonged to his sister.

The legal might of the Romeros was primed and ready for a fight, because the last will and testament of José Romero was being bitterly contested.

As for Carmen…

At twenty-six, she was the baby of the family. She had always been fiery, and sided with Sebastián's strong stance against Maria, but since her father's passing she'd felt increasingly depleted.

'Carmen,' he warned, 'you need to stay and fight this—not run away.'

'I'm not running away.' Carmen's voice was always a little throaty but this morning it sounded strained and hoarse. 'I just need a break.'

'But why America?' Alejandro asked.

'It's the land of the free,' Carmen responded. She had always liked hearing that at school, and had loved the occasions when she had competed there. 'And I want to be free.'

'But why LA?'

'Maybe I want to be a film star or a model...' She fought a rare blush. 'Maybe I want to dance...'

'Carmen, you hate getting dressed up even for the Romero Ball.'

No one but her brothers would know that.

Her hair, when it was out of its ponytail, was glossy and long, and she dazzled on the red carpet on suitable occasions. Away from the spotlight, though, Carmen lived in jodhpurs, or on particularly hot days a bikini and shorts, but had been trying to be a little more glamorous of late.

'And you *abhor* dancing,' Sebastián added, not noticing the press of her lips as he continued his mini lecture. 'As well as that, you don't take direction...'

Carmen shot her brother a look. 'You have no idea how disciplined riding is.'

'I meant outside of riding.'

'I was joking about being an actress,' Carmen said. 'I'm going to work in a café or a restaurant.'

'But why?' Sebastián gave her a nonplussed look. 'It's not as if you need the money.'

'Perhaps I want to prove that I can make it on my own.'

'Carmen,' he said, glancing at her kitten-soft hands—despite a life spent in the stables, she *always* wore gloves. 'I've never seen you take a cup through to the kitchen, let alone wash it. Anyway, you won't last a morning without a horse.'

'I can barely *remember* a morning without a horse.' Carmen sighed. 'And I've never known a moment when I wasn't a Romero…'

'Meaning?'

Her full name was Carmen Romero de Luca, but in Spain she was Carmen Romero, a brilliant and talented equestrian who had trained and performed with the famous Andalusian dancing horses, as well as competing in dressage at the highest levels.

And she was José Romero's only daughter.

People said she was entitled and spoilt.

And that was all true.

But a deeper truth was that she was lonely and scared and seemed to have the worst luck with relationships.

Carmen had overheard her last boyfriend talking about her, saying how demanding and needy she was. She had covered her mouth to silence her cry of anguish. Her mother had, on more than one occasion, accused her of being the very same. They couldn't both be wrong, could they?

The character assassination hadn't ended there, though. She'd listened to the man she had been planning to lose her virginity to that weekend telling his friend that she always smelt of the stables, and that he practically had to hold his nose to kiss her.

His friend's response: 'Just close your eyes and think of all that Romero money…'

But actually it wasn't her ex who had broken her heart— her mother had inflicted that damage a long time before. And now, at the grand old age of twenty-six, Carmen was starting to believe that it might be safer to carry her broken heart all the way to the grave rather than risk attempting to love again.

She looked at her brothers. They had the same dark eyes as her, the same glossy black hair and olive skin, and they shared the same DNA. Yet even though they came from the same broken home her brothers were so self-assured, so confident…

Carmen only pretended to be.

And, while it was true she was spoilt and precious—she'd been her father's favourite, after all—Carmen would trade it all for peace in her soul.

She wanted to make her own way, earn her own keep—stand on her own two feet, rather than sail on the family's wealth or hide in plain sight on the back of a horse.

'I'm going to be Carmen de Luca in America,' she told her brothers.

'You're going to use *her* name…?' Sebastián frowned. 'But you hate her!'

'Perhaps. But I'll use her name if it buys me a chance of freedom.'

'But you love riding…' Alejandro still insisted.

Did she, though?

Her passion for horses had been fully indulged, yet not a soul knew or understood that at first riding had simply been her one true rebellion…

Carmen had been just a little girl, standing at the top of the stairs, eavesdropping as her *papá* spoke on the phone with her *mamá*. Her heart had started to thump with excitement as she'd heard them discussing her…

'Flamenco lessons?' Papá said. 'She's only four!'

Carmen felt giddy with excitement as she pushed the door of her mother's studio open.

Her mother had abandoned the studio, just as she had abandoned her children, yet Carmen often sneaked in. There was the scent of Mamá in the air, even if Carmen couldn't remember her. There were shawls and castanets and shoes with nails in the heels and toes.

Sometimes she would drape a shawl around her shoulders and push her little feet into the shoes, or tie a faded silk rose into her long dark hair and smile at her plump little body in the mirrored walls. She had painted her lips red once, and her cheeks too, and put on a pretty bead necklace.

Sebastián, who had been a teenager then, had washed the lipstick off her face...

'But I want to dance like Mamá,' she had told him.

After all, Mamá was a world-famous flamenco dancer. She had seen her—and not just in the photos that lined the studio walls and the bar over at the bodega. Carmen had heard her mother's rich voice giving interviews on the radio, and seen her on television. She had even heard her mamá say to a reporter how it broke her heart to be separated from her children.

The reporter had asked if she might one day perform with her daughter. Mamá hadn't answered that question. Instead she had spoken about the devotion that the art of flamenco required. Still, Carmen's little mind had lit up with visions of her on the stage beside her famous and beautiful mamá...

She would be a mini Maria de Luca, and Mamá would scoop her up into adoring arms.

And now Mamá was coming home to teach her.

Carmen's heart soared as Papá came off the phone.

'Mamá has seen the photos I sent her of you. She thinks you're too...' He paused and sounded sad. 'She wants you to start flamenco lessons.'

'Yes!' She jumped up and down in excitement and delight. 'When? When can I start?'

'Soon. I will call Eva.'

'Eva?' Carmen had blinked. Eva was a flamenco dancer who came to the exclusive infant school that she attended, and gave private lessons to some of the children. 'But Mamá is much better than Eva.'

It was that night that she had begun to comprehend that her *mamá* had no intention of coming back.

Yes, Carmen was needy and demanding. And she had screamed that night for her mother, over and over. It wasn't her father, or her brothers, nor Paula, her nanny, she wanted.

'Quiero mi mama!'

I want my mummy!

When it had become evident her *mamá* wasn't coming—

was never coming—Carmen had chopped off all her long black hair, right there in the studio. And on the day of her first private flamenco lesson Carmen had refused to come out of her bedroom.

'Carmen,' her papá had sighed, weary from the antics of his overly dramatic daughter. 'Mamá thinks you need more exercise.'

'I don't want to dance flamenco, like Maria.' It was the first time Carmen had called her mother that. 'I want to ride horses.'

Even at five it had felt like revenge when she'd won her first ribbon. Her father had laughed at his daughter's apparent fear-lessness. In truth, Carmen had been terrified.

She still was, at times, but she would never let anyone see it.

Even though Papá had been proud of her achievements, he had been so depressed, so desperate for his wife's return, that he had just thrown money at the situation rather than offer true guidance.

It was Alejandro who had told her to stop holding out any hope that Maria might one day return, and Sebastián who had had 'the talk' with her about periods. *They* were the ones who had guided her in place of her parents.

And now it was her brothers who were telling her she needed to fight.

'Papá wasn't in his right mind when he made his will,' Alejandro said as they walked back towards the cars.

'He was never in his right mind where Maria was concerned.' Carmen shrugged.

'Perhaps,' Alejandro agreed, 'but he always said this was to be your home.'

Papá *had* said that.

It was clear that this legal dispute had nothing to do with money. This property, the land, were small change in the grand scheme of things.

'This was our home…' Alejandro said as they came to the sweeping driveway.

Carmen could see the pain in his features, knew that the agony of their childhood wasn't solely hers.

Sebastián was less sentimental. 'She had nothing to do with Papá until she discovered he was dying, and she hasn't been near the place in twenty-five years.'

Perhaps he caught Carmen's awkward swallow, or noticed that she'd turned away from her brother's gaze.

'Is there something you're not telling me?'

'Of course not.'

'Because if we do fight her, then it will all come out in court.'

He levelled a shrewd stare at his sister, but Carmen looked away and stood silent as he carried on speaking.

'Fair enough. I get that you need a change of scene. Just don't rush into anything. I'm going to speak with Dante.'

The Romeros really did havé everything: Capitán Dante was the captain of Sebastián's luxury yacht.

'He'll organise a leaving party for you. Anna and Emily will want to see you before you leave.'

'Of course.'

Carmen nodded and kissed Sebastián on the cheek, then watched him walk towards the car. She wished Alejandro would leave with him.

'Carmen,' Alejandro said. 'What's going on?'

'I just miss Papá so much…'

'I know.'

'I feel as if I let him down…'

Her *papá* had always said he wanted to see her married, to walk her down the aisle. But she had balked at the men her father had deemed suitable, or she had tried dating them only for it to end in disaster. Carmen knew she had intimacy issues, and was so terrified of rejection that she simply did not know how to let anyone get close.

And then there had been the endless rows that had soured the time she'd had left with her father following his diagnosis. She had loathed how he had taken back their mother, and how he had continued to defend her and explain away her actions. And now, in Carmen's name, the Romero siblings wanted to dispute their father's will…

'I don't know if I want to fight,' Carmen admitted, wondering where all the anger she'd once nurtured had gone. 'Alejandro, what if she's changed—?'

'Carmen!' he interrupted swiftly. 'You know better than that.'

'Of course. But what if she really wants to come back here…?'

She saw his expression and halted. Of her two brothers, she had thought Alejandro would be the one who might just understand. Despite everything that had happened, the child inside Carmen still wanted to believe her mother had changed, wanted to give her this chance to prove it…

But, no. 'Do not go soft on her now,' Alejandro warned her darkly.

Carmen felt his words like a knife in her heart. Something inside her had changed since her father's death, and she feared that maybe Alejandro was right: she *was* going soft. In fact, scared that she was weakening, she had, unbeknownst to her brothers, already booked her flight.

She was leaving for LA tonight. No sentimental goodbye party on a yacht for her!

She felt it was imperative that she get away as soon as possible.

Alejandro and Emily would soon be taking their baby daughter, little Josefa, on a trip to England. What if they decided to remain there?

Sebastián and Anna were already planning an extended trip on the yacht to celebrate their new family as soon as Willow's adoption came through.

And now her father was gone…

At any moment Maria might return to her beloved flamenco, leaving them again, just as she had all those years ago.

People hurt her or they left. Carmen knew that only too well. That was what they did.

She didn't want to fight any more. Not for a house and land…not to be loved. She was just too tired. Too heartsick. Alejandro was right. She *was* going soft.

But from this day forward, Carmen vowed, she would *always* be the first to leave…

CHAPTER ONE

ELIAS HENLEY HAD attended more awards nights than most movie stars.

Tonight he stood, seemingly relaxed and poised, with Wanda, his regular date for such events, by his side.

His thick brown hair was superbly trimmed, his chiselled jaw freshly shaven, his tuxedo immaculate. He looked every inch the Hollywood heartthrob—for surely someone that good-looking must be famous!

But the glances and whispers as onlookers tried to place him came only from those not in the know.

Those in the know treated him with a certain reverence.

After all, the barrel of his burnished Namiki pen might as well be filled with liquid twenty-four-carat gold, such was the value of Elias Henley's signature.

Yet, whether or not you were in the know, one constant remained: Elias Henley was something of an enigma.

His exquisite face had not been touched by needles, and his hair—including the flash of silver—was all his. The combination afforded him a distinguished edge. Even the slight receding at his temples only made him sexier, unique as it was in this setting. There were real lines at the corners of his eyes, and his brow actually furrowed to indicate emotion...

It did so now.

'Hey, Elias.'

A movie producer came up and shook his hand and suitable small talk was made. Or rather, Elias made small talk. The producer, desperate for news of any progress on the finance he wanted for a script, couldn't hide his impatience.

'I was just talking with your father about—'

'I'm surprised you could find him…' Elias quickly deflected the talk away from the project the producer wanted to discuss and looked over his shoulder. 'Ah, there he is.'

He looked towards his father, William Henley, who was in his utter element, relishing the buzz of the event, while his mother, Eleanor, stood quietly by his side, nodding and smiling.

Tonight was an exclusive event, at which his late grandfather's movie financing company would be recognised and undoubtedly rewarded. For now, though, it was a drinks reception—an opportunity for networking and everything Elias hated.

He intended to leave most of the speeches to his father, who excelled on nights such as these. But there was, though, one speech that Elias was expected to make.

It was the one night a year he detested more than anything else: the occasion when the Henleys would be announcing the recipient of an award named after their late son—a full-ride scholarship to study film at the Californian college many of his successful family had attended.

Elias would thank everyone for their donations and reiterate just how much this scholarship would change the life of its lucky recipient. Then he would acknowledge Seraphina, his late brother's widow, and how hard she worked alongside his mother to make this award a success.

And, despite his seemingly unruffled demeanour, Elias was dreading it.

He stood, utterly unmoved, as the producer reiterated the wonders of the script upon which Elias was about to undertake a full risk assessment.

'It's a guaranteed winner,' he emphasised, assuming they were the words Elias wanted to hear.

But the man was preaching to the wrong choir. Elias was

sick of guaranteed winners, and his father's preference for movies that played it safe.

'We'll be in touch,' Elias said, in a voice that indicated the conversation was over.

He remained unmoved as the producer shuffled off.

'You can be so brusque!' Wanda hissed. 'I wanted a chance to talk to him. You could at least have introduced me. What *is* your problem tonight?'

Where do I start? Elias thought, as he saw that Seraphina and her husband Vincent now stood conversing with his parents.

He would like to be able to say, after all these years, that he wished her well.

But he did not.

It was then that he noticed the slight swell of her stomach beneath her gold dress, and recalled observing Vincent's team toasting and congratulating him a couple of weeks back. While he and Vincent might now be on opposing polo teams, they were old friends...

Elias glanced towards his mother, who was smiling and immaculate, but he knew the strain she was under tonight. Elias hoped, if he was right, that Seraphina and Vincent wouldn't share their happy news just yet. Elias would prefer to break the news to his mother in private. Not that she'd betray any emotion other than sheer delight. But even so, Elias knew the news would hurt her.

Although he looked impressively immaculate, tall and elegant in his tux, and was conversing politely with all and sundry, there was a restlessness to him that made him something of an enigma. He might look the part of red carpet idol, but he would rather be riding—either women or horses.

But he couldn't be described as a playboy—because at thirty-five he was no boy, and he certainly didn't play.

Well, he played polo, but he took that extremely seriously. His current team was relatively new, but they were already making waves...

'Elias?'

He frowned as he saw Seraphina making her way towards him. It was only then that he realised Wanda had seized her chance and was now talking to the producer he'd so recently snubbed.

'On your own tonight?' Seraphina observed, while taking a glass of champagne from a waitress.

Perhaps she wasn't pregnant after all…

Elias stared into her cold blue eyes and her pretty china doll face.

'Go to hell,' he told the woman he loathed.

'I just miss you so much,' she said urgently. 'There isn't a day when I—'

'Do you want me to state it more loudly?' he fired back, his voice low with enough threat that she heeded his warning and walked off.

'Sorry, darling…'

Wanda was back, and she reached out a hand to rearrange his tie, but in a reflex gesture Elias arched his neck and turned his head away.

He *loathed* unnecessary touch.

'If we were a real couple,' Wanda drawled, removing her hand and taking a drink from the proffered tray, 'then the occasional display of affection would be expected.'

'Wanda, if we *were* a real couple,' Elias responded tartly, 'then you'd know by now that I abhor feigned affection and—'

Elias's irritation was abruptly halted as he saw the ghost of a smile on the waitress's full lips.

He wasn't remotely embarrassed that a waitress might have overheard his conversation—hell, this was LA. Everyone gathered here tonight surely knew that he and Wanda were not a couple. She was his date for functions such as these, but no more than that.

Elias Henley was close to no one by choice.

He kept his relationships superficial at best, and with good reason—he didn't trust anyone and nor did he want to.

His arrangement with Wanda benefited them both: he required a beautiful woman on his arm, and she made the most of his network of contacts to further her career in the movie business.

As for sex—it was a basic need. But he wasn't fulfilling it with Wanda.

The waitress's subtle smile remained on her face, and it surprised Elias, for staff at such a prestigious event usually knew better than to eavesdrop quite so obviously.

He lifted his brown eyes to meet her almond-shaped black ones.

She didn't blush, nor drop her gaze, and nor did she swiftly move on. 'Would you care for champagne?' she offered, in a rich Spanish accent.

He gave a curt shake of his head. Really, given there were staff milling about everywhere, there was no need for her to offer. If he wanted a glass of champagne he merely had to reach out for any passing silver tray.

'No, thank you,' Elias said, and turned back to his date.

He frowned, surprised that Wanda didn't appear to have even noticed the waitress—neither her faintly mocking smile nor how she'd hovered…

It was a non-event.

A fleeting moment that should instantly have been forgotten.

And yet Elias found he dwelt on that subtle smile.

It had felt almost as if she shared his attitude towards nights such as this.

And the rich Spanish edge to her voice lingered in his mind even as Wanda asked, 'Have you prepared your speech?'

'No need.' Elias gave a tense shrug. 'It's the same speech I've been delivering for five years now.'

The first year—eight months after the death of his twin— Elias had wished for the glare of a harsh spotlight in his eyes so he could not see the faces looking back at him as he delivered his speech.

His father must have dropped twenty pounds, Elias had thought that night, looking at his unusually gaunt features. His mother, as always, had been immaculate, with pearls at her ears and throat, yet he'd known the supreme effort it had taken for her to attend.

There had been a hush, an air of tense expectancy, for it was the first time anyone from the family had spoken publicly of Joel's sudden and tragic death.

His throat had felt so tight…as if there had been hands around his neck, squeezing, squeezing, *squeezing*…

Elias Henley, who rarely broke a sweat except when he was riding, had felt a cold trickle down his spine and icy shards piercing his temples.

Thanks to a privileged education, he'd been used to public speaking, and had already been holding his own in the family business. Life hadn't been perfect, though, not even before his brother died. He'd felt pressure to dedicate himself to the long-established family business—had felt the tightening of its constraints pulling him into the world of movie finance even as his heart drew him towards polo and horses…

It had been nothing he couldn't handle, though. And then…

Elias reached for a glass of water, rather than champagne, to clear his head and ease his tight throat. He found he was curiously disappointed that it was a different waitress who held the tray.

He wasn't nervous about the speech. Oh, no, his mood tonight was far more dangerous than that.

Elias was angrier than he usually dared to be on a night such as this.

Despite appearances…despite what everyone thought… his seemingly perfect life hadn't ended on the night of his brother's death.

It had ended a couple of weeks before.

'Your father's coming over,' Wanda warned him.

'Yep.'

'A quick word, Elias?' William Henley's smile disappeared as he spoke to his son. 'Your mother might be playing it down, but the foundation's board members have made it clear that if we want the award to continue in its full capacity—'

'I'm well aware,' Elias cut in.

He was more than aware of the financial situation of the foundation. He'd made a huge anonymous donation himself— and not for altruistic reasons. He didn't want his mother to find out that the donors' interest was waning.

'People want more than just the same old cursory speech. Say how much you miss him, or—'

'I've already been well briefed by PR,' Elias snapped.

'If you don't want to talk about yourself…' William gestured with his hand, as if plucking ideas from the air '…then talk about the wedding. Talk about how happy Joel and Seraphina were.'

'That would hardly be fair to her current husband,' Elias replied tartly.

William Henley blew out a tense breath. 'Talk about the last five years, then. How you've dealt with grief. How you've found the strength to move on…'

Perhaps at that moment William saw the flash of warning in his son's eyes, because he took a second to regroup and then played his trump card.

'The award means everything to your mother.'

'I know it does.'

His father screwed his eyes closed in frustration. 'Give them *something*, for God's sake!'

He didn't outright call his son a cold-hearted bastard, but the implication was very much there.

'Would it kill you to show some emotion or to say how you're feeling?'

As Elias's father stalked off, Wanda chimed in with some acting advice. 'Fake it if you have to,' she told him. 'I can give you some pointers.'

Elias pressed his lips together to mask his fury.

There was nothing fake about his emotions.

He was holding them in. He had been holding them in for five years now. If he let them out… If he dared open that box…

Be careful what you wish for, he thought, as he watched his father return to his mother's side.

The reception was over and the guests were being ushered

in for the meal, which would be interspersed with awards. It was always a long and tedious night, but at least soon it would be over for another year.

Elias was thinking of Domitian, a problem stallion he'd recently acquired. The beast would be missing his evening gallop along the beach, and so too was he. Blake, his yard manager was on a day off, and there was no one else who could or even would ride him.

'Elias!' Wanda whispered, pulling his focus back to the ceremony—he saw they were waiting for desserts to come out. 'Would you please get me a lunch or something with that producer?'

Elias knew he was being appalling company tonight, so he nodded, which quickly cheered Wanda up.

'Do you know what I do when I want to look as if I'm upset?' she ventured.

'No.'

This evening could not be over soon enough, Elias thought, his mind drifting as Wanda talked at length about the acting tricks she used to express certain emotions. His only saving grace came as he was watching the desserts being brought out.

There was the mystery waitress.

She was no longer smiling. Her apron was twisted and she was carrying only two small plates, while the other servers were carrying three or four. Her previously neatly tied back hair had begun to unravel, and there was a dark flush to her cheeks.

'Are you listening, Elias?'

He wasn't, and he felt bad at how little attention he had paid Wanda this evening, so he turned to her and forced himself to focus.

There were a lot of awards...

Films backed by Henley Finance scooped up more than their share—as they did most years.

The company Elias's grandfather had founded was still flourishing.

'Look at all these, Elias. Do you really want to leave?' his father said, gesturing to the awards that littered the table.

Elias gritted his jaw. The conversation he'd had with his father, and later his mother, about possibly leaving the company had been a private one.

'Leave?' Seraphina perked up at this snippet of information.

'Those damn polo ponies!' William huffed.

'Vincent's team is doing really well.' Seraphina squeezed her husband's arm. 'I think they'll take the cup.'

She smiled over at Elias, but it only made the bile churn in his stomach.

'It might be your team against Vincent's in the final...'

'Elias?' his mother prompted. 'Seraphina's talking to you.'

'I think I'm about to be called to speak,' Elias said, grateful for the usher who came over and told him he was indeed needed to make his way to the stage. 'Excuse me.'

The audience were undoubtedly expecting the usual polished performance. It was five years now since Joel had died, and Elias had delivered a variation of the same speech every time.

Elias thanked the sponsors and the donors and all the people who had made the award possible. Then he spoke briefly about the selection process and the quality of candidates who had competed to win the scholarship.

He looked to his father, who sat holding his mother's hand. She'd been a much sought-after interior designer before Joel died, and had overseen the impressive refurbishment of Elias's Malibu ranch.

It was the last project she'd undertaken, though, and she had since refused his repeated requests for her help with the restoration of the grooms' lodge. Instead, she had devoted herself to this scholarship, in a bid to keep the perfect memory of her son alive.

With the formalities out of the way, Elias looked out at the now rather bored audience and knew his father was right. Public interest in the scholarship was waning, and he couldn't bear to see his mother's heart broken all over again.

He knew he could do more. *Should* do more...

'After Joel died,' Elias said, in his deep, measured voice, 'it was as if my world stopped turning...'

He moved his tongue over dry lips, unable to tell anyone, let alone an audience of people he cared nothing for, that he'd been lost.

'I moved out of LA in an attempt to get my bearings. And I guess I've never quite made it back...'

He glanced at the audience and it was clear that his attempt to describe, even obliquely, how he'd felt was not going down well. This was his chance to do what his father had suggested.

'People often ask how I dealt with my grief. Joel and I were not only best friends...we worked together, socialised together, played sport together... Well, we did until he fell in love with my mother's new assistant...'

He forced out a smile to indicate that he'd just delivered a good-natured little joke, and glanced towards his family's table, at his late brother's seemingly sweet widow, who was clutching his mother's other hand...

'A few months before Joel died we celebrated his marriage.' He could not bring himself to say Seraphina's name, he realised. 'He was the happiest I've ever—'

Elias swallowed audibly. He attempted to continue, to give the audience what his father claimed they clamoured for, but his mouth was dry...so dry. He was so burdened with the weight of the truth, so weighed down by the secret only he and one other person knew, that suddenly he did not think he could keep the lid on that box of emotions for one second longer.

Because Joel had *not* been happy...

And now, as he stood in front of the podium, attempting to articulate the depth of his loss, all Elias could feel was the same abhorrence and disgust he had felt two weeks before his brother had died.

The sheer disbelief when Seraphina had attempted to kiss him.

Pushing her off, Elias had said two words that no gentleman should ever say to a lady.

Oh, but she was no lady.

'It's you, Elias,' Seraphina had sobbed, *still* reaching for him, *still* trying to kiss him. 'It's always been you… Joel doesn't have to know.'

'You *disgust* me.'

She still did. And there was no one he could tell…

Or could he?

There were awkward coughs from the impatient audience. He glanced at his father.

You want feelings? How about I tell everyone what Joel was really doing on his cell phone when he died? How about I tell them that he was driving and sobbing, asking me if he was going mad or if his new wife had gone cold on him…? Why don't I tell them how it felt to lie to my twin and tell him he was just imagining things? Why don't I describe that brief sense of relief I felt as Joel laughed on the other end of the phone, and agreed with my rallying words?

'You're right,' he said. 'It can't be a honeymoon every day, can it? You won't tell anyone?'

'Joel,' Elias replied. 'Do you even have to ask? Of course I would never tell anyone.'

'Thanks.'

'Give it time,' Elias had said to his brother.

But there had been no more time.

Not for Joel.

Elias had heard Joel's sudden shout of alarm, then a horn blaring and the screech of brakes.

He recalled it now so vividly that he could almost smell the burning rubber…

He hadn't experienced a second of relief ever since.

As he stood at the podium, he felt as if the smoke from the wreck was choking him, filling his nostrils and making his eyes smart.

'On the night my brother died, he called me.'

It was information only those close to the family could possibly know. He looked straight at Seraphina, and he loathed that she had the nerve to look back at him, that she had no idea how close he was to telling all those present what had really occurred.

Nothing had occurred, Elias reminded himself.

But only because of him.

Had it been up to Seraphina…

'Joel had a question for me,' he went on. 'He wanted to know how come his new wife…'

Elias watched her rapid blinking. Perhaps she had begun to sense just how out of control the usually measured and emotionless Elias Henley currently was.

'He wanted to know—'

CHAPTER TWO

'DE LUCA!'

Carmen was certainly not listening to the boring speeches. Even if she was supposed to be as invisible as a ghost, there was still a lot of work to be done.

This was her third job since arriving in America, and she desperately wanted to hold on to this one. *Had* to hold on to this one if she was to keep her promise to herself and not use Romero money.

But it was hard to be treated so badly. And not just by guests: it was the treatment of staff by the owners and managers that had caused her temper to rise until she exploded.

She glanced over to the manager, who nodded towards a table where someone was signalling for more wine. Carmen made her way over with an ice bucket.

The lady shook her head. 'I asked for sparkling water.'

'Of course,' Carmen said, and went and collected the necessary bottle.

But as she started to pour she heard the current speaker—or rather, heard the uncomfortable pause.

Looking over to the stage, she saw that the speaker was the man from before.

He was too good-looking not to recall.

He'd made her smile earlier, with his honest response to his partner.

It had been no more than that.

But now she could see that he was in trouble.

Carmen was more than used to this type of function—had

been to a thousand such events herself. Albeit usually she was seated rather than serving. Still, she was aware—as was everyone else in the room—that this pause in the smooth proceedings had gone on for too long.

The man's brown hair gleamed and his stunning features were amplified by the lighting. He wore his evening suit exceptionally well, and yet despite the excellent cut of the fabric he seemed somehow confined.

Carmen watched as he reached up to adjust his tie, but then changed his mind and awkwardly brought his hand back down to his side.

Was he nervous? she pondered briefly. But why? Perhaps he had forgotten the name of the person receiving whatever award he was presenting?

But now she was really watching—and she saw that he was *not* nervous. He reminded her a little of Sebastián on the day of their father's funeral, attempting to be civil but having to bite his tongue and keep a lid on his deep and complex emotions.

She knew that look.

This speaker was struggling to contain himself...

His hands were clutching the podium, his breathing was shallow, and his eyes were shooting daggers into the audience...

There were three things that hauled Elias back from the brink.

The promise he had made to his brother when he'd identified his body—that no one would ever know about his wife's vile betrayal.

The fact that Elias had sworn to protect his family—especially his mother—from further hurt.

And the sudden distraction near the back of the room, which gave Elias an easy excuse for his extended silence...

'Hey!' the lady cried, as the water Carmen had been pouring spilled over the top of the glass and quickly pooled across the table.

'I'm so sorry!' Carmen offered,

But the woman leapt up, knocking her chair over, furious that her dress was wet.

'I'm drenched!' she shouted into the awkward silence.

'Ma'am, I'm…' Carmen took a breath and reminded herself that she was working.

She hoped to God that she had never spoken to a waitress like that. No. She might be spoiled and difficult, but only with the people she loved.

She clamped her lips shut on the retort she wanted to make, that the woman's dress was barely wet. 'I do apologise, ma'am.'

The manager ran over, followed by a troop of waiters with cloths, but all Carmen was really aware of was that the speaker had found his voice.

As the small commotion at the back of the room faded he apologised for the interruption, checked that he could progress, and said, 'Yes, Joel asked me how come his new wife and he were so fortunate…'

'De Luca!' her manager hissed. 'I'll speak to you in the kitchen. *Now!*'

All eyes must be on the speaker, of course, and yet Carmen felt as if every eye was on her… She was going to be fired, she knew, and she blushed as she made her way between the tables.

As she reached the swing doors to the staff area the speaker was concluding his remarks.

His voice reached her.

'I've been asked, many times, "How do you deal with grief?"'

Carmen, who had been desperate to escape, now found she paused to hear his answer.

The weight of her own grief was unbearable.

Worse even than the day her *papá* had died.

She did not know how to deal with it, and was desperate for answers.

Please, Mr Good-Looking, Carmen thought, *tell me it gets better. Tell me how to deal with this ache in my soul…*

'Five years on…' she heard the slight husk to his tone '… I still don't know the answer.'

His words brought no comfort.

None at all.

She pushed through the swing doors to face her manager.

'De Luca!'

Her boss was awful.

Horrible.

'What the hell were you thinking?' He was right in her face. 'Only, you *weren't* thinking, were you?'

'It was a simple accident,' Carmen said. 'And I apologised immediately.'

'You've been here for a week and there's a disaster every night.'

'I spilt some water. I don't see the issue.'

'I'll tell you the issue…'

And he proceeded to do so, just as he had every night this week.

Carmen had to bite her tongue, so tempted to pull off the apron of this stupid outfit the female waiting staff were made to wear and tell him where he could stick his job.

That was exactly what she'd done at her last job.

And the one before.

She'd pulled rank, told them what they could do with their attitude, and said that if that was the way they treated staff, no wonder they couldn't keep them.

Her fiery nature was returning, she realised, but then she checked herself. Tonight she *would* hold her tongue.

'I am *so* sorry,' Carmen repeated.

'Not good enough.'

He really let her have it then, telling her that she was going to have her wages cut…

They clearly thought she was an illegal worker. That had been the assumption in all the casual jobs she had gone for.

Carmen loathed the way the workers here were being treated.

She looked over at the junior chef, who stood, head down, listening to the manager's tirade. She knew the chef wanted to leap to her defence, but he had a family to support.

She looked at another waitress, Joni, who she knew was trying so hard to stay on the straight and narrow and keep a regular job.

It wasn't just Carmen's fiery nature that was returning, but a deep hatred for injustice that was starting to emerge.

'Do you know why you can't keep staff for more than five minutes?'

Carmen hadn't got where she was in the equestrian world by staying quiet—there she was able to speak her mind, and she would do the same here. She could not keep her silence.

'Because you're a disgrace!' Her lips curled in contempt. 'You berate and you bully!' She spoke for everyone here, because she was the only one who could afford to. 'You take wages and you steal tips!'

'Now, you listen to me—'

'No! I will not!' Carmen shook her head. 'You're going to listen to *me*. I would never speak to my staff the way you do—and I make sure my staff are properly paid. You've held back thousands of dollars in tips in just the week I've been here.'

She told him the amount exactly, and watched the manager's nervous blink.

'How many staff are working tonight?' she demanded.

Nobody responded.

'Very well…' Carmen did the maths herself. 'I think that works out to about one hundred and ten dollars each are owed. Including the staff who are absent tonight.'

'Get out!' he told her.

'You don't know who you are dealing with. I'm not going anywhere until all these staff are paid. Failing that, I'll be reporting you…'

Carmen's tirade built up steam as she listed the authorities she'd be contacting, and then repeated it to the owner of the venue, who had been alerted to the commotion and had come to see what the problem was.

Carmen named the law firm her family used for their professional dealings in LA—the same firm that had swiftly sorted out her temporary work visa.

'I can call them now and get the police to come too…report you for breaking labour laws…' She took out her phone and quickly pulled up her contact at the law firm, to show she meant business. 'Up to you?' Carmen warned.

And finally they conceded.

Carmen stood, arms folded, until all the correct tips were dispersed.

'Take your job…' now she pulled off her apron and tossed it onto the floor '…and your stinking attitude, and shove them. And if I hear there are any repercussions, or that this practice continues, I shall be making several calls. I've got my eye on you.'

Joni was in tears as she followed Carmen out of the back entrance. 'You've no idea how much this means…'

Carmen was starting to. Even though she had grown up a long way from this kind of situation.

'Call me if this nonsense starts again. I'll make sure they won't find out it's you,' she said, and she hugged Joni.

As she stepped out into the night Carmen felt sad rather than proud. She had wanted to make her own way not only as a matter of pride, but because she had wanted to prove to herself that she could do it.

She'd thought coming to LA would give her a new sense of purpose, fix her somehow, or at least make her feel better. Instead, she felt lonelier than ever, and even more lost than the night she'd boarded the plane.

There had been more than a kernel of truth in the manager's words, Carmen reluctantly acknowledged. She was a truly dreadful waitress.

She crossed the strip and took a long look back at the hotel where she'd hoped to somehow prove herself, find herself… but then she did a double take when she saw him.

Him.

He was outside the main entrance of the hotel, where people were milling about and talking. He had stepped aside, away from the bright forecourt lights, and he cut a solitary figure, leaning against the wall, looking out at nothing.

There was something about his stance that stopped Carmen mid-stride.

He looked as if he might be having as wretched a night as she was.

More so, perhaps.

He had made use of the distraction of her water-pouring disaster to explain the momentary lapse in his sleek delivery, but Carmen knew damn well the true order of events.

Her spilling the water had not been the cause.

Yet, there was somehow an effect.

Suddenly he looked over. And she no longer felt like an invisible ghost because he was staring right at her.

Perhaps she should have quickly looked away, but instead she raised her hand and tapped her forehead with the side of her forefinger. It was a Spanish gesture that indicated *fed up to here*, but she realised it must look as if she was saluting him, or something equally bizarre…

But he just smiled. Clearly he'd understood her meaning, because he copied her gesture—he was fed up to *here* too.

She watched as he pushed himself off the wall and straightened his jacket, before strolling confidently back inside as Carmen headed off to catch her bus.

Of course she could order a cab, but there was that little matter of personal pride…

Surely she could last three months without using Romero money? Carmen asked herself when she arrived back at the tiny soulless apartment she had taken on a week-to-week lease. God, she wanted to order food in. But, reminding herself she couldn't afford it, instead she poured a bowl of cereal.

She scrolled listlessly through the job vacancies on her phone, and knew that tomorrow she'd be doing the rounds of restaurants and—

Something caught her eye.

Yard Manager

She read the job description. It was a permanent role, managing a stable.

No.

Hadn't she come here to have a break from horses?

But it was then that it dawned on Carmen that this break from horses had taught her precisely how very much she missed them.

Bowl of cereal forgotten, Carmen scrolled eagerly through various other jobs.

Stable hand... Casual position... Immediate start... Polo experience preferred...

Well, she didn't have any experience of polo, but when she saw the yard was in Malibu, Carmen read on.

Early starts... One day off a fortnight during polo season...

Carmen smiled, because that didn't concern her at all. She knew what that wording *really* meant: must love horses.

And she did.

She really did.

At the age of twenty-six, with a successful equestrian career, it should have been a given, but Carmen had never been free of the nagging suspicion that she only rode because it was a way of getting back at her mother.

But she *did* love horses. So, so much.

A stable hand?

No pressure.

No need to perform in the incredibly highly skilled art of equestrian ballet.

No management responsibilities.

She could just put her head down and get on with it...

Excitement bubbled in her for the first time since Papá had died.

Malibu!

The hills, the oceans, the horses...

Surely there she would be able to find herself?

Carmen de Luca, stable hand.

Why not?

CHAPTER THREE

'YOU HAVE *NO* experience with polo?'

'None.' Carmen shook her head as she walked through the impressive stables with Blake, the yard manager. 'But I have worked with dancing horses.'

'Dancing horses?' Blake gave a slight, almost derisive laugh, perhaps thinking her heavy Spanish accent meant she had chosen the wrong word. 'You mean dressage?'

'Well, yes, that too, but...' She shrugged, remembering that she didn't want to reveal the extent of her real skills or experience. 'Sort of...'

'It doesn't matter,' Blake said. 'We need someone to stay back on game day. We've got a couple of mares in foal, as well as—'

He halted their conversation and called out to one of the grooms to stop letting the horses out.

'Domitian is out,' he said, and then explained what he'd meant to Carmen. 'We have a stallion causing problems. He's usually taken out later in the day, but Elias wanted him to expend some energy before the vet examines him.'

He stopped discussing the stallion and got on with listing the duties Carmen would be expected to carry out.

'Exercising, cooling, settling...'

Carmen hadn't planned to do any riding on her working holiday, so hadn't brought her gear. In keeping with her attempt at budgeting she wore some dreadful brown cotton trousers she'd found in a thrift store, as well as scruffy second-hand Cuban-heeled boots that were just a little too big. She had topped off the look with her favourite T-shirt from home, which was navy and had boldly written across the chest *NO BAILO*. As always, she had on dark leather gloves—her biggest expense as she'd had to buy them new. Her hair was pulled back in a low ponytail and her whole look was such that she was glad there weren't any mirrors around the stable yard.

Furthermore, she had spent a *lot* of hours sitting at a bus stop, so she could arrive fifteen minutes before the start of her early-morning interview ready to prove herself.

Strangely, apart from downplaying her experience of competing and stable management, she felt she was finally being herself—her true and honest self.

So determined was she to get this job that she had packed up her things and given notice on the apartment, knowing they wanted someone who could start immediately. She hoped her backpack indicated as much to the yard manager.

It wasn't her scruffy attire that was the issue, though. He was clearly in doubt as to her ability to manage these very expensive and tempestuous horses.

'You'd be…what…all of a hundred pounds?'

Perhaps the equestrian world was the only one where you could get away with asking someone their weight at a job interview, but just then a rider came into the yard on a steaming black stallion and Carmen acknowledged that Blake's question was possibly merited.

Blake greeted the rider. 'Hey, Elias, how was he?'

'Guess,' came the surly response.

That single word demanded her sudden attention. Because Carmen looked up from the magnificent horse, snorting and blowing, and saw who the rider was.

It was the man from the other night! From the hotel ballroom! Carmen was incredibly grateful that he was too focused on containing the stallion even to notice her.

So, his name was Elias.

And she simply knew that he owned the place.

It was clearly a busy yard, so the interview was being cobbled in between its normal activities, and Carmen took absolutely no offence that she was being ignored. If anything, she welcomed it, for as Blake updated the owner with details about a mare in foal she was able to fight her blush by turning her attention to the stunning stallion.

She was doing her best to dismiss the brief interaction they had shared the other night.

Why did it matter? Carmen pondered.

But that was the moment—at six in the morning in a stable yard in Malibu—that a little bit more of what was missing in her life returned. The other night was forgotten and all her worries drifted away as the stallion sniffed the air in her direction and made his first curious approach.

'Hola, caballo,' she said gently, introducing herself.

He breathed out softly, then moved his head a little closer as he breathed in her scent again, and Carmen took it as a polite greeting. Instinctively, she slowly extended her closed hand to greet him.

'Hola, guapo,' she murmured—*Hello, handsome.*

But before his gorgeous nostrils could make contact, Elias jerked back on the reins.

'Watch it!' Elias barked.

Carmen snatched back her hand, aching to touch the horse. She was about to register a brief protest and point out that mutual contact had been about to be made, but then she saw Elias's dark brown eyes narrowed in warning.

She reminded herself that this was not her yard, and these were not her horses.

Here, by her choice, she did not make the rules.

There was also an inward sense of relief that, as evidenced by his clear lack of interest, Elias hadn't recognised her.

Why it should matter, Carmen didn't really know. She would examine that later. But for now, while she was being interviewed, it simply came as a relief.

It was Blake who explained to her the nature of the beast.

'Dom's a vicious bastard,' he informed her, and glanced at her leather gloves. 'Those won't protect you—he's a biter, amongst other things,' he added, although the last sardonic comment was aimed at Elias. 'Apart from me, Laura's the only one who'll take his feed in. Elias, I'm just interviewing this girl for the stable hand position. No experience with polo and she'd only be a hundred pounds soaking wet...'

'Not a girl,' Carmen corrected. 'And I am one hundred and ten pounds.' Then she added, 'Dry.'

This was the world she was used to—because, far from taking offence, Blake grinned.

Elias did not, however. His jaw seemed to be moulded from granite, Carmen thought as she spoke on. 'As well as that, I'd have no issues feeding him.'

She looked up at Elias but he made no response—at least not to Carmen.

'Let's get him cooled down,' he said, and Blake held Domitian's bridle and reins as Elias dismounted lithely, his long black boots thudding onto the ground. The familiar sound made Carmen jolt with sudden longing, but he paid no heed to her jump, his attention solely on the hot and bothered horse.

Domitian—or Dom—was more aggressive without his rider, she thought, but Elias and Blake took up positions on either side of the stallion's head and together led the unwilling horse into the stable.

Elias held him while Blake hosed him down, although Domitian proved something of a moving target. Carmen stood there feeling rather useless as she watched both men get drenched.

'Can I help?' she asked—and not just because she was still being interviewed. It was more that she simply wanted to be a part of the action again.

Elias was having none of it, though. 'You can help by staying back,' he called over his shoulder, then took the hose from Blake and finished off the horse's neck.

Carmen smiled as he let Domitian chase the hose and take a drink. 'You like that...?' he crooned, and Carmen saw the ghost of a smile on Elias's stern features as he let Domitian play for a couple of moments, biting at the water rather than at people. Then it was time to take him to his stall.

Everyone seemed to be staying well back from the stallion, Carmen noted—all the staff scattered as the stallion was moved through the stable. They were clearly nervous—and with good reason. His tail was swishing and he kept trying to lurch towards the other stabled horses as they passed the various stalls.

It took both men to steer him straight, but finally he was in. If it were her horse, Carmen thought, she would not have housed him in the last stall, where he had to pass all the rest of the horses to be moved in or out.

She was so used to making such decisions that it was going to be hard to hold her tongue.

'Blake!' someone called out, and she was told to 'wait there' as he headed off to do whatever he needed to.

Carmen stood there, feeling redundant, as the yard came to life and the grooms started to let the horses out and the day got underway.

It felt pleasingly familiar to be there, yet frustrating to stand idle and not be a part of it.

She thought not just of her own yard, and of how Presumir would be whinnying and calling out for attention if she was left to stand still doing nothing, but also of the busy mornings she'd spent at the famed equestrian school in Jerez, which had been such a big part of her life.

By now she'd be out riding, or would have just returned, breathless, from taking the most difficult of the mounts out. Or perhaps she would be sipping a well-earned coffee with colleagues and friends before starting schooling or rehearsing for the famous shows. Sometimes she taught a class—never beginners, but riders who had travelled from all across the globe to learn from masters of the art of equestrian ballet...

For six weeks Carmen had told herself that she didn't miss it...that after twenty-two years of riding, she needed time away from the horses...

Now she was trying to fathom how she'd survived so much time apart from them.

She wanted to be the one dealing with Domitian.

She watched as Elias exited the stable, pleased to note that he didn't close the door, thereby letting the horse know he was the boss. When Domitian's black nose appeared, Elias didn't hold a stick, or use the flag that was pinned next to the stable door, but instead lifted an arm and pointed, telling him firmly to get back. Domitian clearly complied, because she heard a snort and the nose disappeared.

Elias stood patiently, refusing to bolt the door closed and walk away until he had control of their relationship. He ran his hand through tousled hair. It had been sleek and brushed back from his face the other night, but it was now black and shining from sweat. His white jodhpurs and black polo shirt were drenched, though how much was exertion and how much was from hosing down the restless horse she wasn't sure.

'Elias?' a female voice shouted. 'Your father's on a video call. He wants you there…'

'Tell him I'm busy,' Elias said, still not closing the stable door.

'I already have,' she called back. 'He says they'll wait.'

'Great…' he muttered under his breath.

Carmen looked over and saw a silver-haired, middle-aged woman poking her head out of the office.

'Give him this,' she said, and threw a bundle to Carmen, who caught it.

She realised it was a towel wrapped around a shirt. A business shirt…

Was she supposed to hand them to him?

Elias wasn't paying attention to her. He was still focused on Domitian, but it was clear the horse was staying well back in the stable.

'Do you want me to feed him now?' Carmen offered. 'While he's back?'

He briefly glanced over. 'You're not to go in with him until Blake or I give the all clear.'

Carmen shrugged. 'Here.' She tossed him the bundle and he caught it.

'Thank you.'

Not *thanks*, as was more commonly used here. For a brief second—*very* brief—she felt his eyes on her, and she recalled that he'd been one of the very few guests at the event the other night to thank her.

For the first time she wondered if perhaps he did, after all, recall her, but then he turned back to Domitian, who was still behaving and staying well back in his stall, despite the other horses being moved through the yard.

Though Elias was sweaty and dishevelled, and still a touch breathless, he looked somehow more at ease than he had the other night. And, to Carmen, ridiculously more handsome—if that were possible. He had been dressed in the finest tailoring then, and yet the jodhpurs showed off long, muscular thighs and taut buttocks.

Just when Carmen was about to look away, Elias made it impossible for her to do so—because he pulled off his drenched top.

Carmen worked with sports people all the time, and was more than used to well-exercised and toned bodies—professionally, a body was simply a vehicle, a machine to be fed, exercised and maintained. Personally, she'd dated all the men her father had approved of, and had spent a lot of time on the beach or at parties, sometimes aboard Sebastián's yacht. She was usually surrounded by a plethora of men who perfected their bodies solely to be seen, or to impress, or to provoke a reaction...

Usually they did not. Not in her.

Carmen had started to wonder if she was actually *capable* of reacting in that way...but now she saw Elias's honey-brown torso and his dark chest hair. She watched him dry himself as he continued to focus on Domitian, warning him now and then to move back and letting him know who was in charge.

He dried his flat stomach, and the curly black hair there, then held the towel in both hands and ran it across his back.

Goodness, he was stunning!

In all the usual ways, but also in ways that were inexplicable to Carmen.

Why did the flat mole on his left shoulder look as if an artist had chosen to place it there? Why did the raising of his arm to warn Domitian to move back, and the glimpse of dark underarm hair, make her feel as she was being pinched between the tops of her thighs? And why did the glint of an expensive watch on his wrist make her think not of its obvious value but instead of him taking it off at night?

These were not the kind of thoughts Carmen was used to. Not at all! So much so that she was ridiculously grateful that her thrift shop boots were a size too big, for there was room for her to curl her toes.

Thankfully, he pulled on his shirt.

Thankfully, because even if hiding away such a vision of male beauty felt akin to closing the shutters on a stunning sunrise, Carmen seemed to have forgotten how to breathe.

He was tucking in his shirt when he glanced over at her, as if suddenly aware of her attention. Carmen had to quickly come up with something to say. 'Your father...' she mumbled. 'He's waiting.'

'So he is.'

He closed up the stable, then headed off.

'Laura?' he called to someone who now stood behind Carmen—the same woman who had thrown her the clothes. 'Make sure Domitian moves to the back of the stall when you feed him.'

'Sure,' Laura said and, holding a bucket of feed, Carmen watched as she took down the flag to wave at the stallion to get it back.

Laura was a little tentative, but actually good with him, but of course Carmen would have done things differently.

Carmen closed her eyes.

I am a stable hand!

It was her new mantra.

She was here to do the grunt work, not run the yard...

She could do that with her eyes closed.

As Laura carried on with her duties, Carmen wandered closer and looked at the many posters tacked to Dom's stable.

STAY BACK!
I BITE!
AUTHORISED EMPLOYEES ONLY

'Those signs are there for a reason…'

She jumped when she heard Elias's voice and swung around.

'I was just admiring him,' Carmen said. 'I thought you had a meeting.'

'It's done.' He refused to meet her eyes. 'Blake's been called away and he's asked that I show you around.'

'I'm sure I can find my way…muck in where needed…'

'This isn't a farm,' he said in a snobbish voice. 'Or some backwater riding school.'

Carmen really had to bite her tongue and stop herself from telling this arrogant man just who was…

She repeated her mantra in her head. *I am a stable hand…*

'Let's get started…'

CHAPTER FOUR

IT WAS CLEAR to Carmen that Elias was reluctant to play guide, but she took no insult. Certainly, she hadn't been expecting the owner to give a new stable hand a tour, but it was obvious something unexpected had happened with Blake, and the yard was a busy one.

'Laura would usually step in—' he nodded to the silver-haired woman '—but she's with the farrier this morning. Laura's our head groom.'

'Hey!' Laura looked up from the horse's leg she was holding and gave Carmen a welcoming smile, then spoke to Elias. 'I'll take over as soon as I can, but if I can't get there she'll be in the attic.'

'The attic?' Carmen asked, but he offered no explanation.

Instead, he asked, 'How many can you take out in a set?'

'A set' was riding one horse and leading the others in order to exercise them.

'Four,' Carmen said. 'Five if I know them.'

'Start with three.'

Clearly he wasn't prepared to take her word. It was fair enough; she wouldn't take on a new hire without observing them at work either.

Next, she was shown the office, which boasted a huge electronic board for updating feed rations and vitamins and such, as well as a scruffy desk. She glanced through a door and blinked at the rather unexpected sight of an additional office that looked better suited to a glamorous city high-rise than a horse yard, no matter how well-heeled.

'Yours, I presume?' she said.

In response to her question he closed the door, making it clear to Carmen that there was much about this man that was off-limits.

Completely off-limits.

Elias had been thinking about the dark-haired beauty since Saturday night—not just their brief exchange outside the venue, but also the subtle smile she'd imparted and her throaty voice as she'd offered him champagne.

It was rare that his mind dwelt on someone like this. He'd trained himself to be impervious to charm—and not just at work. He kept himself distant when it came to sexual partners too.

Riding into the yard, he had recognised her immediately. Dom had been startled at the sudden tension evident in his rider.

Elias had been less than thrilled to find that Blake, who dealt with all the hiring decisions, had already decided to take her on for the position.

'She seems great,' Blake had said during their brief exchange in the office.

'A bit overly confident,' Elias had suggested, but then halted himself—because there was no tangible reason he could call upon that justified why she shouldn't be hired.

There was one intangible one, though: a silent allure.

Oh, yes, he certainly remembered her from the other night.

How could he forget her smile, or the distraction she had caused that had snapped him back to attention, saving him from revealing too much in his speech.

And then there was that moment when he'd stepped outside for air...

It had nothing to do with preferring not to be attracted to a stable hand—it wasn't him being a snob. Elias didn't want to be that attracted to anyone. He didn't even want to be that *aware* of anyone.

Ever.

And he'd been aware of her before he'd so much as met her black eyes. That smile had been enough to draw his gaze upwards…

'I'll put her through her paces on Rocky when I get back,' Blake had said. 'She can only do six weeks, but it gives us time to find someone permanent. After the Martin debacle, I want to take my time and get it right.'

Elias had nodded his agreement. Even though he usually left the hiring and firing to Blake, he'd fired the last stable hand himself.

'You don't mind showing her around?' Blake had checked. 'Erin called, and I do need to go and see her…'

'What about Laura?'

'She's with the farrier. Do you want me to—?'

'It's fine,' Elias had cut in, as if it were no trouble at all.

And now, those dark eyes bored into his back as he picked up a couple of apples and showed her around the yard.

'Most of the horses are out, or waiting for their turn,' he explained.

It was clear to Carmen that his brisk stride was familiar to the animals, because heads came over the stable doors to greet him.

'This is Winnie.' He took an apple and gave it to her. 'She's our top pony. I generally ride her in the first and fourth chukka.'

'I'm completely lost,' Carmen admitted. 'I have no idea what a chukka is.' She couldn't help adding, 'And that's not a pony. She's a horse.'

'Yes, but in polo they're all called ponies,' he explained.

They moved swiftly on past several empty stables. 'You can check they've been fed on the board in the main office, or on here—' he pointed to the tablet beside each stable '—and make sure you update the record or they'll end up being fed twice.'

'Sure.'

'It's not complicated…' he let out a tense breath, '…you just swipe here…'

Carmen suppressed a smile as her impatient teacher showed her how to use a tablet as if she'd never seen one before.

'I think I can manage,' she said. 'But *thank you* for your patience in explaining all this technology to me.'

He looked at her, unsure whether it was merely her rich accent and throaty words that had made her tone seem as if it was laced with sarcasm. And then, of course, there was that smile again—not as obvious as it had been on Saturday night, but there all the same.

'I'll take you in to meet Capricorn,' Elias said, to cover his sudden and unexpected awkwardness.

His march to the next stable had begun, but Carmen didn't rush to follow him. Instead, she gazed up at the magnificent high ceilings and the purpose-built yard that would be any horse-owner's dream.

'What's down there?' she asked.

But she was speaking to thin air, for he had already gone into the stable.

'This is Capricorn,' he said, stroking the neck of a beautiful grey thoroughbred mare who was clearly in foal.

The vet who was with her was taking out some equipment.

'Come over,' Elias invited Carmen. 'If you work here you'll be spending a lot of time with her.'

'Hola, mi belleza,' she said as she approached and, unlike when she'd introduced herself to Dom, and put out a gentle hand, she was not warned to step back.

The mare sniffed the air, and as her velvet nostrils pushed past Carmen's gloves and met the skin of her wrist Carmen almost wept. It had been six weeks of no horses, and for Carmen it suddenly felt as if she'd had six weeks of no sustenance, no food, no contact...

'She's restless,' Elias told the vet as Carmen fussed over her. 'She's not settling at night. Just doesn't want to lie down.'

'Bored?' the vet suggested. 'Perhaps she hates missing out on game day.'

The vet examined her for signs of foaling, but there were none, so he listened for a long time to her heart rate, and that of the foal.

'I'm worried about sleep deprivation,' Elias said. 'She's jumpy...'

'How long does she have to go?' Carmen asked.

'Eight weeks,' the vet responded.

'Is she a maiden?' Carmen asked, and the vet glanced over.

So too did Elias. Capricorn, like some first-time pregnant mares, did not appear to be as advanced as she actually was. Clearly Carmen knew her stuff, but what had Elias frowning in slight bemusement was that the vet, who was generally a man of few words, responded to her readily.

'She is, and though she's hiding it well the foal's a good size.' He carried on talking about position and size, answering all of Carmen's intelligent questions.

Elias could not quite work out what was happening, nor could he hide his increased bemusement at the exchange. Of course the staff often liaised with the vet, and treatments were discussed amongst the team, but this was more than that. There was a certain arrogance to this stable hand—a confidence and a level of experience not quite fitting with someone applying for such a casual role.

And clearly he wasn't the only one who'd noticed—the vet was opening up like a California poppy to the morning sun.

'Capricorn used to be the star here,' the vet explained, 'but then she went lame. She's obviously bored, though, so some gentle walking might do her good?' he suggested. 'Perhaps try her on the water treadmill.'

'She's not keen,' Elias said. 'Thanks to that bastard—'

'Who?' Carmen asked, but he ignored her question. 'What about taking her down to the beach?' she suggested. 'It would be easy on her joints.'

'For sure,' the vet agreed. 'Win-win.' He nodded to Elias. 'Right, let's see Dom, then.'

* * *

Carmen was left outside the stable for that consultation, and amused herself by scrolling through her phone, looking at new pictures of little Josefa and reading about the upcoming Jerez Horse Fair.

It would be the first time since her childhood that she'd missed it. Her heart twisted when she thought of the Romero marquee, where her father and brothers would invite favoured guests—the golden ticket that everyone wanted.

Carmen had usually managed to escape that part—she'd always been too busy at Horse Fair time to attend corporate events and had thankfully been excused. She'd stop by, though—briefly—and her father would smile in delight and introduce her and her beloved horse Presumir, who would be beautifully groomed and looking her best—

'Carmen!'

She looked up and from his impatient stance realised it mustn't be the first time Elias had called her name.

'If you can drag yourself away from your phone, go and saddle up Winnie.'

'Sure.'

'She kicks,' he warned.

'You're giving her Winnie to try out on?' Laura checked, frowning at Elias as they walked past. 'She can be a bit feisty.'

'Good,' Carmen said. 'So can I.'

Unfortunately for Elias, Carmen handled Winnie brilliantly.

So much so that he decided he'd be asking the vet to give his favourite polo pony a once-over—because his usually temperamental mare, who loathed anyone riding her except him, was as docile as a lamb and followed every one of Carmen's instructions.

Damn, she rode like a dream!

For once he wasn't admiring the horse, but the rider. And there was a smile on Carmen's flushed face when, having watched her put the mare through her paces, Elias could not find a single fault.

'Where did you work before?' he asked.

'An event venue in LA.'

Elias refused even to blink. 'I meant what stables did you work at?'

'A few places back home in Spain...'

Carmen wasn't the first casual worker to be evasive.

'A riding school... I have my own horse there... I went through all this with Blake.'

'But you have *no* polo experience?'

'As I said to Blake, none.'

Carmen was smiling on the inside. She knew the job *had* to be hers after the way she had handled Winnie.

And she was not wrong, because with Winnie stabled, and after a glance over to Laura, who was still stuck with the far-rier, Elias said, 'I'll show you where you'll be staying.'

On the way, he pointed out the old riding school and arena.

'It's next to the vet and therapy facilities. We'll probably move Capricorn there soon, but I don't want any unsettling changes for her right now.'

'Your place is gorgeous,' Carmen said, smiling. 'The old riding school reminds me of where I had my first lessons.'

But he clearly wasn't hanging around to hear about that, and she had to run to keep up with him.

They went past the immaculate polo lawn only used on game day, then the practice fields and schooling arenas, and finally, after a morning of seeing the very best of the best, they came to a tall wooden building that had definitely seen better days.

'The front door doesn't work,' he said, and took her around the back, where there was a large covered summer kitchen.

'Everyone takes it in turns to cook,' Elias explained, scrub-bing out what must be her predecessor's name from the chalk-board. 'But I'm sure they'll let you off tonight.'

'I would hope so,' Carmen said, with a flutter of panic erupting in her chest as she realised that she would have to cater for everyone on Mondays.

'I'm sure Laura can better explain. I know they usually make enough for lunch the next day too. Go ahead—' he gestured to a rather flimsy door '—take a look around. I think Laura said you were to have the attic.'

'Aren't you going to show me around?'

'I'm sure you can find your way,' he responded tartly. 'Attics are usually at the top…'

He felt her scowl, and knew it was deserved, but Elias could not face going in there. He stood in the bright morning sun and thought he really didn't care if his tour guide rating would suffer as a result. He hadn't set foot in the place for five years. Not since the night Seraphina had—

He absolutely would not be taking Carmen up the stairs to the attic.

Elias stood there, frozen to the spot, trying not to recall coming out of the bathroom, a towel wrapped around his waist, unaware that Seraphina was planning on betraying her new husband with his own twin…

He felt the churn of bile in his stomach as he couldn't help but remember aggressively wiping from his lips the taste of lipstick that had transferred to his mouth when she'd tried to kiss him. When he had recovered from his shock—at first incredulous, then furious—he'd packed up his things, and had been in the process of departing when Seraphina had confronted him again.

He'd been telling his sister-in-law *exactly* what he thought of her just as Laura had come through the door.

'Where are you going in such a hurry?' she'd asked.

'I'm moving out while the bathrooms are being renovated,' he'd said, and had watched Laura's expression change as Seraphina had come down the stairs behind him…

The slam of a door brought him back to the present, and he saw Carmen walking towards him—a welcome distraction from the darkness of his memories.

Elias glanced at his watch. 'I have to head into work.' He saw her frown and explained, 'My other office is in LA.'

'Oh.' She glanced at his attire. 'You're going into the city dressed like that?'

He smiled rather than give an answer—a real smile—and she saw his beautiful teeth. It made Carmen feel all lit up inside...

'Laura will sort you out with a yard uniform.'

'Er...not so fast,' Carmen said, halting him before he could walk off. 'Am I being offered the job?'

'I'll leave the official offer to Blake, but yes.'

'You should have saved some of those posters from Dom's stable to nail to *this* door!' Carmen half joked.

'Excuse me?'

'The whole building should be condemned.' She looked at him challengingly. 'It's a dump.'

'I'm sorry if the *free* board and accommodation isn't up to your usual standard,' he clipped, and then added sarcastically, 'It would seem I've wasted your morning.'

'You haven't,' Carmen said, not remotely perturbed by his haughtiness. 'I'd love to accept the job. But I'm unable to start until tomorrow.'

He didn't so much as blink—just pressed his lips together as she spoke on.

'If I'm expected to sleep here tonight I'll need to clean the bedroom—and also the bathroom.' She looked around the summer kitchen doubtfully. 'As well as in here.'

Elias had *never* met anyone like her. She was tiny—like a little Jack Russell that didn't know its own size, or rather couldn't care less. But, dammit, in this instance he knew she was right. The place had been a dump even five years ago...

'There's no need for that. I'll call my housekeeper and have her send some staff over.'

'Good,' Carmen said. 'And could you ask that she brings fresh linen? I don't believe my predecessor changed the sheets.'

'Fine. I assume you're accepting the position?'

'I am,' Carmen said, and then swallowed. 'Thank you for the opportunity.'

'You're so welcome,' he responded, and gave her a saccharine smile.

But before he headed off Elias knew there was something else that had to be said.

'One more thing...' He looked right at her. 'We need to address the other night.'

Carmen felt the breath still in her lungs. She had honestly thought he hadn't recognised her, or that he'd forgotten. But then again, how could he have? They had stared at each other, assessed each other, just as they were doing now...

'What about it?' Carmen asked.

'I keep my LA life very separate from my life here.'

She guessed he was referring to his date and the conversations she'd overheard.

'At least, I do my level best to do so.'

'I signed an NDA when I was employed by the venue,' Carmen informed him. 'So don't worry—your secrets are safe...' She looked at him. 'Whatever they may be.' She shrugged, as if she couldn't even remember what had been said. 'Do you have any more questions?'

'Just the one.' He glanced down at her T-shirt and then met her eyes again. 'What does "NO BAILO" mean?'

It was the Californian sun hitting her face that set her cheeks on fire, surely? The sun and a fractured night spent at the bus stop, to ensure she made the early-morning interview. That was what had her feeling a little *altered*...

It could not be the feeling of his eyes dusting her body and then returning to her gaze.

Nor could it be the memory of his naked torso this morning...

It was the sun, Carmen told herself. Because it couldn't be anything else.

She'd never known anything else.

And so she dragged her mind back to the question.

'It means,' Carmen said, somehow still holding his gaze, 'that I don't dance.'

Though Elias nodded, there was something in his eyes that told her he believed otherwise…

And there was something about Elias that made Carmen *feel* otherwise…

She pondered that as she watched him walk away.

CHAPTER FIVE

'PAELLA!' CARMEN SAID confidently that evening, when asked what she would cook for them all next Monday.

She even wrote it by her name on the chalkboard.

For tonight, though, it was pizza for all and getting to know the new girl—and, of course, talking about the yard.

Actually, it was mainly talking about the yard.

Carmen was more than used to that, and very happy to eat pizza and glean what she could.

'What did the vet say about Dom?' asked John, one of the ten or so grooms who lived in the lodge. 'Did anyone hear?'

'Gelding…' Laura responded.

'The sooner the better.'

'Even if it's done tomorrow it will still take months for him to calm down,' Laura sighed. 'Elias wants to put some more work in on him first. He's still hoping to sire him.'

'Well, *I'm* not going near him again.' John shook his head. 'That leaves you feeding him, and Blake and Elias riding him. What the hell's Elias going to do with him if it doesn't work out? He can hardly join the Misfits.'

'Misfits?' Carmen checked.

'The horses that end up on Elias's property,' Laura said, laughing. 'They're not exactly the elite.'

'That's putting it mildly.' John rolled his eyes. 'Dom would finish them off in five minutes. I know Blake's had enough of him.'

'Where *is* Blake?' Carmen asked.

'He's got a cottage in the grounds.'

'Well, hopefully it's nicer than here...'

'You've surely seen worse,' Laura said, and Carmen quickly remembered that perhaps, as a young stable hand, she *should* have seen worse.

'Maybe...' Carmen shrugged, but then thought of her own yard. *Her* staff would walk out in protest if she offered them this accommodation. 'Elias doesn't seem to mind spending money on his horses or himself...'

Carmen had glimpsed his sprawling ranch house from the tiny attic, and after six weeks of dreadful bosses she refused to be a slavish devotee—as Laura clearly was.

'The wages are good, and there's no set budget for food like there was with the last owner...' She took another slice of pizza, as if making a point. 'Elias is great.'

'Only because he didn't kick you out when he found you sleeping rough in the barn!' John threw in.

'True...' Laura shrugged and then explained things to Carmen. 'I'd lost my job at the riding school. Well, I had a go at the owner about his training methods.'

It was nice being amongst people who spoke her language again, Carmen thought. To talk about horses and not much else. Although her ears did pick up when Elias was mentioned again.

'Anyway,' Laura continued, still defending her boss, 'Elias doesn't ask us to do anything he wouldn't do himself. He lived here while the ranch was being renovated.'

'For five minutes,' John retorted. 'He took one look at the place and moved to a luxury hotel!'

'No, that was only when Seraphina—' Laura bit down on whatever she'd been about to say. 'He only moved because they were about to start ripping out the bathrooms.'

'Well, the renovations never happened.'

'Because Joel died,' Laura snapped, and stood up. 'I'm on settling duty.'

'I'll come with you,' Carmen offered. 'I'll be doing it myself soon.'

'Ignore John,' Laura told her as they walked towards the yard. 'He thinks I have a crush on Elias.'

'Do you?' Carmen smiled.

'Of course!' Laura laughed. 'Everyone does!'

The yard felt different in the evening. Perhaps it was calmer because Dom was out, and most of the horses were resting. Not Capricorn, though; the pregnant mare was pacing.

'I tried her on the treadmill this afternoon,' Laura said. 'Without water, but she hated it.'

'Why not take her to the beach?' Carmen asked. 'The vet said it was fine.'

'When do I have time to do that?' Laura pointed out. 'It might be easier now you're here. Martin was her main carer.' She glanced over at Carmen. 'Elias fired him.'

'For…?' Carmen asked as Laura tried to soothe Capricorn.

'Capricorn hates the water level on the treadmill going past her hooves, but Elias caught him filling it up just to upset her.'

No wonder Elias had been less than polite when he'd spoken about Martin to the vet.

'I'll take her for a walk on the beach and then settle her,' Carmen said. 'You go to bed.'

'It's your first night…'

'Honestly, I'd love it. It will be nice to get my bearings.'

Laura showed her the track to the beach, and Carmen led the very tense mare down towards it.

'You're okay,' she crooned to her new charge, deciding that Elias was right to be worried about her. 'You need to sleep at night if you're going to have a baby,' she told her, but her words faded as she saw that Elias was on the beach with Dom.

'What *is* it with him?' Carmen asked her charge.

What was it with her? Elias thought as Dom galloped him through the waves and he saw Capricorn walking the shoreline alongside Carmen.

To see one of the grooms walking a horse certainly wasn't an unusual sight—there was nothing nicer than salt water and the ocean, and he could see how relaxed Capricorn appeared, for once… Yet as he pulled Dom into a walk, he didn't do it solely to avoid unsettling the restive mare.

Elias didn't like the way he'd spoken to Carmen this morning, and how it might have soured relations with his newest stable hand. With his head clearer now, thanks to the ride, he wanted to put that right.

'Hey…' he said as he approached.

'She was tense and pacing,' Carmen said. 'I thought a walk might help her.'

'She loves the beach.' He looked at Carmen. 'Thank you.'

'For what?' She smiled at the glorious setting sun. 'It's not as if it's a hardship. You live in a beautiful part of the world.'

'Yes.'

He dismounted and walked the stallion alongside Capricorn. 'How's the lodge looking?'

Though she clearly wasn't about to worship at his feet for providing the basics, she did push out a smile.

'It's better. You have a wonderful housekeeper.'

At first their conversation was awkward, but then she asked him about the upcoming polo semi-finals.

'You're a new team, yes?' she said.

'Three years now.'

'Do you think you have a chance?'

'Absolutely.' Elias nodded assuredly. 'At least that's what I'm telling the team.'

'What's the truth?' Carmen asked.

Nobody got close to his truth.

But Domitian, for once, was relaxed—so much so that he was simply walking, instead of trying to mount poor Capricorn as he usually would.

There was only the beautiful Malibu night, and surely there was no threat in her question.

'We haven't a hope!' He half laughed. 'I can't believe we've even made it to the semi-finals. But if we do win, there's a chance we'll be playing my old team in the final.'

'Are there bad feelings?'

'No, nothing like that… Both my brother and I used to play for them. Mind you, it was more of a hobby for him.'

Elias fell silent then, because there was a deeper truth—one he would *not* be sharing—which was that there was a part of him that didn't even want to make the final.

He still hadn't told his mother that Seraphina was pregnant, but more than that he loathed the fact that, if the two teams did meet in the finals, then *she* would be there—again—with his family. Needling her way in…giving him that seemingly sweet smile that turned his stomach…batting her eyelashes over innocent blue eyes as if she'd completely forgotten how she'd come on to him…

How she *still* came on to him.

Elias knew it was some sort of perverse and twisted game that she was playing, but he had long since given up attempting to work her out.

Certainly, there was no one he could discuss it with.

He'd always been guarded with his feelings, but since Joel's death he trusted no one but himself with the truth. In any case, he wouldn't be discussing such matters with the new stable hand!

With anyone.

'I'd better get Dom back…' He nodded in the direction of the yard.

'Sure,' Carmen said. 'See you tomorrow.'

'No.' He shook his head. 'I'm in the office tomorrow.'

She was squinting in the low sun, and as she put her hand over her eyes she registered her frown.

'LA,' he said.

'Oh, you mean your real job?'

'That's the one.'

'Well, good luck… I guess.'

Elias had left by the time she returned to the yard, and Capricorn, tired from her walk, settled easily.

Just as Carmen slipped her bolt and went to leave, she changed her mind and walked down to the last stall in the row.

She looked at all the warnings posted on Dom's stable—
and promptly ignored them.

She did not look directly at the stallion, just spoke gently,
quietly pleased when he made his confident way over and
snorted at her. And then, just as she'd wanted him to that
morning, he sniffed her outstretched hand.

Blake was right. If he was going to bite her, gloves wouldn't
help much, so she slipped one off.

'Ah, mi guapo. Eres amable?' she asked softly of the handsome animal.

Her question—whether he was going to be gentle—resulted
in a puff of air being blown onto her skin. She moved to stroke
his nose.

It seemed he was indeed going to be gentle with her.

'What happened to you?' she asked, wishing, as she so often
did, that horses could simply tell her.

She felt his velvet nose and his hot breath, and then he
dropped his muzzle down so she could stroke his face. She
chuckled and told him a secret.

'I think I am more scared of your boss than I am of you…'
Carmen whispered.

Or rather, she was scared of these new and unfamiliar feelings.

The wonderful thing about talking with horses here was
that she could do it in her native Spanish, so nobody around
her would understand. She could pour her heart out to them
and they would stand calmly as she did so, accepting her whispered confidences.

Dom was no different, standing quietly as she told him
about her day.

'I'm sure he thinks I grew up in some barn, with a couple
of old horses and donkeys!' she said, and laughed.

Don nudged her hand, wanting more attention.

'Are you looking for a treat?' she asked, and for the first
time looked directly into his dark brown eyes. 'Good boy,'
she said, stroking him, reassuring him that this eye contact
wasn't a challenge.

Dom was true black, with not a single white marking that Carmen could see. He was absolutely beautiful and, yes, he would be an incredible sire.

'I don't blame him for not wanting to give up on you,' she told him.

There would be a lot of work required, though, and even then it might not work. Sadly, some animals could not be fixed. Schooling the stallion, riding him, trying to gain the trust and respect he had clearly lost somewhere, would be the only way.

Elias was completely right—no one should be near him unless they had serious experience.

But Carmen *was* seriously experienced.

And maybe, just maybe, she could work with Dom...

Of course, neither Blake nor Elias would ever agree, unless she revealed to them her true skills...

No!

Instantly, she discarded that idea. She was here to discover herself—not to return to being the old frightened and confused Carmen Romero...

'Tomorrow,' Carmen told the gorgeous stallion, 'I am going to bring you a treat.'

She had bought some hand-made liquorice for Presumir, as a present—it was the only treat she ever used for training...

'And I'm going to make you my project.'

After all, taming an aggressive stallion seemed a far safer bet than falling for the boss.

CHAPTER SIX

FOR THE MOST PART the world felt a little more as if it was in the correct order now that she was back working with horses again.

Each morning Carmen woke on a very uncomfortable mattress to the sounds of Laura and John making out in the bedroom below—though apart from that she'd never have known they were a couple.

When they were finished—and fortunately it was always very quick—Carmen would pull on the yard uniform of cream jodhpurs and the same kind of black polo shirt that Elias wore. Then she would go to the bathroom, brush her teeth and tie back her hair, and then head down the creaky stairs to stand in the outdoor kitchen, gulping coffee with the others as the lunches were handed out.

Lunch was usually leftovers from the previous evening's dinner, in a wrap, as well as fruit and yoghurt or something similar.

Generally by the time they got to the yard Dom had already been ridden, or they'd stand around waiting for him to get back.

'Elias should just get it done,' John would moan, and a few others would agree that Dom was a hopeless case.

Yet Carmen knew different.

She was slipping him treats, even going into his stable at times, and Dom was beginning to give her space…to let her move around him without startling or reacting.

This morning she was taking out Winnie and two others, trailing Laura who, as always, had her earbuds in. Sometimes

Carmen would overtake her, because she loved these mornings, cantering along a stretch of flat, then walking up a long track lined with trees and eventually emerging into sunlight that painted the sky lilac, lavender and then blue. It always took her breath away.

Carmen trotted on, loving the sound of the joyous snorting the animals made as they stretched their legs. She passed other sets and felt her heart rate lifting as she relaxed into the moment. For the first time since her father's death she felt as if she could fully breathe—as if her lungs were filling again after being crushed inside her chest for too long.

LA had been lonely. She was used to her brothers, family and friends, and had loved life until her mother had returned.

Actually, that wasn't true, she acknowledged.

She pulled on the reins and slowed the set to a walk as they looked down at the valley.

Carmen knew she had never truly been at peace...

She'd never truly fitted in...

Some of her 'friends', Carmen knew, liked her only for the invitations to Romero functions—like the parties that had used to be held on her brother's yacht—and Carmen *always* paid for lunch or dinner... As for family... While she loved her brothers, she wished they would stop pushing her to become close with their new wives.

She'd even had a row with Sebastián a couple of weeks before she'd left.

'Would Anna really love you if you weren't a Romero?' Carmen had asked, in her oh-so-direct way. 'Seriously, would she?'

'Do you know what, Carmen?' her brother had said. 'She loves me *in spite* of it.' He had glared at his sister. 'We're not exactly a welcoming lot.'

Yet, despite her inner turmoil, on this beautiful hazy Malibu morning Carmen felt she was starting to know peace.

'How did I ever think I needed a break from you?' she asked the animals she was getting to know.

She breathed in their earthy scent and felt the cool shade

of the forest, waving to Laura, who had turned now to head back, racing with John along the flat.

Then, as it did most mornings, her mind flicked to Elias...

Laura's easy admission that everyone had a crush on Elias had made her smile, and yet for Carmen it was such an unfamiliar sensation.

He was the first man to have sparked her interest since her move to America. In fact, if she were being honest with herself, she had to admit that he was the first man she had *ever* been truly attracted to.

Carmen huffed out a breath and turned her set for home.

She had been on many dates, all vetted by her *papá* or her brothers, that had bored her to tears. She'd been out with a few with guys she knew they didn't approve of too... But she had never once experienced true attraction—that feeling when you actually ached at the sight of his bare skin, or when a mole upon a shoulder became a memory...

She was done with men, Carmen reminded herself, taking out her cell phone.

Laura listened to podcasts as she rode, and some of the others listened to books or music, but Carmen made use of the time difference and often caught up with family as she rode, knowing it was afternoon back in Jerez.

'How's America?' Alejandro asked this morning, and they chatted away in Spanish for a while.

'Better now I'm back with horses.'

'I knew you'd miss them. How is it being a stable hand?'

'Frustrating at times, but mostly I love it.' She told him about her secret work with Dom. 'If the boss decides to geld him I'm blowing my cover and buying him. I want him to sire Presumir...'

They were chatting about little Josefa as Carmen approached the yard.

'Emily sent you some videos,' Alejandro was saying.

'Yes, I meant to message and say thank you.'

'Please do!'

She heard the slight edge to her brother's tone. 'I am working, Alejandro. And I'm very busy. As well as that, I have to cook for everyone tonight.'

'God help them.'

'Do you know how to make paella?' she asked.

'Easy,' Alejandro said. 'You call the chef and say you would like paella.'

That did make her laugh, but her smile was soon wiped off her face as he turned the conversation to Elias.

'I've just been looking up your new boss, Carmen. Steer clear,' he warned. 'He has a worse reputation than I used to...'

'Lo dudo!' she joked. *I doubt it.*

She shrugged and laughed again as she guided Winnie into the yard and dismounted, nodding her thanks to John, who took two of the set from her.

'Believe me,' Alejandro said, 'he's even worse than Sebastián was. From what I can tell, he has a regular date for functions, but—'

'I don't need details,' Carmen interrupted. Did she halt him so abruptly because she knew that already, or because it stung? 'Anyway, he's hardly going to look at a stable hand.'

'True!' Alejandro laughed. 'Still, even if he knew who you were it wouldn't make much difference. I don't think it's conversation he's after...'

Elias wasn't after anything. In fact, he was actively avoiding the new stable hand—or trying to—but Carmen seemed to be everywhere.

The team adored her—possibly because she was one of the few people bold enough to feed Domitian. Elias had called her out on it a couple of times, when he'd seen her coming out of the stallion's stable. He'd been discomfited to notice that the flag the staff generally used to get him to stay back was still hanging by the door.

'What are you doing?' he'd demanded.

'Feeding Dom,' she'd responded.

'You're supposed to just put the bucket down and get out.'

'Don't you like a bit of conversation with your dinner?'

Carmen had asked. 'Does your maid just put down your food, wave a flag in your face and leave?'

There was an air of insolence about her, and he couldn't help but like it—especially when it caused her to shoot him a daring look from under her brows.

And this morning he saw that look again.

His warning to Blake had been right—she was overly confident, blithely chatting away on her phone as she gave Winnie a light tap on her rump to guide her into her stable.

Elias had no choice but to call her out on it.

'Carmen!' He strode over. 'Be more careful,' he warned. 'Don't forget they kick.'

'Donkeys kick,' Carmen said, laughing.

She closed up Winnie's stable and returned to her conversation with Alejandro as she turned to go and check on Capricorn.

But it would seem Elias hadn't got her joke.

'Carmen!' he said. 'Could you get off your cell phone when I'm talking to you?'

'I'd better go,' she said to her brother in Spanish.

'He has no idea of the fire he's playing with,' Alejandro said, and laughed, clearly enjoying the exchange. *'Luego.'*

Carmen didn't respond—not to Alejandro nor to Elias—but she pocketed her phone at least.

Elias, however, had not finished.

'What does that even mean?' he demanded. 'Donkeys kick?'

'It was a joke.' She shrugged, barely looking up as she checked Capricorn over.

'Not a very funny one,' Elias said. 'Winnie's not some little pony at a riding school. You need to be more aware.'

'I am always aware.'

Carmen knew her retort was a little smart, but she was doing her level best not to blush. In truth, she was far too aware of Elias Henley, but determined not to show it.

She did not like playboys, and had already guessed that

Elias was one—even before Alejandro had rather crudely confirmed it.

The last thing she wanted was to be blushing around Elias, because he would sense it, she knew...

'I don't want any of my staff injured through carelessness.'

She felt her lips become almost pinched, and it was as though lemon juice had pooled in her mouth, as she laboured to restrain herself from giving a smart answer.

'I am never careless, sir,' she said. 'But I take your warning. Thank you.'

'Good. I'm bringing out Dom in a moment.'

'Sure,' Carmen said, and then poked her tongue out as he walked off.

She saw his back stiffen, as if he knew what she had just done.

He turned back, and she gave him a butter-wouldn't-melt smile.

Elias didn't return it. 'Is there a problem, Carmen?'

'Not really.' She shrugged. 'Maybe a bit...'

She pinched her lips again, reminding herself that Elias was the owner and she was but a lowly stable hand. But Carmen was very used to asserting herself and not having to justify her actions—especially around horses.

'I was just speaking with my—' She snapped her mouth closed, remembering she was supposed to be refusing to explain herself to him, but then she found she couldn't help herself. 'It feels a lot like...'

Seeing his features tighten, she was sensible enough to stop then.

'Go on,' he invited, his dark eyes still holding hers.

Though she could not be certain, she felt as if he was daring her to continue.

'Say what you were going to say.'

Very well!

'Am I at school?' Carmen asked, and watched his eyebrows rise. 'Because that was the last time I was told off for using my cell phone. I *do* know my way around horses, and I'm confident—'

She did not get to finish.

'There's a difference between confidence and arrogance,' he told her.

She almost laughed at the irony as he pointed his finger. Possibly he saw it too, because he halted the gesture.

'So, in future, get off your damn cell phone when you're in the yard—especially when I'm about to bring Dom out.'

He turned on his booted heel and she turned towards Capricorn.

'Yuck!' she said to the mare once he'd gone. 'Men! Why do we like them?' Carmen asked as she put her arms around the mare's neck. 'I tell you now, if he was in *my* yard…' she looked into the velvet-brown eyes '… I'd fire him.'

She smiled at the very thought.

'No, I would never have hired him in the first place. Too damned good-looking, too cocksure,' she crooned, trying to calm Capricorn with her tone if not with her actual words as Dom was noisily brought out. 'It's fine,' Carmen soothed.

But then, as the yard quietened down once the stallion had been led out, so too did Carmen's indignity at being dressed down by Elias.

'Was I rude?' she asked Capricorn as she mucked her stable out.

After all, it was easy to get complacent around horses; he was simply looking out for the new stable hand, not realising just how expert she was.

And as for accusing her of being arrogant…?

Carmen knew very well that she was!

Should she apologise?

Only, that would mean talking to him.

Taking her lunch from her satchel, she headed over to the north field, where Domitian was running and letting off steam as Elias leant on the gate and watched.

'I apologise if I was rude,' Carmen mumbled as she came to stand beside him.

'Excuse me?'

You heard, Carmen wanted to say.

'I apologise,' she said more clearly. 'I appreciate that you were just looking out for me, although I *was* keeping one eye on Winnie...'

'Fair enough,' he conceded. 'Still, I'd suggest you keep both eyes—' He halted the lecture. 'Look, I'm not a fan of cell phones. Especially when Domitian is around.'

'Believe me, I wouldn't have my cell phone out if I was dealing with him.'

She smiled, and then took off her gloves and opened the lid on her lunch box, ignoring the fruit salad and pulling out a quesadilla filled with cheese and last night's chilli.

'I'm supposed to cook tonight,' Carmen said conversationally. Seeing him glance at her lunch, she held it out. 'Do you want half?'

'No.' He shook his head. 'No, thank you.'

'Where I come from, it's rude to refuse,' she insisted. But he ignored her, so she looked at Dom. 'He's showing off.'

Carmen smiled as she watched the black stallion pick up his legs and prance. Then, perhaps sensing a new audience, he started to canter around the field.

But her smile waned as she felt the discomfort between her and Elias. Perhaps she should take her lunch elsewhere. She had made her apology, after all, but just as she was about to depart, he spoke.

'What are you making?' he asked, and she felt a little light flare in her chest, because he had initiated conversation.

'Paella,' Carmen said. 'A family recipe.'

'Sounds good.'

'They're all very much looking forward to it...' Carmen sighed, trying not to feel daunted, but brightened up as she watched Dom. 'He's done dressage?'

'Yes,' Elias said, briefly turning from Domitian's showing off to take in Carmen's arms, resting on the rails and her face brown with dust and streaked with sweat.

Elias had *not* been eyeing her lunch. Instead, when she'd removed her gloves, he'd noticed her slender hands.

Carmen really was beautiful.

He had known it, of course, but had not properly allowed himself to acknowledge it until now. He was surprised to realise that a glimpse of her slender fingers had him wanting to see her toes...

Damn! The last thing he needed was to have the hots for the new stable hand.

The staff here lived and worked together, but Elias kept himself well away from all that.

LA was for work and recreation.

Malibu was his haven—where he relaxed, where he let his guard down...

Because even when it came to sex, his guard was never down.

As for relationships...?

There was no such thing.

He turned his attention back to Domitian, who had boldly made his way over. The stallion was heading straight for Carmen.

'Whoa!' Elias commanded.

To his credit, Domitian did as he was told, coming to an abrupt halt—albeit with a challenging stare. It was more than a stare. He flashed his teeth and flattened his ears.

Elias, used to it, calmly turned to Carmen, still keeping the stallion in his peripheral vision, but not offering a direct challenge that might cause confrontation. It was an obvious tactic, and he rolled his eyes at Carmen as they looked at each other, both deliberately ignoring Dom's challenge.

'I think he wants a treat,' Carmen said, knowing exactly why Dom had bounded towards her, given that she'd been bribing him with liquorice all week.

'Well, he's not getting one,' Elias said.

'Give him a strawberry,' Carmen suggested, knowing she had some in her lunch box.

'Not when he's staring me down.'

She felt guilty again, knowing exactly why Dom had come over, and told herself that that was why she blushed. 'He's still staring…'

'So we'll just keep ignoring him,' Elias replied. 'As you can tell, the lunatic really has taken over the asylum.'

Carmen laughed. 'At home we say the wolf is guarding the sheep.'

'Where *is* home?' he asked.

'Spain.'

'I had worked that much out, Carmen. Whereabouts in Spain?'

'The south.'

Carmen didn't want to elaborate and was deliberately evasive. Jerez was famous for its dancing Andalusian horses, as well as its festivals, and she didn't want a conversation that would lead them there or give him enough information that he would figure out who she was.

Because Carmen rather liked being here.

She liked who she was here.

Then she met his gaze and acknowledged that she *very* much liked being here.

'Finally!' Elias said, as Domitian snorted and took himself off.

They leant on the fence again, and Carmen ventured a little more about herself, though it was nothing she hadn't already told Blake.

'I've worked with dressage horses before. I could do some work with Dom,' Carmen offered. 'There was a two-year-old Criollo once, and I managed to—'

'Carmen, I hardly think—' He stopped, clearly checking his tone, which she could hear had veered towards derision. 'Criollo are easy-going.'

'Hmm…' she said. She didn't fully agree with him.

'What does *"hmm"* mean?'

'Had you not cut me off, I would have explained further…' she teased him.

It was just banter, she told herself. Because here she was free and could be anyone she wanted to be. She had no intention of revealing the true extent of her skills and training, but the secret knowledge of it gave her the confidence to toy with him.

'So, now you don't get to know.'

He gave a half-smile, clearly not believing a stable hand could really have anything of benefit to offer in this situation.

So she persisted. 'Have you ever considered—?'

'Carmen,' he cut in. 'We're working on it. And, while I can see you have no fear around horses, sometimes a little fear is a good thing.'

'I do have fear,' she corrected.

'Then you do a very good job of hiding it.' He shook his head. 'Look, I've solicited more opinions on Dom than I can count. He's already seeing an equine psychotherapist—'

'Both of you see the therapist together?' Carmen checked, with a mischievous edge to her tone.

'Yep,' he said, laughing. 'And, let me tell you, it's the closest to couple's therapy I'll ever get.'

Carmen laughed too.

'Look, Blake and I are both going to put more time in with him.' Elias let out a breath. 'Well, that's the plan. Depending on…you know…the LA stuff.'

She knew he was referring to his work outside of the polo yard. 'The grooms say you finance movies?'

'Not me personally.' He let out a low, slightly mirthless laugh. 'It's an investment firm. I mainly do the risk assessments.'

It was Elias holding back now. Holding back the fact that he'd far rather be *here* than *there*—how the board were demanding more, his father was demanding more. Not because the firm wasn't doing well, but because they were. And of course they wanted more, more, *more…*

He settled for: 'It's pretty full-on. Of course it's full-on here too, and unfortunately I can't be in two places at once.'

'There needs to be two of you.' Carmen smiled.

'There used to be.'

* * *

Even as her mind translated his words into Spanish she opened her mouth to respond. But for once she was grateful for that slight pause the translation allowed for, because it halted the light-hearted comment she'd been about to make and she recalled something Laura had said.

'You lost someone?'

'Joel—my twin.'

'I'm sorry.'

'You weren't to—' he started, but then took a quick breath. 'You didn't hear my speech at the awards night?'

'No.' She shook her head. 'I was busy getting myself fired.'

'Ah, yes.' He smiled, clearly recalling the small diversion she had caused.

'Well, I heard the bit when you spoke about grief,' Carmen admitted. 'How old was he when he died?'

'Thirty,' Elias said, and then added rather pointedly. 'We were talking on the phone when it happened. He was driving and I was— Well, I heard—'

Carmen swallowed, understanding a little better now why he'd been so cross earlier. 'I'm sorry,' she said. 'That must have been...' Her voice faded. 'I can't think of the right word.'

'I don't think there is one,' he said, 'in either of our languages.'

He turned his attention back to Dom, and although she rather guessed he'd prefer that she leave it there, she couldn't. 'Identical twins?'

'No,' he said, and breathed out a half-laugh that Carmen couldn't decipher. 'We weren't identical in any way...'

He didn't elaborate. But before she knew what he was doing, Elias had jumped the fence and was approaching the stallion, ready to do some work with him.

Playtime was over.

CHAPTER SEVEN

OCCASIONALLY THERE WAS an amnesty between them. Some nights, when they passed each other on the beach, he would nod to her; other nights he would be too far in the distance.

'Look at that,' she marvelled on one such night, more to herself than to Capricorn, as she watched Dom rear up while Elias leaned in and clung on to his back with his strong thighs.

They both looked magnificent, Carmen thought. Elias because he allowed the animal to be himself while remaining in complete control, and Domitian because he was simply a beautiful creature.

Some evenings Elias didn't acknowledge her at all.

'Don't mind him,' said John, who was riding Rocky at the time. He must have seen her face as Elias galloped past without even looking. 'He's like that with everyone. Well, not his fancy friends in the city...'

Carmen wanted to correct John, because that wasn't the man she had come to know, but then she thought of how he'd been when she'd first arrived. And then, as she thought of the awards night when she'd first met him, telling that blonde woman to go to hell and snapping at his date, she wanted to correct John again.

Elias *was* like that with *everyone*.

Though perhaps, at times, not with her...

The next night when it just Carmen and Capricorn on the beach Elias reined Dom into a walk as he approached them. He wore short boots that were as scruffy as her own for his rides on the beach, so it wasn't his casual attire that was different. There was just a more relaxed feeling in the air.

'*Hola,*' Carmen said, and now when she put up her hand to stroke Dom, Elias no longer warned her off.

She gently stroked the soft nose and the stallion nudged at her shorts.

'I had treats in there!' Carmen laughed.

'Not for him, I hope.'

'Of course not,' she lied. 'My boss won't let me,' she said with a wry smile.

She stroked Dom's ears and, although she spoke to the horse, it was clear for whom her words were intended.

'I'd love to work with you, Dom, if only your owner wasn't so determined to keep you all to himself.'

'Carmen, even *I* can't handle him some days! His previous owner was going to destroy him. And he threw your predecessor—'

'From everything I've heard, *I* would throw Martin.'

'Maybe…' Elias laughed and jumped down.

It was as though, on occasion, they called a truce, he thought. On certain evenings he found the opportunity to be on the receiving end of a dose of her opinionated conversation irresistible.

The fact was, she turned him on, just not in the usual way.

It wasn't simply about chemistry—though there was plenty of that. It was that she turned him on with her laugh, and the way she nudged him and pestered him to let her ride the stallion. It was the way they caught up on stable yard gossip— nothing indiscreet, just everyday chatter.

'I hear you made the most amazing paella,' Elias said now.

'I did!' Carmen smiled, hoping he couldn't see her burning cheeks.

It was the only time since she'd got to America that she'd cheated. Instead of foisting her lack of culinary skills on her hungry, hardworking housemates, she'd caved and arranged a secret delivery from a very swish restaurant.

'What are you making next week?' he asked.

'I haven't decided...'

He loved how she blushed as she lied, and laughed silently to himself at how the entire staff had seen the restaurant truck rumbling up the drive and the driver unloading not bags of ingredients but dishes of food.

She was a mystery—one that made him smile.

He enjoyed the view as she bent to pick up a piece of sea glass from the beach. It wasn't just the backs of her toned thighs that tightened his groin, but the pout on her lips as she examined it, the scrutiny in her eyes as she held up the piece of glass to the light before discarding it with a huff.

'Brown!' she scowled, and tossed it back.

'What's wrong with brown?'

'It's everywhere. I'm always looking out for orange.'

'Why orange?'

'Because in the olden days they didn't make many orange things.' Carmen shrugged. 'It's very rare. There's lots of brown sea glass, and I have a few turquoise pieces too, but no orange.'

'What about this one?' he asked a while later.

She was about to tell him that green was as common as brown, and that she had a hundred pieces like this, but suddenly she knew there could never be one as beautiful as this, because this one came from long fingers that had selected it just for her...

She saw that the hairs on his knuckles were gold from the sun, that his nails were neat, but the skin on his palms was strong and rough.

Carmen wore gloves for a reason.

She had to present herself as picture-perfect at family events. But Elias...

She looked at his hands again and wanted so badly to touch them, to know how that tough skin felt against hers.

'It's beautiful,' she said, and took the glass from him, slipping it into her pocket.

She knew that her plan not to like him was fading as fast as the setting sun.

* * *

'Do you miss Spain?' he asked one night, having returned to the ranch following a long day of meetings in LA.

'Yes!'

She knew she sounded surprised, and saw him turn and look at her.

'Had you asked me a couple of weeks ago, I would have said no. But since working here, at the yard…'

She went misty-eyed as she thought of Presumir.

'How long are you in the US for?'

'Three months,' Carmen said. 'Well, I guess there are only a few weeks left now…'

Her voice faded away as it dawned on Carmen that she was going to miss being here too.

Miss moments like this…

'She's tired,' Carmen said, referring to Capricorn, whose pace had started to drop off. 'I should get her back.'

'Sure.'

But in her stable Capricorn refused to settle.

'Lie down for me, girl,' Carmen said to the mare.

But even when she got the pregnant mare to lie down, she was still unsettled—as though the second Carmen left she might stand up again.

'I used to be like that,' Carmen said, and she lay down with the tired mare.

She told her about the nanny who had raised her after her mother left.

'As soon as Paula tried to turn out the light I would sit up and ask her a question or ask for some water.'

She lay there, remembering, but was brought suddenly back to the present as the little foal within Capricorn moved. Carmen smiled, as the mare lay quietly, accepting the movement and completely unfazed.

'You're going to be a wonderful mother,' Carmen said, and Capricorn responded with a breathy *hmmph*. 'Better than mine, anyway.'

It was Carmen who hmmphed this time.

She could hear the yard quietening down as the soft light of evening fell. She took out her phone and saw that there was another message from Emily, which included some more photos of her little niece.

Josefa was eight months old now, but she had been born twelve weeks early, so was still tiny. She was catching up fast, though, and for the very first time Carmen saw herself in her niece. She was blonde, like Emily, but she had dark almond-shaped eyes and was starting to get fat cheeks...

Carmen loved little Josefa with all her heart, but this evening the sight of her niece made her want to cry. The little girl was so close to the age Carmen had been when her mother had walked out...

'How could you leave a little girl like that?' she asked a dozing Capricorn, who of course didn't reply.

How could her mother have just decided, when Carmen had been less than a year old, that she wanted no part in her life?

And then twenty-five years later decide to return?

She heard hooves then, and the sound of boots. She sat up, only realising then that she'd been crying.

'Maldito,' she cursed, and quickly wiped her eyes as she stood up, certain that Elias wouldn't appreciate finding her lying down with one of the horses—or ponies, or whatever they were called here.

'Carmen?' he said, frowning when he glanced in and saw that she was there.

'Capricorn took a while to settle,' Carmen said, letting herself out.

He looked at the straw in Carmen's hair and she knew he'd guessed she'd been lying down with the pregnant mare. He looked as if he was about to tell her off, but perhaps he saw how red her eyes were, and that her lashes were damp and decided she did not need scolding right now.

'She looks peaceful,' Elias said.

'Yes,' Carmen agreed.

She took a deep breath to calm herself, and it was at that very second that she fully encountered his scent. Cologne, she guessed, left over from his day spent in meetings in LA. She picked up little notes of citrus and wood—or was it wood smoke? The kind you encountered when you rode through the hills in winter? And there was another scent…one she had never really been aware of before…which she knew had to be the potent edge of masculinity, because it made her want to step closer and breathe deeper.

And then she recalled the chest and back and flat stomach she had seen that first morning…

'I'm just going to do a final check and then head to bed,' Carmen croaked. 'It's good to finally be tired.'

'Yeah,' he said.

'I mean…'

She opened her mouth to explain that her head was not tired—that it hadn't been for most of her life, and certainly not since her father died. That she meant *physically* tired, and that felt like a blessing.

'It doesn't matter…' She put up a hand, as if to say it was too hard to explain, but…

Elias nodded.

'Yep.'

He'd kill to be tired tonight.

Instead of hard for Carmen.

CHAPTER EIGHT

'YOU'RE SURE ABOUT TOMORROW?' Blake checked as Carmen headed out for her evening walk with Capricorn. 'I can get someone in…'

'No need.' Carmen shook her head. 'I wouldn't know how to…' She paused to recall one of the many new expressions she had learnt. 'How to "man the line". It all sounds very chaotic.'

'We wouldn't have you manning the line.' Blake grinned. 'There's always a lot of other stuff to do, though, and—'

'Well, I'm sure Laura's busy enough without training me on the job at a semi-final.'

'Fair enough,' Blake said. 'I'll see you bright and early tomorrow.'

'I'll be up long before it's bright,' Carmen said with a smile.

But as soon as she walked away she let her smile drop.

Elias hadn't been at the yard today, and she had missed seeing him far too much for comfort.

So, no, she did *not* want to be at the polo semi-final tomorrow and get caught up in this intriguing sport. Nor did she want to watch Elias compete…

Carmen attempted to switch off that thought but it wasn't as easy as turning off her smile. Her mind kept flickering towards it as she took Capricorn out a little deeper into the sea, pleased that the mare was really enjoying it.

'See?' Carmen said as she stood waist-deep in the ocean next to the gentle horse. 'It's nice for your legs and that big belly…'

Capricorn had certainly got a lot bigger in the past couple of weeks.

Today had been Carmen's first taste of a really hot Californian day, so it could well be the case, she told herself, that the weather was to blame for her pensive mood now. She wore denim shorts and a yellow bikini top, and for once was without her phone.

She was sick and tired of the pressure from her brothers to get the legal ball rolling over the house, as well as exhausted by calls from Maria, pleading her case.

'Carmen, I know was absent, I know that I hurt you, but I came back. I was there for your father and I'm trying to be here for you now. You're the one who's left...you're the one in America...'

'Nice?' she said to Capricorn, scooping water over her back.

Yet even with Capricorn's antics Carmen struggled to smile.

It wasn't just her family issues niggling at her...

She looked at her arms and, though they were still slender, saw that her biceps were certainly coming on. Taking sets of four or five horses out for hours each morning and wrestling their different temperaments along with their reins was good for her.

'Maybe I *could* man the line,' Carmen grumbled, suddenly upset with herself for refusing Blake's offer, knowing it had confused him, and no doubt the other grooms too...

Why *wouldn't* she want to go and watch the game they'd spent hours of every day preparing the horses for?

But, no, she didn't want to be dripping sweat and covered in horse hair and worse while all those elegant beauties were cool in the shade or under a gorgeous hat, sipping champagne...

Would Wanda be there? Or would it be one of his in-betweens?

Carmen was jealous, and she knew it. Though she firmly told herself it wasn't because she *liked* Elias. Of course it wasn't *that*, she scoffed. She was jealous of his confidence, his inhibition. She wished she could date casually, like he did...

'Why shouldn't I?' Carmen said aloud, leaving Capricorn

to kick her hooves in the shallows while she took a seat on the beach.

She picked at the coral varnish on her toenails, wishing she'd brought her phone so she could try this internet dating that Laura kept telling her about...

But wasn't Laura sleeping with John?

And she was fifty years old!

Not that age had ever stopped her parents. They'd been having sex when Papá had died—as Maria loved to reveal to anyone who stood still long enough to breathe in her presence.

Carmen had sworn off men and relationships a long time ago, and yet her twenty-six-year-old body seemed to have decided otherwise...

What is this sex thing we've been missing out on? it enquired as she lay in bed at night. *Why do you have to take it all so seriously?* it demanded, as she woke to the sound of Laura and John...

And now, with her ocean-soaked shorts riding up uncomfortably as she sat on the beach, those night-time thoughts were creeping in to her days too.

She turned when she heard Dom's now familiar gait, and was surprised by the unexpected sight of Elias on the eve of the semi-final.

'Hey,' he said, having pulled Dom to a halt.

'Hola,' Carmen said, annoyed at how her heart leapt. 'She's cooling off,' Carmen said, nodding towards Capricorn.

'I might let him go in too,' Elias said.

Dom needed no encouragement or goading. As soon as he was unsaddled he went straight in, and Carmen laughed at the stallion's obvious delight as he rolled onto his back and scissored his front legs.

With Dom safely loose in the water, Elias tried not to notice Carmen's bare stomach, or that her nipples were pebbled beneath the wet bikini top. He took off his scruffy boots and joined her in sitting on the shoreline, pretending to be engrossed in the horses' antics, while noting that even her feet were sexy.

'How's the real job?' Carmen asked.

'I signed off on a big project today,' he said, nodding.

'You did your risk assessments?'

'This one's a pretty safe bet.'

'Is there such a thing in movies?'

'Yep,' he said, nodding again.

That producer had been right; the script was a guaranteed winner.

'Well, so long as the leading actor doesn't fall off the wagon…'

He sighed and closed his eyes, as if to shut out the long and tedious past couple of weeks.

Carmen's arrival had been something of a saving grace…

'Are you looking forward to tomorrow?' she asked.

'Not really,' Elias replied, his eyes still closed. He was surprised by his own honesty.

'You'll miss him…?'

'Yep.' He didn't pretend not to understand her meaning. 'Joel would rock up in the morning with these disgusting vitamin juice drinks…'

'I made them for a while,' Carmen said with a snort. 'When I first came to the States I got a job in a juice bar. They're disgusting.'

'I used to feed mine to Homer.'

'Who's Homer?'

'My horse before Capricorn,' he said, and then frowned, trying to fathom why he felt that she ought to already know that. Had she really only been here for a couple of weeks? 'My parents always come for a final.'

'Will they be there tomorrow?'

'They'll be there,' he said. 'The first time they'll have been to a match since—' No, he was definitely not looking forward to tomorrow. 'You're not coming?'

'Someone has to stay back.'

'Blake said he offered to get in a casual.'

'I told him there was no need for that. I'm more than happy to stay.'

Elias leant back on his forearms and turned his head to look at her, but it was as if Carmen refused to look back at him. 'You don't want to see what all the fuss is about?' he asked.

'Not really.' Carmen shrugged.

Elias wasn't sure if it was her shrug that irked him, or his own disappointment that she wouldn't be there tomorrow to watch him play. 'You're really not interested in watching a polo match?'

'Not particularly,' Carmen stated, staring out at the rolling waves and wondering why, on a hot Malibu night, she could be so cold. She was unsure too as to why her defences were suddenly up. 'Anyway, I doubt I'd get to see much. It sounds like the grooms are kept rather busy.'

They loved it, though, Carmen knew, but there was something gnawing at her that kept her from relaxing.

She turned and gave him a tight smile. 'What happens if you win tomorrow?'

'We make the grand final. It's being held the following week.'

'I know that. I mean what happens after the match?'

'Oh.' He thought for a moment. 'There's an after-party at Ramone's—though I suspect it'll be our opponents celebrating.'

'Ramone's?' Carmen frowned. 'Isn't that quite a formal venue? I thought Laura said everyone usually just headed to a bar.'

'The grooms do their own thing. Still, there's a grand ball after the final, for all the teams that took part. The grooms go too.'

Carmen pulled a face. 'Well, if you make it, I'll be putting up my hand to stay back for the final too. I don't exactly have a ballgown stashed in my backpack. Anyway, I hate formal functions,' she told him. 'What about you?'

'I don't mind them. It's part of the tournament.'

'You looked pretty miserable the other week.' She glanced over. 'Both you *and* your partner…'

He stared ahead in silence and Carmen knew she'd crossed a line few would dare.

'I wouldn't call her that.'

'What, then?'

He didn't answer for a very long time. In fact, when he spoke he didn't answer at all. 'You ask a lot of questions.'

'I'm just making conversation.'

But Carmen knew then what was really churning her insides.

'Wanda accompanies me to formal functions and such.'

Carmen pursed her lips.

Elias never usually explained himself, yet somehow he felt it necessary. 'She knows that I don't want to be tied to any other person.'

'That sounds very definite.'

'Because I *am* very definite.' He made it a warning.

'Why?' Carmen turned to him. 'Don't you believe in romance or love?'

'It's not for me.'

'Why?'

'Isn't that what three-year-olds do?' He tried to deflect her. 'Ask why? Why? Why?'

'Oh, I was a lot younger than three when I started asking *por qué?*' Carmen told him. 'And I've never stopped.'

He smiled at her persistence. 'I'd just prefer not to get that close to anyone.'

'Have you ever been?'

'Not really…' He pondered her question. 'I was seeing someone when Joel died, though we broke up soon after.'

'Por qué?' Carmen asked.

He gave a reluctant laugh. 'When we were first going out I was living the LA life—I would came here at weekends, but it was more of a hobby. Then, after Joel died, I spent more and more time here... At the end of the day, I didn't want to involve anyone else in how I was feeling. And I still don't.'

It was another warning.

'So, is Wanda a paid escort?'

'Carmen!'

'Excuse me!' She gave him a small, apologetic smile. 'My English is terrible sometimes. I know that I can come across as too direct.'

His eyes narrowed, and she saw a reluctant smile on his lips, even though he clearly knew she was lying. 'Your English is excellent, Carmen.'

'Thank you.'

'And no, I don't pay for company. I have to go to these events and Wanda likes to network, so it benefits us both.'

'So, do you sleep together?'

'I'm not discussing that.'

They sat in silence for a very long time.

It was Elias who spoke first. 'Do you?'

'Do I what?'

'Believe in love and romance.'

Carmen gave a scoffing laugh. 'No.' She shook her head. 'I've given up on dating.'

She scuffed the sand with her heel and then, sitting up, pulled up her knees and rested her head on them, turning to look over at him.

'My father desperately wanted to walk me down the aisle. He saw every man I dated as a future husband.'

'What about you?'

'I wanted to make my father happy.'

'Wanted?'

Carmen nodded. 'He died last year.'

'I'm sorry.'

'Please don't...'

She put up a hand to halt his sympathies. It still felt too new, too raw, to talk about. But it wasn't just words he was offering, because his hand gently rested on her bare shoulder.

Usually Carmen pulled away from physical contact, but

there was comfort in his hand, and it steadied her enough to dwell on the moment. Elias was the first person she'd told about her father who had never met him. It felt like some bizarre milestone...one she didn't want to unpick.

Then he removed his hand, but that rare feeling of comfort remained.

A lovely wave came and kissed her toes and Carmen smiled, saying, 'The tide is turning.'

She closed her eyes, missing his hand on her shoulder, knowing his eyes roamed her body, feeling her spine tingling as if he'd run a light finger down it.

'My father had terrible taste. He adored the last boyfriend I had, but...'

'Did you?'

'We weren't together for long, but I actually thought he was a nice guy for once.'

Why she was sharing her shame, Carmen didn't know. Well, she wouldn't tell him about the money, because she didn't want to reveal her background, or how well-known she was back in Spain. The only alternative was to reveal the part of her life that had stung the most.

'I overheard him telling his friend that I smelt of the stables and that he had to— Well, anyway, some other not nice things too.'

Telling Elias, watching his reaction, she felt her embarrassment over the long ago incident evaporate. *Poof!* Gone.

Because he just looked at her.

And *how* he looked...

Carmen had never been looked at like that before. It was as if he wanted to lean over and inhale her neck, or lift her arm and kiss the tender inside and say, *I beg to differ...*

There was nothing she could pinpoint, no apparent change in his demeanour, but he looked, and she smouldered beneath his gaze. She saw the dark ring around his chocolate irises and felt something heavy in the air between them. She felt the weight of her own lips, and as the object of his studied attention she felt...

Wanted.

She felt kissed.

For a moment, just a second—it didn't even equate to time—Carmen felt wanted in a way she'd never known before. So wanted that the most natural thing to do was surely to move her face towards his...

She'd never met such power. The ocean was a mere puddle compared to the absolute pull that shot through her, and it made her want to lean in and know his kiss for real.

It took everything she had to resist, to remind herself that she had no idea what she was doing...

'I should get going...' she croaked.

'Of course,' Elias said calmly as Carmen stood up.

She had known she had a crush on him. Was attracted to him. With his looks and charm it was perhaps a matter of course. Yet what she had felt just now had been far from a matter of course. To kiss him would have felt natural.

Normal.

Necessary.

Her cheeks were suddenly stinging, her legs felt unsteady and her voice quivered as she called Capricorn in from the water.

'Enjoy your night,' she said to Elias.

'And you.'

Capricorn settled easily, thank goodness, because Carmen didn't want to be around when Elias returned. Or rather, she desperately *did* want to be around when Elias returned. Because she wanted to revisit that moment and claim the kiss she felt she had denied by walking away.

She made her way to the lodge, thankful that everybody else was either out or already in bed.

Using her cell phone to light the way, she climbed the creaking steps. In her attic room she peeled off her damp shorts and bikini top and hung them over a chair, then pulled on a T-shirt and climbed into bed.

'I don't like you, Elias,' Carmen said aloud, as she slid

into the dip in the middle of the lumpy mattress, her words a vain attempt to remind herself of her determination not to let anyone in.

She lay there, her body prickling from its first real exposure to the Californian sun. She sat up and took off her T-shirt to relieve her skin...

Only that didn't help. And Carmen knew it wasn't the sun that had turned her body to fire.

And it was there, lying naked in the soft darkness of the night, that it dawned on Carmen that she was finally finding herself...

With Elias, it felt as if she was discovering the sensual side of herself.

Carmen hadn't even been aware that she could feel like that...like this... She had told herself that Elias would never deign even to look at a stable hand...

Yet he had.

That someone as worldly and sexy as Elias might actually want her, purely for herself, felt liberating. That she, Carmen, could be caressed with his eyes when he knew nothing about her family, her money, her inheritance...

She rolled onto her stomach and pressed her forehead into her arm, willing sleep to come.

She wanted to know his kiss...

More than his kiss.

Carmen had come to America to discover herself, to find out what kind of person she was without the Romero name opening doors for her. And now that she was actually starting to... Well, it turned out that she *was* capable of attraction and lust and all the things that had eluded her until now.

Next time he looked at her like that...

She lay there, on fire, certain of one thing: there absolutely would be a next time.

And when that next time came, Carmen wanted more than a kiss...

CHAPTER NINE

Elias didn't feel as if it was semi-final day.

'No green juice for you,' he said to Homer as he gave the Misfits their treats and then headed over to the yard.

And no parents dropping by, as they always had when he and Joel had played for the old team.

'Hola!' Carmen was tying Winnie's tail as if she'd done it a thousand times. 'She's on fire this morning. She could make it to Vegas and back.'

'Good to know!'

'Vegas?' Laura looked up from the horse's leg she was strapping. 'You so have to go there, Carmen.'

'Oh, I'm going to,' Carmen said assuredly.

'I saw the best psychic there.'

Elias had rolled his eyes, because Laura was clearly about to start a monologue on her favourite pastime, when Carmen chimed in, 'Well, I want to see a show and play the tables.'

Why, Elias pondered, when he had a million things to do, was he standing here listening to his head groom and his junior stable hand chatter on? And, more to the point, why was he joining in?

'Red or black?' he asked.

'Red,' Carmen said. 'Every time.'

'Do you gamble?' he asked.

'Never.' She shook her head. 'But if I did, it would be—' Her voice halted as Blake called out for him. 'Blake's calling.'

'Yep,' he said, nodding, and tore his focus away from Carmen.

He reluctantly got back to his busy day as his yard manager made his way over.

'Laura, the truck's ready. Elias, Wanda's calling; she can't get you on your cell phone.'

'Sure.'

Carmen found she was biting her lip as she finished off Winnie's tail. She kept telling herself it didn't matter as she helped load the horses into a huge, luxurious horse truck and the rest of the team went off to get changed.

Elias had changed too, and came out of his office in fresh attire and long, gleaming black boots. And Blake was looking very smart.

'It's a shame you're missing it,' he said as he went to do a final check on the animals before the truck headed off with its precious cargo.

Oh, no, it wasn't, Carmen thought.

It hurt her that Wanda would be there.

Bitterly.

More than that, it angered her.

Oh, she hadn't expected flowers and romance from a playboy, but common decency would do! She knew she hadn't imagined that moment on the beach last night.

Not that she would let on.

Carmen pushed out a smile for Blake. 'Good luck!'

And she said the same to each member of the team as they piled into the coach that would take them to the venue.

'Why aren't you coming?' John asked.

'Because…' Carmen took a breath, her anger building. She wished everyone would simply go, so she could run into a field and scream…

'If we win, we'll let you know where the party is!' Laura called.

'I hate parties.'

Carmen waved them off in the coach, then turned and found herself face to face with Elias's scent and his chest.

'Shouldn't you already be gone?' she asked.

'On my way…'

He looked stunning…elegant and polished. He stood there, waiting for her to speak, and she knew damn well what he expected. After all, she'd spent the last fifteen minutes wishing everyone else luck, and now she stood before the owner of the team.

But Carmen was too angry to play nice. 'Yes?' she said, rather directly. 'Is there something you need?'

'Nothing.' He went to go but then clearly changed his mind. 'Wishing someone good luck is generally considered polite…'

'You don't need luck, Elias.' She took a tense breath. She knew he was probably as superstitious before an event as she was, and she wouldn't want to feel responsible for him losing. *'Buena suerte,'* Carmen snapped. 'I wish you luck in Spanish.'

'Hey!' Elias frowned. 'What *is* your problem?'

'No problem,' she said, all too aware that if she blew her temper now, it would be the fourth job she'd lost…

Only, this had nothing to do with work.

Nothing.

Her eyes met his and she could feel her chest rising and falling, hear her own breath in her chest. Suddenly, she couldn't stop herself.

'How dare you look at me as you did last night and then expect me not to be angry when I hear your date waits for you today!'

'What the hell…?'

'You heard me,' Carmen said. 'You kissed me last night with your eyes—you know damn well that you did.'

'What does that even *mean*?'

'You know exactly what it means—and you know too that we could have taken it all the way to bed!' She was furious. 'You're damn lucky I won't be at the match today. Because if I'd seen her there I'd have slapped your cheek!'

'And that,' Elias snapped, 'is exactly why I don't do relationships! We haven't even kissed and you expect me to answer to you?' He turned on one booted heel. 'You're unreal,' he called out as he walked off.

'I'm right!' she called out. 'And you know it.'

Illogical?

Maybe.

Over the top?

Carmen did not care.

She had standards, and she was setting them for herself, here in this beautiful land where she was finding herself. Her heart was shattered, yet bit by bit she felt as if it was beginning to beat again…as if a brave new heart was blossoming…

'Your master is an arrogant bastard,' she told Dom as she fed him a treat before heading over to Capricorn. 'I hate men,' she told the mare, who nudged her to go for a walk. 'Come on, then,' she said.

But walking Capricorn on the beach did little to cool her temper. Worse, though, embarrassment was starting to emerge. Carmen knew that she'd revealed to Elias how attracted she was to him, and as well as that she knew she could be demanding.

But he'd probably laughed the whole episode off by the time he'd got to his vehicle, no doubt used to the hired help having a crush on him…

Her phone rang.

'What?' she snapped as she answered Alejandro's call.

'Just reminding you it's Emily birthday…'

'I know. I've sent her a present.'

'No,' Alejandro said. 'You messaged my assistant and asked her to get something.'

'What do you want from me, Alejandro? Am I to call and sing "Happy Birthday"?'

'She'd love it if you did. You can be so damned selfish, Carmen. Emily doesn't have any family.'

'And if you break up? Am I still to ring and wish her Happy Birthday next year?'

'Why do you always have to assume the worst?'

Because it was all she knew.

Carmen's day didn't get better after that, and the news that the team had won the match did little to improve her mood.

For all the excited chatter that came with the win, there were still tired horses to be unloaded and cared for.

'You should have seen them!' Laura was beaming. 'They won every chukka. Elias smashed it.'

'Fantastic!' Carmen beamed back.

'Elias said we can have the coach for the night, so we can party anywhere we like…'

John, like Carmen, was perhaps a little tired of hearing Laura rave about their super-talented and generous boss, because he snapped, 'We get the coach, and he's getting suited up for the after-party at Ramone's.'

'We're in the final!' Laura just laughed at his grumpy mood. 'Win or lose, next week we're going to a proper ball.'

'Lucky us,' John muttered.

As they all headed off to get changed, Carmen pushed out a smile as she once again declined Blake's kind offer to get someone in so she could join in with the celebrations.

'No need. I want to go to Santa Monica tomorrow, and I don't want to have a hangover on my day off.'

'Fair enough.'

She wasn't just cross with Elias, Carmen realised as her colleagues left, all showered and scented and ready to party… She was fed up with being seen in either dirty jodhpurs or scruffy shorts. She'd always loathed dressing up, but tonight Carmen found that she missed it—and that made her even more annoyed. She was tired of being a grubby stable hand and embarrassed at the thought of facing Elias again, having practically accused him of cheating on her after a mere look.

Carmen opened the fridge and ate a leg of chicken, then headed up the stairs to the attic and looked out towards the ranch, wondering if he was in there, celebrating with Wanda…

Of course he was, Carmen decided.

So what if he'd told her she accompanied him to formal functions but they weren't in a relationship? He hadn't denied that they were sleeping together, had he?

Or was she a media and family-friendly front to hide his appalling reputation?

Alejandro had had Mariana for events like that, and they certainly had been sleeping together. Sebastián hadn't even bothered with a regular date for appearances' sake; he'd been an unashamed playboy where women were concerned.

Her brothers' past behaviour was part of the reason why Carmen didn't want to get close to Emily or Anna. They might *appear* different now, but who was to say that they would stay faithful to their wives?

She stomped to the shower, peeling off her filthy, smelly clothes. Of course there was no hot water left, after the whole team had showered and gone out, and a cold shower did nothing to cool her temper down.

Pulling on a denim skirt and vest top, she lay on the saggy bed and tried to take deep, calming breaths. She picked up her phone, put a smile on her face and made the necessary call.

'Cumpleaños feliz...' she sang, and Emily laughed. She knew Alejandro would get the joke, and laugh too, because singing was so unlike Carmen. *'Cumpleaños feliz...'* she sang again, but then felt herself choking up.

And now Emily was crying too.

'Thank you,' she tearfully said. 'It's so lovely to hear from you. How is it there?'

'Oh, you know...' Carmen shrugged, but of course Emily didn't know. How could she? 'Emily, how did you—?' She stopped herself from asking, how shy, sweet Emily had dared risk her heart in the hands of a playboy and instead asked, 'How are you celebrating?'

'Didn't Alejandro tell you?' Emily said. 'We're in London!'

'Oh? When did you get there?'

'I didn't know anything about it. It was a surprise this morning. We're spending the day here, and tomorrow we're going to show Josefa where I grew up, and see Anna's parents.'

To Carmen's wounded, abandoned heart, Emily's words sounded like a threat. Her throat tightened. What if her brothers moved to England?

What was to stop two best friends deciding they both missed home?

There was no point getting close to anyone. Not when they would only leave her in the end.

'Well, I won't keep you…it sounds incredible.'

'Carmen?' Emily said hurriedly before Carmen could hang up. 'What are you doing? Do you ever get time off?'

'Not much,' Carmen said. 'In fact, I have to go and check on the horses for the night. Have a great trip.'

'Thank you for the perfume.'

'You're welcome. *Ciao!*'

The horses were all tired; even Capricorn was snoring. The only exception was Domitian, and she stood admiring possibly the most magnificent horse she had ever seen.

'Apart from Presumir!' she warned him, feeling his warm breath on the backs of her hands. 'I think I'll have to leave,' she told him. 'I made a fool of myself today.' She took a breath. 'So I'm never going to get to ride you.'

But why be sensible now?

She'd already made a mess of this day.

So she slipped into his stable…

'Come on,' she said, putting a soft bridle on him. 'Let's see what you can do.'

Carmen led him out to the old riding school arena, walking as casually as if she were taking Capricorn to the beach, but her heart was pounding.

There was little that was more unnerving than this—walking into an empty arena with a horse she knew could turn on her at any given second.

She turned on the lights and walked him to the centre of the arena. She held out her hand with a treat and spoke to him for a few moments, telling him what she meant to do. But then came the terrifying part.

Carmen turned her back on the stallion and walked away from him, eventually coming to a stop and standing motionless. It was a move meant to show Domitian that she had no fear, and that she expected him to respect her.

Domitian had to know he had her trust.

She could hear the blood whooshing in her ears as she stared at a knot in the wood of the gate, and then she swallowed as she felt Domitian's attention on her. He might attack, or kick. He might drag her around the arena, or slam her straight into the gate and crush her...

All this Carmen knew well, and yet this was what she did for a living...these were the animals she loved.

And here was her reward: the nudge of his nose in her back and his magnificent head coming down over her shoulder.

'*Hola, caballo,*' she crooned, and there were tears in her eyes as she turned and buried her face in his neck. 'Are you going to be good for me?

He was better than good.

Domitian was stunning.

She worked with him for a full hour, lightly instructing him with a stick, or a click of her tongue, loving how receptive he was.

'Are we really going to do this?' she asked, as he came over once more.

Without thinking twice, she gripped his mane and mounted him—no saddle, and certainly no stirrups. She was just trying him out, moving with him.

'Clever boy,' she said.

And he was such an incredible horse that she took him through a few basic movements.

And then some more.

When she did some flyover changes, it felt as if she was asking a high school student to spell *cat*. There was nothing this horse could not do.

Let's see...

She gave him an instruction and his hindquarters lowered.

'You complete star!' Carmen said, patting his neck. 'You could dance if I had time to train you.'

Gosh, he really was perfection, Carmen thought, and decided to try a levade—a move where the hindquarters were lowered fully and the front legs were lifted.

She held on to his mane and gave the signal. And she felt the absolute beauty as Dom moved and then brought his front legs up…

What the hell…?

Elias didn't even know if he'd said it out loud, but as he watched Dom rear up his impulse was to dash forward. And yet he knew it was imperative that he stay calm, so as not to spook the stallion.

Elias had felt pure terror once—the night Joel had died. Tonight, he felt it again.

Seeing that Dom was missing from his stable, and the lights were on in the old riding school arena, at worst he'd thought he might be about to catch Carmen doing some ground work with the bad-tempered beast. But not…*this.*

It was then that he realised he hadn't spoken out loud, for horse and rider hadn't noticed him, and he stood in silent awe, watching true poetry in motion.

He'd known Dom was stunning and had great potential, but it was the sight of Carmen that had reduced him to silent awe.

She was perfection…barely moving as the horse moved, an utter master as she brought him up again, onto his hindquarters, and then cantered around the arena a couple of times.

Even her long black hair barely rippled, and her brown legs were relaxed. She gracefully brought him to a halt and then did the manoeuvre again.

Elias wasn't sure if it was Dom or Carmen who saw him first, but there was a slight wobble and a less than perfect landing as the horse lowered himself down.

'Good boy,' Carmen said, stroking his mane, and then added 'I think we've been busted.'

'Carmen…' he said, keeping his voice even with great difficulty. Even though his heart was still thumping in terror, he refused to be provoked, knowing that anything could unsettle Domitian. 'Get off him. *Now!*'

'I don't want to,' she said.

'Get. Off. Him.'

'We're fine.'

'Oh, I'm not asking,' he warned, and finally she met his eyes.

No, Elias was not asking; he was ordering her to get down.

He watched her dismount, as lightly as a cat jumping from a table, and then she calmly took some liquorice from her pocket and fed Domitian a treat.

'I'm taking him in,' Elias told her.

'I can manage,' she responded tartly. She looked at him again. 'Shouldn't you be at your after-party?'

'Do I look as if I've been at a party? Or going to one?'

Her eyes took in his attire, and he knew she must see that he was still in his match gear, but it didn't change her stance.

'I told you. I know what I'm doing.'

He said nothing. Just took a very pleased with himself and surprisingly well-behaved two-thousand-pound stallion back to his stable and bolted him in.

'Now he needs another treat,' Carmen said, and had the audacity to reach into the pocket of her skirt and take out some more liquorice.

'Is that what you've been bribing him with?' Elias snapped, and took the damned treat from her.

He patted and stroked the horse then, pretending that everything was completely fine, so as not to confuse the horse.

'Good boy,' he said nicely. 'Well done for not killing Carmen. Good Dom.'

Then he turned with eyes blazing.

'My office—now!'

He practically marched her there, and when she stepped into his office for the first time she saw not the gleaming desk, nor the leather chairs and sofa, only the blaze of his eyes.

'Clearly,' he said, 'you have no idea what you're doing!'

Carmen blinked. Elias was white-faced—she assumed it was with anger.

'You could have been killed!' he shouted. 'I swear to God,

Carmen, if you've been taking him out alone, with no one around…'

He was livid, she could see that, and trying to contain it.

'You had no business taking him out without permission!'

'Would you have agreed if I'd asked?'

'We both know the answer to that,' he snapped. 'Can you imagine how it would have felt for Laura or Blake to find you unconscious on the floor? Or dead?'

He sucked in a tense, shuddering breath and closed his eyes for a moment, as if envisaging just that.

'Damn it, Carmen!'

There was only the sound of his heavy breathing in the silence that followed these words.

'Where do you think you're going?' he demanded as Carmen turned to leave.

'The animals are all settled,' she called over her shoulder. 'I'm now officially on my day off. You can get back to your date.'

'Date? What date? What the hell do you think I'm doing here?'

'I've no idea.'

'I came to say…' He took a breath. 'I came to say that you're wrong.'

She knew exactly what he was referring to. How could she not? It was all she had thought about all day long.

'No, no, no…' She shook her head. 'Listen to me, you arrogant man. I don't expect flowers, and I don't give a damn about your past, or what you do after I'm gone, but don't make out with your eyes and then go off with your date—'

'On that point you are correct,' he said. 'And that is why I called Wanda last night and told her…'

'Told her what?'

'That our arrangement is over.'

'So why did she call you today?'

'Because I promised her an introduction to a producer she's been trying to impress!'

And then, just like that, he did what they both knew was

inevitable—what she had ached for last night. He kissed her fiercely, his mouth so full of demand that had he not held her so tightly she would have toppled over.

His jaw was rough and his tongue was probing—but then he suddenly pulled back, conflicted. 'We can't do this.'

'Why not?' she asked.

He stared down at her.

'You *know* why! Carmen, I don't want to mess things up here.'

She could see he was struggling to explain.

'I don't do relationships…' he said.

'I already know that.' She stared back at him. 'And I told you last night that I don't either.'

His mouth came down on hers again, and the kiss felt like an elixir, like nectar, and she kissed him back as if she knew how…because with Elias she did.

The skin of his neck was warm, and she coiled her slender arms around it and whimpered in relief as his hands slid beneath her T-shirt to her breasts.

'Oh…' she moaned as he freed her from her bra. 'Please…'

She straightened her arms above her head as he slid off her T-shirt and then greedily tugged at his, unable to wait a moment longer to feel his naked chest on her skin.

When it finally happened, it was sublime.

Bare skin…pressing, touching, sliding…but then he pulled his mouth away.

'Don't stop!' she panted, stunned that she could so readily want this. It was as if he had found the lost key to her defences, and she was terrified to lose the moment. There was more than a kiss required to soothe this burning.

'I want this…'

He crushed her lips with his mouth then, and she felt all his power. She liked it that he hadn't made promises that he would never keep—Carmen had had a lifetime of that. And she liked it that he did not want to invade her world.

'I want you…now…'

Now.

Her loneliness was hushed. Not just the ache for home, but the dark pit of emptiness was gone too, as if she'd come alive under his mouth and the grip of his hands.

He kissed her as he lowered her down onto the couch and she wrapped her legs around his waist. Deep, hungry kisses that made her feel both soothed and desperate. The best kisses possible because their faces were level.

His impatient hands lifted her skirt, so that it bunched around her hips.

If this was what she had been scared of, what she had avoided, then she did not know why. Because this was incredible.

She was the one driving this forward as she unhooked his jodhpurs. It had been on the cards, she realised, since the moment she had arrived in his pristine yard, and now all order and control was gone.

Elias had spent half a decade holding himself in check, never allowing himself to sink into the moment, or lose himself to pure pleasure. From every angle and in every way he exerted control. But now he felt it slipping away...

His office, his order—all was forgotten as they explored each other's mouths and bodies. He felt her hand gripping him, stroking him, too tentative and delicate a touch when his body was on fire.

He slid his hand into her knickers and felt that she was ready, so wet and ready, and he heard her throaty gasps as he encircled his base.

'Please...'

He could wait no longer. He pulled her knickers aside and eased himself into position—then thrust in with all the passion she demanded.

He was shocked at what could only be the tearing of virgin flesh...

Carmen had expected it to hurt, and it did, but it was also delicious—as if every star in the sky was spinning.

But she was hauled back down to earth by the question in his voice.

'Carmen?'

She opened her eyes and locked her gaze with his for a moment. He seemed…angry. But she had no breath in her to respond to anything other than the feel of him inside her as she tried to acclimatise to this new sensation.

'Elias…' she begged as he pulled back, desperate to hold him inside her still.

She did not want him to stop, and he clearly got the message, because now he pushed in deeper, and it felt as if he were prising open the black sky.

'Dios…' she said, because the sensation was exquisite.

She buried her face in his shoulder as he pushed again, all the way in this time, and then out, and then in again, each measured, slow thrust stretching her, taking her deeper than she had ever thought possible, to new experiences and new places she had waited so long to explore.

Slowly, she wanted to say. But she had forgotten not just the English word but the Spanish word too. She couldn't speak. So instead she met his thrusts…moving with him, joining him.

It was like pushing off from a cliff-edge, diving into the freedom he gave.

'Elias…' She cried out his name as she shuddered inside, sensation sparking every cell in her body.

He took her to oblivion, and his groan as he came inside her was met by her startled shout of pleasure as she climaxed. The strength of her first orgasm, the pulses of pleasure, was so deep and unexpected that all she could do was collapse into it.

Elias lifted his head. 'Carmen, I…'

She did not want it to be over—not least because she knew he would have questions—so for now they both just sucked in air, eyeing each other and panting.

He pulled out and looked down at the blood, and then back at her.

'I think I must be getting my period…'

'Don't lie!' he warned as he tucked himself back in to his boxers. 'Not about this.'

'Elias…' She was trying to get her breath. 'Please don't make a big deal of it.'

'Don't even try to tell me I'm making a big deal of it.' He ran a hand through his shock of dark hair. 'If I had known you were a virgin—'

'What? You wouldn't have taken me, here in your office?' She laughed in his face. 'You'd have been all tender and—'

'I wouldn't have had sex with you in the first place.'

'Worried my heart can't take it?'

'Something like that.' He nodded.

'We both enjoyed it, Elias. That's all. Don't worry—I'm not going to fall in love with you.'

'Carmen, for goodness' sake!'

'No!' She stared angrily at him. 'I wanted you and you wanted me—and that's it. The end. You're the one who is complicating things.'

She got up and pulled on her top, heading for the door.

'We are going to talk,' he told her.

'About what?'

She was stunned—not at his reaction, but at the power of what had taken place. Intimacy was a huge issue for her, and she had never been so overtaken by desire, so utterly lost in the sensations of her body, wanting…

And Carmen did not want to explain it to him.

'I don't want commitment or promises. I never have. So don't worry about things changing, Elias.' She shook her head. 'I wanted sex, and so did you.'

'Don't walk away.'

'Go to your party,' Carmen replied.

'Don't be ridiculous.'

'What?' she said. 'Are we really going to sit down and talk now?'

It was the last thing she wanted. She didn't want to spoil the memory of what they had shared by putting it into words. She needed time and space to process it on her own first.

'I said I don't want to talk about it, Elias.'

Carmen wrenched open the office door and marched back to her attic room in the lodge. Even as she undressed and showered she could not quite believe the woman he'd made her tonight. She ran her hands over her skin under the spray of water and wondered at what she had just experienced.

And as she crawled into the most uncomfortable bed she'd ever slept in, she still couldn't understand her own lack of inhibition, the depth of her own desire.

Some things didn't need to be put into words...they could just *be*.

CHAPTER TEN

IT WAS HER one day off in a fortnight and Carmen was in agony.

'That bastard!' she said, because it stung her to wee. 'What has he given me? *This* is why men cannot be trusted!'

Carmen feared the worst—because everything she was feeling right now was a first for her.

The lodge wasn't empty this morning, of course. John was there, eating from a bag of pretzels, and Carmen could barely manage a polite good morning, let alone ask about last night.

Not even picking out all the marshmallows from the box of cereal cheered her up.

'Any plans for today?' John asked.

'I'm going to Santa Monica.'

'There's a bus at ten.'

'Thanks.'

It was hell being poor—or pretending to be poor—Carmen thought as she stood waiting for a bus along with several others.

She was in agony. She was sore and swollen down below. And now she could ruefully admit to herself that she understood where Elias's anger had come from last night. After all, it had all been very fast and hard. She was paying for it now.

She winced again, and was tempted to cheat on her promise to herself not to spend more than she made. Unable to bear the wait for the bus any longer, she took out her phone, and she was just about to order a cab when a familiar silver car slid to a halt beside her.

Elias.

The window slid down.

'What?' Her tone was curt.

'Get in.'

He wore a black linen shirt and dark glasses, but even so she could tell his expression was forbidding. She rather suspected she was going to be told off.

'My bus is due any second, and if I miss it I'll have to wait for ever for another.'

'Just get in, Carmen.'

'But I want to go to Santa Monica.'

'I'll take you to Santa Monica,' he said tersely. 'And you and I are going to have a talk on the way.'

'We have nothing to discuss.'

'Carmen,' he warned, 'get in now, or we will have this discussion right here at the bus stop. Either way, *we are going to speak*.'

Carmen looked at the curious faces behind her and then acquiesced, sliding into the passenger seat. One-nil to Elias. But she stared rigidly ahead and tried to breathe only through her mouth and not her nose.

Damn him for smelling so fantastic! Not woodsy or citrussy, just soapy, and so devastatingly sexy that Carmen knew she would do last night all over again—even with the accompanying aches and pains.

'Are you okay?' he asked.

'I'm fine.' She glanced over. 'I still don't want to talk about it.'

'You don't want to talk about anything,' he pointed out. 'You don't say where you're from, you're posing as a stable hand when you're clearly—'

'I *am* a stable hand here,' she protested. 'I wanted a break from riding professionally back home. I came here to clear my head and try something new.' She picked at the hem of her skirt. 'But I missed the horses. I'm not lying. I'm not a wanted felon, or married or anything…'

'I had worked that last one out,' he snapped. 'If you were, it must have been a very unsatisfactory honeymoon.'

He drove fast, oblivious to the glorious ocean beside him, and Carmen guessed he wanted this conversation over and done with.

'You should have told me,' Elias started.

'So you've already said.'

'I'm guessing you're not on the Pill?'

'Actually, I am,' Carmen said. 'I like to know when—' She halted, because this was not the type of thing she discussed with anyone.

Ever.

Sebastián had gruffly attempted to tell her about periods when she was younger, but Carmen had pointed out to her brother that she did work with animals and knew how bodies worked, thank you very much.

'That's good,' Elias said, and she felt him turn and glance at her. 'At least one of us had our head on straight...'

'You think?' Again, she came out fighting. 'We should have used a condom. I'm going straight to a clinic,' Carmen said. 'Not today, though.' She gave a hollow laugh. 'I'm a bit sore. God knows where you've been...'

'Carmen,' he said. 'You don't have to worry about that.'

'Oh, please!' she responded tartly, but was a little stunned when the car slowed and he pulled over.

Perhaps he wasn't entirely oblivious to the view, because he looked out to the bright blue of the ocean for a full moment before turning to face her.

'Listen to me. I've never had sex without a condom before.'

'I have two very corrupt brothers,' Carmen said. 'And I've worked in stables for a long time. I know the rubbish men say—'

'Well, in this instance it's true. I don't have unprotected sex.' He took a tense breath. 'Ever.'

'Then why does it sting when I wee?' she asked accusingly.

'Because I was rough. Because it was new.'

She liked it that he didn't blush, or back off. He went on to tell her that she was just bruised and sore, and that it was normal to be, especially as it was her first time.

'Not that I know much about that, but—'

'You don't sleep with virgins?'

'No.'

'Were you *ever* a virgin?'

He smiled at her loaded question, his first smile of the day, and she wished she could see his eyes.

'Not for long.' Then he was serious. 'Carmen, I date women who know what they're getting into. Who understand that I mean it when I say I don't want to get involved—'

'Then I'm glad you were my first,' Carmen cut in. 'Because I don't want a relationship either, Elias, and I don't want to get involved. I'm here in America to get to know myself better—not anyone else.'

'Fair enough.'

'I have a lot going on at home, and I—' Carmen halted herself. 'I don't want to talk about it.'

'I had noticed.'

'What's the point?' She turned accusing eyes to him. 'We both agree we don't want to get involved, so…' She held out her hands, palms up, and shrugged.

'Agreed, but that doesn't exclude all conversation. Carmen, neither of us wants anything long term, but there's one hell of a difference between commitment and connection,' Elias said. 'We connected long before last night.'

Carmen blinked at the impact of his words. 'True,' she acknowledged quietly, because there *was* a connection, and there had been since the moment they'd met. 'I wanted to come over to you when I saw you outside that night…'

'I wanted you to come over,' Elias replied. 'But we're not dogs in the street,' he said. 'We're capable of conversation. And you should have told me that you'd never had sex before.'

'I disagree.' She shook her head. 'Because if I had told you then I'd *still* be a virgin.'

Yes, Carmen, you would be, Elias was about to say. Because absolutely he should have walked away.

Yet that would make him a liar. Because that was what he

would have done *before* he'd met Carmen—before this stunning woman had dropped into his life.

Elias wasn't certain he'd have walked away at all.

'I don't know,' he admitted. 'Maybe.'

When she smiled at his answer, he returned it.

'Can I get back to you on that one?' he asked.

'You may.'

Elias looked at her mouth, and then back to her very black eyes. He'd stopped making out in cars close to two decades ago, so instead he clicked on the indicator and pulled back out onto the highway.

And then he made an attempt at something rather more challenging than kissing.

Getting to know Carmen.

'So, two brothers…?' he asked when his attention was safely back on the road, and she nodded. 'Corrupt?' he checked, repeating what she had said.

'I meant depraved,' she corrected. 'Though not any more. They're both married.' She rolled her eyes. 'You know how sanctimonious ex-smokers can be?'

He laughed, clearly understanding exactly what she meant. 'I do. Joel was the same.'

'I miss just having brothers. Now I have to ask how is Anna, how is Emily? And I'm reminded to call them on their birthdays.'

'Don't you get on with their wives?'

'Yes and no.' Carmen shrugged. 'They're English, and they were best friends before they met my brothers.'

'You feel left out? You don't fit in?'

'I don't want to fit in,' Carmen declared. She glanced over to him. 'Did you get on with your brother's wife?'

'Not really,' Elias admitted, and even if it was a huge understatement, it was more than he'd ever revealed before. 'I never told him, though.'

'But I thought you were close? I've told my brothers what I think of their partners.'

'And how's that working out?' he said drily.

'Not very well,' she admitted. 'But I don't see the point in being warm with them.'

'Warm?'

'Yes.' She nodded. 'I don't want to develop friendships based on the strength of their marriages to my brothers.'

Elias had long since considered himself closed off, but Carmen really was an island, with every drawbridge pulled up and defended.

He couldn't stop himself wanting to prise her open, just a chink—just enough to know her a little more. But that meant opening up himself...

'I didn't tell Joel that I didn't like his wife because it didn't really matter at first. When I first met her she was working for my mother,' he told her. 'I had a big project on—the ranch— and my mother was an interior designer.'

'Was?'

'She hasn't worked since Joel died. Now her main focus is keeping his name alive and staying in with his widow...'

'Staying in?' Carmen repeated. 'I don't understand...'

'It doesn't matter.'

'So, they stay in...?'

'They stay *involved*,' he snapped, certain she must be pretending. He glanced over. 'You have selective comprehension, Carmen. You choose when to understand, don't you?'

'Sometimes.'

Carmen smiled, and when she smiled like that it remained in his head, even as he turned back to the road.

'So she worked for your mother?'

'Yes. I had to go to Europe to do a big assessment, and by the time I got back from my trip she and my brother were about to get engaged and everyone loved her...'

'But not you?'

'Nope.' He shook his head. 'I found her to be...'

'What?'

'Fake,' he said. 'But she was engaged to my twin and working for my mother...'

'What about your father?'

'He adored her and still does.' Elias found he was being more honest than he'd intended to be. 'I did try to tell Joel once. It didn't go down well…'

'Did you fight?'

'No.' He laughed. 'It wasn't pistols at dawn.'

'It would be with my brothers,' Carmen said. 'It was for a while—and they work together. The bodega was not a happy place.'

'Bodega?'

Carmen quickly looked out of the window and he saw her blush, as if she wanted to cover up what she'd just said. 'I think you call it a deli here,' she said hurriedly.

'Take a look,' Elias said, because gorgeous Santa Monica was coming into glorious view, its pier stretched out to the horizon and people milling about.

'Wow!' Carmen groaned. 'How have I never been here?'

'Incredible, isn't it? A bit wild…'

'Wild?' Carmen checked. 'I love wild.'

And even though he could have dropped her off and carried on with his day, he parked. 'I know a nice place where we can get brunch.'

'No, thank you. I want a day to myself.'

She really was like no one he had ever met. 'You're very standoffish, Carmen.'

'No.' She shook her head. 'I'm just being honest. I have one day off a fortnight, and I don't want to have to be on my best behaviour just because I am out with the boss.'

'Since when did you behave?'

'Look, I just want to wander…buy some souvenirs, explore the place. Laura's told me about a few things to do…'

He knew Laura's idea of fun! 'You're not going to see a psychic, are you?'

'Maybe,' she teased. 'I just want to soak it all up.'

'Carmen.'

He halted her, even though he was unsure quite what to say. As someone who knew the pain of loss, knew how vulnerable a person could be in the immediate aftermath of a bereavement, he knew he had to speak up. If she was grieving, she could be easy prey.

'I can come with you...'

'No way!' She actually laughed. 'We have sex once and now you want to come in to see a clairvoyant with me? Do you want the passcode to my cell phone too?'

She made him smile.

'I'll be fine,' she told him.

He relaxed at that. He should leave her be, really. Carmen was right: what she did with her day off had nothing to do with him.

He looked out at the busy street and beyond to the vibrant pier. On the right day it was an incredible place, the best of the best. But on the wrong day...

Or was that just an excuse he was giving himself?

CHAPTER ELEVEN

THERE WERE LITTLE POODLES in tutus, walking on their hind legs, street performers, people on stilts, lovers, colourful stalls and the stunning ocean as a backdrop...

There was nowhere to pause, though. Nowhere to gather her thoughts. It was all music and noise, and Carmen realised her emotions were in tumult.

She leant on the pier and looked at the ocean, but it was as choppy as she felt inside rather than calming.

She had wanted to say yes to Elias's offer of brunch, but she also wanted some time to clear her head. She knew he felt bad about what had happened last night, only there was no need. Carmen had no regrets about what had taken place. She might have been a virgin, but she wasn't a child.

It was her feelings *now* that troubled her.

She had been so sure she could separate her heart and her body, the way her brothers had for so many years.

And yet there was a reason she was twenty-six and, until last night, had been a virgin.

She'd never wanted anyone the way she wanted Elias.

It wasn't just sex. It was the sound of his voice, his scent... how a light seemed to flare inside her whenever she saw him... how somehow she felt as if she shone like a star when she met his eyes...

'Hey, pretty lady!'

A guy joined her as she leant on the pier, and Carmen straightened up and abruptly walked off.

She just wanted a moment of peace, but she was fast realising that wasn't what you came to the pier for.

A woman jogging through the crowd almost collided with Carmen, and she felt an odd flutter akin to panic.

'Slow down!' another woman called out to the jogger's departing back, and then she smiled at Carmen. 'Why would you try to exercise here?'

'No idea,' Carmen admitted.

'Is it your first time on the pier?' she asked.

'Is it that obvious?' Carmen forced out a smile, but it faded as she glanced at the parted curtains behind the woman and saw a table with a crystal ball on it.

'Come through,' the lady said.

'No, thanks.'

'You're worried that he'll never propose…'

'Really, no!' Carmen laughed, and moved to walk away, but she still felt that flutter of panic.

'I see a bull… Taurus?'

Carmen turned back.

'Yes…' Carmen admitted, a little stunned that this woman could know that, but then she gave herself a little shake. 'I really have to go.'

'I have someone who needs to speak to you.'

Perhaps it was precisely *because* Elias had warned her not to that Carmen nodded and went through. Or was it just for the fun of it? It wasn't the type of thing she usually did, but she was in America to have new experiences, wasn't she?

Carmen could feel her own sudden desperation, and an unbearable ache to hear from her father, so she paid and sat down, still telling herself it was just for fun, even though her hand was shaking…

'I see a dark-haired gentleman…'

'For sure,' Carmen said, and pulled at a strand of her hair. 'There are a lot in my family.'

'Sassy!' The woman smiled. 'Now a lady is coming in. She tells me she watches over you,' the clairvoyant said. 'Your grandmother?'

'I never met my grandmother.' Carmen shook her head, knowing this was a stupid idea. And, worse, now she felt foolish, and knew she was being played.

That panicked feeling gripped her as she fought to stay in control.

'She says that your mother worries about you…'

'Well, now I know for sure that you're making this up,' Carmen said, and abruptly stood up.

To her horror, she started to cry. She stumbled out of the tent, blinded by the sudden bright sun and her tears.

'Carmen!'

She was pulled against Elias's chest, enveloped by his scent. Too upset to make a wisecrack, she sank with relief as he took her in his arms.

'Say it,' she said, as she wept into his shirt. *'I told you…'*

'I told you,' he said gently, and then he held her so tight.

Carmen hadn't properly cried since her father had been laid to rest—at least not like this. Or was it that she'd never been held quite like this before? As though he was her shield and she could let down her defences because he would protect her.

'She said that my mother worries for me, but it's all lies—lies, lies!'

'You're okay…'

'No,' she refuted. 'I'm clearly not.'

She pressed her face into his chest and moaned out a sob, feeling as if her knees were buckling, but he held her firmly, and she cried and cried, nestled in his arms, letting herself go…

Really, truly letting herself go.

And there *was* peace to be found on Santa Monica Pier.

It was a comfort she had never known before. And it was beautiful to cry and to be held, not to be hushed or told to be calm, just to be held in solid arms while she cried herself out.

'I'm sorry,' she said, feeling more stunned at her emotional collapse than by losing her virginity last night. She knew she was coming back to herself when she said, jokingly, 'Stalker.' He didn't reply, so she softened and said, 'Thank you for looking out for me.'

'Come on,' he said, and with his arm around her he guided her off the pier. 'Do you want that brunch?'

'I can't go like this.'

'You can,' he said and gave her his sunglasses. 'We'll get a table at the back.'

At a very quiet table, in a cool and shady corner of a beautiful restaurant, she sipped iced water to cool her flushed cheeks while he ordered for them.

'Coffee and…' He glanced over at her. 'Pancakes?'

She didn't nod or shake her head.

'Pancakes,' he said to the waiter.

'With…?'

'Ice cream, syrup…whatever you have. Thank you.'

'I'm so embarrassed,' she said.

'For crying?' he asked.

'More for being such a fool…' Carmen said. 'I can't believe that I was taken in for even one second. She said she knew I was a Taurus, and I am. I don't know how she knew that, but—'

He reached over and took off the sunglasses. When he saw her red eyes and wet lashes he thought of her lying down with Capricorn. He knew this wasn't the first time since her arrival in Malibu that Carmen had cried, and vowed that if he could help her, then he would.

After last night, he could do at least that much.

'Tell me what she said.'

'Just that… The first thing she said was that I am a Taurus.'

But Elias shook his head. 'What else?'

'She told me if I was worried that a man would never propose.'

'Well, you should have known you were being ripped off right away.'

'I know.' Carmen gave a half-laugh. 'I told her no, and I walked off, but then she called out that I was a Taurus.'

'If you tell me everything that was said, I can tell you how she knew.'

'How?'

'That's what I do at work,' he said. 'I look at all the things that will work, and all the things that won't work, and then again at the things that might… It's risk assessment.'

'It's hardly the same thing.' Carmen shook her head, refusing to believe him. 'You crunch numbers.'

'I do,' he agreed.

'It's not the same as seeing into a heart,' Carmen said.

'It's exactly the same,' Elias told her. 'I get lied to for a living. I get told what's going to be the next best thing, a sure thing, and I get told what doesn't have a hope. And then, if something gets far enough to land on my desk, I get to look at it from every angle. And I'm very good at what I do,' he informed her as their pancakes were served.

'Well, I don't need some *assessment* to know how she did it,' Carmen told him, as she dived in to the most perfect, fluffy, syrupy pancakes. 'These are so good,' she told him.

But Elias ignored the plate in front of him and sipped black coffee.

'I know she was making it up,' she said, embarrassed to admit it. 'She just took a lucky guess with my horoscope sign—a one in twelve chance.'

'She'd be laughed off the pier in five minutes if she tried to con everyone with a guess. It wasn't some lucky guess,' he told her. 'You try it. What's my star sign?'

'Scorpio,' Carmen declared, because his words stung a little, but he simply stared back at her. 'Gemini,' she attempted, and then flushed, because wasn't that the sign of the twins? 'Sorry, I didn't mean to—'

'Ten more to go.'

'You wouldn't tell me even if I was right,' Carmen huffed.

'Exactly. And that's why your friend on the pier wouldn't bother to try her luck with me.'

'Okay, Mr Logical, tell me how she knew.'

And Carmen told him everything—about how she'd been jostled by the jogging woman, how she'd tried to assert herself by pointing out her hair and scoffing at the idea of a proposal from a gentleman.

Elias said nothing all the way through—just listened. He didn't eat his pancakes. He just drank coffee as she gave her account.

'She called me sassy,' she said.

'Then what?'

'She said something about my mother.' Carmen took a breath. 'But I was already walking out by then.'

Carmen looked at the black linen shirt that had provided the nicest refuge, and then looked up to his chocolate eyes.

'Was the jogger a part of it?'

'I doubt it.' He put down his cup.

'So you don't know?'

'She knew you were Spanish, yes?'

'Not necessarily,' Carmen refuted. 'A lot of people here think I'm Mexican.'

'These are clever people. They know different accents; that's the sort of thing they pick up on. What do you think of when you think of Spain?'

'Home.'

Carmen thought of home, of the bodega, with a moment of such longing that it brought tears to her eyes. But as she reached for his sunglasses again he halted her, and handed her a napkin which she pressed into her eyes.

'What do tourists think of when they think of Spain?'

'Horse festivals?' she said.

'No.'

'Flamenco?' she asked, because that was massive in Jerez.

But he held up his hand in a wavering gesture. 'Try again,' he said, and then picked up his own napkin and held it to the side like a matador.

'Please!' Carmen laughed. 'Not bull fighting.'

'I'll tell you now, if you hadn't lit up like a Christmas tree when she said Taurus, the next thing she'd have tried would have been Spain and bulls.'

'Well, I would have walked off then.'

'When you laughed about a proposal she knew you weren't worried about a guy. You'd practically told her that wasn't what was on your mind. So she deduced that you were wavering about going in because you were grieving.'

'Yes!' Carmen said, seeing it all so clearly now.

'And then, when you got "sassy" about your hair, she took a guess that you'd given your mother some trouble growing up.'

'No.' Carmen shook her head. 'She walked out when I was a baby.'

He offered her a grim smile—the only glimpse of emotion he'd shown since she'd told her little tale.

'She had me at Taurus!'

'Indeed. She could have said the sky was purple and you'd have looked up to check.'

'I hate it that she played me,' Carmen admitted. 'And I hate it that I've eaten all my pancakes and you still haven't touched yours.'

'I don't share,' he said, as her fork hovered over his plate. 'That's why I don't get played.'

Instead, he ordered her some more pancakes.

Brunch after sex was irregular enough, without sharing his pancakes on a Sunday!

'Don't be so hard on yourself,' he told her. 'Grieving is hell.'

'I can't imagine you ever went in for a psychic reading.'

'No,' he agreed, 'but I did talk to my brother a lot in my head, and kept waiting for him to answer.'

'Do you still?'

'Sometimes,' Elias admitted. 'Were you close with your father?'

'Most of the time.' Her breath quivered as she thought of how difficult things had been between them after her mother had come back into their lives. 'We were arguing near the end, but...'

'I'm so sorry.'

'I feel like we're still arguing now. You see, my brothers and I are contesting his will. He's left the family home to my mother, when he always said he'd leave it to me.'

Carmen knew it sounded dreadful, but she did not care

what Elias thought—or perhaps she did, because she suddenly found herself trying to explain.

'They were separated for twenty-five years! She only came back when she found out my father was dying.'

'Do you *want* to contest it?'

'My brothers want to. It's all tied up with the—'

'Deli?'

'Yes. The deli.' She looked away as she said it.

'What do you want to do?'

'I want to believe her.'

'I meant about the house.'

He was too logical for words, and Carmen just shrugged. 'I came here to figure all that out. I thought I wanted a break from riding.'

'Your mother?' he asked. 'Did she ever come and watch you ride, or…?'

Elias was trying to gauge just how little contact there had been between Carmen and her mother. It was none of his business, Elias kept telling himself, but with so many rules broken already, what was another one?

'No,' she said, shaking her head. 'I wish she had. My father and my brothers tried to come for the important events, though.'

'You're close?'

'Mainly with Alejandro. We talk most days…'

'So I've seen.'

'I certainly gave *them* a lot of trouble when I was growing up.'

She launched into what she clearly thought was a funny story.

'One time I was told off by the riding instructor. He suggested, in front of everyone, that perhaps I needed *un sostén*. You know…a bra.'

'Oh?'

'I said, "I thought you were focusing on my riding position!" But really I was so embarrassed. I called Sebastián and I made him go out and buy me a bra!' She gave a little laugh. 'It was not the right one for an eleven-year-old. He didn't know there was such a thing as a sports bra, or about different sizes…'

Elias didn't laugh. He could barely stretch his lips into a smile.

'I wanted her to be there…' Carmen didn't seem to know how to explain her own confusion. 'And yet now she *is*…'

'You hadn't seen her in all that time?'

'No,' Carmen said, and then swallowed.

He got the sense that that wasn't quite true.

'A couple of times…'

Her face was bright red. Elias could almost feel the heat from her blush.

'I'd skipped school. Maths,' she added, as if that explained everything. 'I thought Papá was at work, but I could hear sounds coming from his bedroom. I was honestly pleased, because I wanted my father to meet someone, so he wouldn't be so lonely, but then *she* came out of the bedroom, wearing his robe.'

'Did she see you?'

'Yes. She didn't even seem startled when she saw me.'

'Did she say anything?'

'No.' Carmen shook her head. 'She just gave me this strange smile—I don't even know if it *was* a smile, or just a smug expression…like she'd won something.'

Oh, Elias knew that kind of black smile. He had been the recipient of it many times from Joel's widow, Seraphina. But to get it from your own mother…

He might not be one for sharing plates, or holding hands in public, but in this instance, Elias made an exception.

He reached over and took her hands across the table. 'I get it.'

'Believe me, you don't.'

Elias didn't correct her. He knew she was partially right— because he didn't know her family, or all that had gone on.

'You didn't tell your father you'd seen her?'

Carmen shook her head. 'Nor my brothers. Though maybe I should have. Perhaps they were long-time lovers…' She rolled her eyes. 'If they were, it will all come out in court. Maybe I should tell them, so they are prepared for it?'

'Well, given you're so vocal to them about their wives,' he teased gently, 'why don't you?'

'Can we not talk about this any more, please?' Carmen said abruptly, and removed her hands.

Elias knew that that encounter with her mother was what had really hurt her.

It was the reason that this incredible, open, confident, beautiful young woman had closed off a part of herself.

Usually Elias resisted deep conversations like this, because they created expectations that he had no intention of meeting.

But, Elias acknowledged, there was a responsibility that came with what had happened last night, and he'd felt her pain when she'd sobbed in his arms on the pier.

There was something about Carmen that meant he couldn't just walk away.

Elias signalled the waiter for the bill.

Carmen instantly regretted breaking contact.

If she could have done it without him noticing, she would honestly have just slipped her hands back between his, but it was far too late.

'I guess that's why I went into the psychic's tent,' Carmen said, unsure if she was trying to resurrect the conversation or just not wanting their time together to end. 'I wanted answers.'

'We don't always get them, Carmen.'

His voice startled her, hauling her out of her introspection. And as she looked over at him she saw again the man she'd first met at that awards night. Not the terse man who'd refused a drink from her tray, nor even the man who'd stood on stage and talked about grief, desperately needing a distraction so he could compose himself. She saw the man who had leaned against the wall of the venue, staring out into the night...

And Carmen wished—how she wished—that they'd still been holding hands. Because the husk in his tone told her that he might need it more than she did.

CHAPTER TWELVE

VENICE BEACH WAS INCREDIBLE. They walked along the vibrant boardwalk and onto the sand, wandering far enough away that the crowds thinned out.

Then they sat watching the roaring waves and the huge jets in the sky.

'That will be me in a few weeks,' Carmen said wistfully.

'Are you looking forward to going back?'

'Yes,' Carmen said. 'And no.'

She didn't need to explain that she had been lucky enough to have seen many beautiful beaches in her life, but had never sat on one and felt like this before, because she knew Elias felt exactly the same way.

There was an undeniable connection.

And for Elias, who hadn't felt even remotely connected to the world for years, and who could only snatch brief moments of stillness when galloping on an untamed horse, it was like a rare gift.

'If we're putting last night down to a one-night stand,' he told her as he lay back on the sand, 'we're still technically within that window…'

'What window?' Carmen asked.

'This one,' he said, and pulled her down by his side.

It was so good to lie there by his side.

'You scared the life out of me on Dom last night,' he admitted.

'I knew what I was doing. But, yes, I agree. It was a little foolish to take him out with no one around.'

'A *little* foolish?' he repeated.

He stroked her hair and she could see the steady thump of his heart in his throat.

'You are an incredible rider,' he told her.

'Can I take Dom out again, then?'

'You can do some basic work with him, so long as someone else is there.'

She pulled a face. 'Some risk-taker you are!'

'Just basic work,' he said again.

The boring stuff, the repetitive stuff, the over and over and over stuff—that was how conversation usually felt for Elias. An effort. But not of late.

'This beach is more comfortable than my mattress,' Carmen told him. 'Why don't you sort out the accommodation in the lodge?'

'I keep hoping my mother might change her mind and take it on.'

'While you're waiting for that, your staff are sleeping on deck rope.'

He smiled ruefully. 'I know I have to sort the lodge out.'

'Do,' Carmen said, standing up for her colleagues while understanding now that he had hoped his mother might take on the task. 'I'm so pleased I came to Malibu,' she told him.

'So am I.'

'I have the most beautiful horse in the world at home.'

'What's his name?'

'*Her* name is Presumir,' Carmen said. 'It means to show off, and she does it very well. She's being looked after by a friend while I'm here, being very spoiled.'

'You miss her.'

It was a statement, not a question.

'I feel like I'm having a heart attack when I think of her,' she admitted. 'But I just needed to get away. We have a saying in Spain: *Huye de las personas que apagan tu sonrisa*—run away from the people who turn off your smile. And since my mother returned, since my father died, I'd stopped smiling.'

'So you *were* running away?'

'Maybe,' Carmen said. 'Or maybe I just needed space to make my own decisions…to know my own mind. My brothers are very decisive, but in this case the decision is mine. I don't know why I'm fighting my mother. She's been so much better lately.'

'You said that growing up there were a *couple* of times you saw her?'

She shook her head.

'You can tell me.'

But he paused then, because he understood her dilemma. Wasn't he torn in just the same way? He was keeping his own truths buried deep inside, and yet he was encouraging her to reveal hers to him.

He marvelled at how connected he felt to Carmen; at how he had felt that way since the first moment he saw her at the awards ceremony. Of all people, she was the one he could open up to, wasn't she? The one who would understand?

I won't tell her everything, Elias assured his brother in his head, *but I need to talk to someone.*

He said out loud to Carmen, 'I know that smile.'

'What smile?'

'The one you said your mother gave you. When you saw her coming out of your father's room.'

'How?'

'Seraphina. My brother's widow. When she gets her way, or gets the reaction she wants…' He shook his head.

'You really don't like her.'

'I really don't,' he confirmed. 'And she's everywhere. If I push too hard for my mother to do the lodge she suggests I use Seraphina, because she has her own business now.'

Elias stared blankly at the clear blue sky and knew his face was dark with anger.

'Now she's married a friend of mine—someone from my old polo team. She'll be at the final, and I swear to God…' He swallowed, unable to continue.

'Have you two ever…?' She trailed off, unable to voice the final words and she sat up.

'Nothing like that.'

The look on Carmen's face told him she wasn't sure she believed him.

'You really can't avoid her?' she asked.

'I try to,' Elias said. 'I'm just saying that I know that smile you described, and the damage a person like that can do.'

'Yes.' Carmen agreed. 'Can't you talk to your mother?'

'I've tried. She's not very good at talking about things. She puts on a front…'

'We all put on a front,' Carmen said. 'I am very lucky to have my brothers, because they know what my mother can be like and we can talk about things. Well, argue about things.'

Elias smiled.

'Talk to your mother,' Carmen said. 'Find out how she is feeling…'

'Maybe. What was the other time you saw your mother?' he asked again, changing the subject.

She lay back down and sighed. 'I went to see her when I was a teenager. I wanted to know about make-up and clothes… maybe get closer to her, you know…?'

'What happened?'

'She said I was demanding and needy.' Carmen let out a breath. 'It's true! I am!' She half laughed. 'If you did date, believe me, you would *not* want to date me.'

'So that was it?'

'Pretty much,' Carmen said. 'And then, years later, my father got ill and she returned. I was terrified for him that she'd change her mind and leave—but, to be fair, she stayed.'

There was a pained and careful balance to her words, Elias thought. Every thought weighed out, considered, analysed.

'They were making love when he died. And since he died she hasn't run off. She's still in the house.'

'Why can't you tell your brothers that she was there that day?' he asked, and he felt her body tense. 'What difference would it make now?'

But she chose not to answer. Instead, she lifted her head and looked at him.

'Do you think people can change?'

'Of course they can,' he said. 'But I would never, ever count on it.'

'What do you mean?'

'I don't believe in second chances. People can change all they like, but it won't affect me. Once I'm done with someone, I'm done.'

'Well, *I* believe in second chances,' Carmen said, and removed herself from his arms and lay back on the beach.

'You've already given her a second chance—'

He halted himself. He had no right to interfere with her decision. He had no stake in this; they weren't close enough for that.

He rolled over and went up on his elbow, so he could look at her as he warned, 'Just be careful how many chances you give…'

'Yes,' she said distractedly, and Elias knew she wasn't listening. 'Just kiss me…'

He was the ultimate distraction. This beautiful, sexy man who kissed her so passionately, so softly. And his tongue tasted of the ocean air they were both breathing.

There was no place nicer than Venice Beach if she could be in his arms. He kissed her as if he were stroking her soul, and she felt at peace.

'More,' Carmen said, because his tongue was sublime.

His leg came over her thighs and she brushed his left shoulder, wishing she'd kissed that dark mole just once…

'Don't tell Laura I went to—'

'Shh…' he said, kissing her neck.

'Don't tell anyone about this day.'

'Do you think for a moment I would?'

His hand was on her waist and his tongue was wet and gently probing. Oh, this man…this man who could charm every secret out of her heart and ease the turmoil in her soul. He was so very, very dangerous.

Carmen shuddered. She knew she had to hold on to her heart, because it would not be safe in this man's hands.

'Not here…' she said, but she was weak from his kiss.

How could she be so turned on just from a kiss? So close to coming? He had truly unleashed something inside her, this dangerous, dangerous man.

He stopped kissing her then, seeming to understand her meaning without her having to say it out loud.

They watched the sunset instead. And, oh, it was spectacular. Yet still nothing compared to the bliss of being held in his arms…

But sunsets were safer.

They don't make you vulnerable, Carmen thought as they headed back to the car.

After one last look at the beach as they drove off, Carmen watched the lights from a jet, glinting in the night sky, soaring away from LA.

Soon that would be her…

All the trouble at home was still there, waiting for her return. And she wanted to be ready to face it… Not giddy in lust with a self-confessed commitment-phobe who had a reputation so bad it rivalled that of her notorious brothers.

She wanted to think and to heal.

Not lose herself in his kisses.

Nor did she want to spoil things by getting too close…

Oh, and she knew she would…

Carmen knew she would fall for his charms. She would adore him, and then—because that was what he so clearly did—he would shatter and break her heart.

And his rejection would be more than she could deal with right now.

It was surely better to end things before she was abandoned.

She wasn't a baby screaming in her cot. She was a woman now.

Elias indicated, turning into the white drive that led up to the ranch house.

'Come in and have a drink?' he said.

'Thank you, but I don't think I should.'

She would be sensible here.

He slowed the car to a stop. 'It's up to you, but I have to see to this lot first, then I'll drop you back at the lodge.'

He nodded his head to the horses who were already making their way over to the fence. As Carmen got out the car and joined him she saw they were far from the prime thoroughbreds she had been dealing with.

Well, one was.

'Who are all these…?' And Carmen smiled as she realised she was meeting the Misfits.

There was fat little miniature pony, a very old donkey, and a beautiful roan whom Elias stroked tenderly.

'Hey,' he said to the handsome horse. 'It's night-time, my old friend…'

She watched as the roan sniffed the air, nuzzling Elias's hand. When he turned towards her she felt a huge lump fill her throat as she saw that he was blind.

'He's not used to me bringing guests this late.'

'Then it would be impolite not to introduce me,' Carmen said, muddled by curiosity and relief as she realised that this was not a place he would have brought any of the women he'd dated.

This really was his haven.

'Homer,' he said to the beautiful roan. 'This is Carmen. When I met her she was pretending to be a waitress, and now she's trying to pass herself off as a stable hand.'

'He's beautiful.'

She looked next at the mini horse, and couldn't quite say the same, because the fat pony had her tongue lolling out on one side of her mouth and eyes that were too far apart.

'What's this one called?'

'Gollum,' he said quietly, and gave a low laugh. 'But to her face we call her Pixie.'

Carmen laughed, but soon it faded away. There was something about seeing his home—the trees and the plants and the Misfits—that reminded Carmen of her own.

'I miss home,' Carmen said as she stroked Homer, wondering what on earth she was doing here when her family was on the other side of the world. Why was she fighting her mother when in truth she had only ever wanted to get closer to her? 'I might head back…'

'To Spain?'

She could tell she had taken him by surprise.

'No! To the lodge.' She laughed. 'But, yes, eventually to Spain.'

'Come in.'

She shook her head, too nervous to glimpse more of his private world. She knew where that would lead.

'No, I have to be up early tomorrow,' Carmen said. 'Today has been lovely, but it's not going to be repeated and I don't want people talking…'

His eyes narrowed just a little. Perhaps he had not been expecting that. She doubted Elias got turned down often.

'I live *and* work with my new friends. We share a house and everything is good—I don't want all that to change.'

'I'm not suggesting you move in!'

'I know,' Carmen said. 'I just don't want to be treated differently by them. And I don't want you to treat me differently at work.'

'I'm barely going to be there this week,' Elias said. 'And why would I treat you differently?'

'Because I'd *expect* you to,' Carmen stated tartly. 'If I was in your bed at night I would not appreciate being ignored the next day. I'd want flowers and dinners and more than you want to give. And how could Blake tell me off if I overslept when I was in your bed? That wouldn't be fair to him. Or to me.'

He looked at her assessingly. Admiringly.

'I'm here in America to make my own way…to work things out… I don't need the distraction of you.'

'Touché,' he said. 'You're okay, though? I mean, after last night, this morning, the pier…'

'I feel better,' she said with a smile. 'I think I overreacted this morning because I felt overwhelmed. I accused you of terrible things…'

'I wish you'd—'

'I know. You wish I'd told you. Thank you for a wonderful day,' Carmen said, 'and a wonderful time last night.' She meant that. 'I don't regret a thing.'

She soon might, though, Carmen knew. If she started to develop real feelings for him.

Hadn't she sworn off even the notion of love? Even dating?

'Night,' she said, and instead of heading to his ranch, where it felt as if her heart was pulling her, she walked across the grounds.

But when she got to the lodge, instead of heading up to her attic room she sat outside in the quiet summer kitchen, thinking about home.

She didn't want to be cynical and mistrusting, like Elias.

Whatever he might say, Carmen believed in second chances, and she desperately, fervently, wanted to believe in love.

Though perhaps not with a playboy...

Decision made, she took out her cell phone and tapped on Maria's name.

'Hola, Mamá,' Carmen said, for the first time since she was a child—not that Maria seemed to notice.

'I am meeting with my lawyer in the morning,' Maria said directly. 'He agrees that you have no right to remove me from the home where I had my babies...where my husband died by my side—'

'Mamá,' Carmen interrupted. 'I'm not going to fight you.' She looked out at the starry night. 'Papá made his wishes clear. He wanted you in Jerez, with your family.' She heard her mother gasp. 'I am going to call Sebastián and tell him to instruct our lawyers to desist.' Carmen took a breath. 'I know things haven't been great between us, but maybe as adults we can do better?'

'Carmen!'

She looked again at the stars, and the beautiful ranch, and thought of Elias and Venice Beach and how cleansed she'd felt having cried. She knew who she was and what she wanted. America had shown her that. No, she thought, Elias had shown her that. It had been absolutely the best night and day of her life.

No regrets...

CHAPTER THIRTEEN

PERHAPS A *TINGE* of regret...

She didn't see him at all on Monday, and that was actually a relief. Carmen didn't know if she could manage not to blush, or light up in his presence. Could she really play it casual?

As well as that, she was fielding irate calls from Sebastián and Alejandro, who clearly thought she had lost her mind.

'It's my decision,' Carmen said. 'I have to listen to my heart.'

'Use your head instead!' Sebastián snapped.

She did not need to be warned, because where Elias was concerned she was frantically trying to do exactly that.

He was a playboy, and he had outright told her he did not want to get involved with anyone...

So why was she regretting not accepting his invitation last night? Why, when she finished early in order to cook dinner for everyone, was she looking towards the ranch and wishing she was there tonight instead?

Why did she droop a little in disappointment when she saw there were no flowers waiting for her...not even a little note pushed under the door?

Anything to show her that their time together had meant something to him too...

But then Maria called, and her heart felt happy. Carmen was confident she was making good decisions in her life, and that made her feel that running away to America had been the best thing she could have done—so much so that she was actually relaxing in her room when Laura came flying through the door.

'We're getting mattresses delivered. Now! You just have to give your permission.'

'Of course!' Carmen nodded, flustered.

'And strip your bed,' Laura said. 'Don't forget to hide anything...' She waggled her eyebrows. 'You know...'

'Like what?'

'Anything you don't want the delivery guys to see!'

Carmen had no idea what she was talking about. Her only concern was getting Laura and the rest of the grooms out of the way before the restaurant delivery arrived...

'Wait a second... I thought you were cooking tonight?' Laura said, pausing before she went down the stairs.

'I'm just about to start,' Carmen replied as she hastily stripped her bed. 'Do I have to do any of the other beds?'

'Of course not.'

The other grooms arrived in dribs and drabs to strip their beds, but finally Carmen had the place to herself—apart from the burly men bringing mattresses...and, better still, new bedlinen for everyone.

Carmen smiled as she peeled the lids off the many boxes of *albondigas* she had ordered, which had just been delivered. She hoped no one would notice the delivery van amidst the confusion of the mattress delivery. She tipped the Spanish meatballs into the huge pot they all used to cook for everyone, then turned the stove to low, and popped the herbed bread into the oven to warm up.

Elias's cell phone number was on the chalkboard, along with Blake's, for any horse emergency. Carmen tried to ignore it, but it kept flashing at her like a beacon.

While the food was warming up she went to peek at her gorgeous new bed, which was now made up with gorgeous sand-coloured linen. It wasn't exactly flowers, or a note pushed under her door, but she knew it was a little message for her all the same.

Dared she listen to her heart and pursue this...just a little?

She took out her phone, afraid of the pitter-patter of her heart as she composed her text.

Now I won't feel like La Princesa y el Guisante

She didn't have time to look up the translation for him because the hungry troops were already coming through the door, so she closed her eyes and hit 'send'.

Don't let me like you too much, she thought. Or rather, she amended, because it was already way too late for that, *Don't let it show...*

It had been a long day in the office...

Elias hadn't been deliberately avoiding Carmen. God knew there was a mountain of work for him to do in the real world. And yet he'd found himself distracted in a boardroom in Century Park, and instead of arguing with his father about the latest project he'd asked his PA to sort out new mattresses for the lodge.

And now, while it should feel good to be home, as he stroked Homer's soft nose he could hear laughter coming from the summer kitchen, and he felt an unfamiliar thump of loneliness in his chest...

He glanced at his messages as he walked to the ranch and stilled when he saw her name.

He had to look up the translation.

The Princess and the Pea...

Pouring himself a drink, he replied.

What did you make for dinner tonight?

He awaited her response.

Albondigas. Spanish meatballs in a flavourful tomato and red wine sauce with crusty herb bread...

He adored how badly she lied...how she practically recited the restaurant's own menu. He knew it was an expensive restaurant that did not normally do deliveries like this.

He wanted to type, Who are you, Carmen?

No, he wanted to head over there and pull up a chair, laugh with them all into the night...

And then bring her back to his bed.

He glanced at his occasional table and the array of pictures there. There was one he would prefer to smash, or turn to the wall, but his family dropped in now and then, and the house-keeper might talk...

He looked at the photograph of his brother, so proud of his radiant bride, and his face hardened.

That was the reason why he should not go over to the lodge and join in.

That was why he should not text Carmen back.

He would never give someone the keys that would let them destroy his family.

Identifying his twin's body had been a life lesson he had not wanted.

But only immediate family could do it.

'I can't,' Seraphina had said.

His father, grey and shaking as he held his wife's hand, had whispered, 'I'll go.'

He'd tried to stand, but his strength had failed him, evidence of the toll taken on him by the death of his son.

'I'll go,' Elias had said, knowing it would be something his father would never get over. 'I'll do it.'

He'd braced himself not to be able to recognise Joel—in truth, he hadn't really recognised his brother since Seraphina had come into his life—but as he'd walked into that room there had been one faint whisper of relief beneath the grim horror.

His brother's face had not been ruined after all.

'It's him.' Elias had formally identified his twin for the re-cord. 'Can I have a moment...?'

'Of course,' someone had said. 'We're just...'

Outside?

Watching behind a screen?

Elias hadn't cared.

It had been devastating.

Rearranging the sheet around his brother was the hardest thing he'd ever done.

He had not been able to protect his brother in life, but he had vowed to protect him in death.

'You won't tell anyone?'

Elias could almost hear his brother's desperate voice as he replayed, as he had a million times, their final conversation.

'Do you even have to ask? I never would...'

A vow between two brothers.

Twins.

Elias knew how proud of his marriage Joel had been. So he'd promised to take his secret to the grave. But sometimes he felt that in doing so he'd dug his own.

With Carmen he'd found himself opening up, and that would never do...

There was no one better at bland, unprovocative responses than Elias.

Sounds great.

CHAPTER FOURTEEN

ELIAS HAD stayed the hell away.

But by Friday he had no real choice but to go into the yard. It was the eve of the final and he didn't want to leave all the preparations to Blake.

But he arrived to find the yard in perfect calm order.

'Where's Dom?' he asked Blake when he returned from the empty stable.

'In the arena with Carmen, the other dark horse,' Blake said. 'She told me she had your permission.'

'Yep.'

'What is she? Some sort of Spanish horse whisperer?'

'Something like that.' Elias shrugged. 'Who knows with Carmen?'

He walked into the arena and took a seat in the stands. Dom was skipping like a kid on his way to school while Carmen stood in the centre. She had on the yard uniform but had made it her own, with the polo shirt knotted under her bust and her scruffy Cuban-heeled boots elongating her legs.

'Do you want a go?' she asked, smiling and looking up. 'I can show you my technique.'

'I'll just watch for now.'

He could watch her all day, Elias realised.

Could he do this? Could he enjoy the little time they had *and* keep the promise he'd made?

'Are you all ready for the final?' Carmen called up to him in the stands.

'Pretty much.' He looked down at her. 'You know there's a ball afterwards...'

'I told you. I hate things like that.'

'Why?'

'I just do.' She tapped Dom on the rear and he crossed the arena on the fly. 'I like staying here with the animals.' She looked up. 'Well, I did last time.'

He laughed, trying and failing not to recall what had happened that night.

'Come to the ball,' he said.

'I don't have ballgown.'

'I can take care of that.'

'I don't need you to dress me up, Elias.' She stared up at him. 'If I were to go to the ball, I would choose my own clothes.'

'Just offering.'

'Well, don't.'

She was the moodiest, most difficult, intriguing woman he'd ever met.

And stunningly direct at times. For now she looked up.

'Don't you think rumours would start flying if you bought me a dress and we danced together?'

'I'll dance with all the stable hands. Well, apart from John...'

She laughed. 'I don't know...' she said, and clicked Dom on.

But a week avoiding her had been too long and seeing her again, Elias could not wait for the possibility of a couple of dances tomorrow night, so he took out his phone and texted her.

Come over tonight...

Carmen read it and laughed and then shook her head. She stood, lips pursed, as he came down the stairs into the arena.

He was in his suit and looked incredible. Always lean, he looked as if he'd lost weight in the last few days, and she guessed he must have been training for the final. But when he moved closer she saw dark shadows under his eyes, and a longing in them that had her swallowing down the lump in her throat.

'Carmen…' He took the rope from her hand and secured Dom, and then moved her to the side, his hands warm on her waist.

'Not here…' she whispered.

'Then come over tonight.'

'Elias,' she prevaricated, 'I don't know if it's such a good idea.'

'I do,' he said. 'You know I said I'd get back to you?'

She frowned.

'About whether I would I have slept with you if I'd known you were a virgin?'

'I think we both know the answer to that.'

'Yes,' he said firmly. 'I would have.'

'You would have run a mile.'

'No,' he shook his head. 'But if I'd known I'd have made love to you properly.'

He made her breath hitch in her chest, and she felt herself light up and shine. He kissed her, and she felt ripples of lust course through her as he stroked his hands over her waist.

'Someone might come…'

'Then let's do this tonight.' He looked right at her. 'A proper first date. You can make paella.'

'I'm not cooking on our date!'

'Okay.' He smiled. 'I'll make paella. Even if we're going nowhere, you deserve better than a quick shag on the office sofa…'

'I loved our "shag" on the office sofa.' Carmen smiled at the new word, but her heart was thumping.

These weeks in Malibu had been so healing to her heart… amongst the happiest she had ever known…

She was starting to find out who she was.

The Carmen without the family fortune behind her and the glittering career.

The Carmen who wasn't abrupt and upfront because she

had Romero name behind her but because she was simply abrupt and upfront.

The Carmen who had never felt comfortable with any man until Elias…

He didn't even know her real name!

She didn't want anything to change. And change it would, Carmen was certain, when she told him about the bodega, the properties, the jet-set lifestyle, the family feuds…

'I don't want to spoil things,' Carmen admitted.

'We're not going to spoil things.'

She looked doubtful.

'One date. We can do things right for one night. Surely?'

'What about tomorrow?'

'A couple of dances with everyone else around—not exactly a date.'

She stared back at him. For the first time in her life, she felt a wobble of excitement at the thought of dressing up for a ball.

She was listening to her heart when she nodded, even while she was lying to herself when she argued that she wasn't playing with fire, nor at risk of falling in love with this man…

'Do I bring wine tonight?'

'Whatever you want. Do you want some time off?'

She frowned.

'To get a dress for the ball…?'

'If you get out your wallet, there's no date tonight,' Carmen warned.

'It's quite an event, Carmen. I would do this for all—'

'Don't say it,' Carmen warned. 'Just don't. I shall see you tonight at…?'

'Seven.'

'Perfect.'

Elias left the arena.

Damn!

Now she had a date tonight, and a ball to get ready for tomorrow, and she'd declined his offer to skip work.

'Dom,' she growled, 'what the hell am I supposed to do?'

She took out her phone, aching for advice.

Anna… Emily… She scrolled past their names.

Maria.

'Hola, Mamá.'

'Carmen! Cómo estás?'

Her mother asked how Carmen was, but didn't wait for her answer.

'I can't talk for long…'

'That's okay. I just wanted to ask… You know those modern flamenco dresses…?'

'I have just taken delivery of one now,' Maria said excitedly. 'It is silver. My designer is a magician. I was about to try it on when you called.'

'Who is your designer?' Carmen asked. 'I might be going to a ball tomorrow and—'

'Carmen, these dresses take weeks to make. And anyway, you don't dance!'

'I might try.' She felt emboldened. 'Emily took it up.'

'Hmm…'

'I don't know what to wear to this ball.'

'Well, with your figure, maybe not a flamenco dress. Those dresses are better on a woman with soft lines…very feminine, you know.'

How did happiness just squeeze out like air from a leaky old balloon whenever her mother was involved?

'You're in LA!' Maria said. 'Go shopping in Beverly Hills.'

'I'm working.'

'You don't *have* to work, Carmen. I must go. I'm very busy. You take care and I shall—'

'We'll speak soon,' Carmen said, but her *mamá* had already gone.

Carmen was tense, but in a very particular way. Her chest felt constricted, and she hadn't felt that in a long time. Not since she'd arrived in America, in fact.

No regrets, she reminded herself. *It was just Mamá's ways. People don't change overnight.*

'How do I get a ballgown in time?' she asked Dom. 'And shoes?'

She thought of her wardrobe full of outfits at home, but there wasn't time. And anyway, she wanted something new, something *red*...

She did not trust her brothers to get this right, nor their wives.

She dialled another number.

'Capitán?' Carmen said to the captain of her brother's beloved yacht. *'Por favor...'*

She might not have wanted a leaving party on the yacht, but Carmen had a favour to ask, and Dante was the only person she knew who could pull it off.

'Is there time?' she asked.

'Leave it with me, Carmen.'

She let out a breath of relief.

Capitán Dante knew exactly how things should be done. *Exactly.*

Carmen had never looked forward to a date the way she did this one.

She ordered flowers, chocolate and wine, with strict instructions for their delivery. Then she spent a long time in the shower, where she shaved her legs carefully, used a whole tube of hand cream on her skin, and then put her head upside down and blasted dry her hair.

From her backpack she took a black slip dress that folded up to little more than the size of a handkerchief, and some flat ballet pumps she'd bought for her waitressing jobs. She had no bra to go with the dress, so she went without, and pulled on the prettiest knickers she had.

'Wow!' Laura said as she came down the very creaky chairs.

'Hey!' said John. 'Where are you going?'

'To meet some guy I've been talking to online,' Carmen smiled. 'Tell me, do American men expect you to split the bill?'

'I wouldn't if *you* showed up!' John said. 'Though I might if it was Laura...'

Laura laughed and threw a shoe at him, and Carmen knew

very well they'd be at it the moment she'd gone—she had the room above Laura, after all.

'Here's my ride,' she said, picking up her bag. 'Don't wait up…'

The poor driver was a bit bemused that Carmen had wanted flowers, chocolate and wine inside the car, and that she wanted to be driven out of the grounds and then back in, this time using the long drive.

She asked him to stop about two-thirds of the way up.

'I have nosey housemates,' she explained, handing him a tip. 'Thank you so much.'

Elias watched her get out of the car. He had no idea how she did it, but she might have been walking into any restaurant in Beverly Hills, ready to be taken straight through to the best table.

Yet still she stopped and gave all the Misfits a treat, and with slavish devotion they accompanied her—on their side of the fence—up the last part of the drive.

Forget *The Princess and the Pea*…he now had on his hands a very sexy Snow White.

Carmen took her time giving the Misfits their treats. She had never needed courage from her friends more.

'I don't want to spoil things,' she said, more to herself than to the oddball trio. 'I have to play it cool and I don't want to get hurt.'

She climbed the wooden steps onto the porch and looked down at stunning mosaic tiling. An intricately carved wooden door had been left ajar, and it was so vast she felt it might belong to a castle.

It opened without her knocking.

'Hey,' Elias said, and she smiled, because that was how he made her feel. He wore dark trousers and a pale linen shirt and he smelt divine—as if two seconds ago he had splashed on cologne. She kissed him on the cheek, because she knew she'd drop her gifts if she met his mouth.

'For you,' Carmen said. 'I don't think men get given enough flowers.'

'True,' Elias said, and looked at the bunch of red roses and carnations. 'Isn't it a bit early for roses?'

'Not for a first date in Spain,' she told him. 'And we love our carnations.'

'Well, thank you. I don't know where the vases are kept…'

'Something smells nice.'

'I told you,' he said. 'I've made paella. Come through.'

'In a moment.'

She stood there, taking it all in for a moment. Carmen had assumed, from the vantage point of the attic, that the ranch building was a couple of storeys high, yet it was actually all on one level, with soaring ceilings, almost cathedral-like, held up by wooden beams.

Carmen was used to luxury, but this was more than indulgence or hedonism. This was both magnificent *and* a home.

Yes, a home.

The distinguished bodega in the heart of the exquisitely private Jerez hacienda she had grown up in was luxurious to the extreme and, despite refurbishments and modernisations, the essence of its glorious past was enshrined in the fabric of the building.

But this…this was absolutely a home, and not even close to what Carmen had expected.

'Un reloj de pie…' she said, gazing up at a grandfather clock that told her it was five minutes after seven.

He led her through to the living area.

And, oh, *how* he lived in it.

The magnificent ocean view was its backdrop, but her eyes were drawn to all that made it his. For despite the huge area there were beautifully defined spaces, and the solid redwood floors were softened with silk rugs. The lighting was subtle, yet she could make out a library, as well as a dining area, and her eyes were drawn to a central sunken lounge, with huge leather sofas and winged chairs.

How she'd love to curl up in that lounge, with its fireplaces so high she would have to stand on tiptoe to reach the carved mantelpieces.

And yet despite its grandeur and size, despite the art on the walls and the silk rugs scattered on the floor, it was his home.

'Your home is beautiful,' she said.

'Thank you.'

She followed him into the lounge and looked at the central log fire. 'It must be wonderful in winter.'

'It is.' He nodded. 'You'll be pleased to know I've finally persuaded my mother to oversee refurbishments at the lodge.'

'How?'

'I had a long conversation with her this week.'

'Oh!' She looked at him. 'I did with mine too. We're no longer arguing.'

'Great,' Elias said unenthusiastically. He took the stopper out of a decanter. 'Do you want a drink?' he asked, and splashed amber fluid into a heavy crystal glass.

Carmen nodded. 'A sherry, please.' And then she added without thinking, 'Romero, if you have it.'

'I'm not a sherry connoisseur,' he said, and walked over to a bar that would not have been out of place in the restaurant at the bodega. 'But I have this?'

He held up a brown bottle. One that would not be welcome in the Romero bodega.

Yikes!

But she nodded and watched as he went to find a glass.

'A wine glass will do, if you don't have the correct—' she started to say, but then halted as he handed her a very small glass…the type the English would use.

If my brothers could only see me now!

'Why are you smiling?' Elias asked.

'I just…' She took a sip of her drink.

Perhaps he saw the slight pull of her lips. 'Not to your liking?'

She shrugged. 'It's adequate,' she said, then realised how rude that must sound. He couldn't know that the mixed blend was like sandpaper to her skilled palate. 'I mean…'

'Carmen, it's fine.' He smiled and took a sip of her drink himself. 'Oh, that's awful.'

He accepted her. Carmen felt it then.

He didn't know her name, but he knew who she was, and he simply accepted her ways. She could not explain what a gift that was.

Unlike the sherry, dinner was incredible.

A candle in the centre of a beautifully laid table made her ask, 'Your housekeeper?'

'Yes,' he said as he pulled out a chair for her and then brought in dinner—a gorgeous paella with the perfect crust at the bottom.

'You made this?' Carmen queried. 'I don't believe it.' She scooped out a mussel. 'It's almost as good as mine.'

'Thank you,' he said, and they drank the delicious Malbec she had brought.

'So…' He looked at her. 'Am I allowed to ask where you're from?'

'Jerez,' Carmen said. 'It's in the south of Spain and it's very beautiful.'

'And you have always loved horses?'

'No,' Carmen admitted. 'I started riding at four, but it was not until I was a teenager that I felt confident. Honestly, I was terrified of them!'

'So did your father want you to ride?'

'No,' she said, scooping up the sauce with crusty bread. 'Did you make this bread as well?'

'I can't take the credit for that.'

She was utterly certain Elias had used the same restaurant as her, but was in no position to say!

'So, he didn't push you to ride?' he asked.

'No. He wanted me to start dance classes.' She took a breath and decided that this she could tell him. 'My father had sent my mother some photos of me—I think I was four—and she called him and said I needed dance lessons because I was fat… or, as my father would say, *cute*. Anyway, I thought she was going to come and teach me flamenco, and I was so excited. But, no. She wanted me to take lessons from someone else. I was so upset that I chopped off my hair and said I wanted to learn to ride instead.'

'But you actually wanted to dance?'

'Maybe I did. I don't know. Sometimes I wonder.'

'You dance with your horses,' he said. 'I know because I've seen you…'

'Yes.'

Carmen nodded and felt a flutter. Because she wanted him to see her perform, to really see what she could do. She wanted to whip out her phone and show him how good she was—but that would surely only spoil things?

'When did you start riding?' she asked him.

'I was about ten,' Elias said. 'Summer camp. Then later I used to go and man the line at polo, working for the team I eventually went on to play for. My old team.'

'You loved it?'

'I did,' he agreed. 'To the great annoyance of my father. He wanted both his sons in the family business. Unfortunately, only one of them really loved it…'

'You don't?'

'There are parts of it I enjoy.' He looked at her. 'I'd like to take more risks, but my father always wants to play it safe. Joel did too.'

'Oh!' Carmen frowned. 'I thought you would be the conservative one?'

'Why?'

'I don't know… I don't think of you as taking a lot of risks.'

'Carmen,' he said, 'that was you, wasn't it? In the office that night we had sex on the couch?'

'I believe it was.' She nodded. 'That wasn't a risk. I was a sure thing.'

She'd made him laugh.

'And do you not think my walking away from a brilliant career to run a polo yard is a bit of a risk?'

'Maybe,' Carmen said. 'Although I would call it following

your heart.' She thought for a moment. 'Do you think your parents resent that it was Joel who died?'

If it had been anyone else asking that question Elias might not have given a polite response, and if it really had been a first date he'd have been calling for the bill. But he was crazy about Carmen, and starting to get her sometimes dark take on life.

'No,' he said calmly. 'My parents were just devastated that they'd lost a son. I've never for a moment thought they'd have preferred it to have been me.' He smiled at her then. 'I do need to talk to my father about work, though.'

'Are you going to leave?'

Ten minutes ago he'd have nodded, but after hearing more about Carmen's mother, Elias knew how lucky he was to have his parents.

He put down his glass. 'I don't know,' he admitted. 'Maybe I can tell him I'm cutting down on some of it. If I could only get rid of that damn scholarship!'

He tapped his forehead in what he had come to think of as *their* gesture—indicating he was fed up to here.

'Win tomorrow, then,' Carmen said. 'Start something you love in Joel's name instead.'

He looked at her and told her the truth. 'You're a brilliant first date.'

'Only because you know you'll get me into bed.'

But not yet. Because tonight they were fixing the world, lying on his couch, eating chocolates, talking about anything and everything, her head in his lap as they listened to music she had never heard before.

'I don't like it.' She shook her head.

'It's romantic…'

She screwed up her nose.

'It is,' he insisted. 'I looked it up especially for tonight.'

'No, it's not.' She took his phone and found something else. '*That's* romantic.'

'Carmen!' He looked at her selection. 'That's a brass band!'

'It's perfect.'

She closed her eyes and Elias knew then that he was in serious trouble. Because one date wouldn't be enough.

Right now it felt as if a thousand wouldn't be enough.

Carmen felt his hand on her face and the music stroking her soul. She never wanted this perfect night to end…

He touched her shoulder, and through the silk slip dress he stroked one breast, till she ached for him to touch the other. But instead she felt the heat of his palm on her stomach, and then the ache of his fingers tracing light circles.

She knew when he lifted the hem of her dress that he was watching her.

'Don't stop,' she said.

'Shh…' he told her, and she felt his fingers slip inside her knickers.

'Take them off,' she told him.

'Quiet,' he said.

And she screwed her eyes closed as his skilled finger slid down and in, knowing just where to touch.

She wanted to call out, but she bit down on her lip, because it felt as if he was drawing invisible threads from her thighs, to her stomach, right up to her breasts.

'If I'd known it was your first time,' Elias said, and she felt his fingers sliding in and out, in and out, 'I'd have done this…'

She was raising her hips to meet his palm.

'With no kiss?' she accused, and opened her eyes. She stared at him for a moment, but then she closed them again to the bliss he delivered, till the thread was pulled so tight that she lifted her hips to a flood of warmth. She knew he watched her as she came against his palm.

'Bed,' he said, and tipped her off the couch.

He led her on shaky legs to places unknown. He could have led her off a cliff and she'd have gone, but instead she got the treat of seeing the master bedroom, with low lights and curtains drawn against the night. Even the bed was turned back.

'Housekeeper?' Carmen asked, as he took off her dress and removed her knickers.

'*I* got the bedroom ready,' he informed her and she felt her throat constrict as he took off his heavy watch and placed it bedside, then he started to unbutton his shirt.

'Let me,' Carmen said, undoing the annoying buttons and sliding the shirt down his arms.

Finally she touched the mole on his shoulder, and his flat nipples, and she breathed against his chest just to inhale him.

Elias dealt with the rest of his clothes as she explored him with her hands, and when they were naked together for the first time it felt as if a wrong had just been made right.

'I should have kissed you like this,' Elias said, and his mouth met hers.

He kissed her on the lips, so measured and so deliciously slow that she felt as if she might cry…for she'd had never dared imagine that the severe man she'd first met could be so tender.

He took her to the bed, nudging her there with his body, and she held on to his neck even as he lowered her down.

She had to touch his body, to feel his shoulders, his back… She whimpered into his mouth as he gave her his tongue, parting her legs, needing more, needing him, needing *this*…

'If I'd known…' he said, and he entered her so slowly it made her cry out at the exquisite bliss of him squeezing into her.

She closed her eyes to the sound of his breath in her ear, but then he lifted his head.

'Look at me…'

She was too nervous to look at him. Because she knew now that she had loved him on sight, and she no longer knew how to deny it.

'You don't have to hide here…' he said.

Oh, but she did. Because with each deep thrust she felt as if he were approaching her dangerous truth, and she feared she might blurt out that she loved him, wanted him, and did not know how to keep her promise to herself to be the first to leave.

But there was no place to hide as he shifted her legs higher, and she moaned in pleasure at the new sensations Elias gave her as he moved deep within her.

'Slowly…' she begged, and yet he was taking her faster.

She'd wanted to retain some semblance of control, because she was losing it now. She wanted promises and for ever and for this never to end…

They were way beyond *slowly*.

Her hands dug into his buttocks, every thrust a jolt of pure pleasure as she wrestled with herself, angry at her own devotion. She almost laughed, because his rapid strokes were setting her alight. She was playing with fire and she liked being this close to the flames.

She was the risk-taker, Carmen knew, because she was gambling with her heart.

'Carmen…'

She heard the call of her name and clenched her teeth, maybe to halt her own verbal response, or maybe in ecstasy.

She knew not.

Then she heard his loud, breathy shout and she gave in…just let her body sink into the deep pleasure of intimate pulses as he shot inside her…just caved in, moaning unformed thoughts that he'd somehow dragged out of her.

'No me dejes ir,' Carmen pleaded as he stroked those last drops of pure pleasure into her, and she felt every last flicker before he collapsed on top of her.

She closed her eyes and tried to remember again how to breathe.

Elias lay there. He knew he was by far too heavy for her, but for now he was unwilling or unable to move.

He was not quite ready to return to the soft lights and the bedroom he'd thought he knew, because the world felt rearranged. The grandfather clock was chiming that it was two in the morning, and he felt as if he didn't quite know where they'd just been.

Then he felt her wriggle beneath him, and he rolled off her, still catching his breath—or was it his thoughts? Because he knew he wanted more brass bands and odd conversations in his life.

'Can I tell you something?' she said.

'Yes.'

'Never to be repeated.'

'Agreed.' He was ready, in this moment, to hear anything.

'Every morning I hear John and Laura having sex…'

He gave a low laugh.

'It's my alarm clock,' Carmen said. 'It's all very…' She turned and looked at him. 'I wouldn't like to be in the room above us.'

'Better than the room below,' he said. 'Where do they all think you are tonight?'

'I said that I'd met some guy online.' She told him about the car, and the flowers, and all her efforts to hide where she was really going.

'You really don't want this getting out?'

It was a first for him to be with a woman who wasn't looking for more from him than he wanted to give.

'I don't,' Carmen told him. 'I don't want to change things at work or complicate things for us…'

That much was certainly true.

He still didn't even know her real name.

And even if he somehow understood her reasons for lying, how long till he got bored with her needy, demanding ways?

Carmen lay there, replaying how she had begged as she orgasmed, and took a moment to be grateful that she'd been pleading in Spanish.

'No me dejes ir.'

Don't let me go.

Who said that on a first date?

Or second, or third…?

Surely it was better to leave than to watch it all fizzle out?

'Carmen?' he said, and she turned and faced him.

They stared at each other in a way Carmen did not recognise. It wasn't invasive. It wasn't even questioning. It was, Carmen thought, more complex than that. She'd caught the eyes of competitors before, as they tried to size each other up, though this didn't quite compare...

She had never held a gaze more readily—even if she was unsure of its meaning.

They were gauging each other, Carmen realised, staring as one might into a glassy ocean and trying to fathom its depth.

'What?' she asked to the demand of his eyes.

'I was thinking...'

Carmen dared not hope, because her starving heart might devour this precious moment and misinterpret it as love.

'Why don't I take a couple of weeks off work?' he said. 'After the final.'

'For...?'

'To spend some time together?'

Carmen swallowed. 'What would we do?'

'Find orange sea glass... Have a lot of sex...'

He smiled that slow smile that made her stomach turn over on itself and she knew her heart was screaming for her to say yes.

But her head was yelling its familiar warning.

Do not love him.

The prospect truly terrified her.

'You should get some sleep,' Carmen said. 'You've got a big match today!'

'I'm glad you'll be there this time.'

'I can't wait,' she admitted.

She lay there, awake in his arms, listening to the thump of his sleeping heart, and she desperately wanted to take this chance, to follow her heart...

It had worked with her *mamá*, hadn't it? Taking a risk that someone could change?

Carmen got up and padded out of his bedroom, picking up a towel from the bathroom and wrapping it around herself. She poured herself a glass of icy water from his fridge and walked to the French windows to look at the view.

She moved to place her glass on an occasional table. It was filled with photos, and she picked up one of Elias and a boy who surely must be his brother. Two little boys…one blond and smiling, one dark and scowling…

Carmen smiled when she thought of his wry laugh when he'd told her they weren't identical in any way.

She picked up another picture, an old black-and-white photo of a distinguished-looking man who looked like Elias would maybe thirty years from now. And there went her greedy heart. Because she was *already* thinking of the future, and how she wanted to be part of those thirty years in between…

Stop! Carmen told herself.

And then she picked up another photo and looked at Joel, smiling and proud on his wedding day, and Elias, presumably his best man.

He must miss him so much…

Then her eyes fell on the bride. Seraphina. She'd looked absolutely beautiful on her wedding day, with smiling blue eyes. Carmen saw that the picture was moving. Her hand was shaking as she found out that his secret was possibly bigger than her own.

Seraphina was the woman he'd been speaking to on that first night.

The woman he'd told to go to hell.

It had been Seraphina telling him how much she missed him…

She hastily put the photo down, her head spinning, desperate not to think the worst. But as she went back to the bedroom and dressed quickly and quietly in the dark she knew it was too late for that.

His loathing for his late brother's wife and Laura's comments suddenly made more sense now…

Seraphina had been there at the lodge when he'd suddenly left for a hotel…

'Where are you going?' he asked sleepily.

'I have to be up in a couple of hours.' She was surprised at how normal her voice sounded. 'Go back to sleep.'

'Think about what I said.'

He caught her hand and pulled her in for a kiss, but Carmen pulled back.

'I have to go.'

She left, feeling dazed. His brother's *wife*?

She kept looking for explanations—kinder ones, nicer ones—but her mind couldn't find one that would fit...

She'd been about to hand over her heart to a man who'd had an affair with his own brother's wife.

And then she saw three missed calls from her own brothers, and several messages.

She called Alejandro.

'Hola,' she said. 'How is Josefa?'

'Noisy,' he said. 'Have you spoken to Sebastián?'

'No, why?' Instantly her guard was up. 'Is there something wrong?'

'Nothing's wrong,' Alejandro said. 'Well...' He paused for a moment. 'Maria called Sebastián.'

'And?'

'Carmen...she's gone. Owning the property is apparently too much of a commitment while she's on tour.'

Even though she knew her brother was speaking, it felt as the sound had been sucked from the air and she barely made out his words...just snatched little pieces of his conversation.

'Maria wants her name to remain on the sherry label, and in return she will gift you your home.'

'What do you mean, she will "gift" me my home?'

Her voice was angry, mocking, and yet she could feel the sting of tears. It felt like acid raining down on her cheeks and it had nothing to do with money.

'Carmen...' Alejandro tried to comfort her. 'Perhaps she knows we're right and that it's rightfully yours.'

'Please don't.'

She stared out at the night and knew her mother's version of the story was one so many would believe—she was making a generous and magnanimous gesture, letting her daughter have the family home...

No. She'd left. Again.

It hurt no less that in her heart of hearts Carmen had always known she would.

'Are you there?' Alejandro asked.

'Yes.' She looked up at the stars. 'Is Sebastián cross?'

'Not with you. He's worried. He'll call soon and talk through your options.'

'What options?'

'You love the hacienda, the stables…' He paused.

'It was never about that.'

'I know. We miss you, Carmen.'

'I miss you all too.'

'Come home,' Alejandro said.

Right now, they were the only words that made sense.

'Carmen?' Alejandro said, and she turned and looked back at the ranch, and the man she had thought she might dare to trust. 'Carmen?' he said again, with concern.

'I'm fine,' Carmen told him. 'I'm just never listening to my heart again.'

CHAPTER FIFTEEN

'READY FOR THE FINAL?' Blake asked when she walked into his office just a couple of hours after she had decided her heart was closed for ever.

He was updating the huge screen with all the feeds and medications.

'Blake,' Carmen said, 'could I have a word?'

'Of course.' He turned, and then blanched when he saw her red eyes. 'What's wrong?'

'It's a private matter.' She took a breath. 'I hate to let you down... I know I said I'd be here for longer, but...'

'You're leaving?' He frowned. 'Carmen?'

'I can work today...but then I have to go.'

'Don't worry about that for now. Is there anything I can do?' She shook her head.

'Can I help in anyway?'

'No,' Carmen said. 'Actually, yes. Can I stay back today? I don't want to come to the match.'

She wanted to say goodbye to the horses...especially to Capricorn and Dom.

'Whatever suits you. I'll make a few calls.' He looked at her. 'Carmen...'

'Blake, please.' She didn't want his concern. It might crack her open to show weakness now. 'I'm just a casual and I can leave without reason.'

'Sure,' he said. 'Of course. I just hope you're okay. The guys will want to say goodbye.'

'Please...' She shook her head. 'I don't want any fuss.'

He agreed, and she went to start her chores for the day.

Blake might be willing to let her go without giving a reason, but she knew Elias wouldn't. She was carrying hay when she heard the ring of his boots and the anger in his stride. She just spread the fresh hay.

'What the hell?' he said, confronting her. 'You're leaving?'

'Yes.'

'And you told Blake and not me?'

'Blake hired me.' Carmen shrugged. 'I don't believe you generally deal with the hiring of junior staff.'

'Carmen!' He took the hay from her and tossed it down. 'Were you going to say anything to me?'

She didn't answer.

'Carmen?' he demanded.

'No.' She shrugged, as if it mattered little. 'I assumed you'd hear. And anyway, we always knew it was a temporary job…'

'I don't get it.'

'Elias, we've had sex a couple of times and that's it. Am I supposed to come to you and give a detailed explanation about why I'm leaving? Do you discard all your women so thoughtfully? Do you give them written warning that you are about to—?'

'Carmen!' He shook his finger at her. 'This has nothing to do with other women and everything to do with us.'

She took in a long breath through her nostrils and looked at the finger he pointed at her. There was a part of her that admired him for coming to confront her.

Her father… Well, he had always just sighed wearily and given in.

And her brothers accepted her demanding ways and simply rolled their eyes.

But here Elias stood, refusing to let her divert the issue.

'I know we're not in a relationship,' he started. 'But—'

'We're not,' Carmen interrupted. 'I don't have to report to you.'

He stared at her for a long moment, to black eyes that had

clearly been crying, yet refused to meet his, then lowered his hand to his side, the fight almost leaving him.

Usually he would shrug and walk away. Or rather, usually it wouldn't have even gone this far.

She was leaving.

So what?

Yet in *this* case it mattered.

And, despite her clear defiance, he saw there was turmoil in her eyes.

'Why?' he said. 'Why would you leave now?'

I'm leaving before you lie to my face! Before you hurt me! she wanted to shout. *Before you change your mind and decide I am too much trouble, too much work, or simply tire of me!*

'I have to go.' She went to push past him, but he caught her wrist. 'And so do you. You have your match to get to.'

'I cannot believe you'd do this today.'

She was shaking inside, and feeling so conflicted.

'I'm not your lucky charm, Elias.'

He took her chin and lifted her head, but she would not look at him.

'What the hell happened between me falling asleep and you leaving?'

She looked right at him then, her top lip curling in distaste and then said, 'Take Wanda to the match.' She narrowed her eyes. 'She can be your human shield to protect you from your late brother's *wife.*'

'Nice,' Elias said, and he removed his hand but not his gaze. 'You could have just asked me about it.'

He was icily calm, but his breathing was short and fast and she could tell she'd really hurt him.

'Keep your secrets, Carmen, if they're so important. Carmen from the south of Spain. Carmen the stable hand. Carmen who runs away instead of talking.'

He stalked off, and she watched his back as he went.

CHAPTER SIXTEEN

CARMEN HATED THAT ROW.

Hated every word she'd said.

So much so that when she had the yard to herself she was sick.

'Oh, God,' she said as she threw up.

And as she clung to the toilet she knew, without a doubt, that he would never have done the same thing to her on a day like today. The Elias Henley she knew would have wished her good luck and quietly dumped her afterwards.

'Hello?'

A casual worker had shown up at the yard, because of course he had been booked so that she could attend the match today.

It was perhaps just as well, Carmen thought, her heart hammering as she packed up her backpack, because she couldn't bear to say goodbye to the horses.

All she wanted to do was leave.

Run away.

Only, she'd run away to here.

To the happiest place she'd known. And now she had so badly messed up that she felt as if there was no place left in the world to run.

Carmen wanted to call Maria, to hurl her rage at the person who really deserved it, but she was out of emotion for her mother today.

Oh, what had she done?

On the morning of the grand final. A match he had wanted to win for his late brother...

She thought about her own preparations before a big event, how she had to have the right boots, the right scarf, the right brush for Presumir...

She could never make that row right. Carmen knew that. But she had to at the very least apologise.

'Good luck,' said Elias's father, shaking his hand. 'Proud of you.'

'We haven't won yet...'

'I'm proud of you whatever the result today.'

'Thank you,' Elias said.

'You're very pale,' observed his mother.

'It's the grand final, Mom.'

Elias could not give a damn about the grand final.

He wasn't angry, he wasn't shaken—he just knew he was in the wrong place.

Carmen was no doubt packing that backpack and heading to LAX, and he was about to play a silly game while she was leaving him.

All the molecules and atoms in his world felt misaligned: the immaculate green grass was too vivid, the world not quite right without Carmen here.

Laura was missing her too, and obviously sulking. 'Carmen would be much faster. Why did Blake let her stay behind? She should be here.'

'Well, she's not,' Elias said, and mounted Winnie, who was so full of energy that he possibly *could* ride her to Vegas...

Their names were being called over the speakers.

'You've got this,' Blake said, as he always did before a match.

'Good luck!' Laura stopped sulking long enough to give him her best wishes.

'Buena suerte!'

He heard her voice and turned to see Carmen, smart in her uniform, her hair in a ponytail. But her face was grey. She was patting Winnie's neck, and although she was looking towards him, she did not look directly at him.

'Thank you.'

I'm so sorry, she mouthed.

But he said nothing, just gave a very brief nod.

And then John caught sight of her.

'Carmen, thank God you're here!' he shouted.

It was the craziest, most dangerous game she had ever seen, and so fast that her head was spinning. She watched them deliberately crashing into each other, and it was hard to make sense of it when her career was one of perfect formations, with beautiful dancing horses…

'I thought it was seven and a half minutes?' she said.

'Plus fouls,' Laura said.

She saw Elias and three others go from standing still into a full gallop, and she felt electricity shoot down her neck…

Far from being a good luck charm, it seemed she had only made things worse. They were one chukka down as Elias jumped off Winnie and changed horses.

'Elias is off his game,' John said, cursing. 'What's going on?'

Elias's team were still down at half-time, but there was barely time for Carmen to register it and not a moment to breathe. There were legs to be unstrapped, tails and manes to be un-braided, and horses to be cooled down.

It was the most incredible, exhilarating game, and she could barely take it in. The crowd was cheering, hooves were thundering, and Carmen could not believe she had ever asked to stay away from seeing this game.

Because she absolutely loved it.

And him.

But there was just no time to worry about her heart, because the opposition had scored again and John declared the match lost.

'It's over… They can't come back from this.'

'Misery!' Laura exclaimed.

There wasn't any time to feel—not for Carmen, as she prepared Winnie for the final chukka. And then Winnie did what horses sometimes did when you were bandaging their back legs and messing with their tails...

'Carmen!' Laura shrieked, and turned the hose on her to wash off the worst of it.

But there really wasn't time to care. And Carmen, who had thought she would never smile again, and certainly not today, found that she was laughing.

'Good God!' Elias said when he saw her.

'I probably deserved it,' Carmen said, and he gave her a brief flicker of a smile.

And then it was all about the match.

'Come on!' John was shouting.

And the line was barely being manned any more. Duties were suspended as they stood cheering on the team, and Carmen watched as Elias charged through the opposition and smashed it.

Carmen started whooping, as she would have done at home.

'They're going to do it!' Laura was calling out. 'Come on, Elias! Go, *go*!'

John was shouting too. 'Go! I think he might... It looks like they might... Yay!'

Then a siren went off.

'They've won!'

Carmen's heart was in her mouth, because it was the most exciting thing she'd ever witnessed. But, oh, it was bittersweet too. Because everyone was so happy, clapping him and supporting him... And Carmen would never forgive herself for throwing him off his game with her personal dramas.

So she put her head down and worked hard with the rest of the staff to rub down the horses and prepare them for transport back to the stable.

And then it was the prizegiving ceremony, and Elias went up to receive the trophy.

'Thank you,' he said in his speech, 'to everyone.'

They all got a mention—his team mates, Blake and his wonderful grooms. But even though he glanced over, he did not look at her.

'Why don't I get a proper mention?' Laura grumbled. 'I'm head groom.'

'And thank you to my parents…' Elias paused for a moment, then, 'We're going to be starting a new venture,' he explained.

He kept it brief, because this was clearly not the right time to announce the launch of something new, and although he did not outright say that the scholarship was being dropped, it was clear that this was implied.

As he spoke, Carmen looked over and saw Seraphina's tight lips. She knew she'd been told.

'My incredible head groom used to teach riding for young people facing challenges…' everyone clapped Laura '…so I'm sure she'll have a lot of ideas, which we'll be discussing. But we want the yard to honour Joel.' He lifted up the trophy. 'This is for my brother. For Joel.'

Vincent was gallant in defeat. 'Congratulations, Elias. I thought we had you, but we'll have to come back fighting next year to challenge you. The win is well deserved, my friend.'

'Wonderful…congratulations.' Seraphina smiled and kissed Elias's cheek, and then turned to greet his mother.

'Eleanor…'

It was no surprise to Elias when she chose this moment to do the most damage.

'We wanted to tell you in person—'

She was about to share the news of her pregnancy, he knew, and Elias had never been more proud of his mother—because she got there first.

'I hear you two are the ones who deserve congratulating!' Eleanor smiled. 'Wonderful news. Congratulations.'

He had found a quiet moment earlier that morning to prepare his mother, and he had also discussed winding down the scholarship fund and starting something new instead. Better to get it all over in one go, he had thought.

Everything was all kisses again, and Elias looked away—to discover that there was no Carmen in sight.

'We're thrilled.' Vincent was clearly delighted at the prosepct of being a father.

'Are you going to ask Elias?' Seraphina prompted him, but then she did it herself. 'Elias, Vincent and I—'

'I hope you're not about to ask me to be godfather,' Elias interrupted. 'I'm far too irresponsible!'

There was a moment's awkwardness, but it was worth the trade, because he saw the rapid blink of relief in his mother's eyes. He was so grateful that Carmen had pushed him to open that door. He could see now that perhaps the strain had been upon her too, and he wished they had spoken about it earlier to save them both some agony.

'Right,' his father said, 'let's head to the hotel. We'll follow you, Elias.'

'I'll meet you there,' Elias said. 'I've got some things to take care of first.'

He found her on the beach back at the stables. She was sitting with her chin on her knees, her face brown from the dust and from Winnie's little gift, and streaked from crying…

'We seem to do better on the beach,' he said.

She gave him a thin smile. 'We do.' Carmen took a breath. 'I would like to apologise.'

'Thank you.'

'Congratulations,' she offered, but he didn't respond. 'They are all fighting for the shower and getting ready for the ball.' She furrowed her brow. 'I thought you were heading straight to the hotel?'

'I was, but now I'm here.'

'I should have told you myself that I was leaving.'

'Have you booked your flight?'

She didn't answer.

'Fine. You don't have to tell me anything.' He shrugged. 'That was the deal we made.'

'You were right about me not giving my mother any more chances. She's gone, of course.'

'So why are *you* leaving?'

'Because of this morning…'

'Come off it, Carmen. You booked your flight before that row. Talk to me,' he said. 'I'm not leaving you like this.'

'I'm hardly going to go to the ball now!'

'Not if you really don't want to, but you can come to the hotel.' He was being practical. 'You can take a bath, have something to eat—just don't be here on your own tonight.'

'You're very kind, but—'

'Actually, I'm not a very kind person,' Elias corrected. 'I have no issue in not going. They can go ahead without me.'

'But it's your team. Your friends and family.'

'Then come to the hotel. You don't have to see anyone.' He wasn't moving. 'All right, we'll just sit here instead.'

And he was more stubborn even than she, because he ignored his buzzing phone.

'Can I ask you one thing?' he said. 'You don't have to answer, but can I at least ask?'

'I saw Seraphina in their wedding photo.'

Carmen seemed certain that was what he wanted to know.

'I recognised her from the awards ceremony.'

'I'm not asking about her—or that. Why won't you tell your brothers that you saw your mother that day? You tell them what you think about their wives…you tell me what you've decided I've done… You say you can talk to them about everything, why not that?'

'Because I'm ashamed!'

'Why?' He didn't get it. 'Because you heard them having sex?'

'No!' She covered her face. 'Nothing like that.'

'Then what?' His voice was hoarse. 'Carmen?'

'She came home for sex. She came home for her husband. But she didn't come for *me*. Not once. Only for Papá…for sex. She didn't love me even that much.' She held up her thumb and finger. 'I hate her.'

'You love her.'

'Both,' Carmen admitted, and started to cry.

'Come with me.' He stood and lifted her into his arms and held her. She didn't resist.

'I have to get my clothes…'

'And your passport,' he added drily. 'Carmen, I'll drive you to the airport myself, if that's what you want, but I'm not leaving you here upset like this.'

They walked back to the lodge, and for once it was fragrant, with all the soap and perfume in the air, but everyone had already headed off.

'I shan't be long…' she told him.

She went up to the little attic, where her backpack was already packed, and saw there was a large box sitting on her bed.

Carmen Romero
From Capitán Dante

'Ready?' Elias asked.

'Yes.'

He'd already guessed she was leaving, but he knew for sure as they drove down the long driveway.

She couldn't look at Homer sniffing the air… Nor at Pixie, with her short, fat legs trying to catch up with the car.

'I'll just stop and let—'

'Please don't.'

She couldn't bear to say goodbye, Elias realised.

From the basement car park at the hotel they were whisked up by a private elevator to his suite, and he wondered just who she was back home in Spain. Because she had a grubby backpack and also a big, fancy box. She was filthy, and yet as they stepped into the penthouse she managed to smile confidently at the butler.

'Can I get you anything, ma'am?' he said.

'A sherry, please.'

'I'll sort it,' Elias said. 'Could you excuse us?'

A maid came out then, and announced, 'The bath is drawn, ma'am.'

'*Gracias,*' Carmen said with a smile, but when they were alone she rolled her eyes. 'Why do they assume it's for me?'

'It *is* for you!' He was on his cell phone and firing off texts. 'I might only have time to brush my teeth…'

'Elias, you smell too,' Carmen said, but not unkindly as her ex once had.

'I know. Go and have your bath and I'll be in soon.'

'I'll wait till you're gone.'

'Up to you.'

Only, Carmen ached, and she was so filthy that when she headed into the bathroom she peeled off her clothes and climbed into the lovely, soapy water. She knew she was a coward for not telling him that she would be flying home *tonight*. But she had never learned how to say goodbye, and she still didn't know how.

To people.

Or to horses.

But especially to him.

Elias's phone was lit up like a Christmas tree, but he made only a few quick calls as he sorted out his suit.

He glanced again at the backpack and the box…

Carmen Romero

So that was her name, was it?

He poured her a drink, and now he saw it was Carmen's phone that flashed a message, inviting her to check in for her flight.

Her flight *tonight*.

First class!

Well, that explained a few things…

'Here.' Elias came in with a bottle and a proper sherry glass. 'That sherry you like.'

'Oh!'

'Is it adequate?' he quipped.

'Perfect,' she said, and then blushed. 'You saw my name

on the box.' She turned the bottle so the image of her mother faced away. 'My full name is Carmen Romero de Luca.'

'And the bodega's not a little corner deli, I take it?'

'No…' She gave a soft laugh. 'That is my mother on the label.' She watched him glance towards the bottle. 'She would like to remain there. My oldest brother disagrees.' She shrugged. 'That's the next legal battle.'

'Yikes…'

'And then we shall have nothing left to fight over.'

'Oh, there'll be something. There's always something.' He looked over at her, naked in the bath. 'I'm going to tell you something that I swore I never would tell a soul. I made the promise to my brother when I identified his body—'

'Please don't break your promise because of me.'

'I want to,' he admitted. 'I trust you.'

'How can you after this morning? And when I've only just told you my real name? I haven't been honest all along…'

'You haven't lied, Carmen, you just haven't opened up.' Elias paused and looked at her again, lying stretched out in the bath, and then he amended that. 'Fully.'

Carmen wasn't sure she was up to any confessions right now. She didn't think she'd be able to say the right thing. But then she looked at the trouble swirling in his velvet brown eyes. Even if what Elias told her wasn't what she wanted to hear, the very least she could do was listen. She looked at Elias—really looked at him—and knew that it wasn't just about trusting another person, but about trusting yourself also. Trusting that you would do your best, even if faced with something that wasn't what you wanted, because you cared so very much.

'You can tell me.' She gave a small nod.

'Seraphina…' He swallowed and his voice was hoarse. She could see his guilt and his agony.

'Okay…' Carmen said, in a voice that was gentle rather than shaking with fear, even if she was more terrified than when she'd first turned her back on Domitian.

'A couple of weeks before Joel died, she came on to me…'

Carmen actually wanted to stand up, climb out of the bath

and walk away before he revealed what she knew was coming, but she owed it to him not to flinch or show fear…

'I was staying at the lodge, and she was there, measuring up something or other. I didn't even know she was there. I came out of the shower, heading up to the attic, and she was on the stairs…'

Carmen could picture it exactly…knew the squeak of every stair between the bathroom and the little attic bedroom. She lay so still that the water didn't so much as ripple, yet she felt as if she was being pulled into his hell.

'Nothing happened. I pushed her away. I was so shocked, and I might have been a bit rough…'

Carmen felt as if the oxygen masks had fallen down on a plane, but she was too scared to reach for one in case the motion betrayed her terror. Now she was afraid that he'd find out she'd believed the very worst of him.

But, given her cruel words this morning, he already knew that.

'Elias…' She touched his arm. 'I am so sorry for what I said.'

'Carmen, I get it. I would have thought the same. But nothing happened. At first I was so shocked that I couldn't move. She said it had always been me…that Joel would never have to know.' His voice really was hoarse now. 'She was his *wife*. He was my *twin*. I mean…what the actual hell?'

'You didn't tell Joel?'

'Hell, no!' He shook his head, and then he looked at her with eyes that showed he had wrestled with that question all alone for so long. 'Should I have told him?'

'How could you have?' She thought of her brothers in that situation. 'No, you couldn't tell him. Have you told *anyone*?'

'You.'

She heard the single word.

Not, *Just you*.

Just, *You*.

'Joel called me on the night of his accident. He was a mess… crying. He said that since they'd got back from their honeymoon things had changed between him and Seraphina. He was asking for my advice. I just told him to give it time...that marriage couldn't all be a honeymoon. He agreed—he even laughed. He asked me not to tell anyone that he'd had doubts.'

Elias buried his head in his hands.

'I swore I wouldn't. And then...then I heard the accident...'

It felt as if the hot water she lay in had risen to a boil...as if the steam had taken the oxygen from the air as she glimpsed his hell.

Carmen asked the bravest question. '*Was* it an accident?'

'Yes!'

He pulled his head from his hands and looked at her. He nodded, certain.

'I heard it all happen, and when I got there I found out that a truck driver had crossed lanes. It turned out he'd been drifting for a few miles and had fallen asleep. Joel was on his cell phone... Both of them were in the wrong...'

He took the hand that was resting on his arm and toyed with her fingers. He turned her hand over and looked at her palm.

'You have a long lifeline.'

'You don't believe in all that!' Carmen joked, but she knew he was just taking a moment...focusing on the irrelevant for a moment before diving back into hell.

'I made a decision to keep it all to myself,' Elias told her. 'Once it was clear it had been a dreadful accident, I didn't see the benefit in telling anyone the content of our conversation, or about what Seraphina had tried to do.'

'Why?'

'I didn't want to hurt my parents any more than they already were. But mainly for Joel...because he was so proud of his marriage. He loved her... When I went to identify his body, I swore to him that I'd take it to the grave...'

'Some secrets need to be shared,' Carmen said.

'Yes, they do.' He nodded. 'Carmen, I'm not saying this just for me...' He looked at her. 'I'm not unburdening myself out of guilt. I'm telling you this because of what you told me.

Your brothers should know. You have nothing to be ashamed of. It's her shame, not yours.'

'I'm sorry I left you like that.'

'Just try asking me next time.'

'I asked you about Wanda,' she pointed out.

'We weren't together then,' he said. 'Anyway, you've got a first-class ticket out of here, so you don't get to hold that over me.'

'How do you know that?'

'I was going through your phone,' he teased, then gave her a look that told her it was a joke. 'I saw the message flash up.' He stood up. 'I have to get ready for the ball now.'

'I know. Will Seraphina be there?'

'Yep,' he said, stripping off. 'Trying to get a moment alone with me, no doubt.'

'I'd love a moment alone with Seraphina,' Carmen muttered. 'I would finish her.'

'You probably would!' He snorted, smiling.

She watched him turn on the huge shower in the centre of the bathroom, but then he came over and picked up the sherry bottle.

'What are you doing?' she asked.

'Putting your mother outside while I get naked!'

It made her laugh, and she lay watching him stand beneath a cloud of water, soaping his chest, his underarms, and then he looked at her and soaped his stomach…and then lower.

It would be so easy to climb out of the bath and go over and hold his lovely soapy body…

'Thank you for bringing me here with you…'

'Thank you for coming.'

She watched as he brushed his teeth and picked up the brush to soap his face before shaving. And then she was out of the bath and running her fingertips over that mole.

Her hands closed around the shaving brush. 'Let me.'

'I am not letting you shave me!'

She soaped his neck, and a little of his jaw, and then they

sank into toothpaste kisses. She felt her damp body so receptive to his.

'Careful!' he said as she kissed his neck. 'I have to look nice tonight.'

'You always look nice,' Carmen said, kissing his chest and his flat nipples.

Her hands slipped down to the curly hair on his stomach and then she held him.

'Yes…' he groaned.

'You'll be late…'

'Do I look like I care?'

He nudged her legs apart and brushed his fingers over her dark triangle, parting her intimate lips. She'd never seen herself so pink and turned on before.

Carmen held on to the marble counter, and watched as he shifted her bottom right to the edge. She bit down on her lip as he took his time, slowly nudging in.

'More…'

'Just watch,' he told her, and she could not believe she didn't feel shy as they watched together.

When it was time, she looked at him instead, and let him take her to the places only he could, right there, on the marble countertop, pressing into her again and again and again.

And she did not want them to ever end.

'I've got to go,' he said as reluctantly led her through to the bedroom.

'I know.' She lay back on the bed and watched him dress. 'You still have to shave…'

'Too late.'

He was doing up his tie.

'So what else haven't you told me?' he joked as he pulled his jacket on.

'I'm rich…'

'Brilliant.' He smiled. 'What else?'

'I'm a better rider than you.'

'Ha!'

'I can't cook…'

'Neither can I!' He laughed. 'Nothing else?' he checked.

What should she say? Did she dare to tell him she loved him?

'Carmen, I know your flight's at midnight…'

Carmen pressed her lips closed, relieved she hadn't bared her heart…

'So this is goodbye?' he said.

She nodded.

'Here.' He went to the bench and picked up his wallet. 'I was going to give you this later.'

He took out a dark stone and handed it to her.

'Sea glass!'

'*Orange* sea glass!' he said.

'Brown,' Carmen corrected, and then realised how ungrateful that sounded. 'But I love it. I really do…' She fell silent as he turned on the overhead light. 'Oh!'

It really was orange. Well, maybe…at a push. It was a dark, golden orange—a colour her beady eyes had scanned every beach for.

'Do you know how rare this is?'

'Yep.'

'I mean it, Elias. This is seriously rare.'

'Very,' he agreed. 'And so is this chance…'

He took her chin and looked right into her eyes, but if she couldn't quite look back at him.

'Why *are* you leaving tonight, Carmen?'

'I have things to sort out at home.'

'That's an excuse.'

'It's my home,' she attempted, but he would not let her hide. 'I've got a family at home who loves me.' She could hear her own plea for guarantees and hated her desperation. 'If I stay here and we get closer, it will make it harder to leave…'

'It's the same for me.'

'No…'

'Yes.'

He picked up the sherry bottle and looked at the dark-haired woman on the label and the swirl of her orange flamenco dress. He took out his pen...

'Don't!' she warned as he scribbled on it. 'Don't erase her.'

She went to reach for the bottle, angry at his disrespect, but he turned wide shoulders to her.

'That's my *mamá*!'

'I know.' He took a swig of sherry from the bottle and pulled a face. 'You're right. Maybe we could never work. That's dreadful...'

'Hey!' Carmen warned as he grimaced, but then she smiled.

He spoke in Spanish then. '*Huye de las personas que apagan tu sonrisa.* Run away from the people who turn off your smile.'

Carmen frowned, wondering if he'd misunderstood what she'd been trying to say that day...if somehow the translation had been lost.

But no.

'I turn on your smile, Carmen, and you know it. So why would you run away?' he asked, and then he shrugged. 'I might see you later.'

And then he walked out. And the only indication that he was angry was the silence he left behind.

If he loved her, he'd stay, Carmen decided.

But she knew that wasn't fair.

There was a ballroom full of people waiting for him.

She was sick of running away...

And she could not stand for this to be goodbye!

The *capitán* of her brother's yacht was used to demands from his spoilt guests—and Carmen had been one of those on many occasions. And yet there was so much care wrapped up in this package, because he had sent her favourite red velvet dress.

Perhaps he had spoken to her brothers? Or had he relied on a memory?

Also in the package was her eighteenth birthday present from Papá—gorgeous diamond earrings—as well as her twenty-first birthday present—a necklace, also from Papá...

There was nothing, not even a hairpin, from Maria. Not even a card.

There was, though, a card from her sister-in-law Anna…

Capitán Dante asked for some help with the underwear! I remember you taking me shopping once. I hope these are to your taste, Anna x

Carmen laughed, and then looked at the X, the little kiss from her sister-in-law. They'd gone out dancing once, and had got on well, yet Carmen still held back, also with Emily…

There was another package, a small one, containing red lipstick from Emily.

Her favourite, the note said, rather cryptically. And another X.

Were they her family?

She wanted to dress up, to dance, to truly be Carmen Romero…

Carmen blasted her long black hair dry, and then combed it smooth.

Again she was grateful that she always wore gloves when working in the stables. Her nails might not be done, but her hands were always ready to go out, presenting the Romero brand.

She pulled on the brand-new lilac underwear, and then the long dark red gown and high-heeled shoes…

She would be herself tonight.

Her new self.

Usually she loathed all this, but tonight she was shaking with excitement…

Carmen poured another small sherry, to raise a glass to Papá, but then she saw that Elias hadn't been scribbling a moustache or scratching out her mother's eyes. Instead there was some writing on the bottle.

I want to dance with Carmen.

She scanned the label, looking for a little love heart, a clue, even a moustache on her *mamá*.

There was no hate in his words. No ultimatum. No threat. No challenge. No comparison or competition.

Elias Henley wanted to dance with a woman who insisted she didn't want to...

But desperately did.

Carmen looked in the mirror at her rather too tanned shoulders, and possibly too muscular arms, and then she took out the lipstick from her sister-in-law and painted her full lips red.

She picked up her phone to text Seb and tell him she was ready to take things from here, but she didn't want that tonight...

Alejandro, maybe. She would tell him she would not be heeding his warning about a certain playboy...

Then her mind flicked to Maria, to her *mamá*. No, her mother wouldn't be excited for her tonight...

So she started a new group: Carmen, Anna, Emily... And she attached a photo of herself in her velvet gown, her diamonds, and her red lips with their very wide smile.

Allá voy. Deséame suerte!

Then Carmen had a little panic. Because she'd written, *Here goes. Wish me luck!* in Spanish, and they were, of course, both English, and she didn't want them asking her brothers to translate.

But the replies were instant...

Hearts.

Shining eyes.

Kisses and best wishes.

It made her feel braver to know she had them on her side.

Putting down her phone, she took one more breath and looked in the mirror—and there she was.

Carmen.

Who just happened to love Elias—the man who turned on her smile.

And if it didn't work out...?

Instead of running from the thought, she faced it. Faced herself in the mirror.

'You'll survive,' she said aloud.

CHAPTER SEVENTEEN

'WHERE'S WANDA?' asked his mother, when she saw Elias was attending one of these functions for the first time without a date.

'We broke up,' Elias said, offering no more than that.

'Darling…' Eleanor said. 'You didn't say!'

He took a drink and all he could think about was Carmen… that she might right now be in a car on the way to LAX.

He could not understand why Carmen was leaving tonight… how she could walk away from such promise and hope… But his mother was giving him a tiny smile, a supportive smile, and although she was difficult at times, even through hard times Elias knew she had always loved him.

He would never take her for granted.

'I am sorry…' Eleanor sighed. 'How long were you and Wanda…?'

'It's fine.'

'I knew there had to be a reason.' Eleanor sighed again. 'You haven't even shaved…' Then she smiled at him. 'Well done again for today!'

'Thanks.' He looked at his father, and then back to his mother, and knew how lucky he was. 'It means a lot that you're here.'

'Of course,' his father barked, and even though William Henley loathed the way his son's passion had taken him away from the family business, he was still here, supporting him.

Elias went over to join some of his teammates, and right

on cue, Seraphina made her way towards him. 'I just heard about you and Wanda.'

Elias said nothing. Refused to react.

'I thought you'd been a little off lately...'

Seraphina spoke in a little girl's voice at times, and if there was one thing he couldn't abide it was grown women doing that.

'What happened?' she asked.

She put a hand on his arm and Elias wanted to brush her off, or get in some dig about how he'd met someone else, someone with integrity... He wanted to turn and look into her Machiavellian eyes and tell her he'd found love...

But there was someone else who deserved to hear that first. *Needed* to hear that, perhaps.

Of *course* Carmen wanted guarantees, Elias realised—she was terrified to bare her heart.

'Excuse me, but I really need to—'

He was going to leave and to hell with the speeches. If Carmen had left already, then he'd head straight to LAX.

But even as his decision was made there was a stir in the room...

'Look at you!'

He heard Laura's incredulous voice and he turned.

And there was Carmen.

She certainly did not need a trip to Beverly Hills with his credit card...

Her black hair was gleaming and there was dark red lipstick on her sultry lips, and even though she hadn't so much as looked in his direction she wore a smile that he knew was just for him.

'Who's that?' Seraphina exclaimed.

Elias didn't even answer her. For five years now he'd been trying to come up with the right words to say to his ex sister-in-law, but there were two little words that came easily tonight.

'Hold that.'

He handed Seraphina his glass, then made his way over to

the undisputed belle of the ball, who was now standing with her colleagues and friends.

'Look at you, Carmen!' Laura was beaming. 'How did you get that dress in a backpack?'

'Well,' she said in her rich throaty voice, 'it's best to be prepared...'

He didn't know how she'd managed it, but he did know it had taken every last nerve she had to walk into the ball.

After a lifetime of rejection, she had chosen to risk her heart to him.

He would never, ever let her down.

'You look incredible,' he told her.

'So do you.'

She put her hand up to his jaw. He didn't pull his head away because this was no feigned affection.

'You still haven't shaved?'

'I was a bit busy...' He looked at her shining black eyes. 'Did you get my message on the bottle?'

'That's why I'm here.' Carmen smiled. 'To claim my dance.'

On this beautiful night the ballroom lit up, and she leant on his chest and danced in his arms.

'Thank you for not leaving tonight...'

'We deserve a chance.'

'We're more than a chance,' Elias said. 'I love you.'

'Don't say that just because you've won today or—'

'I love you,' Elias told her again.

'Never take that back.'

It was an odd response, perhaps, especially from someone who looked so confident and poised. But he took her plea seriously, and understood that her doubts came from a world before him.

He said it a third time, right into the shell of her ear. 'I'm going to love you for ever.'

CHAPTER EIGHTEEN

CARMEN HAD THOUGHT—or rather she'd been told since she was a little girl—that she would marry in Jerez and her father would give her away.

'I always thought I'd have a reception at the bodega, like you did,' she said to Emily, who was taking her wedding dress out of its reams of tissue paper. 'I don't know what Papá would say about a wedding in Malibu!'

'I think he'd be thrilled to see you so happy,' Anna said.

'We couldn't leave Dom, you see. Not when he's doing so well. It would really have set him back...'

Her voice trailed off. Her brothers and their wives had all been a little baffled and trying not to be when she'd explained that they couldn't leave Dom just now.

After all, Anna had left her daughter, Willow, to attend Emily's wedding.

She smiled now at Willow, her bridesmaid—she was officially her niece now, because the adoption had finally come through.

'You look like a flamenco dancer,' Carmen told her.

'I *am* a flamenco dancer!' Willow exclaimed.

And then she looked at Emily, who was holding Josefa.

They seemed like sisters, even if they didn't quite understand each other yet.

They were there for each other.

Her family was here in Malibu for this very special wedding.

In a few weeks they would take a honeymoon in Jerez, and

sort out the transfer of Carmen's horses to Malibu... For now, though, it was all about today.

It had been four weeks since Elias had told her that he would love her for ever. Four weeks of drama. Because when Sebastián had heard she was engaged to marry he'd been all set to board the next flight...

Anna had talked him down.

Alejandro had been stuck at home with the lawyers, battling Maria, but Emily and little Josefa had come out early, the week before the wedding, and helped get things ready.

Their wedding was to take place on the ranch, but with such a rushed event the numbers were still a little up in the air, and even on the day of their wedding there were still responses to come.

'She hasn't even responded,' Carmen had said, when Elias's assistant had confirmed last week that Maria had failed to RSVP. 'It was such short notice, though. Knowing Maria, she might just turn up at the last minute and surprise everyone...'

Then her voice had faded. She doubted she'd come, but was still hoping she might...

'It's fine,' Elias had said. 'There's plenty of room if she does come.'

'In the attic!' Carmen had snapped, though the barb hadn't been aimed at him.

'No, I've kept one of the guest suites for your mother. She's always welcome in our home...'

He accepted that Carmen loved her, even if it could never, ever work out.

'Guess who *has* responded?' Elias had gone on. 'Seraphina and Vincent can't come.'

'Oh, that's a shame...'

'They're off on a babymoon—whatever that means. It was booked as soon as they found out they were expecting, apparently.'

'Oh, well...' Carmen had said, and then had turned away so he wouldn't see her sudden blush.

'What *is* a babymoon?' Elias had asked.

'A holiday before the baby comes...'

And now their not very long-awaited wedding day was here.

Carmen sat in a robe, her black hair slicked back into a low bun. Though Emily had tried, Carmen took over and tied a large red silk rose to the base of the bun, so it sat at the side.

'Ready for the dress?' Emily asked.

'One moment,' Carmen said, and slipped into the en suite bathroom.

As she turned the lock she stood for a moment, looking at one of the drawers and knowing what she'd hidden there. She'd bought the pregnancy testing kit yesterday, and had been telling herself to wait until tonight, or tomorrow, or...

Except she had no patience!

Carmen stood there, hearing Willow laughing and little Josefa singing, and her sisters-in-law chatting in the bedroom as she watched the lines appear and found out that she was to be a mother.

There was no fear, nor any worry as to what Elias would say.

Their love might be new, but it was by far too certain for her to worry about that.

Just for a moment, as she found out she was to be a mother, she wished she had her own mother to share it with. But then the string quartet started playing, and she peered out of the window to see the gathering congregation.

Carmen knew that she had a village to support her...

More than that, soon she would have a family of her own.

Both Sebastián and Alejandro walked her towards Elias. The brothers who had argued with her, parented her, loved and supported her and would never let the miles separate them from her took her arms and walked her down the aisle to the delicious strains of the quartet.

There were so many smiling faces in the congregation, but they were all a bit blurry for Carmen.

Her focus was on him alone.

'Carmen,' Elias greeted her. 'You look wonderful.'

She wore a little bit of home—a modern ivory Flamenco

dress and a shawl—because even if she'd rejected it out of hand flamenco was something she secretly loved too.

Elias looked incredibly handsome, in a charcoal-grey tailored suit and a silver tie, and she put her hand up to his freshly shaved chin and loved the way he captured her hand and held it there. That was all it took to know they were real.

It was gorgeous and low-key.

There was some beautiful music, and the celebrant told the congregation a little of their story.

'Elias and Carmen didn't actually meet here,' she told everyone. 'Carmen was waitressing…'

She spoke about those who were absent, about Joel and José, and Carmen looked up and saw the only tear she had ever seen in the darkness of his eyes.

'Carmen and Elias miss them today and every day,' the celebrant said on their behalf.

That would always be true.

'And now they've written their own vows…'

Elias went first. 'Carmen…'

He took her hands. He'd been thinking about what to say for four weeks. He'd spoken with his mother, her family, and he'd read books. He'd thought of the many weddings he'd been to and now he had quite a speech written in his head.

But then he looked at her waiting eyes and he thought of her standing in her crib as a baby, needing and demanding love…

'Carmen, I love you,' he told her. 'I want to walk with you and our horses and I want to dance with you, and I can't wait to go to Jerez and learn to love sherry…' He saw her smile. 'But first, last and always, I love you. That will never change.'

'Thank you.'

'Carmen?' The celebrant prompted.

'Elias…' Carmen took a breath. *'Eres el amor de mi vida…'* He squeezed her hand. 'You are the love of my life. I've waited so long to meet you.'

Their rings were simple—Californian gold for Carmen and Spanish gold for Elias—and they slipped on easily. Then Elias took out another ring—the gorgeous orange sea glass he had found on the beach and had had set in delicate gold.

Well, it was more brown, although neither would ever actually admit it, and they would keep looking for a true orange one.

Elias didn't wait to be told he could kiss his bride, and Carmen closed her eyes in bliss as his mouth came down on hers...

'I don't understand...' Eleanor Henley was on her second glass of Romero sherry and trying to work out how Spanish surnames worked. 'So you keep the father's surname and drop...?' She looked up as Carmen came and sat down. 'So you'll be Carmen Henley Romero?'

'No.' Carmen shook her head. 'I'm going to be Carmen Henley, but professionally I will stay as Carmen Romero.'

Carmen was holding little Josefa, who was standing on her lap. She had grown so much in just a few weeks.

'She's trying to stand already.'

'She's making up for being early,' Emily said and smiled.

'Have a drink,' Sebastián said.

But Carmen shook her head. 'I'm sticking with water...'

'No, look.' Sebastián pushed the sherry bottle forward, and then looked at his sister. 'Look at the bottle.'

'What?' Carmen said, and then shook her head. 'Let's not talk about the label today...'

'Just *look*!'

She turned it around and there, dancing on the label, was her *mamá*. But on the other side was Carmen, in a print out of a photo taken just now on the dance floor, her white dress swirling, utterly happy and free...

Maria might not like sharing the spotlight, but in Carmen's eyes they were finally dancing together...

'I love it!' Carmen smiled and clapped her hands.

'Me too,' Emily said and then gazed at the dreamy view. 'It's so beautiful here.'

'It is,' Carmen agreed. 'Though, I can't wait to show Elias around Jerez, I think we will be spending a lot of time there—

especially for the horse festival.' She looked over to Anna. 'How's the new home?'

Sebastián and Anna had taken over the hacienda, and it was perfect for their little family. Willow was delighted by her life and being spoilt rotten by Carmen's, oh, so strict brother...

Carmen's niece had a wonderful new adoptive father. Yet as a brother he was still protective, and still looking out for Carmen.

'Why,' he asked, 'is your new husband on his phone on his wedding day?'

Carmen looked over and saw a flash of concern cross Elias's features. She knew the only reason he'd be gazing at his phone today.

Handing Josefa back to Emily, she went over. 'Capricorn?' she checked, and looked at the video. The mare was pacing the stable—and not in the way she did when she was tired...

'I'll let Blake know,' Elias said, but Blake was enjoying the party, and anyway Carmen was already walking towards the stables.

'This is *not* how you're supposed to be spending your wedding day!' Elias said as they entered the stable...

'It's the perfect way,' Carmen said, holding Capricorn's neck and soothing her. 'We're here, darling...'

'She's close,' Elias said. 'Where's the vet?'

'Up to no good with one of the grooms, I should think!'

'Carmen?' He looked over at her. 'Do you have something to tell me?'

'Yes.'

'And...?'

'I told Seraphina to go and take a babymoon.'

'What?'

'She called to congratulate us and ask for the wedding date and I suggested she book something right away and tell her husband how much she needed a break.'

'You said that?'

'Oh, yes.' Carmen nodded. 'I didn't want her here today. I wasn't having her ruining this for a second.'

They watched as Capricorn began labouring and pushing, until a tiny grey foal slipped out. What a privilege it was to watch Capricorn nudge her foal and see two shaky little front legs pushing up, the back legs unfolding into a stand…

'He's tiny!'

'Not for long,' Elias said. 'Dom's going to have his work cut out in a couple of years.'

He looked at his wife who was smiling and crying and totally happy to get messy on her wedding day.

'What do we call him?'

'Taurus,' Elias said. 'You had me at Taurus too.' Carmen smiled when she thought back to that day on the pier and understood he had fallen in love then too. 'I decided that before I even proposed.'

'What if I'd said no?'

'Then I'd have had a constant reminder of the one I let get away.' He looked at her. 'Carmen, I saw the pregnancy testing kit in the drawer last night.'

'I was going to wait till after the wedding…'

'And did you wait?' He gave her a look. 'Of course you didn't.'

'Of course I didn't,' Carmen agreed, and as he wrapped her in his arms and she breathed in his delicious scent she told him the wonderful news.

'We're going to need a babymoon of our own. But the honeymoon comes first!'

So much to do…

So many reasons to love.

* * * * *

COMING SOON!

We really hope you enjoyed reading this book.
If you're looking for more romance
be sure to head to the shops when
new books are available on

Thursday 21st
December

To see which titles are coming soon, please visit
millsandboon.co.uk/nextmonth

MILLS & BOON®

Coming next month

AN HEIR MADE IN HAWAII
Emmy Grayson

A dull roaring drowned out the sounds around her. Each beat of her heart felt magnified, thundering inside her body as Anika stared at him.

'What?' she finally managed to gasp.

'You want me. I want you.'

'I never said I wanted you,' she sputtered.

Nicholas watched her, his fingers pressing more firmly against her back, his eyes glowing with that same predatory light she'd glimpsed on the catamaran.

'You also never said you didn't. So tell me now, Anika. Tell me you haven't thought about me kissing you. Tell me,' he continued, his husky voice washing over her and sending sinful shivers racing over her body, 'you didn't think about how we'd be together when you were in my arms on the boat. That you didn't imagine me tracing my fingers, my lips, over every inch of your incredible body.'

Say something!

But she couldn't. Not when her imagination was conjuring up carnal images of her and Nicholas entwined, arms wrapped around each other as he trailed his lips over her neck, her breasts, his hips pressing against hers without any barriers between them.

'Ah.' His smile deepened. 'So you have thought about it.'

Continue reading
AN HEIR MADE IN HAWAII
Emmy Grayson

Available next month
www.millsandboon.co.uk